P9-DGQ-575

Surprise Me

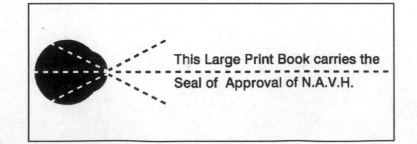

This Large Print Book carries the
Seal of Approval of N.A.V.H.

SURPRISE ME

SOPHIE KINSELLA

THORNDIKE PRESS
A part of Gale, a Cengage Company

Farmington Hills, Mich • San Francisco • New York • Waterville, Maine
Meriden, Conn • Mason, Ohio • Chicago

Copyright © 2018 by Madhen Media Ltd.
Thorndike Press, a part of Gale, a Cengage Company.

ALL RIGHTS RESERVED
Surprise Me is a work of fiction. Names, characters, places, and incidents are either the product of the author's imagination or are used fictitiously. Any resemblance to actual events, locales, or persons, living or dead, is entirely coincidental.
Thorndike Press® Large Print Basic.
The text of this Large Print edition is unabridged.
Other aspects of the book may vary from the original edition.
Set in 16 pt. Plantin.

LIBRARY OF CONGRESS CIP DATA ON FILE.
CATALOGUING IN PUBLICATION FOR THIS BOOK
IS AVAILABLE FROM THE LIBRARY OF CONGRESS.

ISBN-13: 978-1-4328-4874-3 (hardcover)

Published in 2018 by arrangement with The Dial Press, an imprint of Random House, a division of Penguin Random House LLC

Printed in the United States of America
1 2 3 4 5 6 7 22 21 20 19 18

To Henry

"Twenty-year-olds are three times more likely to reach 100 than their grandparents, and twice as likely as their parents."

— UK Office for National Statistics report, 2011

"All our institutions, including that of marriage and the family, are historically based on short and vulnerable lives. . . . The twenty-first century has to adapt all of these institutions to deal with longer and longer lives."

— Sarah Harper, professor of gerontology, University of Oxford

PROLOGUE

I have this secret little vocabulary for my husband. Words I've invented, just to describe him. I've never even told him about them: They just pop into my head now and then. Like . . .

Scrubcious: the adorable way he scrunches up his face when he's confused, his eyebrows akimbo, his gaze imploring, as if to say: *Explain!* Dan doesn't like to be confused. He likes everything straight. Clear. Out in the open.

Tentery: that taut, defensive way he behaves whenever the subject of my father comes up in conversation. (He thinks I don't notice.)

Shoffed: when life has turned round and punched him in the face so hard, his breath is literally taken away for a moment.

Actually, that's more of an all-purpose word. It can apply to anyone. It can apply to me. Right now, it *does* apply to me.

9

Because guess what? I'm shoffed. My lungs have frozen. My cheeks are tingling. I feel like an actor in a daytime soap, and here's why: 1. I'm prowling around Dan's office, when 2. he's out at work, oblivious to what I'm doing, and 3. I've opened a secret locked drawer in his desk, and 4. I can't believe what I've found, what I'm holding, what I'm seeing.

My shoulders are rising and falling as I stare at it. My brain is shouting panicky messages at me, like: *What? And: Does that mean . . . ? And: Please. No. This is wrong. This has to be wrong.*

And, almost worst of all: *Was Tilda right all along? Did I bring this on myself?*

I can feel rising tears, mixed with rising incredulity. And rising dread. I'm not sure yet which is winning. Actually, yes, I am. Incredulity is winning, and it's joining forces with anger. "Really?" I feel like shouting. "*Really,* Dan?"

But I don't. I just take some photos with my phone, because . . . just because. Might come in useful. Then I put what I found back, shut the drawer, lock it carefully, check it again (I'm slightly OCD over locked doors, turned-off washing machines, that kind of thing — I mean, not a big deal, I'm not *crazy,* just a bit . . . you know), and

10

back away, as though from the crime scene.

I thought I knew everything about my husband and he knew everything about me. I've seen him cry at *Up*. I've heard him shout, "I *will* vanquish you!" in his sleep. He's seen me wash out my knickers on holiday (because hotel laundry costs are ridiculous), and he's even hung them up for me on the towel rail.

We've always been *that couple.* Blended. Intertwined. We read each other's thoughts. We finished each other's sentences. I thought we couldn't surprise each other anymore.

Well, that shows how much I knew.

ONE

Five Weeks Earlier

It begins on our tenth anniversary. Who would have thought?

Actually, there are two things going on here: 1. Who would have thought it would all kick off on such an auspicious day? And 2. Who would have thought we'd make ten years in the first place?

By ten years, I don't mean ten years since our wedding. I mean ten years since we first met. It was at my mate Alison's birthday party. That was the day our lives changed forever. Dan was manning the barbecue and I asked him for a burger and . . . *bam.*

Well, not *bam* as in instant love. *Bam* as in I thought, *Mmm. Look at those eyes. Look at those arms. He's nice.* He was wearing a blue T-shirt, which brought out his eyes. He had a chef's apron round his waist, and he was flipping burgers really efficiently. Like he knew what he was doing. Like he was king of the burgers.

The funny thing is, I'd never have thought "ability to flip burgers" would be on the list of attributes I was looking for in a man. But there you go.

Watching him work that barbecue, cheerfully smiling all the while . . . I was impressed.

So I went to ask Alison who he was ("old college friend, works in property, really nice guy") and made flirty conversation with him. And when that didn't yield any results, I got Alison to invite us both to supper. And when that didn't work, I bumped into him in the City "by accident" twice, including once in a very low-cut top (almost hookerlike, but I was getting a bit desperate). And then finally, *finally,* he noticed me and asked me out and it was love at, you know, about fifth sight.

In his defense (he says now), he was getting over another relationship and wasn't really "out there."

Also: We have slightly edited this story when we tell other people. Like, the low-cut hooker top. No one needs to know about that.

Anyway. Rewind to the point: Our eyes met over the barbecue and that was the

14

beginning. One of those kismet moments that influence your life forever. A moment to cherish. A moment to mark, a decade later, with lunch at the Bar.

We like the Bar. It has great food and we love the vibe. Dan and I like a lot of the same things, actually — films, stand-up comedy, walks — although we have healthy differences too. You'll never see me getting on a bike for exercise, for example. And you'll never see Dan doing Christmas shopping. He has no interest in presents, and his birthday becomes an actual tussle. (Me: "You must want something. *Think.*" Dan [hunted]: "Get me . . . er . . . I think we're out of pesto. Get me a jar of that." Me: "A jar of *pesto*? For your *birthday*?")

A woman in a black dress shows us to our table and presents us with two large gray folders.

"It's a new menu," she tells us. "Your waitress will be with you shortly."

A new menu! As she leaves, I look up at Dan and I can see the unmistakable spark in his eye.

"Oh really?" I say teasingly. "You think?"

"Easy." He nods.

"Big-head," I retort.

"Challenge accepted. You have paper?"

"Of course."

15

I always have paper and pens in my bag, because we're always playing this game. I hand him a rollerball and a page torn out of my notebook and take the same for myself.

"OK," I say. "Game on."

The pair of us fall silent, devouring the menu with our eyes. There's both bream and turbot, which makes things tricky . . . but even so, I *know* what Dan's going to order. He'll try to double-bluff me, but I'll still catch him out. I know just how his mind weaves and winds.

"Done." Dan scribbles a few words on the page and folds it over.

"Done!" I write my answer and fold my own paper over, just as our waitress arrives at the table.

"Would you like to order drinks?"

"Absolutely, and food too." I smile at her. "I'd like a Negroni, then the scallops and the chicken."

"A gin and tonic for me," says Dan, when she's finished writing. "Then the scallops also, and the bream."

The waitress moves away and we wait till she's out of earshot. Then:

"Got you!" I push my piece of paper toward Dan. "Although I didn't say G&T. I thought you'd have champagne."

"I got everything. Slam dunk." Dan hands

me his paper, and I see *Negroni, scallops, chicken* in his neat hand.

"Damn!" I exclaim. "I thought you'd guess langoustines."

"With polenta? Please." He grins and refreshes my water.

"I know you nearly put turbot." I can't help showing off, proving how well I know him. "It was between that and the bream, but you wanted the saffron fennel that came with the bream."

Dan's grin widens. Got him.

"By the way," I add, shaking my napkin out, "I spoke to —"

"Oh, good! What did she —"

"It's fine."

"Great." Dan sips his water, and I mentally tick that topic off the list.

A lot of our conversations are like this. Overlapping sentences and half thoughts and shorthand. I didn't need to spell out, "I spoke to Karen, our nanny, about babysitting." He knew. It's not that we're *psychic* exactly, but we do tend to sense exactly what each other is going to say next.

"Oh, and we need to talk about my mum's —" he says, sipping his drink.

"I know. I thought we could go straight on from —"

"Yes. Good idea."

Again: We don't need to spell out that we need to talk about his mum's birthday gathering and how we could go straight on from the girls' ballet lesson. We both know. I pass him the bread basket knowing that he'll take the sourdough, not because he likes it particularly but because he knows I love focaccia. That's the kind of man Dan is. The kind who lets you have your favorite bread.

Our drinks arrive and we clink glasses. We're both pretty relaxed this lunchtime, because we've got the afternoon off. We're renewing our health insurance, and so we both need a medical, which is slated for later today.

"So, ten years." I raise my eyebrows. *"Ten years."*

"Unbelievable."

"We made it!"

Ten years. It's such an achievement. It feels like a mountain that we've scrambled to the top of. I mean, it's a whole *decade.* Three house moves, one wedding, one set of twins, about twenty sets of Ikea shelves . . . I mean, it's practically a lifetime.

And we're very lucky to be here, still together. I know that. A few other couples we know who started off around the same time as us weren't so fortunate. My friend

Nadia was married and divorced within three years. Just didn't take.

I look lovingly at Dan's face — that face I know so well, with its high cheekbones, sprinkling of freckles, and healthy glow from all the cycling he does. His sandy, springy hair. His blue eyes. His air of dynamism, even sitting here at lunch.

He's looking at his phone now, and I glance at mine too. We don't have a no-phone rule on dates, because who can go a whole meal without looking at your phone?

"Oh, I got you something," he says suddenly. "I know it's not a real anniversary, but whatever. . . ."

He produces a gift-wrapped oblong and I already know it's that book about tidying your house that I've been meaning to read.

"Wow!" I exclaim as I unwrap it. "Thanks! And I got you a little something too. . . ."

He's already smiling knowingly as he feels the heft of the package. Dan collects paper-weights, so whenever he has a birthday or a special thing, I get him one. (As well as a jar of pesto, obviously.) It's safe. No, not *safe* — that sounds boring, and we're definitely not boring. It's just . . . Well. I know he'll like it, and why waste money on taking a chance?

"Do you love it?"

"I love it." He leans over to kiss me and whispers, "I love you."

"Love that Dan," I whisper back.

By 3:45 P.M. we're sitting in a doctor's office, feeling pretty marvelous about everything, in the way you only can when you've got the afternoon off work, your children are at a playdate after school, and you're stuffed with amazing food.

We've never met Dr. Bamford before — the insurance company chose him — and he's quite a character. He brings us both into the room together, for a start, which seems unconventional. He does our blood pressure, asks us a bunch of questions, and looks at the results of the fitness tests we did earlier. Then, as he writes on our forms, he reads aloud in a rather theatrical voice.

"Mrs. Winter, a charming lady of thirty-two, is a nonsmoker with healthy eating habits. . . ."

Dan shoots me a comical look at "healthy eating habits," and I pretend not to notice. Today's our anniversary — it's different. And I *had* to have that double chocolate mousse. I notice my reflection in a glass cupboard door and immediately sit up straighter, pulling in my stomach.

I'm blond, with long, wavy hair. I mean

really long. Waist-length. Rapunzel-style. It's been long ever since I was a child, and I can't bear to cut it. It's kind of my defining feature, my long blond hair. It's my *thing*. And my father adored it. So.

Our twin girls are also blond, and I make the most of it by putting them in adorable Scandi stripy tops and pinafores. At least I did until this year, when they both decided they love football more than anything and want to live in their lurid blue nylon Chelsea shirts. I'm not blaming Dan. Much.

"Mr. Winter, a powerful man of thirty-two . . ." Dr. Bamford begins on Dan's medical form, and I stifle a snort. *Powerful.* Dan will love that.

I mean, he works out; we both do. But you wouldn't call him massive. He's just . . . he's right. For Dan. Just right.

". . . and there we are. Well done!" Dr. Bamford finishes writing and looks up with a toothy grin. He wears a toupee, which I noticed as soon as we walked in but have been very careful not to look at. My job involves raising funds for Willoughby House, a very tiny niche museum in central London. I often deal with wealthy older patrons, and I come across a lot of toupees: some good, some bad.

No, I take it back. They're all bad.

"What a delightful, healthy couple." Dr. Bamford sounds approving, as though he's giving us a good school report. "How long have you been married?"

"Seven years," I tell him. "And we dated for three before that. Actually, it's ten years exactly since we met!" I clutch Dan's hand with a sudden swell of love. "Ten years today!"

"Ten years together," affirms Dan.

"Congratulations! And that's quite a family tree the pair of you have." Dr. Bamford is looking at our paperwork. "All grandparents still alive or else died at a very good age."

"That's right." Dan nods. "Mine are all still alive and kicking, and Sylvie's still got one pair going strong, in the south of France."

"They're pickled in Pernod," I say, smiling at Dan.

"But only three remaining parents?"

"My father died in a car crash," I explain.

"Ah." Dr. Bamford's eyes dim in sympathy. "But otherwise he was healthy?"

"Oh yes. Very. Extremely. He was superhealthy. He was amazing. He was . . ."

I can't help it; I'm already reaching for my phone. My father was so handsome. Dr. Bamford needs to see, to realize. When I meet people who never knew my father, I feel a weird kind of *rage* almost that they never saw him, never felt that firm, inspiring handshake, that they don't understand what has been lost.

He looked like Robert Redford, people used to say. He had that glow. That charisma. He was a golden man, even as he aged, and now he's been taken from us. And even though it's been two years, I still wake up some days and just for a few seconds I've forgotten, until it hits me in the guts again.

Dr. Bamford studies the photo of my father and me. It's from my childhood — I found the print after he died, and I scanned it into my phone. My mother must have taken it. Daddy and I are sitting outside on the terrace of my old family home, underneath the magnolia. We're laughing at some joke I don't remember, and the dappled summer sun is burnishing both our fair heads.

I watch Dr. Bamford carefully for his reaction, wanting him to exclaim, "What a terrible loss to the world. How did you bear it?"

But of course he doesn't. The longer you've been bereaved, I've noticed, the more muted the reaction you'll get from the aver-

23

age stranger. Dr. Bamford just nods. Then he hands the phone back and says, "Very nice. Well, you clearly take after your healthy relatives. Barring accidents, I predict nice long lives for both of you."

"Excellent!" says Dan. "That's what we want to hear!"

"Oh, we're all living far longer these days." Dr. Bamford beams kindly at us. "That's my field of interest, you know, longevity. Life expectancy is going up every year. But the world really hasn't cottoned on to the fact. The government . . . industry . . . pension companies . . . none of them has properly caught up." He laughs gently. "How long, for example, do you expect to live, the pair of you?"

"Oh." Dan hesitates. "Well . . . I don't know. Eighty? Eighty-five?"

"I'd say ninety," I chime in boldly. My granny died when she was ninety, so surely I'll live as long as her?

"Oh, you'll live beyond a hundred," says Dr. Bamford, sounding assured. "A hundred and two, maybe. You . . ." He eyes Dan. "Maybe shorter. Maybe a hundred."

"Life expectancy hasn't gone up *that* much," says Dan skeptically.

"Average life expectancy, no," agrees Dr. Bamford. "But you two are way above aver-

age in health terms. You look after yourselves, you have good genes . . . I fully
believe that you will both hit one hundred.
At least."

He smiles benevolently, as though he's
Father Christmas giving us a present.

"Wow!"

I try to imagine myself, aged 102. I never
thought I'd live that long. I never thought
about life expectancy, full stop. I've just
been going with the flow.

"That's something!" Dan's face has
brightened. "A hundred years old!"

"I'll be a hundred and *two*," I counter
with a laugh. "Get me with my super-long
life!"

"How long did you say you've been married?" says Dr. Bamford. "Seven years?"

"That's right." I beam at him. "Together
for ten."

"Well, just think what good news this is."
Dr. Bamford twinkles in delight. "You
should have sixty-eight more wonderful
years of marriage!"

Wh—

What?

My smile kind of freezes. The air seems to
have gone blurry. I'm not sure I can breathe
properly.

Sixty-eight?

Did he just say —

Sixty-eight more years of marriage? To Dan?

I mean, I love Dan and everything, but . . .

Sixty-eight more years?

"I hope you've got plenty of crossword puzzles to keep you going!" The doctor chortles merrily. "You might want to save up some of your conversations. Although there's always the TV!" Clearly he thinks this is hilarious. "There are always box sets!"

I smile weakly back and glance at Dan to see if he's appreciating the joke.

But he seems in a trance. He's dropped his empty plastic water glass on the floor without even noticing. His face is ashen.

"Dan." I nudge his foot. "Dan!"

"Right!" He comes to and gives me a rictus smile.

"Isn't that great news?" I manage. "Sixty-eight more years together! That's just . . . I mean . . . Lucky us!"

"Absolutely," says Dan, in a strangled, desperate voice. "Sixty-eight years. Lucky . . . us."

Two

It's good news, obviously. It's great news. We're superhealthy, we're going to live long . . . we should be celebrating!

But sixty-eight more years of marriage? Seriously? I mean . . .

Seriously?

On the car journey home, we're both quiet. I keep sending little glances to Dan when he's not looking, and I can feel him doing the same to me.

"So, that was nice to hear, wasn't it?" I begin at last. "About living till a hundred, and being married for . . ." I can't say the number out loud, I just can't. "For a while longer," I end tamely.

"Oh," replies Dan, without moving his head. "Yes. Excellent."

"Is that . . . what you imagined?" I venture. "The marriage bit, I mean? The . . . uh . . . the length?"

There's a huge pause. Dan is frowning

27

ahead in that silent way he gets when his brain is dealing with some huge, knotty problem.

"I mean, it's kind of long," he says at last. "Don't you think?"

"It's long." I nod. "It's pretty long."

There's a bit more silence, as Dan negotiates a junction and I offer him gum, because I'm always the gum-giver in the car.

"But *good* long, right?" I hear myself saying.

"Absolutely," says Dan, almost too quickly. "Of course!"

"Great!"

"Great. So."

"So."

We lapse into silence again. Normally I would know exactly what Dan's thinking, but today I'm not quite sure. I look at him about twenty-five times, sending him tacit thought-wave messages: *Say something to me.* And: *Start a conversation.* And: *Would it kill you to look this way, just once?*

But nothing gets through. He seems totally wrapped up in his own thoughts. So at last I resort to doing the thing I never do, which is to say: "What are you thinking about?"

Almost immediately I regret it. I've never been that wife who keeps asking, "What are

28

you thinking about?" Now I feel needy and cross with myself. Why *shouldn't* Dan think in silence for a while? Why am I prodding him? Why can't I give him space?

On the other hand: What the hell *is* he thinking about?

"Oh." Dan sounds distracted. "Nothing. I was thinking about loan agreements. Mortgages."

Mortgages!

I almost want to laugh out loud. OK, this just shows the difference between men and women. Which is something I don't like saying, because I'm very much *not* a sexist — but honestly. There I am, thinking about our marriage, and there he is, thinking about mortgages.

"Is there an issue with the mortgage or something?"

"No," he says absently, glancing at the satnav. "Jeez, this route is going *nowhere.*"

"So why were you thinking about mortgages?"

"Oh, er . . ." Dan frowns, preoccupied by his satnav screen. "I was just thinking about how before you sign up for one" — he swings the wheel round, doing a U-turn and ignoring the angry beeps around him — "you know exactly how long the loan period is for. I mean, yes, it's twenty-five years, but then it's done. You're out. You're free."

Something clenches my stomach, and before I can think straight I blurt out, "You think I'm a *mortgage*?"

I'm no longer the love of his life. I'm an onerous financial arrangement.

"What?" Dan turns to me in astonishment. "Sylvie, we're not talking about *you.* This isn't about *you.*"

Oh my God. Again, I'm really not being sexist, but . . . *Men.*

"Is that what you think? Do you not *hear* yourself?" I put on my Dan-voice to demonstrate. " 'We're going to be married for a massive long time. Shit. Hey, a mortgage is really good because after twenty-five years, you're out. You're free.' " I resume my normal Sylvie-voice. "Are you saying that was a random thought process? Are you saying the two are unrelated?"

"That is *not* —" Dan breaks off as realization catches up with him. "That is *not* what I meant," he says, with renewed vigor. "I'd actually forgotten all about that conversation with the doctor," he adds for good measure.

"You'd forgotten it?" I shoot him a skeptical look.

"Yes. I'd forgotten it."

He sounds so unconvincing, I almost pity him.

"You'd forgotten about the sixty-seven more years we've got together?" I can't help laying a little trap.

"Sixty-eight," he corrects instantly — then a telltale flush comes to his face. "Or whatever it is. As I say, I really don't remember."

He's such a liar. It's etched on his brain. Just like it is on mine.

We arrive back in Wandsworth, find a parking spot not too far from the house, and let ourselves in. We live in a smallish three-bedroomed terraced house with a path up to the front door and a garden at the back, which used to contain herbs and flowers but now is mostly filled with the two massive Wendy houses my mother bought the girls for their fourth birthday.

Only my mother would buy two socking great identical Wendy houses. And deliver them in the middle of their birthday party as a surprise. All our guests were speechless as three deliverymen manhandled in the candy-striped wall panels and roofs and cute little windows and made them up while we all gawped.

"Wow, Mummy!" I exclaimed, after we'd

said our fulsome thank-yous. "I mean, they're wonderful . . . absolutely amazing . . . but . . . two? Really?" And she just blinked at me with her clear blue eyes and replied, "So they don't have to *share,* darling," as though it was perfectly obvious.

Anyway. That's my mum. She's adorable. Adorably annoying. No, maybe annoyingly adorable is a better way to put it. And, actually, the second Wendy house is pretty useful for storing my gym mat and weights. So.

As we enter the house, neither of us seems to have much to say. While I'm leafing through the post, I catch Dan looking around our kitchen as though he's seeing the house for the first time. *As though he's getting to know his prison cell,* I find myself thinking.

Then I chide myself: *Come on, he doesn't really look like that.*

Then I exonerate myself, because in fact he really does. He's pacing around like a tiger, eyeing the blue-painted cabinets morosely. Next he'll be scratching a mark on the wall. Starting the tallies to mark our ceaseless, weary march down the next sixty-eight years.

"What?" says Dan, feeling my eyes on him.

"What?" I counter.

"Nothing."

"I didn't say anything."

"Nor did I."

Oh God. What's happened to us? We're both irritable and wary. And it's all that bloody doctor's fault for giving us such good news.

"Look, so we're going to live practically forever," I burst out. "We have to *deal* with it, OK? Let's just talk this out."

"Talk what out?" Dan feigns innocence.

"Don't give me that!" I erupt. "I *know* you're thinking, *Bloody hell, how the hell are we going to last that long?* I mean, it's wonderful, but it's . . ." I circle my hands. "You know. It's . . . it's a challenge."

I slowly slide down the kitchen cabinet I'm leaning against, so I'm on my haunches. After a moment, Dan does the same.

"It's daunting," he agrees, his face relaxing as he admits it. "I feel a bit . . . well . . . freaked out."

And now, finally, it's out. The honest, deep-down truth. We're both shit-scared of this epic, *Lord of the Rings*–scale marriage we suddenly appear to find ourselves in.

"I mean, how long did you *think* we'd be married for?" I venture after a pause.

"I don't know!" Dan throws up his hands as though in exasperation. "Who thinks about that?"

"But when you stood at the altar and said, 'Till death us do part,'" I persist. "Did you have, like . . . a ballpark figure in mind?"

Dan screws up his face, as though trying to cast his mind back. "I honestly didn't," he says. "I just envisaged . . . you know. The misty future."

"Me too." I shrug. "I was totally vague. I suppose I imagined we might reach our silver wedding one day. When people reach their twenty-fifth wedding anniversary, you think, *Wow. They've done it! They're there!*"

"When we reach our silver wedding anniversary," says Dan, a little grimly, "we won't even be halfway there. Not even halfway."

We're both silent again. The ramifications of this discovery just keep on coming.

"Forever is a lot longer than I thought," says Dan heavily.

"Me too." I slump against the cabinet. "*So* much longer."

"It's a marathon."

"A supermarathon," I correct him. "An *ultra* marathon."

"Yes!" Dan looks up in sudden animation. "That's it. We thought we were running a 10K and now we've found out we're in one of those nutty hundred-mile ultramarathons in the Sahara Desert and there's no getting out of it. Not that I *want* to get out of it," he adds hastily, at my glance. "But nor do I want to . . . you know. Collapse with a stroke."

Dan really knows how to pick his metaphors. First our marriage is a mortgage. Now it's going to give him a stroke. And by the way, who's the Sahara Desert in all this? Me?

"We haven't paced ourselves properly." He's really warming to his theme. "I mean, if I'd *known* I was going to live that long, I probably wouldn't have got married so young. If people are all going to live until a hundred, then we need to change the rules. For a start, don't commit to anyone till you're at least fifty. . . ."

"And have babies at fifty?" I say, a little cuttingly. "Heard of the biological clock?"

Dan is drawn up short for a moment.

"OK, that doesn't work," he concedes.

"Anyway, we can't go back in time. We are where we are. Which is a *good* place," I add, determined to be positive. "I mean, think of your parents' marriage. They've been married for thirty-eight years and counting. If they can do it, so can we!"

"My parents are hardly a good example," says Dan.

Fair enough. Dan's mum and dad have

what you might call a tricky relationship.

"Well, the queen, then," I say, just as the doorbell rings. "She's been married for a zillion years."

Dan just stares at me incredulously. "The queen? That's all you can come up with?"

"OK, forget the queen," I say defensively. "Look, let's discuss it later." And I head to the front door.

As the girls burst joyously into the house, the next sixty-eight years or whatever suddenly seem irrelevant. *This* is what matters. These girls right now, these rosy-cheeked faces, these fluty high-pitched voices calling, "We got *stickers*! We had *pizza*!" They both drag at my arms, telling me stories and firmly pulling me back toward them when I try to say goodbye to my friend Annelise, who's dropped them off and is waving cheerily, already heading back to her car.

I hold them to me, feeling the familiar squirm of their arms and legs, wincing as their school shoes trample on my feet. They've only been on a two-hour playdate. It was nothing. But as I clasp them to me, I feel like they've been away for ages. Surely Anna's grown? Surely Tessa's hair smells different? And where did that little scratch on Anna's chin come from?

Now they're talking in that almost-secret twins' language they have, their voices overlapping, strands of their blond hair meshed as they gaze reverentially down at a sparkly seahorse sticker on Tessa's hand. From what I can hear, I think they're cooking up plans to "share it forever, till we're grown up." Since it will almost certainly disintegrate as soon as I take it off, we'll need a diversion, or there'll be howls. Living with five-year-old twins is like living in a Communist state. I don't *quite* count out the Shreddies into the bowls every morning to make sure things are equal, but . . .

Actually, I did once count out the Shreddies into the bowls. It was quicker.

"Right!" says Dan. "Bath time? Bath time!" he corrects hastily. Bath time is very much not a question. It's an absolute. It's the lodestone. Basically, the entire edifice of our household routine is based on bath time happening.

(This isn't just us, by the way; it's every other family I know with young children. The general perception is that if bath time goes, everything goes. Chaos descends. Civilization disintegrates. Children are found wandering the street in tatters, gnawing on animal bones while their parents rock and whimper in alleyways. Kind of thing.)

37

Anyway, so it's bath time. And as our nightly routine gets under way, it's as though the weirdness of earlier on never happened. Dan and I are operating as a team again. Anticipating each other's every thought. Keeping communication brief in our almost-psychic parent code.

"Shall we do Anna's —" Dan begins, as he passes me the hair detangler.

"Did it this morning."

"What about —"

"Yup."

"So, that message from Miss Blake." He raises his eyebrows.

"I *know.*" By now I'm combing detangler through Anna's hair with my fingers, and I mouth over her head: *Hilarious.*

Miss Blake is our headmistress and her message was in Anna's home message book. It was a typed memo to all parents, asking them please NOT to discuss or gossip at the school gate about a certain incident, which had absolutely NO FOUNDATION.

I had no idea what she was talking about, so I immediately emailed round the other parents, and apparently Miss Christy, who teaches the top year, was seen googling one of the dads on the classroom computer, not realizing it was linked to the whiteboard.

"Can I have the —"

Dan hands me the shower attachment and I blast Anna's head with warm water, while she giggles and yells, "It's raining!"

Were we always so psychic? So in tune with each other? I'm not sure we were. I think we changed after we had the girls. When you have baby twins, you're in the trenches together. You're feeding, changing, soothing, passing babies back and forth in rotation, round the clock. You hone your routines. You don't waste words. When I was breastfeeding Anna and Tessa and too tired to even *talk,* Dan could pretty much tell just from my expression which of the following I meant:

1. Could I have some more water, please? Six pints should do.
2. And a couple of Galaxy bars? Just shove them into my open mouth; I'll suck them in.
3. Could you please change the TV channel? My hands are full of baby and I've watched thirteen straight hours of Jeremy Kyle.
4. God, I'm exhausted. Have I said that more than five hundred times today?
5. I mean, do you realize the *levels* of exhaustion I'm talking? My bones

have collapsed inside my body, that's how tired I am. My kidneys are slumped against my liver, weeping gently.

6. Ow, my *nipple.* Ow. *Ouch.*
7. *Owwwwww.*
8. I know. It's natural. Beautiful. Whatever.
9. Let's not have any more after this, OK?
10. Did you get that? Are you paying attention, Dan? NO MORE BABIES, EVER.

"Argh!" My reminiscing comes to an end as Tessa swooshes the water so hard out of the bath, I'm drenched.

"Right!" snaps Dan. "That's *it.* Get *out* of the bath, both of you."

At once, both girls start wailing. Wailing happens a lot in our house. Tessa is wailing because she didn't mean to splash me so hard. Anna is wailing because she always wails when Tessa does. They're both wailing at Dan's raised voice. And, of course, they're both wailing because they're exhausted, though they'd never admit it.

"My sti-icker," says Tessa in choked tones, because she always brings every calamity she can think of into the frame. "My sti-i-i-i-cker bro-oke. And I hurt my thu-u-umb."

"We'll take it to the sticker hospital, remember?" I say soothingly as I wrap her in a towel. "And I'll kiss your thumb better."

"Can I h-h-h-have an ice lolly?" Her eyes slide up to me, spotting an opportunity.

You have to admire her chutzpah. I turn away to hide a giggle and say over my shoulder, "Not right now. Maybe tomorrow."

While Dan takes over story duty, I go to change out of my wet clothes. I dry myself off — then find myself moving over to our mirror and staring at my naked body.

Sixty-eight years. What will I look like in sixty-eight years' time?

Cautiously, I press the skin together on my thigh until it's all wrinkled up. Oh *God*. Those wrinkles are my future. Except they'll be all over my body. I'll have wrinkly thighs and wrinkly boobs and . . . I don't know . . . a wrinkly scalp. I release my wrinkles and survey myself again. Should I start more of a beauty regimen? Like exfoliation, maybe. But, then, how's my skin going to last me till the age of 102? Shouldn't I be building *up* layers, not scrubbing them away?

How do you keep your looks for a hundred years, anyway? Why aren't they telling us *this* in the magazines?

"OK, they're settled. I'm going for a run."
As Dan comes in, he's already peeling off
his shirt, but he stops when he sees me
standing naked in front of the mirror.

"Mmm," he says, his eyes gleaming. He
throws his shirt on the bed, comes over, and
puts his hands around my waist.

There he is in the mirror. My handsome,
youthful husband. But what's *he* going to
look like in sixty-eight years' time? I have a
sudden dismaying image of Dan all elderly
and wizened, batting at me with a stick and
yelling, "Humbug, woman, humbug!"

Which is ridiculous. He'll be old. Not
Ebenezer Scrooge.

I shake my head sharply to dispel the image. God, *why* did that doctor ever have to
mention the future in the first place?

"I was just thinking . . ." I trail off.

"How many more times we're going to
have sex?" Dan nods. "I already worked it
out."

"What?" I swivel to face him. "I wasn't
thinking that! I was thinking —" I stop,
intrigued. "How many times is it?"

"Eleven thousand. Give or take."

"Eleven thousand?"

I feel my legs sag in shock. How is that
even physically possible? I mean, if I thought

42

exfoliation was going to wear out my skin, then surely . . .

"I know." He takes off his suit trousers and hangs them up. "I thought it'd be more."

"More?"

How could he think it would be more? Just the thought of it makes me feel a bit dizzy. Eleven thousand more shags, all with Dan. Not that — I mean, obviously I *want* them to be with Dan, but . . . *eleven thousand times*?

How will we even have the time? I mean, we have to eat. We have to hold down jobs. And won't we get bored? Should I be googling new positions? Should I install a TV on the ceiling?

That figure *can't* be right. He must have misplaced a zero.

"How did you work that out?" I demand suspiciously, but Dan ignores me. He runs his hands down my back and cups my bottom, his eyes full of that intent, single-purpose look he gets. The thing about Dan is, you can only talk about sex with him for about thirty seconds before he wants to be doing it, not talking about it. In fact, he views talking about sex, generally, as a total waste of time. (I rather love talking about it, but I've learned to do that *afterward.* I lie in his arms and tell him everything I think about . . . well, everything, and he says, "Mmm, mmm," until I realize he's fallen asleep.)

"Maybe I'll put off my run," he says, kissing my neck firmly. "It *is* our anniversary. . . ."

And it is. And the sex is great — we're pretty psychic at that, too, by now — and we lie in bed afterward and say things like, "That was amazing," and "I love you," and everything that happy couples say.

And it was amazing.

And I do love him.

But — totally, absolutely honestly — there's also another tiny voice in my head. Saying: *One down. Only another 10,999 times to go.*

THREE

I wake up early to find that Dan is ahead of me. He's already got out of bed and is sitting in the little wicker chair in our bay window, staring morosely out the window.

"Morning." He turns a smidgen toward me.

"Morning!" I sit up, already alert, thoughts buzzing around my head. I reckon I have this whole living-forever thing worked out. I was thinking hard about it while I was drifting off to sleep, and I have the answer!

I'm about to tell it to Dan — but he gets in first.

"So basically I need to work till I'm about ninety-five," he says, in the utmost gloom. "I've been doing sums."

"What?" I say uncomprehendingly.

"If we're living forever, that means we've got to work forever." He gives me a baleful look. "To fund our ancient, elderly lifespans.

45

I mean, forget retiring at sixty-five. Forget retiring altogether. Forget taking it easy."

"Stop being so miserable!" I exclaim. "It was *good* news, remember?"

"Do you want to work till ninety-five?" he shoots back.

"Maybe." I shrug. "I love my job. You love your job."

Dan scowls. "I don't love it *that* much. My dad retired at fifty-seven, do you know that?"

His attitude is really starting to piss me off.

"Stop being negative," I instruct him. "Think of the opportunities. We have decades and decades in front of us! We can do anything! It's amazing! We just have to plan."

"What do you mean?" Dan gives me a suspicious look.

"OK, here are some of my ideas." I shuffle forward in the bed and fix my gaze on his, trying to inspire him. "We divide our life into decades. Each decade we do something different and cool. We achieve things. We push ourselves. Like maybe for one whole decade, we speak only Italian to each other."

"What?"

"We speak only Italian to each other," I repeat, a bit defensively. "Why not?"

"Because *we don't speak Italian,*" says Dan, as though I'm totally nuts.

"We'd learn! It would be life-enhancing. It'd be . . ." I gesture vaguely.

Dan just gives me a look. "What are your other ideas?"

"We try new jobs."

"What new jobs?"

"I don't know! We find amazing, fulfilling jobs that stretch us. Or we live in different places, maybe. What about one decade in Europe, one decade in South America, one decade in the States. . . ." I count off on my fingers. "We could live everywhere!"

"We could travel," Dan allows. "We should travel. I've always wanted to go to Ecuador. See the Galápagos Islands."

"There you go, then! We go to Ecuador."

For a moment we're both silent. I can see Dan digesting this thought.

His eyes start to gleam and he suddenly looks up.

"Let's do it. Fuck it, Sylvie, you're right. This is a wake-up call. We need to *live* life. We'll book flights to Ecuador, take the girls out of school, we'll be there by Monday. . . . Let's *do* it."

He looks so excited, I don't want to dampen his enthusiasm. But wasn't he listening? I was talking about the next

47

decade. Or possibly the one after that. Some far-off, unspecified time. Not *this week.*

"I definitely want to go to Ecuador," I say after a pause. "Absolutely. But it would cost a fortune —"

"It's a once-in-a-lifetime experience." Dan bats my objection aside. "We'd manage. I mean, *Ecuador,* Sylvie."

"Totally!" I try to match his level of animation. "Ecuador!" I leave a pause before I add, "The only thing is, Mrs. Kendrick doesn't like me taking unscheduled holidays."

"She'll live with it."

"And it's the girls' school play. They *can't* miss it, and they need to be at rehearsals. . . ."

Dan makes a small, exasperated sound. "OK, *next* month."

"It's your mother's birthday," I point out. "And we've got the Richardsons for dinner, and the girls have got sports day. . . ."

"All right," says Dan, sounding as though it's an effort to stay calm. "The month after that. Or in the summer holidays."

"We're going to the Lake District," I remind him, and wince at his expression. "I mean, we could cancel, but we've paid a deposit. . . ." I trail away.

"Let me get this straight." Dan speaks

evenly, but he sounds like he wants to explode. "I have endless years ahead of me, but I can't fit in one spontaneous, life-enhancing trip to Ecuador?"

There's silence. I don't want to say what I'm thinking, which is: *Obviously we can't fit in a spontaneous, life-enhancing trip to Ecuador, because, hello, we have lives.*

"We could go and eat at an Ecuadorian restaurant," I suggest brightly.

Although from the look Dan shoots me, maybe I should have just kept quiet.

At breakfast I pour muesli for myself and Dan and add some extra sunflower seeds. We're going to need good skin if we're going to last another sixty-eight years.

Should I start getting Botox?

"Another twenty-five thousand breakfasts," Dan suddenly says, staring into his bowl. "Just worked it out."

Tessa looks up from her toast and regards him with bright eyes, always ready to find the joke.

"If you eat twenty-five breakfasts, your tummy will explode!"

"Twenty-five thousand," corrects Anna.

"I *said* twenty-five-a-thousand," Tessa instantly retorts.

"Honestly, Dan, are you still thinking

about that?" I give him a pitying look. "You really have to get past it."

Twenty-five thousand breakfasts. Shit. How am I going to keep *that* interesting? We could start having kedgeree, maybe. Or spend a decade eating Japanese food. Tofu. Things like that.

"Why are you wrinkling your nose?" Dan stares at me.

"No reason!" I hastily brush down my pink floral skirt. I wear a lot of floral skirts to my office, because it's that kind of place. Not that there's an official dress code, but if I'm wearing anything spriggy or rosy or just pretty, really, my boss, Mrs. Kendrick, will exclaim, "How lovely! Oh, how *lovely*, Sylvie!"

When your boss is the owner of the business and has absolute power and has been known to fire people on the grounds that they "didn't quite fit in" . . . you want to hear her saying, "How lovely!" So in the six years I've worked there, my wardrobe has become more and more colorful and girly.

Mrs. Kendrick likes lemon yellow, periwinkle blue, Liberty print, frills, pearl buttons, and pretty bow clips decorating your shoes. (I found a website.)

She really *doesn't* like black, shiny fabrics, low-cut tops, T-shirts, or platform shoes.

("Rather *orthopedic,* dear, don't you think?") And as I say, she's the boss. She may be an unorthodox boss . . . but she's the boss. She likes things done her way.

"Ha." Dan gives a snort of laughter. He's been opening the post and is looking at an invitation.

"What?"

"You'll love this." He gives me a sardonic look and turns the card round so I can read it. It's a reception for some new medical charity being launched by an old friend of my father's called David Whittall, and it's taking place at the Sky Garden.

I know about the Sky Garden. It's thirty-five floors above-ground and it's all glass and views over London. And just the thought of it makes me want to clutch for my chair and anchor myself safely to the ground.

"Sounds just up my street," I say with an eye roll.

"That's what I thought." Dan grins wryly, because he knows, only too well.

I'm so scared of heights, it's not funny. I can't go out on high balconies. I can't go in a transparent lift. If I watch TV programs where people skydive or venture out on wires, I get all panicky, even though I'm sitting safely on the sofa.

I wasn't always like this. I used to ski, cross high bridges, no problem. But then I had the children and I don't know *what* happened to my brain, but I started feeling dizzy even if I went up a stepladder. I thought it would pass in a few months, but it didn't. When the girls were about eighteen months, one of Dan's colleagues bought a new flat with a roof terrace, and when we went to the housewarming, I couldn't go near the ledge to look at the view. My legs just froze. When we got home, Dan said, "What's *happened* to you?" and I said, "I don't *know*!"

And I realize it's something I should have sorted out by now. (Hypnosis? CBT? Exposure therapy? I do look it up on Google occasionally.) But it hasn't exactly been a priority recently. I've had other, more pressing concerns to deal with. Like, for example . . .

Well. OK. So, a key fact about me: When my father died, two years ago, it was a bit of a thing. I "didn't cope well." That's what people said. I heard them. They'd whisper it in the corner: "Sylvie's not coping well." (My mum, Dan, that doctor character they brought in.) Which started to annoy me, actually. It raised the question: What's "coping well"? How does anyone "cope well" when their father, their hero, just suddenly dies in a car crash with no warning? I think people who "cope well" are either deluding themselves, or they didn't have a father like mine, or perhaps they just don't have feelings.

Maybe I didn't *want* to cope well. Did they think of *that*?

Anyway, things went a bit haywire. I had to have some time off work. I did a couple of . . . stupid things. The doctor tried to put me on pills. (No, *thanks.*) And in the scheme of things, a fear of heights didn't seem like such a major inconvenience.

I'm fine now, absolutely fine. Apart from the heights issue, obviously, which I will deal with, when I have time.

"You should really go and see someone about your phobia," Dan says, reading my thoughts in that spooky way he has. "PS?" he adds, when I don't answer at once. "Did you hear me?"

PS is Dan's occasional nickname for me. It stands for "Princess Sylvie."

Dan's whole riff is that when we met, I was the princess and he was the poor working guy. He called me "Princess Sylvie" in his wedding speech and my father chimed in, "I guess that makes me the king!" and everyone cheered, and Dan did a charming mock bow to Daddy. The truth is, Daddy *looked* like a king, he was so distinguished and handsome. I can remember him now, his golden-gray hair burnished under the lights, his morning coat immaculate. Daddy was altogether the best-dressed man I've ever known. Then Daddy said to Dan, "Carry on, Prince Daniel!" and twinkled in that charming way he had. And later on, the best man made a joke about this being a "royal wedding." It was all really funny.

But as time has gone on — maybe because I'm a bit older now — I've got tired of being called Princess Sylvie. It rubs me up the wrong way, makes me flinch. I'm wary of saying anything to Dan, though, because I have to be tactful. There's a bit of history. A bit of awkwardness.

No, not *awkwardness*. That sounds too extreme. It's just . . . Oh God. How do I put this, without —

OK. Another key fact about me: I was brought up in a fairly privileged way. Not spoiled, definitely not spoiled, but . . . treated. I was Daddy's girl. We had money. Daddy originally worked in the airline industry as an executive, then received some huge windfall of shares when his airline was taken over, and he started his own consultancy. And it did brilliantly. Of course it did. Daddy had the kind of magnetic personality that attracted people and success. If he was traveling first-class with a celebrity, by the end of that flight he'd have that celebrity's card and an invitation to have drinks.

So we didn't just have money, we had perks. Expensive flights. Special treatment. I have so many photos of me as a child in the cockpit of some plane or other, wearing the captain's hat. In my early childhood we owned a house in Los Bosques Antiguos, that gated development in Spain where famous golfers get married in *Hello!* We even hung out with a few of them. We had *that* kind of life.

Whereas Dan . . . didn't. Dan's family are lovely, really lovely, but they're a sensible, modest family. Dan's father was an accountant and he's very big on saving. *Very* big. He started saving for his house deposit when he was eighteen. It took him twelve hard years, but he did it. (He told me that story the very first time I met him and then asked if I had a pension.) He would never whisk the whole family off to Barbados on a whim, like my father did once, or go shopping at Harrods.

And don't get me wrong: I don't *want* trips to Barbados or shopping trips to Harrods. I've told Dan that a million times. But, still, Dan is a bit . . . what's the word? *Prickly.* That's it. He's prickly about my background.

What's frustrating is that he wasn't like that when we first got together. He and Daddy really got on. We'd go out sailing, all four of us, and have a great time. I mean, Daddy was obviously far better at sailing than Dan, who'd never done it before, but it was OK, because they respected each other. Daddy would joke that he could do with Dan's eagle eye overlooking his accounts team — and he did genuinely ask Dan's advice a few times. We were all relaxed and easy.

But somehow Dan got pricklier as time went on. He stopped wanting to go sailing. (To be fair, it was harder once we had the girls.) Then three years ago we bought our house — using an inheritance from my granny as a deposit — and Daddy offered us a top-up but Dan wouldn't take it. He suddenly got all weird and said we'd relied on my family quite enough. (It didn't help that Dan's dad arrived to see the house and said, "So *this* is what family wealth buys you," as though we were living in a palace, not a three-bedroom house in Wandsworth on a mortgage.)

After Daddy died, everything was left to my mother and she offered us money again — but Dan wouldn't touch that either. He was even more prickly. We had a bit of a row, in fact.

I can understand that Dan is proud. (Sort of. Actually, I don't relate to it at all, but maybe it's a male thing.) What I do find hard, though, is the way he's so defensive about my father. I could see their relationship becoming strained, even when Daddy was alive. Dan always said I was imagining things — but I wasn't. I just don't know *what* happened or why Dan got so tentery. (That's when I invented the word.) It was like he began to resent Daddy, or something.

And even now it's as if Dan still feels threatened. He'll never sit down and reminisce about my father — not properly. I'll sit down and start scrolling through photos, but Dan won't focus. After a while he always makes an excuse and moves away. And I feel a little ache in my heart, because if I can't reminisce about my father with Dan, who can I do that with? I mean, Mummy . . . She's Mummy. Adorable, but you can't actually have a *conversation* with her or anything. And I don't have any siblings.

Being an only child used to bother me. When I was little I pestered and pestered

Mummy for a baby sister. ("No, darling," she would say, very sweetly.) Then I even invented an imaginary friend. She was called Lynn, and she had dark bangs and long eyelashes and smelled of peppermints and I used to talk to her in secret. But it wasn't the same.

When Tessa and Anna were born, I watched them lying face-to-face, already locked into a relationship no one else could penetrate, and I felt this huge, visceral pang of envy. For all that I had as a child, I didn't have *that*.

Anyway. Enough. I've long got over being an only child; I've long grown out of my imaginary friend. And as for Dan and my father . . . Well. I've just accepted that every relationship has some little fault line or other and this is ours. The best thing is just to avoid the topic altogether and smile when Dan calls me "PS," because what does it actually matter?

"Yes," I say, coming to. "I'll go and see someone. Good idea."

"And we'll decline this." Dan taps the Sky Garden invitation.

"I'll write to David Whittall," I say. "He'll understand."

And then Tessa spills her milk, and Anna says she's lost her hair clip and she only wants *that* hair clip, because it has a *flower* on it, and the morning routine takes over.

Dan's changed his job since we first met. Back then, he worked in a huge property-investment company. It was lucrative but fairly soul-destroying, so he put money aside every year (like father, like son) and finally had enough to start his own company. They make self-contained, prefabricated, sustainable office units. His office is on the river in east London and he often drives the girls to school, because it's on his way.

As I'm waving goodbye from the front doorstep, I see our next-door neighbor Professor Russell picking up the paper. He has a comical tuft of white hair that makes me smile every time I see him, although as he turns, I quickly put on a straight, grown-up face.

Professor Russell moved in earlier this year. He's in his seventies, I'd guess. He's retired from Oxford University, where he taught botany, and apparently he's the world expert on some kind of fern. Certainly his garden is full of a massive new greenhouse and I often see him in it, pottering among the green fronds. He lives with another white-haired man, who was just introduced as Owen, and I guess they're a couple but I'm not totally sure.

I'm actually a bit wary of them, because pretty much the first thing that happened after they moved in was that Tessa kicked a football over the fence and it landed on the roof of the greenhouse. Dan had to get it, and he cracked a pane of glass as he was climbing up. We paid for it to be replaced, but it wasn't the *best* start. Now I'm just waiting for them to complain about the girls' screaming. Although maybe they're a bit deaf. I hope so.

No, scratch that. I don't *hope* they're deaf. Obviously not. I just . . . it would be convenient.

"Hello!" I say brightly.

"Hello." Professor Russell gives me a pleasant smile, although his eyes look abstracted and distant.

"How are you enjoying Canville Road?"

"Oh, very much, very much." He nods. "Very much."

His gaze has already slid away again. Maybe he's bored. Or maybe his mind isn't what it was. I can't honestly tell.

"It must be strange, though, after Oxford?" I have a vision of Professor Russell wandering through an ancient quad, wearing a sweeping black gown, lecturing a bunch of undergraduates. To tell the truth, that vision suits him more than this: standing on his front doorstep in a little street in Wandsworth, looking like he's forgotten what day it is.

"Yes." He seems to consider this as though for the first time. "Yes, a little strange. But better. One has to move on." His eyes suddenly fix on me, and I can see the wink of sharpness in them. "So many of those fellows stay on too long. If you don't move on in life, you atrophy. *Vincit qui se vincit.*" He pauses as though to let the words breathe. "As I'm sure you're aware."

OK, so his mind has definitely *not* gone.

"Absolutely!" I nod. "*Vincit . . .* er . . ." I realize too late that attempting to repeat it was a mistake. "Definitely," I amend.

I'm wondering what *vincit*-whatsit means and whether I could quickly google it, when another voice hits the air.

"Toby, are you listening? You need to take the rubbish out. And if you wanted to help me, you could pop and buy a salad for lunch. And where are all our mugs? I'll tell you where. On the floor of your room is where."

I turn to see our other neighbor, Tilda, leaving the house. She's winding what seems like an endless ethnic-looking scarf

61

around her neck and simultaneously berating her son, Toby. Toby is twenty-four and he finished at Leeds University two years ago. Since then he's been living at home, working on a tech start-up. (Every time he tries to tell me what exactly it is, my brain glazes over, but it's something to do with "digital capability." Whatever that is.)

He's listening silently to his mother, leaning against the front doorway, his hands shoved in his pockets, his expression distant. Toby could be really good-looking, but he's got one of those beards. There are sexy beards and there are stupid beards, and his is stupid. It's so straggly and unformed, it makes me suck in breath. I mean, just trim it. Shape it. Do *something* with it. . . .

". . . and we need to have a chat about money," Tilda finishes ominously, then beams at me. "Sylvie! Ready?"

Tilda and I always walk to Wandsworth Common station together in the morning and have done for six years. Tilda doesn't actually take the train — she works from home as a remote PA to about six different people — but she likes the walk and the chat.

We've only been next-door neighbors for three years, but before Dan and I bought our house, we lived opposite, in a flat, and we got to know Tilda then. In fact, Tilda was the one who told us about our house being for sale and begged us to come and live next door. It's the kind of thing she does. She's impulsive and demonstrative and opinionated (in a good way) and has become my best friend.

"Bye!" I wave goodbye to Professor Russell and Toby, then start striding along. I'm wearing trainers, with my kitten heels in my bag, along with a turquoise velvet hair band, which I'm going to put on at the office. Mrs. Kendrick loves velvet hair bands, and she gave me this one for Christmas. So although I'd rather die than wear it at home . . . if it makes her happy, why not?

"Nice highlights," I say, eyeing up Tilda's hair. "Quite . . . bright."

"I *knew* it." She clutches her head in dismay. "They're too much."

"No!" I say quickly. "They brighten your complexion, actually."

"Hmm." Tilda plucks at her hair dubiously. "Maybe I'll go back and have them toned down."

Tilda is a bit of a contradiction when it comes to looks. She dyes her hair religiously but rarely wears makeup. She always wears a colorful scarf but doesn't often wear jewelry, because she says it reminds her of all the guilt presents her ex-husband bought her. At least, she realizes they were guilt presents now. ("I wish he'd bought me kitchen equipment!" she once exclaimed furiously. "I might have a KitchenAid!")

"So," I say as we turn the corner. "This quiz."

"Oh my God." Tilda rolls her eyes in horror. "I know nothing."

"I know less than nothing!" I counter. "It's going to be a disaster." Tilda, Dan, and I have volunteered to be in a team for a charity quiz tomorrow night. It's at the pub at the end of our road, and it happens every year. Simon and Olivia across the road organized our team, and they lured us in by saying the standard was "pitifully easy."

But then yesterday morning, Simon saw Tilda and me on the street and totally changed his tune. He said some of the rounds might be "rather tough" but not to worry, as we'd only need "a bit of general knowledge."

The minute he'd walked away, Tilda and I looked at each other in horror. A "bit of general knowledge"?

Maybe I had a bit of general knowledge once. In fact, I once learned one hundred capital cities for a school competition. But since having babies, the only information I seem able to store is:

1. That Annabel Karmel recipe for chicken fingers.
2. The theme tune to *Peppa Pig*.
3. What day the girls have swimming (Tuesdays).

And, truthfully, I sometimes get the *Peppa Pig* tune confused with the *Charlie and Lola* tune. So. Hopeless.

"I've told Toby he has to be on the team," says Tilda. "Actually, he likes the food at the Bell, so he didn't need much persuading. He knows about music, that kind of thing. And it'll get him out of the house, at least. *That boy.*" She makes a familiar frustrated sound.

To say that Tilda and Toby get on each other's nerves would be an understatement. They both work from home, but from what I can gather, there's a slight clash of working cultures. Tilda's culture is: Work in your home office in an orderly, contained way. Whereas Toby's culture is: Spread your crap all over the house, play loud music for inspiration, have sessions with your business partner at midnight in the kitchen, and don't actually make any money. Yet.

Yet is Toby's watchword. Anything he

hasn't done in life, he was totally planning to; he just hasn't done it *yet*. Even I've heard him bellowing it, through the party wall:

"I haven't cleared up the kitchen yet! *Yet!* Jeez, Mum!"

He hasn't found funding for his start-up *yet*. He hasn't considered any other careers *yet*. He hasn't thought about moving in to a flat *yet*. He hasn't learned how to make lasagna *yet*.

Tilda has an older daughter, too, called Gabriella, and by the age of twenty-four she was working for a bank, living with her boyfriend, and giving Tilda advice on useful gadgets from the Lakeland catalog. Which goes to show. Something.

But what I've learned with Tilda is: When she starts on a Toby rant, you have to quickly change the subject. And, actually, there's something I want to ask her. I want someone else's opinion on this whole marriage thing.

"Tilda, when you got married," I say casually, "how long did you imagine it would last? I mean, I know, 'forever.'" I make quote marks in the air. "And I know you got divorced anyway, so . . ." I hesitate. "But on your wedding day, when you couldn't see any of that coming, how long did you think 'forever' would be?"

"The honest truth?" Tilda says, shaking out her wrist. "*Shit.* My Fitbit's stopped working."

"Er . . . yes. I suppose."

"Is it the battery?" Tilda clicks with annoyance. "How many steps have we done?" She bangs her Fitbit. "It doesn't count unless it goes on my Fitbit. I might as well not have bothered."

Tilda's Fitbit is her latest obsession. For a while it was Instagram, and our daily walk was punctuated by her taking endless photos of raindrops on leaves. Now it's steps.

"Of course it counts! I'll tell you how many we've done when we reach the station, OK?" I'm trying to haul her back on track. "So, when you got married . . ."

"When I got married," Tilda repeats, as though she's forgotten the question.

"How long did you think 'forever' would be? Like, thirty years?" I venture. "Or . . . fifty?"

"Fifty years?" Tilda makes a sound which is half snort, half laugh. "Fifty years with Adam? Believe me, fifteen was quite enough, and we did well to last that long." She shoots me a sharp look. "Why do you ask?"

"Oh, I don't know," I say vaguely. "Just thinking about marriage, how long it goes on for, that kind of thing."

"If you *really* want my opinion," says Tilda, striding more briskly, "the whole system is flawed. I mean, forever? Who can commit to forever? People change, lives change, circumstances change. . . ."

"Well . . ." I trail off. I don't know what to say. I *have* committed to forever with Dan.

I mean, haven't I?

"What about wanting to grow old together?" I say at last.

"I've *never* understood that," says Tilda emphatically. "It's the most gruesome life aim I can think of. 'Growing old together.' You might as well say you want to 'keep your own teeth together.' "

"It's not the same thing!" I object, laughing, but she doesn't hear me. Tilda often gets on a bit of a roll.

"All this nonsensical emphasis on 'forever.' Well, maybe. But isn't 'till death us do part' a bit overambitious? Isn't it a bit of a gamble? There are a lot more likely scenarios. 'Till growing our separate ways us do part.' 'Till boredom us do part.' In my case: 'Till thy husband's wandering penis thee do part.' "

I give a wry smile. Tilda doesn't often talk about Adam, her ex-husband, but she once

68

gave me the whole story, which was funny and lacerating and just really sad.

He's married again, Adam. Has three small children with his new wife. Apparently he looks exhausted all the time.

"Well, here we are." As we arrive at the tube station, Tilda bashes her Fitbit against her wrist. "Stupid bloody thing. What have you got on this morning?"

"Oh. Just a coffee with a supporter." I show her my phone, which is open on my pedometer app. "There you go — 4,458 steps."

"Yes, but you probably ran up and down the stairs six times before we started," retorts Tilda. "Where are you going for coffee?" she adds, giving me such a raised-eyebrow, sardonic look that I laugh. "Where?" she persists. "And don't pretend it's Starbucks."

"Claridge's," I admit.

"Claridge's!" exclaims Tilda. "I knew it."

"See you tomorrow." I grin at her and head into the station. And as I'm reaching for my Oyster card, I can still hear her voice behind me:

"Only you, Sylvie! Claridge's! I mean, *Claridge's*!"

I do have quite a jammy job. I can't deny it.

Literally jammy. I'm sitting at a table in Claridge's, surveying a plate of pastries and croissants with apricot jam. Opposite me is a girl called Susie Jackson. I've met her quite a few times now, and I'm telling her about our upcoming exhibition, which is of fans from the nineteenth century.

I work for a very small charity called Willoughby House. It's been owned by the Kendrick family for years and is a Georgian townhouse in Marylebone, stuffed full of art and treasures and — slightly bizarrely — harpsichords. Sir Walter Kendrick had a fascination for them, and he began a collection in 1894. He also loved ceremonial swords, and his wife loved miniatures, and they both loved bringing souvenirs back from their travels. In fact, basically the whole family was a load of compulsive hoarders. Except we don't call their stuff a "hoard." We call it a "priceless collection of artwork and artifacts of national and historical interest" and put on exhibitions and talks and little concerts.

It suits me perfectly because my background is history of art. I studied the subject at university and I'm never happier than when I'm surrounded by things that are beautiful or historically significant, or both, which is the case for many of the pieces at Willoughby House. (There are also a fair number of pieces which are ugly and totally irrelevant to history, but we keep them on display because they have *sentimental* significance. Which, in Mrs. Kendrick's world, counts for far more.)

Before Willoughby House, I worked for a prestigious auction house, helping to put catalogs together, but I was based in a totally separate building from the actual auctions and I never saw or touched any of the pieces. It was a pretty drab job, to be honest. So I leapt at the chance to work for a smaller outfit, to be more hands on, and also to gain experience in a development role. Development means raising money, only we don't put it like that. The very word *money* gives Mrs. Kendrick a pained look, along with the words *toilet* and *website*. Mrs. Kendrick has a very distinct way of doing things, and after six years working at Willoughby House, I've learned her rules perfectly. Don't use the word *money*. Don't call people by their first names. Don't shake collecting tins at people. Don't make speeches asking for funds. Instead: *Build relationships.*

That's what I'm doing today. I'm building a relationship with Susie, who works for a large charitable trust, the Wilson-Cross

Foundation, whose remit is to support culture and the arts. (When I say "large" I mean about £275 million, and they give a chunk away every year.) I'm gently reeling her in to the Willoughby House world. Mrs. Kendrick is all about being subtle and playing the long game. She positively forbids us from asking for donations at first. Her argument is: The longer you've known the patron, the more they'll give, when the time comes.

Our secret dream is another Mrs. Pritchett-Williams. She's the legend of Willoughby House. She came to every event for ten years. She drank the champagne, ate the canapés, listened to the talks, and never gave us a penny.

Then, when she died, it turned out she'd left the house £500,000. Half a million!

"Have some more coffee." I smile at Susie. "So, here's your invitation to the launch of our antique-fan exhibition, Fabulous Fans. I do hope you can make it!"

"It looks amazing." Susie nods, her mouth full of croissant. She's in her late twenties, I'd say, and always has some amazing new pair of shoes on. "Only, there's a thing on at the V&A that night that I've been invited to."

"Oh really?" My smile doesn't waver,

although inside I'm seething. There's always a bloody thing on at the bloody V&A. And half our patrons are V&A supporters too — in fact, more than half, probably. We spend our whole life changing our events calendar so as not to clash. "What's that?" I add lightly. "I hadn't heard about it."

"Some textiles exhibition thing. I think they're giving away scarves to all the guests," she adds, her gaze shooting sharply to me. "Like a goody bag."

Scarves? Damn. OK, think, quick.

"Oh, didn't I mention?" I say casually. "We're giving away a wonderful gift for supporters at our launch. It's actually . . . a handbag."

"A handbag?" Her head pops up.

"Inspired by the exhibition, of course," I add, lying through my teeth. "They're rather beautiful."

Where I'm going to find thirty handbags that look like they were inspired by an exhibition of antique fans, God only knows. But I do *not* want to lose Susie Jackson to the V&A, let alone all our other patrons.

I can see Susie mentally weighing her options. Scarf from the V&A versus handbag from Willoughby House. A handbag's *got* to win. Surely?

"Well, I might be able to fit it in," she allows.

"Great!" I beam at her. "I'll put you down as an acceptance. It'll be a lovely evening."

I ask for the bill and finish my croissant, allocating this meeting a B plus in my mind. When I get back to the office I'll write my report and tell Mrs. Kendrick about the clash. And find thirty appropriate handbags to give away.

Maybe I'll try the V&A shop.

"So!" says Susie with a weird, sudden brightness as the bill arrives. "How are your children? I haven't heard about them for ages. Have you got a photo? Can I see?"

"Oh," I say, a bit surprised. "They're fine, thanks."

I glance down the bill and hand my card to the waiter.

"It must be so cute, having twins!" Susie is babbling. "I'd love to have twins, you know, one day — of course I'd have to find a man first. . . ."

I'm half-listening to her and trying to find a picture of the girls on my phone, but something's bugging me . . . and suddenly I have it. *How* much was that bill? I mean, I know this is Claridge's, but even so. . . .

"Could I see that bill again?" I say to the waiter. I take it back and read down the list.

Coffee. Yes.

Pastries. Obviously.

Coffee gâteau costing £50? *What?*

"Oh," says Susie in a weird voice. "Oh. I meant to . . . um . . ."

I slowly lift my head. She's staring at me defiantly, her cheeks getting pinker and pinker. But I still don't understand what's going on, until another waiter approaches holding a huge patisserie box tied up with ribbons and hands it to Susie.

"Your cake, madam."

I stare at it, speechless.

No *way.*

She's ordered herself a cake and put it on *our bill?* At bloody *Claridge's?*

The nerve. The absolute, copper-bottomed nerve. That's why she started babbling: She was trying to distract me from looking at the bill. And it nearly worked.

My smile is still fixed on my face. I feel slightly surreal. But I don't hesitate for a moment. Six years of working for Mrs. Kendrick has taught me exactly how to proceed. I punch in my PIN and beam at Susie as the waiter gives me the receipt.

"It was *so* lovely to catch up with you," I say as charmingly as I can. "And we'll see you at the launch of Fabulous Fans, then."

"Right." Susie looks discomfited. She eyes

the cake, then looks up warily. "So, about this cake . . . they put it on your bill, I don't know why!" She gives an unconvincing stab at laughter.

"But of course!" I say, as though astonished she's even bringing it up, as though buying fifty-quid coffee cakes for people is what we do all the time. "I wouldn't hear of anything else! It's *absolutely* our treat. Enjoy it."

As I head out of Claridge's, I'm seething with fury. We're a charity! A bloody charity! But as I arrive back at Willoughby House twenty minutes later, I've simmered down. I can almost see the funny side. And the plus is that Susie definitely owes us one now.

I pause at the front door, put on my velvet hair band, and slick my lips with pink lipstick. Then I head into the spacious tiled hall, which is staffed by two of our volunteers, Isobel and Nina. They're chatting away as I enter, so I just lift a hand in greeting and head up to the office on the top floor.

We have a lot of volunteers — women of a certain age, mainly. They sit in the house and drink tea and chat and occasionally look up to tell visitors about the items on display. Some have been volunteering for years, and they're all great friends and this is basically their social life. In fact, sometimes the house gets so full of volunteers we have to send some home, because there's no room for visitors.

Most of them hang out in the drawing room, which has the Gainsborough landscape in it, and the amazing golden stained-glass window. But my favorite room is the library, which is stuffed full of old books and diaries written by family members, in old scratchy copperplate. It's barely been changed over the years, so it's like walking back in time when you go in, with glass-cased bookshelves and the original gas-lamp fittings. There's also a basement, which has the old servants' kitchen, preserved just as it was, with ancient pans and a long table and a terrifying-looking range. I love it and sometimes go downstairs and just sit there, imagining what it was like to be the cook in a house like this. I once even suggested we have an exhibition of the servants' life, but Mrs. Kendrick said, "I don't think so, dear," so that was the end of that.

The stairs can seem endless — there are five floors — but I'm pretty used to it now. There *is* a cranky little lift, but I'm not wild about cranky little lifts. Especially cranky little lifts which might break down and leave you trapped at the top of a lift shaft, with no way down . . .

Anyway. So I take the stairs every day, and it counts as cardio. I arrive at the top, push my way into the light attic-level office, and greet Clarissa.

Clarissa is my colleague and is twenty-seven. She's the administrator and also does a bit of fundraising, like me. There's only the two of us — plus Mrs. Kendrick — so it's not exactly a huge team, but we work because we're all *simpatico*. We know Mrs. Kendrick's little ways. Before Clarissa, a girl called Amy joined for a while — but she was a bit too loud. A bit too sassy. She questioned things and criticized our methods and "didn't quite fit in," according to Mrs. Kendrick. So she was axed.

Clarissa, on the other hand, fits in perfectly. She wears tea dresses a lot and shoes with buttons, which she gets from a dance-wear shop. She has long dark hair and big gray eyes and a very earnest, endearing way about her. As I enter, she's spritzing the plants with water, which is something we have to do every day. Mrs. Kendrick gets quite upset if we forget.

"Morning, Sylvie!" Clarissa turns and gives me a radiant smile. "I've just got back from a breakfast meeting. It was *so* successful. I met six prospects, who all promised to put Willoughby House in their wills. *So* kind of them."

"Brilliant! Well done!" I would high-five her, but high fives are very much *not* a Mrs. Kendrick thing, and she might walk in at any moment. "Unfortunately, mine wasn't quite so good. I had coffee with Susie Jackson from the Wilson-Cross Foundation, and she told me the V&A are having an event the same night as our Fabulous Fans launch."

"No!" Clarissa's face crumples in dismay.

"It's OK. I told her we'd be giving away handbags as a gift and she said she'd come to ours."

"Brilliant," breathes out Clarissa. "What kind of handbags?"

"I don't know. We'll have to source some. Where do you think?"

"The V&A shop!" suggests Clarissa after a moment's thought. "They have *lovely* things."

"That's what I thought." I nod.

I hang up my jacket and go to put my receipt for coffee in the Box. This is a big wooden box which lives on a shelf and mustn't be confused with the Red Box, which sits next to it and is cardboard but was once covered with red floral wrapping paper. (There's still a snippet of it on the lid, and that's how it got the name the Red Box.)

The Box is for storing receipts, while the Red Box is for storing faxes. And then next to them is the Little Box, which is for storing Post-it notes and staples but *not* paper clips, because they live in the Dish (a pottery dish on the next shelf up). Pens, on the other hand, go in the Pot.

It sounds a bit complicated, I suppose, but it's not, when you get used to it.

"We're nearly out of fax paper," says Clarissa, wrinkling up her nose. "I'll have to pop out later."

We get through a lot of fax paper in our office, because Mrs. Kendrick sometimes works from home and likes to correspond backward and forward with us by fax. Which sounds outdated. Well, it *is* outdated. But it's just the way she likes to do things.

"So, who were your prospects?" I ask, as I sit down to type up my report.

"Six lovely chaps from HSBC. Quite young, actually." Clarissa blinks at me. "Just out of university. But *terribly* sweet. They all said they'd make us legacies. I think they'll give thousands!"

"Amazing!" I say, and draw up a new document. I've just started typing when there's the sound of unfamiliar feet on the staircase.

I know Mrs. Kendrick's tread. She's coming up to the office. But there's another person too. Heavier. More rhythmic.

The door opens, just as I'm thinking, *It's a man.*

And it's a man.

He's in his thirties, I'd say. Dark suit, bright-blue shirt, big-muscled chest, dark cropped hair. The type with hairy wrists and a bit too much aftershave. (I can smell it from here.) He probably shaves twice a day. He probably heaves weights at the gym. Looking at his sharp suit, I decide he probably has a flash car to match. He is so not the kind of man we usually get in here that I gape. He looks all wrong, standing on the faded green carpet with his shiny shoes, practically hitting the lintel with his head.

To be truthful, we rarely get any kind of man in here. If we do, they tend to be gray-haired husbands of the volunteers. They wear ancient velvet dinner jackets to the events. They ask questions about Baroque music. They sip sherry. (We have sherry at all our events. Another of Mrs. Kendrick's little ways.)

They don't come up to the top floor at all, and they certainly don't look around, like this guy is doing, and say, "Is this supposed to be an *office*?" in an incredulous way.

At once I prickle. It's not "supposed" to be an office; it *is* an office.

I look at Mrs. Kendrick, who's in a floral print dress with a high frilled collar, her gray hair as neatly waved as ever. I'm waiting for her to put him right, with one of her crisp little aperçus. ("My dear Amy," she said once, when Amy brought a can of Coke in and cracked it open at her desk. "We are not an American high school.")

But she doesn't seem quite as incisive as usual. Her hand flutters to the purple cameo brooch she always wears, and she glances up at the man.

"Well," she says, with a nervous laugh, "it serves us well enough. Let me introduce my staff to you. Girls, this is my nephew, Robert Kendrick. Robert, this is Clarissa, our administrator, and Sylvie, our development officer."

We shake hands, but Robert is still looking around with a critical gaze.

"Hmm," he says. "It's a bit cluttered in here, isn't it? You should have a clean-desk policy."

Instantly I prickle even more. Who does this guy think he is? Why should we have a clean-desk policy? I open my mouth to

82

make a forceful riposte — then close it again, chickening out. Maybe I'd better find out what's going on first. Clarissa is looking from me to Mrs. Kendrick with an open-mouthed, vacant expression, and Mrs. Kendrick abruptly seems to realize that we're totally in the dark.

"Robert has decided to take an interest in Willoughby House," she says, with a forced smile. "He will inherit it one day, of course, along with his two older brothers."

I feel an inner lurch. Is he the evil nephew, come to close down his aunt's museum and turn it into two-bedroom condos?

"What kind of interest?" I venture.

"A dispassionate interest," he says briskly. "The kind of interest my aunt seems incapable of."

Oh my God, he *is* the evil nephew.

"You can't close us down!" I blurt out, before I've considered whether this is wise. "You mustn't. Willoughby House is a slice of history. A sanctuary for culture-loving Londoners."

"A sanctuary for gossiping freeloaders, more like," says Robert. His voice is deep and well educated. It might even be attractive if he didn't sound so impatient. Now he surveys me with an unfriendly frown. "*How* many volunteers does this place need?

Because you seem to have half the retired women of London downstairs."

"The volunteers keep the place alive," I point out.

"The volunteers eat their body weight in biscuits," he retorts. "Fortnum's biscuits, no less. Isn't that a bit extravagant for a charity? What's your biscuit bill?"

We've all gone a bit quiet. Mrs. Kendrick is examining her cuff button and I exchange shifty looks with Clarissa. Fortnum's biscuits *are* a bit of a luxury, but Mrs. Kendrick thinks they're "civilized." We tried Duchy Originals for a bit but then went back to Fortnum's. (We rather love the tins too.)

"I'd like to see a full set of accounts," says Robert. "I want cash flow, expenses . . . you do keep your receipts?"

"Of course we keep our receipts!" I say frostily.

"They're in the Box," confirms Clarissa, with an eager nod.

"I'm sorry?" Robert looks puzzled, and Clarissa darts over to the bookshelf.

"This is the Box. . . ." She gestures. "And the Red Box and the Little Box."

"The what, the what, and the *what*?" Robert looks from Clarissa to me. "Is any of this supposed to make sense?"

"It does make sense," I say, but he's stalking around the office again.

"Why is there only one computer?" he suddenly demands.

"We share it," I tell him.

Again, this is a bit unconventional, but it works for us.

"You share it?" He stares at me. "How can you *share* a computer? That's insane."

"We make it work." I shrug. "We take turns."

"But . . ." He seems almost speechless. "But how do you send each other emails?"

"If I want to correspond with the girls from home, I send a fax," says Mrs. Kendrick, a little defiantly. "Most convenient."

"A *fax*?" Robert looks from me to Clarissa, his face pained. "Tell me she's joking."

"We fax a lot," I say, gesturing at the fax machine. "We send faxes to supporters too."

Robert walks over to the fax machine. He stares at it for a moment, breathing hard.

"Do you write with bloody quill pens too?" he says at last, looking up. "Do you work by candlelight?"

"I know our working practices may seem a bit different," I say defensively, "but they work."

"Bollocks they do," he says forcefully.

"You can't run a modern office like this."

I don't dare look at Mrs. Kendrick. *Bollocks* is very, very, very much not a Mrs. Kendrick word.

"It's our system," I say. "It's idiosyncratic."

Beneath my defiance, I do feel a tad uncomfortable. Because when I first arrived at Willoughby House and was shown the Boxes and the fax machine, I reacted in the same way. I wanted to sweep them all away and become paperless and lots of other things too. I had all kinds of proposals. But Mrs. Kendrick's Way ruled, as it does now. Every idea I put forward was rejected. So gradually I got used to the Boxes and the fax machine and all of it. I suppose I've been conditioned.

But, then, does it matter? Does it *matter* if we're a bit old-fashioned? What right does this guy have to come and swagger around and tell us how to run an office? We're a successful charity, aren't we?

His gaze is sweeping around the room again. "I'll be back soon," he says ominously. "This place needs knocking into shape. Or else."

Or *else*?

"Well!" says Mrs. Kendrick, sounding a little shell-shocked. "Well. Robert and I are going out for lunch now, and later on we'll have a little chat. About everything."

The two of them turn to leave, while Clarissa and I watch in silence.

When the sound of their footsteps has disappeared, Clarissa looks at me.

"Or else what?" she says.

"I don't know." I look at the carpet, which still bears an impression of his big, heavy man-shoes. "And I don't know what right he has to come and order us around."

"Maybe Mrs. Kendrick is retiring and he's going to be our boss," ventures Clarissa.

"No!" I say in horror. "Oh my God, can you *imagine* him talking to the volunteers? 'Thank you for coming; now please all fuck off.'"

Clarissa snuffles with giggles, and she can't stop, and I start laughing too. I don't share my slightly darker thought, which is that there's no way Robert wants to run this place, and it's a prime piece of London real estate, and it always comes down to money in the end.

At last, Clarissa calms down and says she's going to make coffee. I sit down at my desk and start typing up my report, trying to put the morning's events behind me. But I can't. I'm all churned up. My anxious fears are fighting with defiance. Why *shouldn't* this be the last quirky corner of the world?

Why *should* we conform? I don't care who this guy is or what claim he has on Willoughby House. If he wants to destroy this special, precious place and turn it into condos, he'll have to go through me first.

After work I have to go to a talk on Italian painting given by one of our supporters, so I don't arrive home till nearly 8:00 P.M. There's a quiet atmosphere in the house that means the girls have gone to sleep. I pop upstairs to kiss their slumbering cheeks, tuck them in, and turn Anna the right way around in bed. (Her feet always end up on the pillow, like Pippi Longstocking.) Then I head downstairs, to find Dan sitting in the kitchen with a bottle of wine in front of him.

"Hi," I greet him. "How was your day?"

"Fine." Dan gives a shrug. "Yours?"

"Some pencil pusher is coming to boss us about," I say gloomily. "Mrs. Kendrick's nephew. He wants to 'take an interest,' apparently. Or, you know, shut us down and build condos."

"Did he say that?" Dan looks up, alarmed. "Jesus."

"Well, no," I admit. "But he said we had to change, 'or else.' " I try to convey the menace of those two words with my tone of

voice, but Dan's features have already relaxed.

"He probably meant, 'Or else no Christmas party,' " he says. "You want some?" He
pours me a glass of wine before I can even
answer. As he slides it across the table, I eye
him and then the bottle. It's half empty. And
Dan seems preoccupied.

"Hey," I say cautiously. "Are you OK?"

For a few moments, Dan just stares into
space. He's drunk, I suddenly realize. I bet
he went to the pub after work. He sometimes does, if I'm going to be out and
Karen's on duty. And then he came home
and started on the wine.

"I sat at work today," he says at last, "and
I thought, *Am I really going to do this for
another sixty-eight years? Build offices, sell
offices, build offices, sell offices, build offices . . .*"

"I get it. . . ."

"Sell offices." He finally looks at me. "Forever."

"It's not forever." I laugh, trying to lighten
things. "And you don't have to work till
your *deathbed.*"

"It feels like forever. We're immortal,
that's what we are, Sylvie." He eyes me
moodily. "And you know what the im-
mortals are?"

"Heroic?" I venture.

"Fucked up. That's what."

He reaches across the table, pulls the wine bottle toward himself, and pours a fresh glass.

OK, this is not good.

"Dan, are you having a midlife crisis?" I say, before I can stop myself.

"How can I be having a midlife crisis?" Dan erupts. "I'm nowhere near my midlife! Nowhere near! I'm in the bloody foothills!"

"But that's *good*!" I say emphatically. "We've got so much *time.*"

"But what are we going to *do* with it, Sylvie? How are we going to fill the endless, soulless years of mindless drone work? Where's the *joy* in our lives?" He looks around the kitchen with a questing gaze, as though it might be in a jar labeled *joy,* next to *turmeric.*

"Like I said this morning! We just need to plan. Take control of our lives. *Vincit qui se vincit,*" I add proudly. "It means 'He conquers who conquers himself.' " (I googled it at work earlier, when it was my turn on the computer.)

"Well, how do we conquer ourselves?"

"I don't know!"

I take a slug of wine, and it tastes so good that I take another. I get some plates out of the cupboard, ladle chicken stew out of our slow cooker, and sprinkle it with coriander while Dan reaches in the drawer for cutlery.

"Let *alone* . . . you know." He dumps the cutlery heavily onto the table.

"What?"

"You know."

"I don't!"

"Sex," he says, as though it's obvious.

For God's sake. Sex again? *Really?*

Why does it always come back to sex with Dan? I mean, I know sex is important, but there are other things in life, too, things he doesn't even seem to *see* or *appreciate*. Like curtain tiebacks. Or *The Great British Bake Off.*

"What do you mean, 'sex'?" I counter.

"I mean —" He breaks off.

"What?"

"I mean, sex with the same person forever. And ever. And ever. For a million years."

There's silence. I bring our plates over to the table, put them down, and then pause, my mind circling uneasily. Is that how he sees it? A million-year marriage? I'm remembering Tilda too: *Isn't 'till death us do part' a bit overambitious? Isn't it a bit of a gamble?*

I eye Dan, this man I've gambled on. It seemed like good odds at the time. But now

91

here he is, behaving as though sex with me forever is some sort of punishment, and I feel like the odds are slipping.

"I suppose we could have a sabbatical or something," I say, without even knowing what I quite mean.

Dan lifts his head to stare at me.

"A sabbatical?"

"A relationship sabbatical. Time apart. Be with other people. That could be one of our decades." I shrug, trying to sound cool. "I mean, it's a thought."

I'm sounding so much braver than I feel. I don't *want* Dan to shag other people for a decade. I don't want him to be with anyone except me. But nor do I want him to feel like he's in an orange jumpsuit staring down the barrel of a life sentence.

Dan is just staring at me incredulously. "So what, we talk Italian for a decade, we shag other people for a decade, and then — what was the last one? Move to South America?"

"Well, I don't know!" I retort defensively. "I'm just trying to be helpful!"

"Do you *want* a sabbatical?" Dan focuses on me more closely. "Are you trying to tell me something?"

"No!" I exclaim in frustration. "I just want you to be happy! I thought you *were* happy.

But now you want to leave us —"

"No, I don't!" he says hotly. "You're the one who wants *me* to leave! Would you like me to do that *now*?"

"I don't want you to leave!" I practically shriek.

How has this conversation gone so wrong? I drain my wineglass and reach for the bottle, rewinding back in my mind. OK, maybe I slightly jumped to conclusions. But maybe he did too.

We eat silently for a while and I take several more gulps of wine, hoping it might straighten out my mind. As I do so, a warm sensation creeps over me and I gradually start to feel calmer. Although by "calmer" I really mean "drunk." The two proseccos I had at the talk are catching up with me, but I still drain my wineglass a second time. This is essential. This is *remedial.*

"I just want a long and happy marriage," I say finally, my voice a little slurred. "And for us not to be bored or feel like we're in a jumpsuit, scratching tallies on the wall. And I *don't* want a sabbatical," I add defiantly. "As for sex, we'll just have to . . ." I shrug hopelessly. "I mean, I could always buy some new underwear. . . ."

"I'm sorry." Dan shakes his head. "I didn't mean to . . . Sex with you is really good, you know that."

Really good?

I would have preferred *mind-blowingly awesome,* but let's not pursue that right now.

"It's fine," I say. "We're inventive, right? We can be happy, right?"

"Of course we can be happy. Oh *God,* Sylvie. The truth is, I love you so much, I love the girls so much. . . ." Dan seems to have sailed straight from belligerent-drunk to sentimental-drunk. (I have a word for that too: *wallowish.*) "The day we had the twins, my life just . . . it just . . ." Dan's eyes slide around as he searches for a word. "It expanded. My heart *expanded.* I never knew I could love anyone that much. Remember how tiny they were? In their little plastic cots?"

There's silence, and I know we're both remembering those scary first twenty-four hours when Tessa needed help to breathe. It seems a million years ago now. She's a robust and healthy girl. But still.

"I know." Drunken tears suddenly well up in my eyes. "I know."

"You remember those tiny socks they used to wear?" Dan takes another slug of wine. "You want to know a secret? I miss those tiny socks."

"I've still got them!" I get up eagerly from

the table, half-tripping over the chair leg. "I was sorting out clothes the other day and I put away a whole bunch of baby clothes, for . . . I dunno. Maybe the girls will have children one day. . . ."

I head into the hall, open the cupboard under the stairs, and drag back a plastic bin bag full of baby clothes. Dan has opened another bottle of wine and pushes a full glass to me as I pull out a bundle of sleep-suits. They smell of Fairy washing powder, and it's such a babyland smell, it goes straight to my heart. Our entire world was babies and now it's gone.

"Oh my God." Dan stares at the sleep-suits as though transfixed. "They're so *tiny.*"

"I know." I take a deep gulp of wine. "Look, the one with the duckies."

This sleepsuit was always my favorite, with its pattern of yellow ducklings. We some-times used to call the girls our ducklings. We used to say we were putting them away in their nests. It's funny how things come back to you.

"Remember that teddy-bear mobile with the lullaby?" Dan waves his wineglass er-ratically in the air. "How did it go again?"

"La-la-la . . ." I try, but I can't remember the tune. Damn. That tune used to be ingrained in our psyches.

"It's on a video." Dan opens his laptop and a moment later opens up a video folder, *Girls: First Year.* With no warning I'm looking at footage of Dan from five years ago, and I'm so affected, I can't even speak.

On the screen, Dan's sitting on our sofa, cradling a week-old Anna on his bare chest. She looks so scrawny, with her tiny legs in that froggy newborn position. She looks so vulnerable. They say to you, "You'll forget how small they were," and you don't believe it, but then you do. And Dan looks so tender, so protective. So proud. So fatherly.

I glance over at him, and his face is working with emotion. "*That's* it," he says, his voice all muffled as though he might weep. "That's the meaning of life. Right there." He jabs at the screen. "Right there."

"Right there." I wipe at my eyes.

"Right there," he repeats, his eyes still fixed on baby Anna.

"You're right." I nod emphatically. "You're so, so, *so,* so, so, so . . ." My mind has suddenly gone blank. "Exactly. *Exactly.*"

"I mean, what else matters?" He makes elaborate gestures with his wineglass. "Nothing."

"Nothing," I agree, holding on to my chair to stop the world spinning. I'm feeling just a *bit* . . . There seem to be two Dans sitting in front of me, put it like that.

"Nothing." Dan seems to want to make this point even more strongly. "Nothing at all in the world. Nothing."

"Nothing." I nod.

"So you know what? We should have *more.*" Dan points emphatically at the screen.

"Yes," I agree wholeheartedly, before realizing I don't know what he's on about. "More what?"

"*That's* how we make sense of our life. *That's* how we fill the endless, interminable years." Dan seems more and more animated. "We should have more babies. *Lots* more, Sylvie. Like . . ." He casts around. "*Ten* more."

I stare at him speechlessly. More babies.

And now I can feel tears rising yet again. Oh my God, he's right; *this* is the answer to everything.

Through my drunken haze, I have a vision of ten adorable babies all in a row, in matching wooden cradles. Of *course* we should have more babies. Why didn't we think of this before? I'll be Mother Earth. I'll lead them on bicycle outings, wearing matching clothes, singing wholesome songs.

A tiny voice at the back of my head seems to be protesting something, but I can't hear it properly and I don't want to. I want little feet and ducky-down heads. I want babies calling me "Mama" and loving *me* most of all.

Times ten.

On impulse I reach for the duckling sleep-suit, hold it up, and we both stare at it for a moment. I know we're both imagining a brand-new squirmy baby in it. Then I drop it on the table.

"Let's do it," I say breathlessly. "Right here, right now." I lean over to kiss him but accidentally slide off my chair onto the floor. Shit. *Ow.*

"Right here, right now." Dan eagerly joins me on the floor and starts pulling off my clothes.

And it's not *that* comfortable, here on the tiled floor, but I don't care, because we're starting a new life! We're starting a new chapter. We have a purpose, a goal, a dear little tiny baby in a Moses basket. . . . Everything's suddenly rosy.

Four

OH MY GOD, WHAT HAVE WE DONE?

Am I pregnant?

Am I?

I'm lying in bed the next morning, my head pounding. I feel nauseous. I feel freaked out. Do I feel pregnant? Oh God, *do* I?

I can't believe I'm waking up to this scenario. I feel as though I'm in a video warning teens about accidental pregnancy. We didn't use *any* protection last night.

Hang on, did we?

No. No. Definitely not.

Gingerly, my hand steals down to touch my abdomen. It hasn't changed. But that means nothing. Inside me, the miracle of human conception could have happened. Or it could be happening right now, while Dan sleeps on, blissfully clutching his pillow like our life hasn't just been ruined.

No, not ruined.

Yes, *ruined.* In so, so many ways.

Morning sickness. Backache. No sleep. Baby weight. Those vile pregnancy jeans with the elastic panels. No money. No sleep.

I know I'm fixated by sleep. That's because sleep deprivation is a form of torture. I *can't* do the no-sleep thing again. Plus: The age gap would be six years. So would we have to have a fourth child, to keep the baby company? But four? *Four children?* What kind of car would we need then? Some monstrous minivan. How will we park a minivan in our little street? Nightmare.

Would I have to give up work to look after the brood? But I don't *want* to give up work. My routine works well, and everyone's happy. . . .

A brand-new, horrific thought makes me gasp. What if we have another baby, and then we try for a fourth . . . and *end up with triplets?* It happens. These things happen. That family in Stoke Newington that Tilda met once. Three singletons and then — boom! — triplets. I would die. I would actually collapse. Oh God, why didn't we think this through? Six children? *Six?* Where would we *put* them?

I'm hyperventilating. I've gone from a mother of two girls, keeping her head above water, to a submerged mother of six, with her bedraggled hair in a scrunchie and flip-flops on her pregnancy-ruined feet and a look of meek exhaustion. . . .

Wait. I need the bathroom.

I creep out of bed, tiptoe into the bath-room without waking Dan, and immediately realize: I'm not pregnant. Very much not pregnant.

Which is, oh *God,* such a relief. I sink down on the loo and allow myself to sag, head in hands. I feel as though I've skidded to a halt just before hurtling over the precipice. I'm happy just as we are. The four of us. Perfect.

But what will Dan say? What about the duckling sleepsuit and the dinky little socks and "*That's* how we make sense of our life"? What if he *wants* six children, he just never told me before?

For a while I sit there, trying to work out how I'm going to break it to him that not only are we not having this baby, we're not having any more babies.

"Sylvie?" He calls out from the bedroom. "You OK?"

"Oh, hi! You woke up!" My voice is high and a bit strained. "I'm just . . . um . . ."

I head back into the bedroom, avoiding Dan's eye.

"So . . . I'm not pregnant," I say to the floor.

"Oh." He clears his throat. "Right. Well, that's . . ."

He breaks off into an almighty pause. My breath is on hold. I feel like I'm in an episode of *Deal or No Deal*. How exactly is he going to finish that sentence?

"That's . . . a shame," he says at last.

I make a noise which could sound like agreement although is in fact totally the opposite. My stomach is gnarling up a little. Is this going to turn into the massive deal-breaker of our marriage? Even more than the green velvet sofa? (Total saga. We compromised on gray in the end. But the green would have looked *so* much better.)

"We can try again next month," Dan says at length.

"Yes." I swallow hard, thinking: *Shit, shit, shit, he does want six children. . . .*

"You should probably get some . . . whatsit," he adds. "Folic acid."

No. This is going too fast. Folic bloody acid? Shall I buy some newborn nappies while I'm at it?

"Right." I gaze at the chest of drawers. "I mean, yes. I could do that."

I'm going to have to break it to him. It's like jumping into a swimming pool. Take a

102

deep breath and go.

"Dan, I'm sorry, but I just don't *want* any more children," I say in a burst. "I know we got all sentimental about socks, but at the end of the day, they're just socks, whereas a baby is a massive life-changing commitment, and I've just got my life sorted, and we'd probably have to have a fourth, which might mean six, and we just don't have room in our life for six children! I mean, do we?"

As I run out of steam, I realize that Dan is also talking, just as urgently, straight across me, as though he's jumped into a swimming pool too.

". . . look at the finances," he's saying. "I mean, what about university fees? What about the extra bedroom? What about the car?"

Hang on a minute.

"What are you saying?" I peer at him, puzzled.

"I'm sorry, Sylvie." He looks at me tensely. "I know we got carried away last night. And maybe you want a bigger family, which is something we'll have to talk through, and I'll always respect your views, I'm just saying —"

"I don't want a bigger family!" I cut across

103

him. "You're the one that wants six children!"

"Six?" He gapes at me. "Are you nuts? We had one unprotected shag. Where did *six children* come from?"

Honestly. Can't he see? It's so obvious!

"We have another one and then we go for a fourth, so the baby has a friend, and get landed with triplets," I explain. "It happens. That family in Stoke Newington," I remind him.

At the word *triplets,* Dan looks utterly aghast. His eyes meet mine, and I can see the truth in them: He doesn't want triplets. He doesn't want a minivan. He doesn't want any of this.

"I think another baby is a red herring," he says at last. "It's not the answer to anything."

"I think we were both quite pissed last night." I bite my lip. "We really shouldn't be in charge of our own reproductive systems."

I cast my mind back to the little duckling sleepsuit. Last night I felt so broody. I desperately wanted a brand-new baby inside it. Now I want to fold it up and put it away. How can I have changed my mind like that?

"What about the duckling sleepsuit?" I press Dan, just to make sure he's not concealing some deep, buried desire, which he'll then reveal in some torrent of resentment when it's all too late and we're a faded elderly couple staying by a lake in Italy, wondering where our lives went wrong. (We just did an Anita Brookner novel in our book club.)

"It's a sleepsuit." He shrugs. "End of."

"And what about the next sixty-eight years?" I remind him. "What about the empty interminable decades ahead of us?"

There's silence — then Dan looks up at me with a wry smile.

"Well, like the doctor said . . ." He shrugs. "There are always box sets."

Box sets. I think we can do better than bloody *box sets*.

As I arrive at the Bell for the quiz that evening, I feel fired up on all cylinders. I'm pumping with adrenaline, almost seething. Which, to be fair, is due to all sorts of things, not just dealing with how to be married to Dan forever (and then some).

Mostly, it's my day at work which has got me agitated. I don't know *what's* happened at Willoughby House. No, scratch that, I know exactly what's happened: The evil nephew has happened. I suppose what I mean is: I don't know *what* he's said to Mrs.

Kendrick, because she's transformed overnight, and not for the better.

Mrs. Kendrick used to be the standard bearer. She was the fixed measure for what was Right, according to her. She just knew. She had her Way, and she never doubted it, ever, and we all abided by it.

But now her iron rod is wavering. She seems jumpy and anxious. Unsure of all her principles. For about half an hour this morning, she went wandering around the office as though seeing it through fresh eyes. She picked up the Box and looked at it, as though suddenly dissatisfied with it. She put some old editions of *Country Life* in recycling. (She got them back out again later; I saw her.) She gazed longingly at the fax machine for a bit. Then she turned away, approached the computer, and said in hopeful tones, "A computer is very *like* a fax machine, isn't it, Sylvie?"

I reassured her that, yes, a computer was in many ways like a fax machine, in that it was a great way to communicate with people. But that was a huge mistake, because she sat down and said, "I think I'll do some emails," with an air of bravado, and tried to swipe the screen like an iPad.

So I broke off what I was doing and went to help her. And after a few minutes, when

Mrs. Kendrick tetchily said, "Sylvie, dear, you're not making any *sense,*" Clarissa joined in too.

Oh my God. It eventually turned out — after a lot of frustration and bewilderment on everyone's part — that Mrs. Kendrick had been under the impression that the subject line *was* the email. I had to explain that you open each email up and read the contents. Whereupon she gazed in astonishment and said, "Oh, I *see.*" Then when I closed each email down she gasped and said, "Where's it gone?"

About twenty times.

She was getting a bit hassled by then, so I made her a nice cup of tea and showed her a letter of appreciation that had come in from a supporter. (On paper, written in ink pen.) *That* made her happy. And I know her nephew's probably said to her, "Get with the program, Aunt Margaret, and start using email," but what I would retort is, "For God's sake, let her send faxes to all her friends; what's wrong with that?"

He's coming in again soon to "assess things." Well, two can play at "assessing." And if I "assess" that he's freaking his aunt out for no good reason, I'll be letting him know, believe me.

(Probably in a nice polite email after he's

left. I'm not brilliant at confrontation, truth be told.)

I give my hair a quick smooth-down, then venture into the pub, already deciding that this was a terrible idea but there's not much I can do about it now.

The place has been transformed for the evening, with a glittery banner reading ROYAL TRINITY HOSPICE QUIZ and a little stage in the corner with a PA system. Groups of people are already sitting with glasses of wine and pints, peering at sheets of paper. I see Simon and Olivia sitting with Tilda and Toby and head to the table, giving everyone a kiss.

"Dan's on his way," I say, pulling out a chair. "Just waiting for the babysitter."

What with the cost of babysitting, plus tickets and booze, tonight has worked out pretty expensive for an evening we're both dreading. As I was leaving home, Dan actually said, "Why the hell didn't we just send along a fifty-quid donation, stay at home, and watch *Veep*?"

But I don't divulge this to the others. I'm trying to be positive.

"Won't this be fun?" I add brightly.

"Absolutely," says Olivia at once. "You can't take these things too seriously. We're just here for the fun of it."

I don't know Simon and Olivia very well. They're about Tilda's age and have children at college. He's avuncular and jolly, with curly hair and specs, but she's quite intense and twitchy. She always seems to be clenching her hands, with her knuckles straining at her white skin. And she has this disconcerting way of looking away mid-conversation, with a sudden swooping, ducking gesture of her head as though she thinks you're about to hit her.

The gossip is that they nearly divorced last year because Simon had an affair with his assistant, and Olivia made him go away for a week's marriage therapy in the Cotswolds, and they had to light candles and "brush away his infidelity" with special mystic twig brooms. That's according to Toby, who heard it from their neighbor's au pair.

Although, obviously, I don't listen to gossip. Nor imagine the pair of them brushing away his infidelity with twig brooms every time I see them. (Believe me, if it was Dan's infidelity, I'd want to do a lot more than brush it away with a twig broom. Thrash it with a mallet, maybe.)

"What's your specialist subject, Sylvie?" demands Tilda as I sit down. "I've been boning up on capital cities."

"No!" I say. "Capitals are *my* thing."

"Capital of Latvia," rejoins Tilda, passing me a glass of wine.

My mind jumps about with a little spark of optimism. Do I know this? Latvia. Latvia. Budapest? No, that's Prague. I mean, *Hungary.*

"OK, capital cities can be your thing," I allow generously. "I'll focus on art history."

"Good. And Simon knows all about football."

"Last year we would have won if we'd played our joker on the football round," Olivia suddenly puts in. "But Simon *insisted* on using it too early." She regards Simon with stony eyes, and I exchange glances with Tilda. Olivia is *so* not here for the fun of it.

"Our team is called the Canville Conquerors," Tilda tells me. "Because of living on Canville Road."

"Very good." I take a gulp of wine and am about to regale Tilda with my day at the office, when Olivia leans forward.

"Sylvie, look at these famous landmarks." She pushes a sheet of paper toward me. On it are about twenty grainy photocopied photos. "Can you name any of them? This is the first round."

I peer at the sheet with a frown. It's so badly reproduced I can't even see what anything is, let alone —

"The Eiffel Tower!" I say, suddenly spotting it.

"Everyone's got the Eiffel Tower," says Olivia impatiently. "Look, we've already written it in, *Eiffel Tower.* Can't you get any others?"

"Er . . ." I peer vaguely at the sheet, passing over Stonehenge and Ayers Rock, which have also been written on. "Is that the Chrysler Building?"

"No," snaps Olivia. "It just looks a bit like the Chrysler Building, but it isn't actually it."

"OK," I say humbly.

I'm already feeling a bit hysterical. I don't know anything, nor does Tilda, and Olivia is looking more and more like a headmistress with pursed lips. Suddenly she sits bolt upright and nudges Simon. "Who are *they*?"

A team of guys in matching purple polo shirts walks in and sits down. Half of them have beards and most of them have glasses and all of them look fearsomely bright.

"Shall we not do the quiz?" I say to Tilda, only half joking. "Shall we just be spectators?"

"Welcome, everyone, welcome!" A middle-aged guy with a mustache mounts the tiny platform and speaks into the microphone. "I'm Dave and I'm your quizmaster tonight. I've never done this before — I've stepped in because Nigel's ill — so go easy on me." He gives an awkward half laugh, then clears his throat. "So, let's play fair, let's have some fun . . . please switch *off* your phones. . . ." He looks around severely. "No googling. No texting a friend. *Verboten.*"

"Toby!" Tilda gives him a nudge. "Off!"

Toby blinks at her and puts his phone away. He's trimmed his hipster beard, I notice. Excellent. Now he just needs to get rid of his million grotty leather bracelets.

"Hey, that's Iguazú National Park," he says suddenly, pointing at one of the grainy pictures. "I've been there."

"Ssssh!" says Olivia, looking livid. "Be discreet! Don't yell it out for the whole room to hear!"

I hear someone at the next table say, "Put *Iguazú National Park,*" and Olivia practically explodes in rage.

"You see?" she says to Toby. "They heard! If you know an answer, write it down!" She jabs furiously at the paper. "*Write* it!"

"I'm getting some crisps," says Toby, without acknowledging Olivia at all. As he gets up, I shoot Tilda a collusive grin, but she doesn't return it.

"That *boy,*" she says. She presses her hands against her cheeks, hard, then blows out. "What am I going to do with him? You won't guess his latest. Never."

"What's he done now?"

"Empty pizza boxes. He's been keeping them in the airing cupboard, can you believe? The airing cupboard! With our clean sheets!" Tilda's face is so pink and indignant, I want to laugh, but somehow I keep a straight face.

"That's not good," I say.

"You're right!" she says hotly. "It's not! I started to smell herbs every time I opened the airing cupboard. Like oregano. I thought, *Well, it must be our new fabric conditioner.* But today it started to smell rancid and quite vile, so I investigated further, and what did I find?"

"Pizza boxes?" I venture.

"Exactly! Pizza boxes." She fixes a reproachful gaze on Toby, who sits down and dumps three packets of crisps on the table. "He was disposing of them in the airing cupboard because he couldn't be bothered to go downstairs."

"I was not disposing of them," Toby responds laconically. "Mum, I've explained this to you. It was a holding system. I was going to take them to recycling."

"No, you weren't!"

"Of course I was." He gives her a rancorous glare. "I just hadn't taken them *yet.*"

"Well, even if it was a holding system, you can't have a holding system for pizza boxes in an airing cupboard!" Tilda's voice pitches upward in outrage. "An *airing cupboard*!"

"So, on with the space-and-time round." Dave's chirpy tones boom through the microphone. "And the first question is: Who was the third man on the moon? I repeat, who was the *third* man on the moon?"

There's a rustling and muttering throughout the room. "Anyone?" says Olivia, looking round the table.

"The *third* man on the moon?" I pull a face at Tilda.

"Not Neil Armstrong." Tilda counts briskly off on her fingers. "Not Buzz Aldrin."

We all look at one another blankly. Around the room, I can hear about twenty people whispering to each other, "*Not* Neil Armstrong . . ."

"We know it wasn't them!" snaps Olivia. "Who *was* it? Toby, you're into maths and science. Do you know?"

"The moon landings were faked, so the question's invalid," says Toby without missing a beat, and Tilda emits an exasperated squeak.

"They were *not* faked. Ignore him, Olivia."

"You can live in denial if you like." Toby shrugs. "Live in your bubble. Believe the lies."

"Why do you think they were faked?" I ask curiously, and Tilda shakes her head at me.

"Don't get him started," she says. "He's got a conspiracy theory about everything. Lip balm, Paul McCartney . . ."

"Lip balm?" I stare at her.

"Lip balm *causes* your lips to crack," says Toby dispassionately. "It's addictive. It's designed to make you buy more. You use lip balm, Sylvie? Big Pharma's using you like a puppet." He shrugs again, and I gaze back, feeling a bit unnerved. I always have lip balm in my bag.

"And Paul McCartney?" I can't help asking.

"Died in 1966," Toby says succinctly. "Replaced by a lookalike. There are clues in Beatles songs everywhere if you know where to look for them."

"You see?" Tilda appeals to me. "You see what I have to live with? Pizza boxes, conspiracy theories, everything in the house rewired —"

"It wasn't rewired," says Toby patiently, "it was re*routed.*"

"Question two!" says Dave into the microphone. "Harrison Ford played Han Solo in *Star Wars.* But what character did he play in the 1985 film *Witness*?"

"He was the Amish chap!" says Simon, coming to life and tapping his pen thoughtfully on his fingers. "Or . . . wait. He wasn't Amish; the girl was Amish."

"Oh God." Olivia gives a groan. "That film is ancient. Does anyone remember it?" She turns to Toby. "It was before your time, Toby. It's about . . . What's it about?" She wrinkles her brow. "The witness-protection scheme. Something like that."

"The 'witness-protection scheme,'" echoes Toby sardonically, doing quote marks with his fingers.

"Toby, do *not* start about the witness-protection scheme," says Tilda ominously. "Do *not* start."

"What?" I say, my curiosity fired up. "Don't tell me you have a conspiracy theory about the witness-protection scheme too."

"Does anyone know the answer to the actual question?" Olivia demands crossly, but none of us is paying attention.

"You want to know?" Toby turns his gaze on me.

"Yes! Tell me!"

"If they ever offer you a place in the witness-protection scheme, run for your life," says Toby without batting an eyelid. "Because they're going to get rid of you."

"What do you mean?" I demand. "Who is?"

"The government kills everyone in the witness-protection scheme." He shrugs yet again. "It makes economic sense."

"*Kills* them?"

"They could never afford to 'protect' that number of people." He does his little quotey fingers again. "It's a myth. A fairy tale. They get rid of them instead."

"But they can't just 'get rid' of people! Their families would —" I stop midstream. "Oh."

"You see?" He raises his eyebrows at me significantly. "Either way, they disappear forever. Who knows the difference?"

"Absolute nonsense," snaps Tilda. "You spend far too much time on the Internet, Toby. I'm off to the loo."

As she pushes her chair back, I fold my arms and survey Toby.

"You don't really believe all this rubbish, surely? You're just winding up your mum."

"Maybe." He winks. "Or maybe not. Just because you're paranoid, doesn't mean

117

there isn't a conspiracy against you. Hey, do your girls like origami?" He pulls a piece of paper toward him and starts folding it swiftly. A moment later he's created a bird, and I gasp.

"Amazing!"

"Give it to Anna. Here's one for Tessa." He's making a cat now, with little pointed ears. "Tell them they're from Tobes." He flashes me a sudden smile and I feel a pang of affection for him. I've known Toby since he was a teenager in a school uniform and used to lug a trombone to school every morning.

"Harrison Ford!" Olivia bangs the table to get our attention. "Concentrate, every-one! What character did he play?"

"Actually, I've just seen Dan arriving." I get to my feet, desperate to escape. "I'll just go and . . . er . . . Back in a second!"

OK, I'm never doing a pub quiz again, ever. They're pure evil, sent from Satan. *There's* a conspiracy theory for you.

It's nearly two hours later. We've had about a hundred more rounds (it feels like) and now we're finally on to the answers. Everyone's getting very tired and bored. But proceedings have stalled, because a row has broken out. The question was, "How do you spell *Rachmaninoff*?" and some Russian girl at another table wrote it down in Cyrillic. Now Dave is trying to manage a dispute between her and the purple-polo-shirt team, who are arguing: If no one else in the room understands Cyrillic, how can anyone judge if she's right or not?

I mean for God's sake, *what does it matter*? Give her the point. Give her ten points. Whatever. Let's just move on.

It's not only our marriage which is going to last forever. This quiz is going to last forever. We're going to be trapped at this table for eternity, drinking terrible chardonnay and trying to remember who won Wimbledon in 2008, until our hair goes white and we shrivel up like Miss Havisham.

"By the way, Sylvie, I saw a piece about your father in the local paper," says Simon in an undertone. "About his fundraising achievements. You must be very proud."

"I am." I beam gratefully at him. "I'm very proud."

My father spent a lot of time fundraising for liver cancer. It was his big thing. And being Daddy the super-networker, he did it spectacularly. He launched an annual ball at the Dorchester and managed to corral a load of celebrities into coming along and even got minor royalty involved.

"It said they're naming a scanner suite at the New London Hospital after him?"

"They are." I nod. "It's amazing. They're putting on this big opening ceremony in a couple of weeks. Sinead Brook is unveiling the plaque — you know, the newsreader? It's such an honor. I'm making a speech, actually."

I must finish writing it, it occurs to me. I keep talking confidently about the speech I'm going to make, but all I've written so far is, *My Lady Mayoress, ladies and gentlemen, welcome to what is a very special occasion.*

"Well, it sounds like *he* was pretty amazing," says Simon. "To raise all that money, mobilize people year after year . . ."

"He also climbed Everest, twice." I nod eagerly. "And he competed in the Fastnet sailing race. He raised loads doing that."

"Wow. Impressive." Simon raises his eyebrows.

"His best friend from school died of liver cancer," I say simply. "He always wanted to do something for people with that disease. No one at his company was allowed to raise funds for anything else!"

I laugh as though I'm joking, although it's not really a joke. Daddy could be quite . . . what's the word? Intransigent. Like the time

I suggested cutting my hair, aged thirteen. He got angry that I'd even suggested it. He kept saying, "Your hair is your glory, Sylvie, your *glory.*" And actually he was right. I would have regretted it, probably.

Instinctively, I run a hand through my long blond waves. I could never cut it now. I'd feel like I was betraying him.

"You must miss him," says Simon.

"I do. I really do." I can feel tears brightening my eyes but manage to keep my smile going. I take a sip of wine — then I can't help glancing over at Dan. Sure enough, he's looking tentery. His jaw has tightened. There are frown lines on his brow. I can tell he's waiting for the conversation about my father to pass, like you might wait for a cloud to move.

For God's sake, is he that insecure? The thought shoots through my brain before I can stop it. Which I know is unfair. My father was always so high-octane. So impressive. It must be hard if you're his son-in-law and keep hearing people raving about him, and you're just . . .

No. Stop. I don't mean *just.* Dan isn't *just* anything.

But compared to Daddy . . .

OK, let's be absolutely honest. Here in the privacy of my own mind, where no one else can hear, I can say it: To the outside world, Dan isn't in the same league as my father. He doesn't have the gloss, the money, the stature, the charitable achievements.

And I don't *want* him to be. I love Dan exactly as he is. I really do. But could he just once acknowledge that my father did have these amazing qualities — and realize that this fact doesn't threaten him?

He reacts like clockwork, every time. And now that the subject is safely past, I know he'll relax and lean back in his chair and stretch up with his arms and make that little yawning–yelping sound. . . .

I watch in slight disbelief as Dan does exactly that. Then he sips his wine, just like I knew he would. Then he reaches for a peanut, just like I knew he would.

Earlier on, he ordered a lamb burger for supper, just like I knew he would. He asked them to hold the mayo, just like I knew he would, and joked with the barman, "Is it genuine *London* lamb?" just like I knew he would.

OK, I'm scaring myself here. I may not know the capital of Latvia or how many feet there are in a fathom — but I know everything about Dan.

I know what he thinks and what he cares about and what his habits are. I even know what he's about to do next, right here, sitting in this pub. He's going to ask Toby about his work, which he does every time we see him. I know it, I know it, I know it. . . .

"So, Toby," says Dan pleasantly. "How's the start-up going?"

Argh! Oh my God. I'm omniscient.

Something weird is happening in my head. I don't know if it's the chardonnay or this bloody torturous quiz or my unsettling day . . . but I'm losing my grip on reality. It's as though the chatter and laughter of the pub are receding. The lights are dimming. I'm staring at Dan with a kind of tunnel vision, a realization, an epiphany.

We know too much.

This is the problem. This is the issue. I know everything about my husband. Everything! I can read his mind. I can predict him. I can order food for him. I have shorthand conversations with him and never once does he have to ask, "What do you mean by that?" He already knows.

We're living in marital *Groundhog Day.* No *wonder* we can't face our endless monotonous future together. Who wants sixty-eight more years with someone who always puts his shoes back in the same place, night after night after night?

(Actually, I'm not sure what else he would do with his shoes. I certainly don't want him leaving them all over the place. So that's maybe not the best example. But, anyway, the point still stands.)

I take a swig of chardonnay, my mind swirling around to a conclusion. Because it's actually rather easy. We need surprises. That's what we need. Surprises. We need to be jolted and entertained and challenged with lots of little surprises. And then the next sixty-eight years will whiz by. Yes. This is it!

I glance over at Dan, who is chatting with Toby, oblivious of my thoughts. He looks a bit careworn, it occurs to me. He looks tired. He needs something to ginger him up, something to make him smile, or even laugh. Something out of the ordinary. Something fun. Or romantic.

Hmm. What?

It's too late to organize a strip-o-gram (which, by the way, he'd hate). But can't I do something? Right now? Something to shake us out of our malaise? I take another gulp of chardonnay, and then the answer hits me. Oh my God, brilliant. Simple but brilliant, as all the best plans are.

I pull a piece of paper toward me and start to compose a little love poem.

You may be surprised.
Don't be.
I want you and I always will.
Let's find a moment.
Just be us.
Just be the two of us.
Just be . . .

I pause, peering down at my sheet. I'm running out of steam. I always was a bit crap at poetry. How can I end it?

Just be ourselves, I write finally. I draw a love heart and some kisses for good measure. Then I fold the whole thing up into a smallish oblong.

Now to deliver it. I wait until Dan's looking the other way, then slip it into the pocket of his suit jacket, which is hanging on the back of his chair. He'll find it later, and he'll wonder what it is and slowly unfold it, and at first he won't understand, but then his heart will lift.

Well, maybe it'll lift.

Well, it would probably have lifted more if I was better at poetry, but so what, it's the thought that counts, isn't it?

"Have a toffee," says Toby, offering a bag to me. "I made them myself. They're awesome."

"Thanks." I smile at him, take a toffee,

and put it in my mouth. A few moments later I regret it. My teeth are locked together. I can't chew. I can't speak. My whole face feels immobilized. What *is* this stuff?

"Oh, they're quite chewy," says Toby, noticing me. "They're called 'lockjaws.' "

I shoot him a glare, which is supposed to mean, "Thanks for the heads-up, *not.*"

"Toby!" says Tilda crossly. "You have to *warn* people about those things. Don't worry," she adds to me. "It'll melt in about ten minutes."

Ten minutes?

"All right, people!" says Dave the quizmaster, tapping his microphone to get everyone's attention. His cheerful manner has somewhat faded over the course of the evening; in fact, he looks like he's desperate for it to end. "Moving on, the next question was: How many actors have played Doctor Who? And the answer is: thirteen."

"No, it's not," calls out a fattish guy in a purple polo shirt, promptly. "It's forty-four."

Dave eyes him warily. "It can't be," he says. "That's too many."

"Doctor Who doesn't just feature in the BBC series," says the purple-polo-shirt guy pompously.

"It's fourteen," volunteers a girl at an

adjoining table. "There was an extra doctor. The War Doctor. John Hurt."

"Right," says Dave, looking beleaguered. "Well, that's not what I've got on my answer sheet. . . ."

"It's none of them," says Toby loudly. "It's a trick question. 'Doctor Who' isn't the name of the character; the name of the character is 'the Doctor.' Boom kanani," he adds, looking pleased with himself. "Booyah. In your *face,* everyone who wrote down a number."

"That's a common misunderstanding," says the man in the purple polo shirt, giving Toby a baleful look. "The answer's forty-four, as I said. You want the full list?"

"Did anyone put thirteen?" Dave perseveres, but no one's paying attention.

"Who the hell are you, anyway?" retorts a man in a flowery shirt, who is quite red in the face. He waves a belligerent hand at the purple-polo-shirt team. "This is supposed to be a local friendly quiz, but you come marching in with your matching bloody shirts, picking fights. . . ."

"Oh, don't like strangers, do you?" The purple-polo-shirt guy glowers at him. "Well, sorry, *Adolf.*"

"What did you call me?" The man in the flowery shirt kicks back his chair and stands up, breathing hard.

"You heard." The purple-polo-shirt guy gets up, too, and takes a menacing step toward the flowery-shirt man.

"I can't bear this," says Olivia. "I'm going out for a cigarette." She reaches for Dan's jacket and puts it on — then looks at Simon's, which is almost identical, and back at the one she's wearing. "Wait. Simon, is this your jacket?"

"You're wearing Simon's," says Dan easily. "We swapped chairs. He prefers a lower back."

It's about five seconds before the significance of this hits me. Simon's jacket? That's Simon's jacket? I've put a love poem in *Simon's* jacket?

"Have you got a lighter?" Olivia reaches in the pocket and pulls out my oblong of paper. "What's this?" she says, unfolding it. As she sees the love heart, her whole face blanches.

No. Nooo. I need to explain. I try to wrench my teeth apart to speak, but the stupid bloody toffee is too strong. I can't manage it. I wave my hands frantically at Olivia, but she's staring at my poem with a look of utter revulsion.

"*Again,* Simon?" she says at last.

"What do you mean, again?" says Simon,

who's watching the purple-polo-shirt guy and flowery-shirt man trade insults.

"You promised!" Olivia's voice is so scorching, I feel quite bowled over. "You promised, Simon, never again." She brandishes the poem at Simon, and as he reads it, his face blanches too.

I try to grab at the paper and get their attention, but Olivia doesn't even notice me. Her eyes are blazing and quite scary.

"I've never seen that before!" Simon is stuttering. "Olivia, you must believe me! I have no idea what — who —"

"I think we all know who," Olivia says savagely. "It's obvious, from this piece of illiterate trash, that it's your previous 'friend.' *I want you and I always will,*" she declaims in a syrupy voice. "*Let's find a moment. Just be us.* Did she get it from a Hallmark card?"

She's so mocking, my face flames bright red. At last, with a final wrench, I get my teeth apart and grab the paper from her hand.

"Actually, that's my poem!" I say, trying to sound bright and nonchalant. "It was meant for Dan. Wrong jacket. So. It was . . . it's ours. Mine. Not Simon's. You don't need to worry about . . . Or anything. So. Anyway."

I finally manage to stop babbling and realize that everyone around the table is watching, dumbstruck. The look of horror on Olivia's face is so priceless, I'd laugh if I didn't feel so totally embarrassed.

"Um, so, here you are, Dan," I add awkwardly, and give him the paper. "You could read it now . . . or later. . . . It's quite short," I add, in case he's expecting six verses and metaphors about war, or something.

Dan doesn't look *very* thrilled to be handed a love poem, to be fair. He glances at it and clears his throat and shoves it in his pocket without reading it.

"I didn't mean . . ." Olivia's hands are clenched harder than I've ever seen them. "Sylvie, I'm so sorry. I didn't mean to insult you."

"It's fine, honestly —"

"You're a disgrace to quizzes!" The voice of the flowery-shirted man makes us all jump. "You had that phone under the table all the time!"

"We did not!" the purple-polo-shirt man shouts back. "That's fucking slander, that is!"

He pushes a table roughly toward the flowery-shirted man, and all the glasses jostle and chink together.

"Fight! Fight! Fight!" calls out Toby cheerfully.

"Be *quiet,* Toby!" snaps Tilda.

"So!" Dave is saying desperately into the microphone, over the hubbub. "Let's carry on. And the next question was, Which Briton won an ice-skating gold at the —"

He breaks off as the flowery-shirted guy charges at the purple-polo-shirt team. One of them tackles him, as though they're playing rugby, and the others start roaring encouragement. All around the pub, people start exclaiming and gasping. The Russian girl even shrieks as though someone's stuck a knife into her.

"People!" Dave is imploring. "People, calm down! Please!"

Oh my God, they're fighting. They're actually punching one another. I've never even *seen* a pub brawl before.

"Sylvie," says Dan in my ear. "Shall we go?"

"Yes," I say at once. *"Yes."*

As we're walking home, Dan takes out my love poem. He reads it. He turns the page over as though expecting more. Then he reads it again. Then he puts it away. He looks touched. And a bit flummoxed. OK, maybe slightly more flummoxed than touched.

"Dan, listen," I say in a rush. "I have this

whole big explanation to give you."

"Of your poem?" He looks at me questioningly.

"Yes! Of course of my poem!"

What did he think I meant, of thermocombustion?

"You don't need to explain it. I got it. It was nice," he adds after a moment's thought. "Thank you."

"Not the poem itself," I say, a bit impatiently. "I mean, the concept of the poem. The *fact* of the poem. It's all part of my new brilliant idea which will solve everything."

"Right." He nods, then takes the poem out and looks at it again under the light of a streetlamp, frowning slightly. "Is there supposed to be a second verse?"

"No," I say defensively. "It's pithy."

"Ah."

"And it's only the beginning. Here's my idea, Dan. We need to *surprise* each other. It can be, like, our joint thing. We can call it . . ." I think for a moment. "Project Surprise Me."

To my gratification, Dan looks surprised. Ha! It begins! I was hoping Dan would latch on to the idea straightaway, but he's looking a bit uncertain.

"Right . . ." he says. "Why?"

"To pass the endless weary decades, of course! Imagine our marriage is an epic movie. Well, no one gets bored in a movie, do they? Why? Because there are surprises round every corner."

"I fell asleep in *Avatar,*" he says promptly.

"I mean an exciting movie," I explain. "And, anyway, you only fell asleep in the middle bit. And you were tired."

We're at the front door by now, and Dan reaches for his key. Then, looking over my shoulder, his face changes to one of horror.

"Oh God. Oh my God. What's *that*? Sylvie, don't look, it's *awful. . . .*"

"What?" I swing round, my heart tripping in fright. "What is it?"

"Surprise!" says Dan, and pushes open the door.

"Not *that* kind of surprise!" I say furiously. "Not *that* kind!"

Honestly. He has *completely* missed the point. I meant nice surprises, not stupid wind-ups.

The sitter we used tonight is called Beth, and we've never used her before. As we walk into the kitchen she smiles cheerily, but I can't quite smile back. The whole place is littered with toys. It's toy carnage.

I mean, we're not the tidiest family in the world, but I do like to be able to see *some*

133

floor space in my house.

"Er . . . hi, Beth," I say faintly. "Was everything OK?"

"Yeah, great!" She's already pulling on her jacket. "They're sweet, your girls. They couldn't sleep, so I let them have a little play. We had fun!"

"Right," I manage. "So I . . . see."

There's Lego everywhere. Dollies' clothes everywhere. Sylvanian Families' furniture everywhere.

"See you, then," says Beth blithely, taking the money that Dan is proffering. "Thanks."

"Right. Er . . . see you . . ."

The words are barely out of my mouth before the front door has slammed behind her.

"Wow," I say, looking around.

"Let's leave it," says Dan. "Get up early, get the girls to help. . . ."

"No." I shake my head. "Mornings are such a rush. I'd rather get at least some of it put away now."

I sink to the ground and begin to gather a Sylvanian table and chairs. I set them up together and add tiny cereal packets. After a moment, Dan sighs and starts grabbing Lego bits, with the resigned air of a convict settling in for a day with the chain gang.

"How many hours of our lives . . ." he begins.

"Don't."

I put three teeny saucepans on a teeny cooker and pat them. I do rather love Sylvanian Families. Then I sit back on my heels.

"I'm serious," I say. "We each arrange little surprises for the other. Keep our marriage sparky." I wait for him to put the Lego tub back in the cupboard. "What do you think? Are you up for it?"

"Up for what exactly?" He peers at me with his most scrubcious expression. "I still don't know quite what I'm supposed to do."

"That's the point! There isn't any 'supposed.' Just . . . use your imagination. Play around. Have fun." I head over to Dan, put my arms around his neck, and smile up at him affectionately. "Surprise me."

FIVE

I'm actually quite excited.

Dan said he couldn't launch straight into some program of surprises for me; he needed time to think first. So we've had a week of preparation time. It's been a bit like Christmas. I know he's up to something, because he's been on Google a lot. Meanwhile, I've been all over this project. All over it! I have a special notebook, labeled PROJECT SURPRISE ME. He's not going to know what's hit him.

I'm gazing with satisfaction at my *Surprise Me: Master Plan* page, when Mrs. Kendrick's tread becomes audible on the stairs. I hastily shut my notebook, turn to the office computer, and resume typing out captions for the Fabulous Fans brochure. We'll print the brochure on creamy paper and then write all the labels out by hand in blue-black fountain pen. (Rollerballs are very much not a Mrs. Kendrick thing.)

Nineteenth-century fan, hand-painted by Parisian artist (unattributed).

"Good morning, Mrs. Kendrick." I look up with a smile.

"Good morning, Sylvie."

Mrs. Kendrick is wearing a pale-blue suit, her cameo brooch, and her customary worried frown. Customary as of the evil nephew arriving, that is. Apparently he's staying with her at the moment, which explains why she looks so downtrodden. I expect he lectures her about modern working practices over the toast every morning. She gives the room her usual anxious sweeping gaze, as though to say, "Something's wrong here, but I don't know what." Then she turns to me.

"Sylvie," she says. "Have you heard of 'Museum Selfie Day'?" She utters the words with care, as though they're a foreign language.

"Yes," I say warily. "I have. Why?"

"Oh, just that Robert mentioned it. He thinks we should participate."

"Well." I shrug. "We could. But I'm not sure the patrons would really go for it, do you? I think it's for a certain demographic. I think, to be honest, taking selfies might put some of our patrons off."

"Ah." Mrs. Kendrick nods. "Quite. Quite. Good point." Then she pauses, looking still more worried. "Sylvie, may I ask you . . ." She lowers her voice to a whisper. "What *is* a 'selfie'? I keep hearing this word everywhere, but I've never quite . . . and I *couldn't* ask Robert what it meant. . . ."

Oh God. I bite my lip at the thought of poor old Mrs. Kendrick having some long conversation about Selfie Day with no idea what a selfie is.

"It's a photo," I say kindly. "Just a photo of yourself somewhere. You take it with your phone."

I know this won't mean much to Mrs. Kendrick. In her world, a phone is something that lives on a side table and has a curly wire. She meanders out of the office, probably to go and look dolefully at the Tesco Value biscuits we now offer, and I type another caption.

Feathered fan.

As I type, I feel a bit conflicted. Obviously I still resent this Robert character for trampling into our world and freaking out his aunt. But on the more positive side, if he's suggesting we do Museum Selfie Day, maybe he's not going to turn us into condos? Maybe he actually wants to help?

Should we do Museum Selfie Day?

I try to imagine any of our regular patrons taking a selfie — and fail. I can see where

Robert's coming from, I really can, but hasn't he picked up the vibe? Hasn't he *looked* at our clientele?

Even so, I write *Museum Selfie Day?* on a Post-it and sigh. It's the kind of forward-thinking idea I would have been really excited about when I first joined Willoughby House. I actually wrote a whole digital-strategy document when I arrived, in my spare time. I dug it out last night, to see if there was anything useful in it. But when I read it through, all I could do was wince. It felt so *old.* It referred to websites that don't even exist anymore.

Mrs. Kendrick, needless to say, responded to it at the time with a charming "I don't think so, dear." So we didn't use any of my ideas. Willoughby House just went on its own sweet, quirky way. And we're fine. We're happy. Do we need to change? Isn't there room for one place in the world that *isn't* like everywhere else?

With another sigh, I consult the typed notes which one of Mrs. Kendrick's pet experts compiled for us — but he hasn't added anything about this fan. Honestly. Is there nothing else to say about it? I'm not just putting *Feathered fan.* It sounds totally lame. The V&A wouldn't just put *Feathered fan,* I'm sure of it.

I peer at the photo of the fan, which is large and rather flamboyant, then add, *probably used by a courtesan.*

Which I expect is true. Then my phone buzzes and I see *Tilda* on the display.

"Hiya!" I fit my phone under my ear and carry on typing. "What's up?"

"I have a hypothetical for you," says Tilda without preamble. "Suppose Dan bought you a piece of clothing as a surprise and you didn't like it?"

At once my mind zigzags like lightning. Dan's bought me something! Tilda knows about it. How? Because he asked her advice, maybe. What's wrong with it? What could be wrong with it?

What *is* it?

No. I don't want to know. It's supposed to be a surprise. I'm not going to ruin his surprise.

And, anyway, I'm not the type of person to pick holes in a present just because it's not "perfect," whatever that is. I'm not some kind of mean-spirited control freak. I love the idea that Dan has gone off to choose me something, and I'm sure it's wonderful, whatever it is.

"I'd appreciate it, whatever it was," I say, a little sanctimoniously. "I'd be really grateful he'd bought me something and value his effort and thought. Because that's what presents are all about. It's not the things themselves which matter but the *emotions* behind those things."

I finish my sentence with a flourish, feeling rather noble for being so unmaterialistic.

"OK," says Tilda, not sounding convinced. "Fair enough. But suppose it was really expensive and really hideous?"

My fingers stop, midway through typing the word *embroidered.* "How expensive?" I say, at length. "How hideous?"

"Well, I don't want to give anything away," says Tilda cautiously. "It's supposed to be a surprise."

"Give a little bit away," I suggest, lowering my voice instinctively. "I won't let on."

"OK." Tilda lowers her voice too. "Suppose it was cashmere but a really odd color?"

Again, my mind does lightning zigzags. Cashmere! Dan bought me cashmere! But, oh God, what color? Tilda is actually quite adventurous with color, so if *she* thinks it's bad . . .

"How do you know what color it is?" I can't help asking.

"Dan asked me to take delivery, and the box was already a bit open, so I peeked

141

inside the tissue paper and . . ." She exhales. "I don't know for sure . . . but I don't think you're going to like it."

"What color is it?"

Tilda sighs again. "It's this weird petrol blue. It's horrible. Shall I send you the link?"

"Yes!"

I wait anxiously for her email to arrive, click on the link, and then blink in horror.

"Oh my *God.*"

"I know," comes Tilda's voice. "Awful."

"How did they even create that color?"

"I don't know!"

The sweater itself is quite nice, if a little dull in shape. But that *blue.* On the website, they've put it on this stunning Asian girl and given her blue lipstick to match, and she can carry it off, just about. But me? With my pale skin and blond hair? In *that*?

"They talked Dan into it," asserts Tilda. "I'm sure they did. He told me they were 'very helpful' on the phone. Like hell they were. They had a shedload of vile blue sweaters to sell, and along comes Dan like an innocent lamb, with his credit card and no idea. . . ."

"What am I going to do, Tilda?" My voice jerks in slight panic. "What am I going to do?"

I'm not feeling *quite* as noble as I was. I mean, I know it's the thought that counts and everything . . . but I really don't want an expensive petrol-blue cashmere sweater in my wardrobe, reproaching me every time I don't wear it. Or having to put it on every time we go out to dinner.

Or saying I love it, and then Dan buys me the matching scarf and gloves for Christmas and I have to say I love those, too, and then he gets me a coat and says, "It's 'your color,' darling. . . ."

"Exchange it?" suggests Tilda.

"Oh, but . . ." I wince. "I can't say, Dan, darling, that's amazing, it's perfect, now I'm going to exchange it."

"Shall I say something to Dan?"

"*Would* you?" I collapse in relief.

"I'll say I caught sight of it and I know the company and there's something that would suit you much better. Just a friendly suggestion."

"Tilda, you're a star."

"So what shall I suggest?"

"Ooh! Dunno. I've never looked at this website before."

I'm quite impressed, actually, that Dan headed there. It's not discount cashmere; it's posh, high-end Scottish cashmere.

I flick through a few of the pages and suddenly come across a cardigan called the Nancy. It's stunning. Long-line and flattering, with a belt. It'll look fantastic over jeans.

"Hey, look at the Nancy cardigan," I say in excitement.

"OK, just clicking . . ." There's a pause, then Tilda exclaims, "Oh, that's perfect! I'll tell Dan to order you that instead. *Not* in vile blue. What color do you like?"

I scroll down the color options, feeling like a child in a sweetie shop. Choosing your own surprise present is *fun*.

"Seafoam," I say at last.

"Gorgeous. What size?"

"Ah." I stare at the website uncertainly. "Maybe ten. Maybe twelve. What size is the sweater?"

"It's size ten," reports Tilda. "But it's a bit small-looking. Tell you what, I'll get Dan to order both and then I'll look at them and judge. He can send the other one back. I mean, if you're going to get it right, you might as well get it right."

"Tilda, thank you!"

"Oh, it's no trouble, I'll call Dan now. It's quite fun, secret packages arriving like this. . . ." She hesitates, then adds, "Very nice of Dan to order you a cashmere sweater out of the blue. Is it in honor of anything?"

"Er . . ." I'm not sure how to reply. I

haven't told anyone else about our little project. But maybe I'll confide in Tilda. "Kind of," I say at last. "I'll tell you when I see you."

I'm not expecting to hear any more from Tilda that day, but two hours later, as I'm in the middle of typing out a newsletter, she rings again.

"They're here!"

"What are here?" I say, confused.

"Your cardigans! Dan changed the order, they biked them over and took the first sweater back. It's a good delivery service, I must say."

"Wow. Well, what do you think?"

"Gorgeous," says Tilda emphatically. "My only issue is, which size? I can't tell. And so I was wondering, why don't you pop over quickly and try them on?"

Try them on? I stare uncertainly at the phone. Choosing my own surprise present was one thing. But is trying it on going too far?

"Shouldn't I keep some of the mystery?" I say.

"Mystery?" Tilda scoffs. "There is no mystery! Try them on, choose the one that fits, job done. Otherwise, I'm bound to tell Dan the wrong size and it'll be a great big hassle."

She sounds so matter-of-fact, I'm convinced.

"OK." I glance at my watch. "It's time for
lunch, anyway. I'm on my way."

As I arrive at Tilda's house I can hear
thumping noises coming from upstairs.
Tilda opens the front door, scoops me in
for a hug, then yells, "What are you *doing*?"
over her shoulder.

A moment later, Toby appears on the
stairs. He's in an old white T-shirt and black
jeans and is holding a hammer.

"Hello, Sylvie, how are you?" he says
politely. Then he turns to Tilda, before I
have time to reply. "What do you mean,
'What are you doing?' You know what I'm
doing. We discussed it."

I can see Tilda breathing in and out again,
slowly.

"I mean," she says, "why are you making
so much noise?"

"I'm putting up *speakers,*" says Toby, as
though it's obvious.

"But why is it taking so long?"

"Mum, have you ever put up speakers?"
Toby sounds irritated. "No. So. This is how
long it takes. This is what it sounds like.
Bye, Sylvie, nice to see you," he adds, in his
polite-Toby manner, and I can't help smil-

ing. He turns and marches back upstairs and Tilda glowers after him.

"Don't damage the wall!" she calls. "That's all I ask. Don't damage the wall."

"I'm not going to damage the wall," Toby shouts back, as though highly offended. "Why would I damage the wall?"

There's the sound of a door shutting, and Tilda clutches her head.

"Oh God, Sylvie. He has no idea what he's doing; he's got some set of power tools from somewhere. . . ."

"Don't worry," I say soothingly. "I'm sure it'll be fine."

"Yes." Tilda seems unconvinced. "Yes, maybe. Anyway." She focuses on me as though for the first time. "Cardigans."

"Cardigans!" I echo with a tweak of glee. I follow Tilda into her office, which is yellow-painted and lined with books and has French windows into the garden. She reaches below her desk and pulls out a flat, expensive-looking box.

"They're perfect," she says, as I'm taking off the lid. "The only issue is the fit."

I pull the cardigans out and sigh with pleasure. The color is beautiful and the cashmere is super-soft. How Dan could *ever* have chosen that vile —

Anyway. Not the point.

An almighty whining drilling comes from upstairs and Tilda jumps.

"What's he doing now?" She gazes upward as though in despair.

"It'll be fine!" I say reassuringly. "He'll just be putting brackets up, or something."

I try on the size 10, and then the size 12, and then the size 10 again, admiring myself in Tilda's full-length mirror.

"Stunning." Tilda eyes me curiously. "But you still haven't told me what it's for. Not birthday, not Christmas, not your wedding anniversary, I don't think?"

"Oh." I pause in my preening. I don't mind telling Tilda, I suppose, even though this is quite a private thing. "Well, the truth is, Dan and I have decided to plan some little surprises for each other."

"Really?" Tilda's curious gaze doesn't waver. "Why?"

I won't go into the whole sixty-eight-more-years-of-marriage thing, I decide. It might sound a bit weird.

"Because . . . why not?" I prevaricate. "To keep our marriage alive. Spice things up. Because it's fun."

"Fun?" Tilda looks aghast. "Surprises aren't fun."

"Yes, they are!" I can't help laughing at her expression.

"I understand 'keep your marriage alive.' That I understand. But surprises, no." She shakes her head emphatically. "Surprises have a bad habit of going wrong."

"They do not!" I retort, feeling nettled. "Everyone loves surprises."

"Life throws enough curveballs at you. Why add to them? This won't end well," she adds darkly, and I feel a flinch of annoyance.

"How can it not end well? Look, just because you don't happen to like surprises —"

"You're right." She nods. "I don't like surprises. In my experience, you plan one surprise and end up with a totally different one. When I was twenty-eight, my boyfriend — Luca, his name was, Italian — he threw me a surprise party. But the *big* surprise was that he ended up snogging my cousin."

"Oh," I say feebly.

"While everyone was singing 'Happy Birthday.' "

"Oh God."

"They didn't stay together or anything. Shagged a couple of times, maybe."

"Right." I pull a face. "That's really —"

"And we'd been happy until then," she continues relentlessly. "We'd had three great years together. If he hadn't thrown me that

149

surprise party, maybe I'd have married Luca instead of Adam, and my life wouldn't have been the clusterfuck it has been. He moved back to Italy, it turned out. I stalked him on Facebook. *Tuscany,* Sylvie. I think you need the ten," she adds without taking a breath. "Fits you much better across the shoulders."

"Right." I'm trying to take in everything she's saying, all at once. Tilda is a brilliant multitasker, but sometimes her conversation multitasks a bit *too* much. "If you hadn't married Adam, you wouldn't have Gabriella and Toby," I point out. I'm about to elaborate on this, when there's a thundering down the stairs. The door of Tilda's office bursts open, and Toby surveys her with an accusing look. He has a large piece of plaster in his hair, a light dusting of plaster over his beard, and an electric power drill in his hand.

"These walls are crap," he pronounces resentfully. "They're shoddy. How much did you pay for this house?"

"What have you done?" demands Tilda at once.

"They're flimsy." He scowls, ignoring the question. "Walls should be solid. They shouldn't just break off in chunks."

"Break off in chunks?" echoes Tilda in alarm. "What do you mean, break off in chunks? What have you done?"

"It's not my fault, OK?" Toby exclaims, with a defensive glower. "If this house was a bit more well built . . ." He gestures at the doorframe with his drill and clearly presses the on button by mistake, because it starts drilling noisily into the doorframe.

"Toby!" screams Tilda above the noise. "Stop! Turn it off!"

Hastily, Toby turns the drill off and withdraws it from the hole that it's now made in the office doorframe.

"I don't know how that happened," he says, eyeing the drill dispassionately. "That shouldn't have happened."

"What have you done?" says Tilda for the third time, and this time she sounds quite steely.

"There's a bit of a . . . hole," says Toby. He catches Tilda's eye and gulps, suddenly looking a bit less sure of himself. "I expect I can cover it up. I'll do that. I'll cover it up. Bye, Sylvie," he adds, and hastily backs away.

"Bye!" I call after him, biting my lip. I know I shouldn't laugh. But Tilda's expression is quite comical.

"*How* my life could have been different," she says, apparently to the wall. "I could be in Tuscany. Making my own olive oil."

"Hey, Dan's coming up the path," Toby calls down from the stairs. "Shall I let him in?"

My whole body jolts in shock. Dan? Dan? *Here?*

Wildly, Tilda and I stare at each other. Then Tilda calls back, "No, don't worry, Tobes!" in a slightly strangled voice. "Upstairs," she hisses to me. "I'll get rid of him."

I hurry up the stairs, my heart pounding, hoping frantically that he won't recognize me through the wavy glass of Tilda's front door or look up through the clear fanlight. What's he *doing* here?

"Hello, Dan!" From my vantage point on the landing, I can see Tilda greeting him below. "This is a surprise!"

"I'm just going to Clapham on a site visit," says Dan, "so I thought, why not pick up that package now, while Sylvie isn't about?"

"Good idea!" says Tilda heartily. "Very good idea. It's just through here in my office; come this way. . . ."

My heartbeat is subsiding. OK. No need to panic. He'll just take the box and go and never know I was here. It's quite funny, really, the two of us creeping around after each other.

Tilda leads Dan to her office and I tiptoe

down the stairs a little to listen to them.

". . . very nice," Dan is saying in a voice I can only barely make out. "You're right, the blue was a little . . . blue. So which size do you think I should keep?"

"Definitely the size ten," says Tilda. "I know it'll fit her better."

"Great." There's a slight pause, then Dan says, sounding puzzled, "Er . . . where *is* the size ten?"

Shit! Shit, shit!

I look down at myself in sudden ghastly comprehension. I'm *wearing* the size 10.

"Oh!" says Tilda, her voice a desperate squawk. "Oh! Of course. I took it upstairs to . . . to ask Toby's opinion. I'll just get it. Stay there!" Tilda adds shrilly.

She hurries into the hall and waves her arms at me in mute desperation. Frantically, I unbutton the cardigan, my fingers catching on the buttonholes, and, at last, thrust it at her.

Go! Tilda mouths at me.

As I retreat upstairs to the landing, Dan wanders into the hall, holding the box, and my stomach squirms. That was close.

"Here we are," says Tilda, giving him the cardigan with a rictus smile.

"It's warm." Dan sounds even more puzzled, as well he might.

"It was lying in the sunlight," says Tilda without missing a beat. "Such a lovely present, I know she'll adore it. But I'm afraid I really do have to get back to work now."

I sense a movement behind me and turn to see Toby emerging from a door, covered quite thickly in plaster dust.

"Oh," he says in surprise, "hi —"

Before he can say "Sylvie," I've clamped my hand over his mouth like a mugger.

"No!" I whisper in his ear, with such ferocity he blinks in alarm. He struggles a little, but I'm not letting go. Not till it's safe.

"Right," says Dan, below us in the hall. "Well, thanks again, Tilda. Really appreciate it."

"Anytime." Tilda gives him a quizzical look. "Is it for anything special? Or just a random surprise?"

"Just a random surprise." Dan smiles at her. "Just felt like it."

"Good idea! Nothing like a nice surprise." Tilda shoots a quick, sardonic glance upward in my direction. "See you, Dan." She kisses him briskly on each cheek, then the door closes behind him, and finally I relax my grip on Toby.

"Ow!" he says, giving me an aggrieved look and rubbing his mouth. "Ow!"

"Sorry," I say, not meaning it. "But I

couldn't risk you giving me away."

"What *is* all this?" he demands.

"Just . . . a thing," I say, heading downstairs. "Surprise present. Don't tell Dan you saw me." I squint through the fanlight. "What's he doing? Has he gone? Can you see?"

"He's driving away," reports Tilda, who is peering through the letterbox. She stands up and makes an exaggerated huffing sound. "*What* a palaver. You see? All you're doing is making trouble for yourselves."

"We're not!" I say defiantly. "It's fun."

Tilda rolls her eyes. "So what are you doing for Dan? Getting him cashmere socks?"

"Oh, I'm doing plenty of things." My mind ranges over all my plans for tomorrow, and I give a pleased little smile. "Plenty of things."

Six

My surprise campaign starts first thing, and thankfully my body clock is on my side, because I wake up before Dan. I can hear the girls chatting quietly in their bedroom, but we should have another half hour or so before they start hurling teddies at each other and shrieking.

I creep downstairs, hover by the front door, and spot the Room Service London guy as he pulls up on his motorbike.

"Hi!" I call in hushed tones, and give him a wave. "Here, thanks!"

I'm so pleased with myself. Anyone could make breakfast. Anyone could put together a tray of croissants or eggs and bacon. But I've taken things one step further. I've prepared Dan a surprise international breakfast that will blow his mind!

OK, *prepared* is probably the wrong word. *Ordered* would be more accurate. I used this website where you click on items just like on a room-service menu and they deliver it all in two insulated boxes (hot and cold), complete with a silver tray. (You put down a deposit against the tray, because apparently a lot of people keep them.)

"Shh!" I say, as the delivery guy tramps up the path, still wearing his bike helmet. He's holding two boxes marked *Room Service London,* balanced on what must be the wrapped-up tray. "This is a surprise!"

"Yeah." The guy nods impassively as he puts down his load and holds out his hand-set for me to sign. "We're often a surprise."

"Oh."

"Yeah, we get a lot of wives in southwest London ordering for their husbands. Forti-eth birthday, is it?"

"No!" I say, and give him an affronted glare. First: I thought I was being really unique and individual, not just another "wife in southwest London." Second: Forti-eth birthday? What? Why should I be mar-ried to a forty-year-old? I'm only thirty-two, and I look far younger than that. Far, *far* younger. You know, bearing in mind I've had twins and everything.

Shall I say, "Actually, it's for my twenty-year-old toy boy"?

No. Because I am a mature grown-up and don't care what delivery people think of me.

(Also, Dan might suddenly appear at the door in his dressing gown.)

"Big order." The guy nods at the boxes. "This all his favorite stuff?"

"No, it's not," I almost snap. "It's a bespoke international surprise breakfast, actually."

Ha. Not such a southwest London cliché *now.*

The delivery guy heads back to his bike and I carry the boxes inside to the kitchen. I rip the wrapping off the tray — which is beautiful dull silver with *RSL* engraved at the top — and start assembling dishes. They all come in plain white china (there's a deposit against that too), and there's even cutlery and napkins. The whole thing looks amazing, and my only *tiny* proviso is that I'm not quite sure which dish is which.

Anyway, never mind. I tuck the printed menu into my dressing-gown pocket and decide we can work it all out while we eat it. The main thing is to get it upstairs while the hot things are still hot. It's a bit of a struggle to carry the tray upstairs without overbalancing, but I manage it and push my way into the bedroom.

"Surprise!"

Dan's head turns from where it was buried in the pillow. He sees me holding the tray and his whole expression lights up.

"No way."

"Breakfast!" I nod in delight. "Surprise breakfast!"

I head over to him and dump the tray down on the bed with slightly more force than I was intending, only it was getting heavy.

"Look at this!" Dan somehow struggles to a sitting position without overturning the tray, then surveys it, rubbing his sleepy eyes. "What a treat."

"It's a *surprise* breakfast," I say again, emphasizing *surprise,* because I think this factor needs to be made clear.

"Wow." I can see Dan's eyes ranging over the dishes and landing on a glass full of pink juice. "So, is this . . ."

"Pomegranate juice," I tell him, pleased with myself. "It's totally the thing. Orange juice is over."

Dan sips at the glass and instantly his mouth puckers.

"Great!" he says. "Very . . . um . . . refreshing."

Refreshing in a good way?

"Let me taste," I say, and take the glass. As I sip, I can feel my taste buds shriveling. That is *tart.* It's an acquired taste.

Which we can acquire very quickly, I'm sure.

"So, what *is* all this?" Dan is still peering at the white dishes. "Is there a theme?"

"It's a fusion breakfast," I say proudly. "International. I chose all the dishes myself. Some European, some American, some Asian . . ." I pull the menu out of my pocket. "You've got marinated fish, you've got a German specialty meat dish. . . ."

"Is this coffee?" Dan reaches for the cup.

"No!" I laugh. "Coffee wouldn't be a *surprise*, would it? This is artichoke and dandelion tea. It's South American."

Dan takes his hand away from the cup and instead picks up his spoon. "So this . . ." He prods at a porridge-type substance. "This isn't bircher muesli, is it?"

"No." I consult my list. "It's congee. Chinese rice porridge."

It's not *quite* as appealing as I was expecting. Especially with that gelatinous-looking egg floating on top — which, if I'm honest, turns my stomach. But apparently the Chinese eat it every morning. A billion people can't be wrong, can they?

"OK," says Dan slowly, turning to another dish. "And this?"

"I think it might be the Indian lentil broth." I glance at my menu again. "Unless it's the cheese grits."

Looking at the tray properly for the first time, I have a realization: I ordered too many dishes which are basically a bowl of gloopy stuff. But how was I meant to know? Why doesn't the website have a "gloopy stuff" algorithm? There should be a helpful pop-up box: *Did you mean to order so much gloopy stuff?* I might suggest it to them, in an email.

"You haven't eaten anything yet!" I say, handing Dan a spherical dumpling-like object. "This is an idli. It's Indian. Made from fermented batter."

"Right." Dan looks at the idli, then puts it down. "Wow. This is really . . ."

"It's different, right?" I say eagerly. "Not what you were expecting."

"Absolutely not," says Dan, sounding heartfelt. "Very much not what I was expecting."

"So, dive in!" I spread my hands wide. "It's all yours!"

"I will! I will!" He nods lots of times, almost as though he's having to convince himself. "It's just hard to know where to start. It all looks so —" He breaks off. "What's this one?" He prods the German meat dish.

"Leberkäse," I read from the menu. "It

literally means 'liver cheese.' "

Dan makes a sort of gulpy sound, and I give him a bright, encouraging smile, even though I'm slightly regretting having said "liver cheese" out loud. It's not necessarily what you want to hear first thing in the morning, is it, "liver cheese"?

"Look," I continue, "you love rye bread, so why not start with that?"

I push the Scandinavian dish toward him. It's marinated fish with rye bread and sour cream. Perfect. Dan loads up his fork, and I watch expectantly as he takes a mouthful.

"Oh my God." He claps his hand to his mouth. "I can't . . ." To my dismay, he's gagging. He's retching. "I'm going to . . ."

"Here." In panic, I thrust a napkin at him. "Just spit it out."

"I'm sorry, Sylvie." As Dan finally mops his mouth, he's shuddering. His face has gone pale, and I notice a bead of sweat on his brow. "I just couldn't. It tasted like some kind of decaying, putrefying . . . what *is* that?"

"Have some liver cheese to take away the taste," I say, desperately pushing the plate toward him, but Dan looks like he might retch again.

"Maybe in a minute," he says, looking a little wildly around the tray. "Is there anything . . . you know. Normal?"

"Er . . . er . . ." Frantically I scan the menu. I'm sure I ordered some strawberries. Where the hell are they?

Then I notice a tiny box at the bottom of the menu:

Please accept our apologies. The strawberry platter is unavailable, so we have substituted Egyptian foul medames.

Foul medames? I don't want foul bloody medames. I look at the tray and feel a crash of despair. This whole breakfast is foul. It's gloopy and weird. I should have bought croissants. I should have made pancakes.

"I'm sorry." I bite my lip miserably. "Dan, I'm so sorry. This is a horrible breakfast. Don't eat it."

"It's not horrible!" says Dan at once.

"It is."

"It's just . . ." He pauses to choose a word. "Challenging. If you're not used to it." The color has returned to his face and he gives me a reassuring hug. "It was a lovely thought." He picks up an idli and nibbles it. "And you know what? This is good." He takes a sip of the artichoke tea and winces. "Whereas that's vile." He pulls such a comical expression, I can't help laughing.

"Shall I make you some coffee?"

"I would love some coffee." He pulls me

tight to him again. "And thank you. Really."

It takes me five minutes to make some coffee and spread marmalade on two slices of toast. As I get back upstairs, Tessa and Anna have joined Dan in bed, and the tray of food has been discreetly placed in the far corner of the room, where no one has to look at it.

"Coffee!" exclaims Dan, like a man on a desert island seeing a ship. "And toast too!"

"Surprise!" I waggle the plate of toast at him.

"Well, I've got a surprise for *you*," Dan replies with a grin.

"It's a box," puts in Tessa, in a rush. "We've seen it. It's a box with ribbons on. It's under the bed."

"You're not supposed to tell Mummy!" Anna immediately looks distraught. "Daddy! Tessa told!"

Tessa turns defiantly pink. She may be only five, but she has mettle, my daughter. She never explains, apologizes, or surrenders, unless under severe duress. Whereas Anna, poor Anna, crumples at first glance.

"Well, Mummy knew already," Tessa asserts boldly. "Mummy *knew* what it was. Didn't you, Mummy?"

My heart flips over before I realize this is just Tessa being Tessa and inventing an instant, plausible defense. (*How* are we going to cope with her when she's fifteen? Oh God. Better park that thought for now.)

"Know about what?" I sound totally fake to my own ears. "My goodness, a box? What could *that* be?"

Thankfully, Dan has leaned under the bed and can't see my substandard acting face. He hauls out the box and I unwrap it, trying to pace my reactions, trying to look genuine, aware of Tessa watching me beadily. Somehow my children's little penetrating eyes are a lot more unnerving than Dan's trusting ones.

"Oh my GOD!" I exclaim. "Wow! *Cashmere?* Is this a . . . cardigan? It's just . . . Oh my God. And the color's perfect, and the *belt . . .*"

Too much?

No, not too much. Dan looks replete with happiness — and the louder I exclaim, the happier he looks. He's so easy to fool. I feel a fresh wave of fondness for him, sitting there with his piece of toast, unaware that I'm lying through my teeth.

I honestly don't think it could go the other way. Dan is transparent. He's guileless. If he was lying through his teeth, I'd know. I'd just *know.*

165

"Tilda helped me choose it," he says modestly.

"No way!" I gasp. "Tilda? You and Tilda were in league over this? You!" I give him a little push on the arm.

Too much?

No, not too much. Dan looks even more delighted. "You really like it?"

"I love it. *What* a brilliant surprise."

I give him a huge kiss, feeling satisfied with myself. We're doing it! The plan's working! We're spicing up our marriage. OK, so the breakfast was a slight misfire, but otherwise, bull's-eye. I could *easily* face another sixty-eight years of marriage if every day started with Dan giving me a cashmere cardigan.

No, OK, rewind, obviously I don't mean that literally. Dan can't give me a cashmere cardigan every day; what a ludicrous idea. (Although: Every six months, maybe? Just a thought. Just putting it in the mix.) I suppose what I mean is, I could easily face another sixty-eight years of marriage if they all began like today has. All happy and connected.

So. Actually, I'm not sure where that gets us, but I feel as though I'm Thinking Through Our Issues, which has got to be a good thing, no?

"So." Dan drains his coffee cup and puts it down with a dynamic air. "I must get going. I have a mystery errand to complete." His eyes flash at me, and I beam back.

"Well, I have a mystery task too. Will you be back for lunch?" I add casually. "I thought we'd have pasta and pesto, nothing fancy. . . ."

Ha! Ha! *Not.*

"Oh, sure. I'll be back by noon." Dan nods.

"Great!" I turn my attention to Tessa and Anna. "Right! Who wants breakfast?"

Saturday morning is when I catch up with boring household tasks, while Tessa and Anna play with all the toys they don't have time for during the week. Then we have an early lunch and I take the girls to their 2:00 P.M. ballet lesson.

But not today!

The minute Dan's left the house, I get cracking. I've been meaning to change the kitchen curtains forever, and this is my perfect excuse. I've also bought a coordinating tablecloth, some new candlesticks, and a lamp. I'm giving the kitchen a whole makeover, like in that interiors show I always watch in bed when Dan is downstairs watching the rugby. Our new-look kitchen will feel bright and fresh and new and Dan will love it.

I'm hot and sweating by the time everything is done. It's taken a bit longer than I expected and I've resorted to letting the girls watch CBeebies — but the place looks amazing. The curtains are a really funky print from John Lewis, and the neon rubber candlesticks add a pop of color. (I got that from the TV show. It's all about "pops of color.")

When Karen, our nanny, arrives, I lean nonchalantly against the counter and wait for her to exclaim in admiration. Karen is quite into design and stuff. She always has interesting-colored trainers or nail polish on, and she reads my *Livingetc* after me. She's half Scottish, half Guyanese, and has lots of dark curly hair, which Anna loves decorating with hair slides. Sure enough, she notices the makeover at once.

"Awesome!" She looks around, taking in all the details. "I love those curtains! Really awesome!"

Karen's thing is that she adopts a word and then uses only that word for about a week and then moves onto a new one. Last week it was "trashy"; this week it's "awesome."

"Awesome candlesticks!" she says, picking

one up. "Are those from Habitat? I was looking at those last week."

"I think they add a pop of color," I say casually.

"Awesome." Karen nods and puts the candlestick down. "So, *what* exactly is happening today?"

She sounds a bit puzzled, and I don't blame her. We don't normally employ her on Saturdays, nor do I normally send her texts beginning *Don't tell Dan I'm texting you!!*

"I wanted to give Dan a surprise," I explain. "Take him out somewhere special."

"Right." Karen opens her mouth as though to say something — then closes it again. "Right. Awesome."

"So, if you could give the girls lunch, take them to ballet and then maybe the park? We'll be back at four-ish."

"OK," says Karen slowly. Again, she looks as though she wants to say something more but isn't sure where to start. She isn't going to ask for a change in hours or something, is she? Because I really don't have time.

"Anyway!" I say briskly. "I must go and get ready. Thanks, Karen!"

I take a quick shower before dressing in capri pants and my new cardigan. Sure enough, a minicab soon pulls up outside our house, and I feel a tweak of glee. Dan will be so surprised! In fact, I'm pretty sure I can hear him arriving home. I'd better get a move on.

It only takes me four minutes to do my makeup and a minute more to put my hair in a knot. I hurry downstairs and pause halfway down, glancing through the landing window. To my surprise, there's now a second cab parked next to the first one.

Two?

Oh my God. Please don't say . . .

As I'm staring at the cabs, Dan comes out of the sitting room. He's wearing a smart blue shirt and linen jacket and his eyes are gleaming.

"You look lovely!" he says. "Which is good news, because . . . drum roll . . . we're not having pasta at home!"

"Dan," I say slowly. "Have you done something? Because I've done something too."

"What do you mean?" Dan says, puzzled.

"Look outside," I say, coming all the way down the stairs. Dan opens the front door and I see him blink at the sight of the two cabs. I'm pretty sure they both come from Asis Taxis, the firm we always use.

"What the *hell*?"

"One of them's mine," I say. "Don't tell me the other one's yours. Have we both organized a treat?"

"But . . ." Dan is staring at the cabs, looking totally scrubcious, his brow furrowed. "But I was organizing lunch," he says at last.

"No, you weren't, I was!" I retort, almost crossly. "It was a surprise. I ordered the cab, I booked Karen —"

"I booked Karen too!" says Dan hotly. "I booked her days ago."

"You both booked me!" Karen's voice comes from behind, and the two of us swivel round. She's gazing at the pair of us and seems a bit freaked out. "You both sent me these texts, saying could I work on Saturday and 'keep it secret.' I didn't know what was going on. So I thought I'd just turn up and . . . see."

"Right," I say. "Fair enough."

We should have known this would happen. We should have made a plan. Only then it wouldn't have been a surprise.

"Well, we obviously can't do both. . . ." Dan suddenly focuses on me. "What's your surprise?"

"I'm not telling you! It's a *surprise.*"

"Well, I'm not telling you mine," he says adamantly. "It would ruin it."

"Well." I fold my arms, equally adamant.

"So what do we do? Toss a coin?"

"I'm not tossing a coin!" I retort. "I think

we should just do my surprise. It's really good. We can do yours another day."

"No, we can't!" Dan seems offended. "What, you're assuming your idea is better than mine?"

"Tickets to Tim Wender's sold-out lunchtime event at the Barbican Comedy Festival?" I want to say. "Our favorite stand-up comedian and lunch? You think you can beat that?"

But obviously I have manners, so I don't. I just give him a little smile and shrug and say, "Mine's pretty good."

"Well, *so's mine.*" Dan glares at me.

"Let me decide!" suggests Karen suddenly. "You tell me the plans and I'll decide which one you should go with."

What? That's a stupid idea.

"Great idea!" says Dan. "I'll go first." And there's something about his ebullient demeanor that makes me wonder for the first time: What's he planned? "We'll go into the sitting room," he adds to Karen, "and I'll pitch you my idea there, where Sylvie can't hear. No listening at the door!" he adds to me.

Pitch? What is this, *Dragons'* bloody *Den*?

As he disappears into the sitting room with Karen, I shoot him a mistrustful look. Then I wander disconsolately into the kitchen, where the girls are hoovering up pasta with pesto and studiously ignoring their carrot sticks.

"What does *virgin* mean?" says Tessa at once.

"Virgin?" I stare at her.

"Virgin." She raises her eyes to mine. "I don't know what it means."

"Oh. Goodness. Right." I swallow, my mind scurrying around. "Well, it means . . . it's a person who hasn't yet . . . er . . ." I trail off and reach for a carrot stick, playing for time.

"It can't be a person," objects Tessa. "How would they fit in?"

"They would be too big," agrees Anna. She measures the width of herself with her hands, then squeezes them together tight. "You see?" She looks at me as though making an obvious point. "Too big."

Fit in? Too big? My mind is ranging uneasily over various interpretations of these remarks. And why is Tessa talking about virgins, anyway?

"Tessa," I say carefully. "Have children been talking in the playground, about . . . grown-up things?"

Do I have to have the whole chat, right here, right now? What *is* the chat, anyway? Oh God. I know you're supposed to start early and be all frank like the Dutch, but I'm not saying the word *condom* to my five-year-old; I'm just not. . . .

"I think it means tomato," volunteers Anna.

"It's not tomato," says Tessa scathingly. "It's green. *Green.*"

Suddenly I realize what they're both looking at. The bottle of extra virgin olive oil sitting on the table.

"Oh, this!" I say, my voice almost giddy with relief. "Extra virgin oil! That just means . . . very new. Nice new olives. Mmm. Yummy. Eat up, girls."

I will be frank when the time comes, I promise myself. I'll be Dutch. I'll even say *condom.* Just not today.

"All done!" Dan comes striding into the kitchen, exactly like someone who just went on *Dragons' Den* and won a million pounds' investment. "Your turn."

I head to the sitting room, to find Karen sitting on a high-backed chair in the middle of the room, holding a pen and an A4 writing pad.

"Hello, Sylvie," she says in formal, pleasant tones. "And welcome. Begin whenever you're ready."

I'm already prickling. Welcome to my own sitting room? And, by the way, what's she writing? I haven't even started yet.

"Whenever you're ready," repeats Karen, and I hastily marshal my thoughts.

"Right," I begin. "Well, I'm planning to whisk Dan off for a fabulous, once-in-a-lifetime treat. We're seeing our favorite comedian, Tim Wender, in a special lunch-time performance at the Barbican Comedy Festival. Lunch and wine are included."

I sound like a competition from daytime TV, I realize. Next I'll be promising him £500 spending money in London's exclusive West End.

"Very nice," says Karen, in the same pleasant, ambivalent tone. "Is that it?"

Is that it? I'm about to retort, "Do you know how many strings I had to pull to get those tickets?" But that might not help my case. (And, actually, it was Clarissa who pulled the strings, because she used to work for the Barbican.)

"Yes. That's it," I say.

"All right. I'll let you know my thoughts presently." She smiles a dismissal and I head back out into the hall, feeling all cross and bothered. This is ridiculous.

"How did it go?" Dan comes out of the kitchen, crunching a carrot stick.

"Fine." I shrug.

"Great!" He gives me his ebullient smile

again, just as the door opens. Karen emerges and looks from me to Dan, her face serious.

"I have come to my decision." She pauses momentously, exactly like a judge on TV. "And today . . . you will be carrying out Dan's plan. I'm sorry, Sylvie," she adds to me, "but Dan's plan just had that extra something."

Dan's plan did?

Dan's plan did?

I can't believe it. In fact, I don't believe it. *Mine* had the extra something. But, just like a TV contestant, I manage to squash my real feelings beneath a vivacious smile.

"Well done!" I kiss Dan. "I'm sure you deserve it."

"I wish we could *both* have won," he says generously.

"You did really well, Sylvie," says Karen kindly. "But Dan just had that extra attention to detail."

"Of course!" My smile becomes even brighter. "Well, I can't wait to see it all in action!"

No pressure. But I have set the bar preeeee-tty high.

"Sylvie surprised me with breakfast this morning," Dan is telling Karen. "So really it's only fair that I should surprise her with lunch."

"Hey, you haven't mentioned my other surprise," I say in sudden realization. Dan was in the kitchen just now. He saw the makeover. So why hasn't he exclaimed over it?

"What other surprise?"

"The kitchen . . . ?" I prompt, but Dan still looks blank. "The kitchen!" I snap. "Kitchen!"

"Sorry, was I supposed to find something in the kitchen?" Dan seems bewildered.

I take a deep breath in and a deep breath out. "The curtains?" I say calmly.

I see a look of panic flash through Dan's eyes. "Of course," he says quickly. "The curtains. I was just going to mention them."

"What else?" I grasp his arm tightly, so he can't move. "Tell me what else I did in there."

Dan gulps. "The, uh . . . cupboards?"

"No."

"Table . . . er . . . tablecloth?"

"Lucky guess." I glare at him. "You didn't notice any of it, did you?"

"Let me have another look," pleads Dan. "I was distracted by this lunch business."

"OK." I follow him into the kitchen, where I have to say, my makeover looks amazing. *How* could he not have noticed it?

"Wow!" he duly exclaims. "Those curtains

are great! And the tablecloth . . ."

"What else?" I press him relentlessly. "What else is different?"

"Um . . ." Dan's eyes are darting around, baffled. "This!" He suddenly seizes a Nigella cookbook lying on the table. "This is new."

"That's not new, Daddy!" Tessa breaks into laughter.

"It's the candlesticks," I tell him. "The *candlesticks.*"

"Of course!" Dan's eyes focus on them, and I can tell he's scrabbling for something to say. "Absolutely! I should've . . . They're so bright!"

"They're a pop of color," I explain.

"Definitely," Dan says uncertainly, as though he's not quite sure what "pop of color" means but doesn't dare ask.

"Anyway, I just thought I'd brighten the place up a bit; I thought you'd like it. . . ." I allow a slightly martyred tone to creep into my voice.

"I love it. Love it," Dan repeats emphatically. "And now, my lady . . ." He gives a little bow. "Your carriage awaits."

Luckily the man on the phone at the Barbican Comedy Festival was really sympathetic and had another couple on standby, who were thrilled to get the Tim Wender tickets. (I bet they were.) The second cab wasn't so thrilled to be canceled, but it's a firm we use a lot, so at last they let us off the fare.

On the plus side, Dan's enthusiasm is infectious, and as we travel along in the cab that *he* booked, I'm really starting to feel excited. He has something major to spring on me, I know it.

Although, weirdly, we're not heading into town, which is what I would have expected. We're heading to an unfamiliar part of Clapham. What goes on here?

The car pulls up outside a small restaurant in a side street. It's called Munch, and I peer out doubtfully. Munch? Should I have heard of that? Is it one of these amazing tiny places where you sit on an uncomfortable bench but the food is award-winning?

"So." As Dan turns to me, he looks all shiny-faced with anticipation. "You wanted to be surprised, right?"

"Yes," I say, laughing at his expression. "Yes!"

OK, I'm properly excited now. What's this all about? What?

Our driver opens the door and Dan gestures for me to get out. As he's paying the cab driver, I scan the menu board on the pavement and see that it's a vegan restaurant. Interesting. Not what I would have expected. Unless —

"Oh my God." I turn to Dan in sudden alarm. "Are you turning vegan? Is *that* your surprise? I mean, if so, great!" I hastily add. "Well done!"

"No, I'm not turning vegan." Dan laughs.

"Oh, right. So . . . you just felt like being healthy?"

"Not that either."

Dan ushers me to the entrance, and I push open the door. It's one of those earthy, worthy places, I can see at once. Lots of terra-cotta. Wooden ceiling fans. A pick-your-own-mint-tea planter. (Actually, that's quite fun. Maybe I'll steal that idea for dinner parties.)

"Wow!" I say. "This is —"

"Oh, this isn't the surprise," Dan cuts me off, almost bursting with pride. "That's the surprise."

He points at a far corner table, and I follow his gaze. There's a girl sitting there. A girl with long brown hair and really skinny legs encased in black jeans. Who is it? Do I know her? I *think* I recognize her —

Oh my God, of course. It's that girl from college. She did . . . chemistry? Biochemistry? What's her name again?

Suddenly I realize Dan is waiting for a reaction from me. And not just any old re-action.

"No . . . way!" I say, mustering all my energy. "Dan! You didn't!"

"I did!" Dan beams at me, as though he's presenting me with all my dreams at once.

My mind is working frantically. What the *hell* is going on? Why is some random person from college sitting at our lunch table? And how do I find out her name?

"So!" I say as we give our jackets to a girl with about sixteen earrings in her right ear. "Amazing! How did you — what —"

"How many times have you said to me you wish you'd kept in touch with Claire?" Dan is pink-faced with delight. "So you know what I thought? I thought: Let's make it happen."

Claire. She's called Claire. Of course she is. But this is nuts! I've never even thought about Claire since college. What on earth —

Oh my God, *Claire.*

He's talking about Claire from the art course.

Somehow, I manage to keep smiling as a waitress leads us toward the corner table. There was this girl called Claire who I met on an art course, years ago. She was really great, with a brilliant sense of humor, and we had a few lunches but then our friendship fizzled out. *She's* the one I've been talking about.

Not this Claire.

Fuck, *fuck* . . .

As we reach the table, my face feels stiff. What am I going to *do*?

"We meet at last!" Dan greets Claire like an old friend. "Thank you so much for going along with all my cloak-and-dagger plans. . . ."

"No problem," says Claire in a flat voice. She always had a flat way about her, Claire. "Hi, Sylvie." She pushes back her chair and stands up, taller than me and makeup-free. "Long time."

I glance at Dan. He's watching the pair of us fondly, as though expecting us to fall into each other's arms like that YouTube video of the pet lion seeing its owners again.

"Claire!" I exclaim, in the most emotional voice I can drum up. "This is . . . It's been too long!" I hug her bony, resistant body. "I just . . . Here you are! I don't know what to say!"

"Well. College was a long time ago." Claire shrugs.

"There should be a bottle of fizz on the table," says Dan fretfully. "I'll just go and sort that out. . . . Claire chose the restaurant," he adds to me. "Isn't it great?"

"Fab!" I say, and take a seat on a really uncomfortable painted wooden chair.

"So, this was a surprise," says Claire impassively.

"Yes! So, what exactly happened?" I try to sound casual. "How did this all get arranged?"

"Your husband messaged me on Facebook and said you really wanted to hang out with me." Claire eyes me. "He said you kept saying what a shame it was that we'd lost touch."

"Right."

I'm still smiling, while my mind darts frenziedly around my options. Do I tell her the truth and have a little laugh and ask her to keep it quiet? No. She's not that sort. She'd blurt it out to Dan in a heartbeat, I can tell, and he'd be crushed.

I have to go with this.

Somehow.

"I thought it was a bit strange, to be honest," says Claire. "Hearing from you."

"Well, you know!" I say, over-brightly. "You get to that age and you look back and you think . . . what *did* happen to Claire and . . . the gang?"

"The gang?" Claire frowns blankly.

"You know!" I say. "Everyone! All our mates! Like . . . er . . ."

I can't remember a single name of anyone who Claire might have known. We hung out in different circles. Yes, we were in the same halls — and didn't we once play in a netball match together, when I was co-opted onto the team? Maybe that's how Dan got confused. Maybe he saw an old photo online. But that was our only point of connection. We *weren't bloody friends.*

"I'm in touch with Husky," allows Claire.

"Husky!" I say shrilly. "How's —"

He? She? Who the hell was Husky? I should look more closely at Facebook. But quite honestly, since the twins, I don't have time to check up on all my 768 "friends" the whole time. I barely keep up with my real ones.

"I'm still in touch with Sam . . . Phoebe . . . Freya . . . all the art history lot," I volunteer. "Phoebe's just got married, actually."

"Right," says Claire, with a dampening lack of interest. "I never really got on with them."

Oh God. This is painful. Where's that bottle of fizz got to?

"You and your husband, you're not *selling* something, are you?" says Claire, eyeing me suddenly with suspicion.

"No!"

"Or trying to convert me? Are you Mormons?"

"No." I half-want to cry and half-want to break into hysterical laughter. *We had tickets for Tim Wender. . . .* "Look, here's Dan with the bottle of fizz. Let's have a drink."

It's an ordeal. The food (mostly beans) is dry and bland. The Cava is acidic. The conversation is sparse and difficult, like digging for carrots in rock-hard soil. Claire doesn't give a lot. I mean, she *really* makes it hard. How on earth does she motivate a research team at GlaxoSmithKline? The only plus of the experience is, it's made me want to call up all my *real* friends and gratefully fall into their conversational laps.

At last we get in the cab that Dan's ordered to take us home and wave goodbye. (We offered a lift to Claire, who declined, thank *God.*) Then Dan leans back on his seat in satisfaction.

"That was amazing," I say hastily. "Just amazing!"

"You liked it, huh?" He grins.

"I was blown away," I say truthfully. "To think you went to all that trouble . . . I'm so touched." I reach over to kiss him. "Overwhelmed."

And I really am. Arranging a reunion was

the most thoughtful thing to do. He couldn't have chosen a better treat. (Except if it was with, you know, someone I actually liked.)

"She's not what I imagined," Dan says curiously. "Was she such a fierce vegan at college?"

"Well . . ." I have no idea. "Maybe not *that* fierce."

"And her views on composting." He widens his eyes. "She's quite vociferous, isn't she?"

Dan just made one flip remark and had to put up with a humorless rant, which he took in the best possible spirit. All for me. I could *see* him peering at Claire, thinking, *Why on earth did Sylvie want to get back in touch with her?*

I bite my lip, trying to quell a rising laugh. One day I'll tell him the truth. Like, in a year's time. (Maybe five years' time.)

"Anyway," says Dan, as the cab swings round a corner. "I have one surprise left."

"Me too." I touch his knee. "Mine's a *sexy* surprise. Is yours?"

"It's pretty sexy." He meets my eyes and I can see the glint in them, and then we're kissing properly, passionately, just like we used to do in taxis all the time, before the "back seat" meant "two car seats and bumper wet wipes, just in case."

My surprise is some tingly massage oil. It's supposed to be "super-stimulating," not that Dan seems as though he needs much extra stimulation today. I wonder what his surprise is? Underwear, maybe? Agent Provocateur?

"I can't wait," I murmur into his neck, and I stay nestled up against him all the way home.

As we head into the house, the girls come running to greet us, shrieking something about a ballet show, and Karen follows behind, her eyes shining in expectation.

"Was it awesome?" she demands, then turns to me. "Now you see why I chose Dan's surprise. A reunion! I mean, a *reunion*!"

"Yes!" I try to match her tone. "It . . . blew me away!"

Dan's phone bleeps with a text and his eyes gleam. "All ready!" he says, then looks up. "Karen, you can go now. Thanks so much for stepping in."

"Of course!" says Karen. "Anytime!"

Dan looks suddenly keyed up, I realize. Really keyed up. As Karen waves goodbye and shuts the door behind her, he starts tapping a text into his phone. Is this about the sexy surprise?

"So, shall we plan the rest of the day?" I

say. "Or . . . ?"

"In a minute," says Dan, as though barely hearing me. "In a minute."

The atmosphere has become weirdly tense. Dan's mouth keeps twitching into a smile. He keeps glancing down at his phone and walking to the front door and back. He seems in such a ferment that I feel a squirm of excitement myself. What on *earth* is his sexy surprise? If it's that epic, should we have gone to a hotel for the night?

The doorbell suddenly rings and we both jump.

"What's that?" I say.

"A delivery." Dan's mouth won't stop twitching. "A very special delivery." He opens the door and a deliveryman in a black anorak nods curtly at him.

"All right? Dan Winter, is it?"

"Yes!" says Dan. "All ready."

"We'll get it out of the van, then. Will we be all right, spacewise?" The guy comes in a step and peers around.

"I think so." Dan nods. "You should be able to get it through the hall."

I'm gaping at them in shock. Get what through the hall? This isn't a set of underwear from Agent Provocateur, is it? It's something that needs two men to haul it out of a van.

Oh my God, it's not some sort of . . . *equipment*? Should I hurry the girls away before they glimpse something that will scar them for life?

"Can you take the girls upstairs, Sylvie?" says Dan in unreadable tones, and my heart flips over. "Just until I say so."

"OK!" I say, my voice a bit strangled. What has Dan *done*?

I hustle the girls into their room and read them a *Winnie-the-Pooh* story in a self-conscious voice, all the while thinking: Erotic chair? Erotic sofa? Erotic . . . oh God, what else is there? A sex swing? (No, Dan *couldn't* have ordered that. Our joists would never support a swing.)

I'm desperate to google *big sex item needs delivery in van* on my phone, only the girls are bound to grab it. (This is the trouble with your children learning to read.) So I just have to sit there, talking about Heffalumps, getting into a lather of suspicion and fantasy . . . when at last I hear the front door slamming and the sound of Dan's tread on the stairs.

"Come downstairs," he says, looking round the door, his whole face glowing. "I have quite a surprise for you."

"Surprise!" yells Tessa joyfully, and I glance at her in alarm.

"Dan, should the girls . . ." I give him a meaningful glance. "Is this *suitable*?"

"Of course!" says Dan. "Go to the kitchen, girls. You won't believe your eyes!"

The kitchen?

OK, I'm really not following this.

"Dan," I demand, as we go downstairs, the girls hurrying ahead, "I don't understand. Is this your sexy surprise?"

"It certainly is." He nods beatifically. "But not just sexy . . . beautiful. She's beautiful."

She?

"Arrrggh! A snake!" Tessa comes bombing out of the kitchen and wraps her arms round my legs. "There's a snake in the kitchen!"

"What?" My heart thumping, I skitter into the kitchen, turn around, and immediately jump back six feet. Oh my God. Oh my God.

Lined up against the wall, where our toy box used to be, is a glass tank. Inside the glass tank is a snake. It's orange and brown and has a black snakey eye, and I think I might vomit.

"Wh— wh—" I'm gibbering. I'm actually unable to form words. "Wh—"

"Surprise!" Dan has followed me in. "Isn't she lovely? She's a corn snake. Bred for captivity, so you don't have to worry about her getting upset."

That's not what I was worried about.

"Dan." Finally I find my voice and grab his lapels. "We can't have a snake."

"We have a snake," Dan corrects me. "What shall we call her, girls?"

"Snakey," says Tessa.

"No!" I'm nearly hyperventilating. "I won't have a snake! Not in the house! I won't do it, Dan!"

At last, Dan looks at me properly. Eyebrows raised innocently. Like *I'm* the one who's being unreasonable. "What's the big deal?"

"You said you were getting something *sexy*!" I hiss furiously. "*Sexy*, Dan!"

"She is sexy! She's exotic . . . sinuous. . . . You must agree."

"No!" I shudder. "I can't even look at her. It," I correct myself quickly. It's an *it*.

"Can we have a dog?" pipes up Anna, who is quite intuitive and has been watching our exchange. "Instead of a snake?"

"No!" cries Tessa. "We have to keep our lovely Snakey. . . ." She attempts to hug the glass tank, and the snake uncoils.

Oh God. I have to look away. How could Dan think a snake was a sexy surprise? *How?*

By the time the girls are in bed, we've

191

reached a compromise. We will give the snake a chance. However, I do not have to feed, handle, or look at the snake. I will never even touch the freezer drawer dedicated to its food. (It eats mice, actual *mice.*) Nor am I calling it Dora, which is what the girls have named it. It is not Dora, it is the Snake.

It's 8:00 P.M. and we're sitting on our bed, exhausted by our negotiations. The girls have finally stopped creeping out of their room to "see if Dora's all right."

"I thought you'd like it," says Dan dolefully. I think the truth has finally dawned on him. "I mean, we talked about having a snake. . . ."

"I was joking," I say wearily. "As I have explained about a hundred times." It never occurred to me he might be serious. I mean, a *snake*?

Dan leans back against the headboard with a sigh, resting his head against his hands.

"Well, I surprised you, anyway." He looks over with a wry smile.

"Yup." I can't help smiling back. "You did."

"And you liked your cardigan, anyway."

"It's stunning!" I say with enthusiasm, wanting to make up for the snake. "Honestly, Dan, I love it." I stroke the fabric. "It's so soft."

"You like the color?"

"I *love* the color." I nod as emphatically as I can. "*So* much better than the bl—"

I stop mid-word. *Shit.*

"What did you say?" asks Dan slowly.

"Nothing!" I paste on a bright smile. "So, shall we watch some TV, or —"

"You were going to say *blue.*"

"No, I wasn't!" I say, but not quite convincingly enough. I can see Dan's mind working. He's not stupid, Dan.

"Tilda called you." The light is dawning on his face. "Of *course* she bloody called you. You two talk about everything." He eyes me balefully. "That cardigan wasn't a surprise at all, was it? You probably —" He breaks off, as though a fresh theory is dawning. I have a horrible feeling it might be the truth. "Is that why it was warm?" He's shoffed, I can tell. He's goggling at me as though his whole world is crumbling about him. "Were you *at Tilda's house*?"

"Look . . ." I rub my nose. "Look . . . I'm sorry. But she didn't know which size to choose, and this way you didn't have to faff around . . . it made sense. . . ."

"But it was supposed to be a *surprise*!" he almost bellows.

He has a point.

For a while we're both silent, staring up at the ceiling.

"My surprise breakfast wasn't any good," I say morosely. "And you didn't even *notice* my kitchen makeover."

"I did!" Dan says at once. "The . . . uh . . . candlesticks. Great."

"Thanks." I raise a wry smile. "But don't pretend. I was deluded to think you'd get excited by a kitchen makeover, of all things."

Maybe I was deluded, or — I'm thinking more honestly to myself — maybe I just wanted an excuse to buy new stuff for the kitchen.

"Well," replies Dan, his hands spreading in acknowledgment. And I know we're both thinking: *Same goes for the snake.*

"And we never went to Tim Wender. . . ." I add mournfully.

"Tim *Wender*?" Dan swivels round. "What do you mean?"

Oh my God. What with all the snake shenanigans, he doesn't even know.

"I had tickets!" I almost pop with frustration. "A special lunchtime performance! It was going to be —" I break off. There's no point rubbing it in. "Never mind. We can go another time." A sudden gurgle of laughter escapes from me. "What a fiasco."

"Maybe surprises are a red herring," says Dan. "It was a fun idea, but maybe we should call it a day."

"No," I retort. "I'm not giving up so soon. You wait, Dan, I'm going to come up with an awesome surprise for you."

"Sylvie —"

"I'm not giving up," I repeat obstinately. "And in the meantime, I do have one more thing up my sleeve." I pull open my bedside-table drawer, take out my tingly massage oil, and throw it to Dan.

"*Now* you're talking." His eyes shine as he reads the label, and I can tell I've scored. The way to Dan's heart has always been through sex. So . . .

Wait a minute. Hang on.

I actually blink as my thoughts crystallize. Why on earth have I bothered with all this other stuff? Why on earth did I think he'd notice a new tablecloth or care what he has for breakfast? I've been a total idiot. Sex is the answer. Like they say: It's all about sex, stupid. *This* is how we keep our marriage alive.

Already ideas are bubbling up in my head. A new strategy is forming. I have the perfect surprise for Dan. The perfect plan. And he'll love it; I just know he will.

SEVEN

I don't get to the sex plan *straight* away, because: 1. We've agreed to have a few days' rest from surprises, and 2. I have a few other things to deal with first. Like giving the girls breakfast and plaiting their hair and stacking the dishwasher, all while avoiding looking at the snake. If I look at the snake, the snake will have won, is how I feel.

Which I know is irrational. But what's so great about being rational? If you ask me, being rational isn't always the same as being right. I'm almost tempted to share my little maxim with Dan, but he's frowning moodily at the Sunday paper, so I don't disturb him.

I know why he's in a mood. It's because we're seeing my mother this morning. I'm actually getting a bit tired of his attitude. It's the same as with Daddy. Dan used to be OK with Mummy — but now, forget it. Every time we visit, this horrible cloud of tension grows around him beforehand. When I ask, "What's wrong?" he scowls and says, "What do you mean? There's nothing wrong." So I persist: "Yes, there is; you're all grouchy," whereupon he snarls, "You're imagining things; it's *fine.*" And I can never face a great big argument, especially when it's the precious weekend (it's always the precious weekend), so we leave it.

And, OK, it's only a tiny kink in our happiness — but if we're going to be married for another zillion years, we really should iron it out. We can't have Dan wincing each time I say, "Let's visit my mother this weekend." Soon the girls will start noticing and saying, "Why doesn't Daddy like Granny?" and that'll be *really* bad.

"Dan," I begin.

"Yes?"

He looks up, still frowning, and instantly my nerve fails. As I've already mentioned, I'm not the best at confrontation. I don't even know where I'm planning to start.

Anyway, maybe I shouldn't tackle this openly, I suddenly decide. Maybe I need to operate by stealth. Build trust and affection between my mother and Dan in some subtle way that neither of them notices. Yes. Good plan.

"We should get going," I say, and head

out of the kitchen — still managing to avoid looking at the snake by fixing my eyes on a distant corner.

As Dan drives us to Chelsea, I stare ahead at the road, mulling on marriage and life and how unfair everything is. If anyone was destined to have a long and perfect marriage, it was my parents. I mean, they were perfect. They could have been married for six hundred years, no problem. Daddy adored Mummy, and she adored him back, and they made an amazing couple on the dance floor, or on their boat in pastel polo shirts, or turning up at school parents' evenings, twinkling and smiling and charming everyone.

Mummy still twinkles. But it's the kind of bright, unnerving twinkle that might shatter at any moment. Everyone says she's coped "marvelously" since Daddy died. She certainly coped better than me, Go-to-Pieces Sylvie.

(No. Not "better." It's not a competition. She coped differently from me, that's all.)

She still talks about Daddy — in fact, she loves talking about Daddy. We both do. But the conversation has to be along her lines. If you venture onto the "wrong" topic, she draws breath and her eyes go shiny and she blinks very furiously and gazes at the window and you feel terrible. The trouble is, the "wrong" topics are random and unpredictable. A reference to Daddy's colorful handkerchiefs . . . His funny superstitions when he played golf . . . Those holidays we used to spend in Spain . . . Topics that seem utterly safe and harmless . . . but no. Each of them has brought on an attack of furious blinking and window-gazing and me desperately trying to change the subject.

Which is just grief, I guess. I've decided that grief is like a newborn baby. It knocks you for six. It takes over your brain with its incessant cry. It stops you sleeping or eating or functioning, and everyone says, "Hang in there, it'll get easier." What they don't say is, "Two years on, you'll *think* it's got easier, but then, out of the blue, you'll hear a certain tune in the supermarket and start sobbing."

Mummy doesn't sob — it's not her style, sobbing — but she does blink. I sometimes sob. On the other hand, sometimes I go hours or even days without thinking about Daddy. And then, of course, I feel terrible.

"Why are we going for brunch?" says Dan as we pull up at the lights.

"To have brunch!" I say, a little sharply. "To be a family!"

"No other agenda?" He raises his eyebrows, and I feel slight misgivings. I don't *think* there's another agenda. On the phone last night I said to Mummy, at least three times, "It is just brunch, isn't it? Nothing . . . else?" And she said, "Of course, darling!" and sounded quite offended.

She has history, though. She knows it and I know it and Dan knows it. Even the girls know it.

"She's at it again," says Dan calmly, as he finds a parking space outside her block.

"You don't *know* that," I retort.

But as we enter her spacious mansion flat, my eyes dart around, searching for clues, hoping I won't find any. . . .

Then I see it, through the double doors. A white kitchen-type gadget perched on her ormolu coffee table. It's large and shiny and looks totally out of place sitting on her old, well-thumbed books about Impressionist painters.

Damn it. He's right.

I deliberately don't see the gadget. I don't mention it. I kiss Mummy, and so does Dan, and we get the girls out of their coats and shoes and head into the kitchen, where the table is laid. (I've finally got Mummy to give up trying to entertain us in the dining room when we have the girls with us.) And the minute I enter the room, I draw breath sharply. Oh for God's sake. What is she up to?

Mummy, of course, is playing completely innocent.

"Have some crudités, Sylvie!" she says in that bright sparkly voice that used to be real — she had everything to sparkle about — and now sounds just a little hollow. "Girls, you like carrots, don't you? Look at these ones. Aren't they fun?"

There are four huge platters on the kitchen counter, all covered in strangely shaped vegetables. There are zucchini batons, etched with a crisscross design. Discs of cucumber with scalloped edges. Carrot stars. Radish hearts (they are super-cute, I must admit). And, as the pièce de résistance, a pineapple carved into a flower.

I meet eyes with Dan. We both know how this is going to go. And half of me is tempted to harden my heart, be brutal, not even mention the extraordinarily shaped vegetables. But I can't. I have to play along.

"Wow!" I say dutifully. "Those are incredible."

"I did them all myself," says Mummy in triumph. "It took me half an hour, if that."

"Half an hour?" I echo, feeling like the second presenter on a QVC show. "Goodness. How on earth did you manage that?"

"Well." Mummy's face lights up. "I've bought this rather wonderful machine! Girls, do you want to see how Granny's new machine works?"

"Yes!" cry Tessa and Anna, who are so easily persuaded into new ventures, it's ridiculous. I know if I said to them, "Do you want to study QUANTUM PHYSICS?" in the right tone of voice, they'd both yell, "Yes!" Then they'd fight over who was going to be first to study quantum physics. Then I'd say, "Do you know what quantum physics is?" and Anna would stare blankly, while Tessa would reply defiantly, "It is like Paddington Bear," because she always has to have an answer.

As Mummy hurries out, Dan shoots me an ominous look.

"Whatever it is, we're not buying it," he says in a low voice.

"OK, but don't . . ." I gesture with my hands.

"What?"

"Be negative."

"I'm not being negative!" retorts Dan — totally lying, as he couldn't *look* more negative. "But nor am I spending any more money on your mother's —"

"Shhh!" I intervene.

"— crap," he finishes. "That applesauce

202

maker . . ."

"I know, I know." I wince. "It was a mistake. I've admitted it."

Don't get me wrong: I'm as big a fan of the heavyweight retro American-style gadget as the next person. But that bloody "traditional applesauce maker" is *huge*. And we hardly ever eat applesauce. Nor do we use it for "all those handy purees" that Mummy kept on about in her sales pitch. (As for the "liquid spice" sachets . . . It's best to cast a veil.)

Everyone works through grief in their own way. I get that. My way was to have a meltdown. Mummy's way is to blink furiously. And her other way is to sell one weird product after another to her friends and family.

When she started holding jewelry parties, I was delighted. I thought it would be a fun hobby and distract her from all the sadness. I went along, I sipped champagne with all her friends, and I bought a choker and a bracelet. There was a second jewelry party, which I couldn't make but apparently it went well.

Then she held an essential-oils party and I bought Christmas presents for all Dan's family, so that was fine. The Spanishware party was OK too. I bought tapas bowls and

I've used them maybe once.

Then there was the Trendieware party.

Oh *God.* Just the memory makes me shudder. Trendieware is a company that makes garments out of stretchy fabric in "modern, vibrant" (vile) prints. You can wear each item about sixteen different ways, and you have to choose your personality (I was "Spring Fresh Extrovert") and then the saleswoman (Mummy) tries to persuade you to throw out all your old clothes and only wear Trendieware.

It was horrendous. Mummy has a sylph-like figure for her age, so of course she can wear a stretchy tube as a skirt. But her friends? Hello? The place was full of ladies in their sixties glumly trying to wrap a lurid-pink stretchy top over their sensible bra, or work out the Three-Way Jacket (you'd need a thesis in mechanics), or else flatly refusing to join in. I was the only person who bought anything — the Signature Dress — and I've never worn it even one way. Let alone sixteen.

Not surprisingly, after that, a lot of Mummy's friends dropped off. At the next jewelry party there were only half a dozen of us. At the scented-candles party it was just Lorna, who is Mummy's oldest and most loyal friend, and me. Lorna and I had a hurried conversation while Mummy was out of the room, and we decided that this selling obsession was a harmless way for Mummy to process her grief and it would come to a natural end. But it hasn't. She keeps finding new things to sell. And the only person dumb enough to keep buying them is me. (Lorna has claimed "no more room" in her flat, which is very clever of her. If I did that, Mummy would come round, clear out a cupboard, and make room.)

I know we need to stage an intervention. Dan's suggested it, I've agreed, and we've sat in bed many times, saying firmly, "We'll talk to her." In fact, I was all geared up for it last time we visited. But it turned out Mummy was having a bad day. Lots of blinking. Lots of window-gazing. She looked so piteous and fragile, all I wanted to do was make her life better . . . so I found myself ordering an applesauce maker. (It could have been worse. It could have been the £900 special-edition retro ham slicer: "a unique and distinctive focus for any kitchen." I'll say.)

"So!" Mummy arrives back in the kitchen, clutching the white gadget that I noticed before. Her cheeks have flushed and she has that focused look she gets whenever she's about to pitch. "You may be thinking this is an ordinary food processor. But let me assure you, the Vegetable Creator is in a league of its own."

"The 'Vegetable Creator'?" echoes Dan. "Are you telling me it *creates* vegetables?"

"We all get so tired of vegetables." Mummy plows on, ignoring Dan. "But imagine a whole new way to present them! Imagine fifty-two different chopping templates, all in one handy machine, plus an extra twelve novelty templates in our seasonal package, free if you order today!" Her voice is rising with each word. "The Vegetable Creator is fun, healthy, and *so* easy to use. Anna, Tessa, do you want to try?"

"Yes!" yells Tessa, predictably. "Me!"

"Me!" wails Anna. "Me!"

Mummy sets the gadget up on the counter, grabs a carrot, and feeds it through an aperture. We all watch speechlessly as it turns into tiny teddy-bear shapes.

"Teddies!" the girls gasp. "Teddy carrots!"

Typical. I might have known she'd get the girls onside. But I'm going to be firm.

"I think we've got too many gadgets already," I say sorrowfully. "It does look good, though."

"A study has shown that owning a Vegetable Creator leads to thirty percent more vegetable consumption in children," says

Mummy brightly.

Rubbish! What "study"? I'm not going to challenge her, though, or she'll start quoting some stream of made-up figures from the Vegetable Creator Real Proper Lab with Real Scientists.

"Quite a lot of waste," I observe. "Look at all those bits of carrots left over."

"Put them in soup," Mummy retorts like a shot. "So nutritious. Shall we try making cucumber stars, girls?"

I'm not buying it. I know I'm her only customer, but I'm still not buying it. Resolutely, I turn away and search for a change of subject.

"So, what else is up with you, Mummy?" I say. I head across to her little pinboard and survey the notices and tickets pinned there. "Oh, a Zumba class. That looks fun."

"All the unused pieces collect in this handy receptacle. . . ." Mummy is still doggedly continuing with her pitch.

"Oh, *Through the High Maze*!" I exclaim, seeing a hardback book on the counter. "We did that at my book group. What did you think? A bit hard going, I thought."

Truth be told, I only read about half of *Through the High Maze,* even though it's one of those books that everyone has read and it's going to be a movie, apparently. It's by this woman called Joss Burton, who overcame her eating disorder to set up a perfume company called Maze (that's the play on words). She's stunning, with cropped dark hair and a trademark white streak. And her perfumes are really good, especially the Amber and Rose. Now she hosts events where she tells businesspeople how to succeed, and I suppose it is quite inspirational — but there's only so much inspiration you can take, I find.

Whenever I read about these super-inspiring people, I start off all admiring and end up thinking, *Oh God, why haven't I trekked across the desert or overcome crippling childhood poverty? I'm totally crap.*

Mummy hasn't responded to my gambit — but on the plus side, she's paused in her chat about the chopper, so I quickly carry on the conversation.

"You're going to the theater!" I exclaim, seeing tickets pinned up. "*Dealer's Choice.* That's the one about gambling, isn't it? Are you going with Lorna? You could get a meal deal beforehand."

There's still complete silence from Mummy, which surprises me — and as I look round I blink in shock. What did I say? What's up? Her hands have frozen still and there's an odd expression on her face, as though her smile has been petrified in acid. As I watch, she glances at the window and starts blinking, very fast.

Oh shit. Obviously I've strayed onto another "wrong" topic. But what, exactly? The theater? *Dealer's Choice*? No. Surely not. I glance at Dan for help, and to my astonishment, he seems frozen too. His jaw has tensed and his eyes are alert. He glances at Mummy. Then at me.

What? What's this all about? Did I miss the memo?

"Anyway!" says Mummy, and I can tell she's pulling herself together with an almighty effort. "Enough of this. You must all be hungry. I'll just tidy up a little. . . ."

She starts sweeping things off the counter with an indiscriminate air — the Vegetable Creator, a load of Tupperware which was out (no doubt to store her vegetable creations), and the copy of *Through the High Maze*. She dumps them all in her tiny utility room, then returns, her face even more pink than before.

"Buck's Fizz?" she says, almost shrilly. "Dan, you'd like a Buck's Fizz, I'm sure. Shall we go through to the drawing room?"

I'm baffled. Isn't she even going to *try* to sell me the chopper thing? She seems to have been utterly derailed, and I can't work

209

out why.

I follow her through to the drawing room, where champagne and orange juice in ice buckets are waiting on the walnut Art Deco cocktail cabinet. (Daddy was very big on cocktails. When he had his sixtieth birthday party, almost everyone who came bought him a cocktail shaker as a present. It was quite funny.)

Dan opens the champagne and Mummy makes the Buck's Fizz and the girls rush over to the big dolls' house by the window. It's all just like normal — except it isn't. Something weird happened just now.

Mummy is asking Dan lots of questions about his work, one after another — almost as though she's desperate not to let any gaps into the conversation. She swigs her entire drink, pours herself another (Dan and I have barely begun on ours), then flashes me a bright smile and says, "I'll make some pancakes in a moment."

"Girls, come and wash your hands," I call to them, and lead them into Mummy's powder room, where they have the usual fight to go first and squirt far too much Molton Brown soap everywhere. Tessa's hair has become a wild tangle, and I go into the kitchen to get my hairbrush from my bag. On the way back, I glance into the drawing room and see something that makes me slow down . . . then stop altogether.

Mummy and Dan are standing close together, talking in low voices. And I can't help it: I inch forward, staying out of view.

". . . Sylvie finds out *now* . . ." Dan is saying, and my stomach flips over. They're talking about me!

Mummy replies in such a quiet voice, I can't hear her — but I don't need to. I know what this is. *Now* I get it. It's one of Dan's surprises for me! They're planning something!

The last thing I want is Dan thinking that I'm eavesdropping, so I hurriedly head back to the safety of the powder room. It's a surprise. What kind of surprise? And then it hits me. Are Dan and I going to see *Dealer's Choice*? That would explain Mummy's frozen expression. She probably pinned the tickets up on her board, not thinking, and then I went and blundered in, asking her about them.

OK, from now on, I'm noticing nothing untoward. *Nothing.*

I tidy Tessa's hair, then lead the girls back into the hall, and my gaze falls on the massive framed photo of Daddy which sits on the hall table like a sentinel. My handsome, dapper, charming father. Killed while he was still in his prime. Before he had a chance to really know his grandchildren, write that book, enjoy his retirement . . .

I can't help it; I'm starting to breathe harder. My fists are clenching. I know I need to let it go, and I know they never proved whether he was using his phone or not, but I will hate Gary Butler forever. *Forever.*

That's the name of the lorry driver who killed Daddy on the M6. Gary Butler. (He was never prosecuted in the end. Lack of evidence.) At the height of my "bad time," as I think of it, I found his address and went and stood outside his house. I didn't do anything, just stood there. But apparently you're not supposed to stand outside people's houses for no reason, nor write them letters, and his wife felt "threatened." (By me? What a joke.) Dan had to come and find me and talk me into leaving. That's when everyone got alarmed and gathered in corners, murmuring, "Sylvie's not coping well."

Dan, in particular, went into overdrive. He's a protective type naturally — he'll always open a door for me or offer a jacket — but this was another level. He took time off work to look after the girls. He negotiated extra leave for me from Mrs. Kendrick.

He tried to get me to go to a counselor. (*Really* not my kind of thing.) I remember the doctor told Dan I needed to sleep (of course I wasn't sleeping; how could I *sleep?*), and Dan took it on as his responsibility, buying blackout blinds and calming music CDs and asking everyone in the street to keep the noise down. He still asks me every morning if I've slept. It's become his habit, like he's my sleep monitor.

Mummy, on the other hand, didn't want to know. I don't mean that to sound bad. She was grieving herself; how could she worry about me too? And, anyway, it's her way. She doesn't cope well with outlandish behavior. We once had a lunch guest who got so drunk he fell over the sofa, which I found hilarious (I was nine). But when I mentioned it the next day, Mummy just closed the conversation down. It was as if nothing had happened.

So when I went to stand outside Gary Butler's house, she wasn't at all impressed. ("What will people *say?*") It was Mummy who was keen for me to take some pills. Or maybe go abroad for a month and come back all better again.

(She herself seemed to process her grief like a caterpillar in a cocoon. She disappeared into her bedroom after the funeral and no one was allowed in for two weeks, and then she emerged, fully dressed, fully made up, blinking. Never crying, only blinking.)

"Grandpa is in heaven," asserts Tessa, looking at the picture of Daddy. "He is sitting on a cloud, isn't he, Mummy?"

"Maybe," I say cautiously.

What do I know? Maybe Daddy *is* up there, sitting on a cloud.

"But what if he falls off?" queries Anna anxiously. "Mummy, what if Grandpa falls off?"

"He will hold on tight," says Tessa. "Won't he, Mummy?" And now both of them are looking expectantly up at me, with absolute trust that I know the answer. Because I'm Mummy, who knows everything in the world.

My eyes are suddenly hot. I wish I were what they think I am. I wish I had all the answers for them. How old will they be before they realize I don't? That no one does? As I survey their questioning little faces, I can't bear the idea that one day my girls will know about all the shit that the world really involves, and they'll have to deal with it, and I won't be able to fix it for them.

"All right, Sylvie?" says Dan, as he and

Mummy come out of the drawing room. He glances swiftly at the picture of Daddy, and I know he's realized my train of thought. Photos of Daddy do tend to catch me out.

Well, to be honest, anything can catch me out.

"Fine!" I force a bright tone. "So, girls, what are you going to put on your pancakes?"

Distraction is crucial, because the last thing I need is Tessa talking about Grandpa sitting on a cloud in front of Mummy.

"Maple syrup!"

"Chocolate sauce!"

Anna and Tessa dash into the kitchen, all thoughts of Grandpa forgotten. As I follow them I glance at Dan, still walking right by Mummy's side, and the sight suddenly cheers me up. Will Project Surprise Me have an unexpected side benefit? Will it bring Dan and Mummy closer together? Seeing them just now, huddled in the drawing room, they had a kind of directness and openness with each other that I've never seen before.

I mean, they *do* get on, as a rule. They *do*. Kind of. It's just . . .

Well. As I've mentioned, Dan can be a bit prickly about Daddy. And money and . . . lots of stuff. But maybe he's over that, I think optimistically. Maybe things have changed.

Or maybe not. By the time we've all finished eating, Dan seems more prickly than ever, especially when Mummy finds out about the snake and teases him about it. I can tell he's struggling to stay polite, and I don't blame him. Mummy has a habit of picking one joke and making it too many times. I almost find myself coming to the wretched snake's defense. (Almost.)

"I always wanted a pet when I was little," I say to the girls, trying to broaden the conversation. "But I didn't want a snake; I wanted a kitten."

"A kitten," breathes Tessa.

"Your snake would probably eat the kitten!" says Mummy merrily. "Isn't that what you feed snakes, Dan, live kittens?"

"No," says Dan evenly. "It is not."

"Don't be ridiculous, Mummy," I say, frowning at her before she freaks out the girls. "Granny's joking, girls. Snakes don't eat kittens! So anyway," I press on, "I wasn't allowed a pet, and I didn't have any brothers or sisters either . . . so guess what? I made up an imaginary friend. Her name was Lynn."

I've never told the girls about my imaginary friend before. I'm not sure why.

No, of course I know why. It's because my parents made me feel so ashamed about it. It's actually taking me some courage to mention her in front of Mummy.

In hindsight — especially now that I have children of my own — I can see that my parents didn't handle the whole imaginary friend thing well. They were great parents, really they were, but that one issue, they got wrong.

I mean, I get it. Things were different then. People were less open-minded. Plus Mummy and Daddy were super-conventional. They probably worried that hearing voices in my head meant I was going mad or something. But imaginary friends are perfectly normal and healthy for children. I've googled it. (Lots of times, actually.) They shouldn't have been so disapproving. Every time I mentioned Lynn, Mummy would freeze in that awful way she had, and Daddy would look at Mummy with a kind of disapproving anger, like it was her fault, and the whole atmosphere would become toxic. It was horrible.

So of course, after a while I kept Lynn secret. But it didn't mean I abandoned her. The very fact that my parents had such an extreme reaction to her made me cling on to her. Embellish her. Sometimes I felt guilty when I talked to her in my head — and sometimes I felt defiant — but I always had a horrible feeling of shame. I'm thirty-two years old, but even now, saying "Lynn" out loud gives me a queasy *frisson.*

I even woke up dreaming about her the other day. Or remembering, maybe? I could hear her laughing that happy gurgle of a laugh. Then she was singing a song that I used to love, "Kumbaya."

"Did you talk to her in real life?" says Tessa, puzzled.

"No, just in my head." I smile at her. "I made her up because I felt a bit lonely. It's perfectly normal. Lots of children have imaginary friends," I add pointedly, "and they grow out of them naturally."

This last is a little dig at Mummy, but she pretends not to notice, which is typical.

I've promised myself that one day I'm going to have it out with Mummy. I'm going to say, "Do you realize how ashamed you made me feel?" and "What was the problem? Did you think I was going *mad* or something?" I have all my lines ready — I've just never quite had the guts to say them. As I say, I'm not brilliant at confrontation, and especially so since Daddy died. The family boat's been unsteady enough without me rocking it more.

Sure enough, Mummy has blanked this entire conversation and now changes the subject.

"*Look* what I found the other day," she says, zapping at the wall-mounted TV, and after a few seconds a family video appears onscreen. It's from my sixteenth birthday — the part when Daddy stood up to give a speech about me.

"I haven't seen this one for ages," I breathe, and we all fall silent to watch. Daddy's addressing the ballroom at the Hurlingham Club, where my party was. He's in black tie, and Mummy's all shimmery in silver, and I'm in a red mini-dress, which Mummy spent Saturday after Saturday helping me look for.

(Now I look back, it *really* doesn't suit me. But I was sixteen. What did I know?)

"My daughter has the wit of Lizzy Bennet . . ." Daddy is saying, in that commanding way of his, "the strength of Pippi Longstocking . . . the boldness of Jo March . . . and the style of Scarlett O'Hara." Onscreen, the guests break into applause and Daddy twinkles at me and I gaze back up, speechless.

I remember that moment. It blew me away. Daddy had secretly gone through all the books in my bedroom, looking for my heroines and writing a speech around them. I glance over at Mummy now, my eyes a little hot, and she gives me a tremulous smile back. My mother can drive me mad — but there are times when no one gets it like she does.

"Good speech," says Dan after a few moments, and I shoot him a grateful smile.

But as we're watching, the screen starts to go blurry, and suddenly the voices are distorting, and the video becomes unwatchable.

"What happened?" demands Tessa.

"Oh dear!" Mummy jabs at the remote but can't improve the picture. "This copy must be damaged. Never mind. If everyone's finished, let's go into the drawing room and we can watch something else."

"The wedding!" says Anna.

"The wedding!" shrieks Tessa.

"Really?" says Dan incredulously. "Haven't we done family DVDs?"

"What's wrong with watching the wedding?" I say. And if I sound a little defensive . . . it's because I am.

So, yet another key fact about my family: We watch our wedding DVD a lot. A *lot*. Probably every other visit to Mummy's place, we all sit down to watch it. The girls love it and Mummy loves it and, I have to admit, I do too.

But Dan says it's weird to keep replaying one day of our life. In fact, Dan hates our wedding DVD — probably for the same reason that Mummy loves it. Because while most wedding videos are about the happy couple, ours is basically all about Daddy.

I never even noticed to begin with. I thought it was just a lovely, well-produced DVD. It wasn't until about a year after our wedding that Dan suddenly flipped out on the way home from some gathering and said, "Can't you see, Sylvie? It's not our DVD, it's his!"

And the next time I watched it, of course, it was obvious. It's the Daddy Show. The first shot of the whole DVD is of Daddy, looking gorgeous in his morning suit, standing by the Rolls-Royce we used to get to the church. Then there are shots of him leading me out in my wedding dress . . . shots of him in the car . . . the pair of us walking up the aisle. . . .

The most moving moment of the whole DVD isn't our vows. It's when the priest says, "Who gives this woman to be married?" and Daddy says, "I do," his resonant voice all choked up. Then all the way through our vows, the camera keeps panning over to Daddy, who is watching with the most poignant expression of pride and wistfulness.

Dan thinks Daddy went into the editing suite and made sure that he featured prominently. After all, he was paying — he was the one who insisted on hiring an expensive video team, in fact — so he could have it just the way he wanted.

I was incredibly upset when Dan first suggested this. Then I accepted that it was possible. Daddy was . . . not conceited, exactly, but he had healthy self-esteem. He liked to be the center of attention, always. Like, for example, he was *desperate* to be knighted. Friends would mention it and he'd brush them off with a lighthearted joke — but we all knew he wanted it. And why not, after all the good he did? (Mummy's really sensitive about the fact that he missed out. I've seen her blinking while reading the honors list in the newspaper. Let's face it — if he had been knighted, she'd be "Lady Lowe" now, which does sound pretty good.)

Even so, I have a different theory about our DVD. I think the video team was just naturally drawn to Daddy, because he dazzled like a movie star. He was so handsome and witty; he whirled Mummy around the dance floor with such aplomb. . . . No wonder the cameraman or editor, or who-ever it was, focused on him.

To sum up, Dan's not the greatest fan. But the girls are obsessed by watching the wedding — by my dress, mainly, and of course my hair. Daddy was insistent that I should wear my hair — my "glory" — down for the wedding, and it did look fairly spectacular and princess-like, all wavy and shiny and blond, with braids and flowers woven through it. The girls call it "wedding hair" and often try to do the same with their dolls.

Anyway. So what usually happens is that we start the DVD, Dan absents himself, and after a while the girls get bored and go off to play. Whereupon Mummy and I end up watching together in silence, just drinking in the sight of Daddy. The man he was. It's our indulgence. It's our tin of Quality Street.

Today, though, I don't want Mummy and me to gorge on watching Daddy, all alone. I want things to be different. Together and relaxed and more . . . I don't know. Uni-fied. Family-like. As we head into the draw-ing room, I put my arm through Dan's.

"Watch it today," I say coaxingly. "Stay with us."

Mummy's already pressed Play — none of us comments on the fact that the DVD was already loaded in the machine — and soon we're watching Daddy and me stepping out of my childhood home in Chelsea. (Mummy sold the house a year ago and moved to this flat nearby, for a "new start.")

"I had the local paper on the phone yesterday," says Mummy, as we watch Daddy posing with me for pictures in front of the Rolls-Royce. "They want to take photos at the opening of the scanner suite. Make sure you get your hair done, Sylvie," she adds.

"Have you mentioned it to Esme?" I ask. "You should do."

Esme is the girl at the hospital who is organizing the opening ceremony. She's quite new at her job and this is her first big event, and almost every day I get an anxious email from her, beginning, *I think I've planned for everything, but . . .* Even over the weekend. Yesterday she wanted to know: *How many parking spaces will you need?* Today it was, *Will you need PowerPoint for your speech?* I mean, PowerPoint? Really?

"Dan, you *are* coming to the ceremony?" Mummy says, suddenly turning to us. I nudge Dan, who looks up and says, "Oh. Yes."

He could sound more enthused. It's not every day your late father-in-law is honored by a whole hospital scanner suite being named after him, is it?

"When I told the reporter everything that your father had achieved in his life, he couldn't believe it," Mummy continues tremulously. "Building up his business from nothing, all the fundraising, hosting those wonderful parties, climbing Everest . . . The journalist said his headline would read, a REMARKABLE MAN."

"It wasn't exactly 'from nothing,' " says Dan.

"Sorry?" Mummy peers at him.

"Well, Marcus had that massive windfall, didn't he? So, not quite 'nothing.' "

I glance sharply round at Dan — and, sure enough, he's all tentery. His jaw is taut. He looks as though he's sitting here under total duress.

Whenever I spend time with Dan and Mummy, my sympathies constantly swing back and forth between the two, like some wild pendulum. And right now they're with Mummy. Why can't Dan just let Mummy reminisce? What does it matter if she's not 100 percent accurate? So *what* if she romanticizes her dead husband?

"That's lovely, Mummy," I say, ignoring Dan. I squeeze her hand, simultaneously eyeing her warily to see if she's going to start blinking. But although her voice is a bit trembly, she seems composed.

"Do you remember the time he took us to Greece?" she says, her eyes lost in memory. "You were quite little."

"Of course I do!" I turn to Dan. "It was incredible. Daddy chartered a yacht and we sailed round the coastline. Every night we'd have these fantastic candlelit meals on the beach. Crabs . . . lobster . . ."

"He invented a new cocktail every night," adds Mummy dreamily.

"Sounds fantastic," says Dan tonelessly.

"Where are you going on holiday this year?" Mummy blinks at him, as though coming to.

"Lake District," I say. "Self-catering."

"Lovely." Mummy gives a distant smile, and I sigh inwardly. I know she doesn't mean to look disparaging. But she doesn't really *get* our life. She doesn't understand living on a budget, or keeping the girls grounded, or taking pleasure in simple things. When I showed her the brochure for a French campsite we went to once, she blenched and said, "But, darling, why don't you hire a lovely villa in Provence?"

(If I said, "Because of the money," she'd say, "But, darling, I'll *give* you the money!" And then Dan would get all prickly. So I don't ever do that.)

"Oh, look." Mummy points at the screen. "Daddy's about to make that funny little joke before you go into the church. Your father was always so witty," she adds wistfully. "Everyone said his speech *made* the reception, absolutely *made* it."

I feel a movement beside me on the sofa, and suddenly Dan has risen to his feet.

"Sorry," he says, heading to the door without meeting my eye. "There's an urgent work call I should make. I forgot earlier."

Yeah, right. I kind of don't blame him. But I kind of do blame him. Couldn't he put up with it for once?

"That's fine." I try to sound pleasant, as though I'm not aware he's just totally invented this call. "See you in a moment."

Dan leaves the room and Mummy looks over at me.

"Oh dear," she says. "Poor Dan seems a little tense. I wonder why?"

This is how she often refers to him: "poor Dan." And she sounds so patronizing — even though she doesn't mean to — that my pendulum instantly swings the other way. I must stick up for Dan. Because he has a point.

"I think he feels . . . he thinks . . ." I trail off and take a deep breath. I'm going to tackle this, once and for all. "Mummy, have you ever noticed that our wedding DVD is quite focused on . . . well, Daddy?"

"What do you mean?" Mummy blinks at me.

"Compared to . . . other people."

"But he was the father of the bride." Mummy still looks perplexed.

"Yes," I press on, feeling hot and bothered, "but there's more of Daddy on the DVD than there is of Dan! And it's his wedding!"

"Oh." Mummy's eyes widen. "Oh, I see! Is *that* why poor Dan is so prickly?"

"He's not prickly," I say, feeling uncomfortable. "You've got to understand his point of view."

"I do not," says Mummy emphatically. "The DVD represents the spirit of the wedding perfectly, and, like it or not, your father was the center of the party. Naturally the videographers chose to focus on the most entertaining character present. Poor Dan is a lovely chap, you *know* I love him to bits, but he's hardly the life and soul, is he?"

"Yes, he is!" I retort hotly, although I know exactly what she means. Dan is really funny and entertaining when you get to know him, but he's not *out there.* He's not going to sweep three women onto the dance floor all at once while everyone cheers, like

228

Daddy did.

"What a ridiculous thing to mind about," Mummy says, with just a trace of disdain in her voice. "But, then, poor Dan *is* a little sensitive, especially about Marcus and all his achievements." She sighs. "Although . . . can one blame him?" She's silent for a moment, and her face becomes softer and more distant. "What you have to remember, Sylvie, is that your father *was* a remarkable man, and we were lucky to have him."

"I know." I nod. "I know we were."

"Of course, Dan has many fine attributes too," she adds after a pause. "He's very . . . loyal." I know she's making an effort to be nice, although clearly in her mind *loyal* ranks several fathoms below *remarkable.*

We lapse into silence as the DVD plays on, and a lump grows in my throat as I watch Daddy onscreen, watching me marrying Dan. His face is noble and dignified. A shaft of light is catching his hair in just the right place. Then he glances at the camera and winks in that way he had.

And even though I've seen this DVD so many times before, I feel a sudden fresh, raw hurt. All my life, Daddy used to wink at me. At school concerts, at boring dinners, as he left the room after saying good night. And I know that doesn't sound like much

— anyone can wink — but Daddy's wink was special. It was like a shot in the arm. An instant spirit-lift.

My inner pendulum has stilled. I'm gazing speechlessly at the screen. Everything has fallen away to the sides of my brain, leaving only the headline news: My father died and we'll never get him back. Everything else is irrelevant.

EIGHT

Next morning, my pendulum is haywire
again. In fact, everything's bloody haywire.
I can't possibly contemplate being married
to Dan for another sixty-eight years. The
last sixty-eight *minutes* have been bad
enough.

I don't know what got under his skin at
Mummy's place yesterday. Ever since, he's
been morose and broody and picky and
just . . . argh. Last night in the car, on the
way home, he started on a thing about how
my family harks back to the past too much
and it's not good for the girls to keep dwell-
ing. He even said, did I have to mention my
imaginary friend? What the hell is wrong
with me mentioning my imaginary friend?

I know what Dan worries about, even
though he won't admit it. He worries that
I'm unstable. Or potentially unstable. Just
because I went and stood outside Gary
Butler's house that one time. And put one

tiny little letter through his letterbox. (Which, OK, I'll admit I shouldn't have done.) But the point is: That was a special case. I was in the throes of grief when I had my "episode" or whatever we call it.

Whereas my invention of "Lynn" was long ago, when I was a child, and it was normal and healthy, because I've googled it, as he well knows, and *what is his bloody problem*?

Which is a basic summary of how I put it to him. Only I was hissing under my breath so that the girls wouldn't hear, and I'm not sure he heard all my nuanced arguments.

Then I woke up this morning, thinking, never mind, new day, new start, and determined to be cheerful. I even said hello to the snake, over my shoulder, with my eyes shut. But Dan seemed even more mired in gloom. He sat silently at breakfast, scrolling through his phone, and then suddenly said, "You know, we've had an offer to expand into Europe."

"Really?" I glanced up from the girls' spelling-test words. *"Took."*

"Tuh-oh-oh-kuh," Anna began intoning.

"There are these guys based out of Copenhagen, who do similar stuff to us. They have a load of projects they want us to team up on, all in Northern Europe. We could end up trebling our turnover."

"Right. And would that be a good thing?"

"I don't know. Maybe. It would be a bit of a punt." Dan had a knotted, unhappy look that sent warning bells off in my brain. "But we've got to do *something*."

"What do you mean?"

"The business won't grow unless we . . ."

He broke off and sipped his coffee and I gazed at him, feeling troubled. As I've mentioned, I know Dan pretty well. I know when his brain is cantering along happily with new, doable ideas, and I know when it's got stuck. Right then it seemed stuck. He didn't look *pleased* about expanding. He looked beleaguered.

"Look," I said to Tessa, and she started sounding out, "Luh-oh-oh-kuh."

"When you say, 'grow,' " I began, over the sound of her chanting, "what exactly —"

"We should be five times the size we are."

"Five?" I echoed, in astonishment. "Says who? You're doing really well! You have lots of projects, a great income. . . ."

"Oh, come on, Sylvie," he almost growled. "The girls' room is tiny. We'll want to move to a new house before long."

"Says who? Dan, what's brought all this on?"

"It's simply about looking forward," said Dan, not meeting my eye. "It's simply about making a plan."

"Right, and what would this plan entail?" I shot back, feeling more and more scratchy. "Would you have to travel?"

"Of course," he said tetchily. "It would be a whole new level of commitment, of investment. . . ."

"Investment." I seized on the word. "So you'd have to borrow money?"

He shrugged. "We'd need more leverage."

Leverage. I hate that word. It's a weasel word. It sounds so simple. You picture a lever and think, *Oh, that makes sense.* It took me ages to realize what it actually means is "borrowing stacks of money at a scary interest rate."

"I don't know," I said. "It seems like a risky thing. When did these Copenhagen guys approach you?"

"Two months ago," replied Dan. "We turned them down. But I'm reconsidering."

And something furious immediately erupted inside me. Why was he reconsidering now? Because we went to my mother's yesterday and she talked about holidays on yachts in Greece?

"Dan." I fixed his eyes with mine. "We have a great life. We have a great work–leisure balance. Your business doesn't need to be five times bigger. The girls like having you around. We don't want you in Copenhagen. And I love this house! We've made it our home! We don't *need* to move; we don't *need* more money. . . ."

I was on quite a roll. I could probably have talked for twenty minutes, except that Anna's little voice piped up, saying, "Seven fifty-two." She was reading the clock on the oven, which is her new hobby. I broke off midstream and exclaimed, "What time? Shugar!" and it was a total scramble to get the girls ready for school.

I never finished testing the girls' spelling either. Great. It's the weekly quiz today. They'll probably get three out of ten. And when the teacher asks, "What happened this week?" Tessa will say in that clear little voice of hers, "We couldn't learn our words, because Mummy and Daddy were arguing about money." And the teachers will bitch about us in the staff room.

Sigh.

Double sigh.

"Sylvie!" exclaims Tilda, as she joins me at her gate. "What's wrong? I've said hello three times. You're miles away!"

"Sorry." I greet her with a kiss and we start on our usual walk.

"What's up, honey?" she says, studying

her Fitbit. "Just the Monday-morning blues?"

"You know." I heave another sigh. "Marriage."

"Oh, *marriage.*" She makes a snorting sound. "Did you not read the disclaimers? 'May cause headache, anxiety, mood swings, sleep disturbance, or general feelings of wanting to stab something.' " Her expression is so comical, I can't help laughing. "Or hives," Tilda adds. "Brought me out in hives."

"I don't have hives," I allow. "That's a plus."

"And another plus, I'm assuming, would be your lovely new cashmere cardigan . . . ?" Tilda prompts, her eyes twinkling. "Did everything go to plan?"

"Oh God." I clap a hand to my forehead. "That feels ages ago now. To be honest, nothing went to plan. Dan found out I tried the cardigan on. And we double-booked lunch. And we've ended up with a snake."

"A snake?" She stares at me. "Did *not* see that one coming."

I regale Tilda with all the events of Saturday, and we both get fits of the giggles, and I feel really quite cheerful again. But then I remember Dan's scratchiness, and my mood sinks once more.

"So, why the blues this morning?" she inquires again. Tilda is one of those friends who like to know for sure you're OK and can't be brushed off and never get offended. The best kind of friend, in fact. "Is it the snake?"

"No, it's not the snake," I say fairly. "I might get used to the snake. It's just . . ." I spread my arms and let them fall.

"Dan?"

I walk a few paces, marshaling my thoughts. Tilda is wise and loyal. We've both shared some sensitive stuff along the way. She might see the situation a different way.

"I've told you before about Dan and my father," I say at last. "And that whole . . ."

"Financial prickliness?" Tilda suggests tactfully.

"Exactly. Financial prickliness. Well, I thought it would get better, but it's getting worse." I lower my voice, even though the street is empty. "Dan's come up with a plan to expand his company. I *know* it's because he's trying to compete with Daddy, but I don't want him to!" I look up, meeting Tilda's shrewd eyes. "I don't want him to work himself into the ground, just to be some version of my father. He's not my father; he's Dan! That's why I love him. Because he's *Dan,* not because . . ." I trail off, not quite sure where I'm going.

We walk in silence, and I can see that Tilda is mulling.

"I watched a documentary about lions a while ago," she says presently. "About the young lions taking over the pride from the older generation. They're vicious to each other. They get horribly injured. But they have to fight it out. They have to establish who's boss."

"So what, Dan's a lion?"

"Maybe he's a young lion with no one to fight," says Tilda, shooting me a cryptic look. "Think about it. Your father died in his prime. He won't ever get old and frail. He won't ever make way for Dan. Dan wants to be king of the jungle."

"But he *is* king of our jungle!" I say in frustration. "Or at least . . . he's joint king with me," I amend, because our marriage is definitely an equal partnership, which is something I really try to get across to the girls in a positive, feminist role-model way. (When I'm not arguing with Dan and neglecting their spelling test, that is.) "We're both the king," I clarify.

"Maybe he doesn't *feel* like he's king." Tilda shrugs. "I don't know. You'd have to ask David Attenborough." She walks a few more steps in silence, then continues, "Or else, you know, Dan should just suck it up and get over himself. Sorry to be harsh," she adds. "You know what I mean."

"I do," I say, nodding. We've reached the station by now, and there's the usual stream of commuters and schoolchildren heading inside. "Anyway," I say to Tilda, above the hubbub. "I've come up with a new plan, and it'll definitely make Dan feel like the king of the jungle. It's another surprise," I add, and Tilda groans.

"No! Not more of this nonsense! I thought you were cured. You'll end up with another snake. Or worse."

"No we won't," I say defiantly. "This one is a *good* idea. It's related to sex, and sex is crucial to everything, agreed?"

"Sex?" Tilda seems simultaneously appalled and fascinated. "*Don't* tell me you've come up with some new sexual maneuver to make Dan feel like the king of the jungle. Frankly, the mind boggles."

"It's not a sexual move. It's a sexual gift." I pause dramatically for effect. "It's *boudoir photos.*"

"What?" Tilda's face is totally blank. "What's that?"

"Boudoir photos! It's a thing. You do it before you get married. You have sexy photos taken of you in stockings or whatever and you give it to your husband in a special book. So you can look back in future years and remember how hot you were."

"And then look at yourself in the mirror and compare and contrast?" Tilda sounds aghast. "No, thanks! Keep it all in the misty memory, that's what I say."

"Well, anyway, I'm doing it," I rejoin, a bit defiantly. "I'm going to google it today. There are special companies who do it."

"How much do they charge?"

"Don't know," I admit. "But what's the price of a happy marriage?"

Tilda just rolls her eyes sardonically. "I'll do it, if you like," she says. "And I won't charge anything. You can buy me a bottle of wine. Nice wine," she clarifies.

"*You'll* do it?" I give an incredulous gasp of laughter. "You just said you hated the idea!"

"For me. But for you, why not? Be fun."

"But you're not a photographer!" As I say it, I suddenly remember all her Instagram efforts. "I mean, not a *real* photographer," I add carefully.

"I have an eye," says Tilda confidently. "That's the main thing. My camera's good enough, and we can hire lighting or whatever. I've been wanting to get more into photography. As for props . . . I've got a riding crop somewhere around." She waggles her eyebrows at me and I dissolve into laughter.

"OK. Maybe. I'll think about it. I must go!"

And I give her a hug and dash into the station, still giggling at the idea.

Although in fact . . . she's got a point. By ten o'clock, I've spent a good hour peering at "boudoir photo" websites on the office computer. (I sent Clarissa off to interview the volunteers on their levels of job satisfaction, to get her out of the way.) First of all, the sessions all cost hundreds of pounds. Second of all, some of them make me cringe: *Kevin, our photographer, will use years of experience* (Playboy, Penthouse) *to guide you sensitively into a series of erotic poses, including advice on hand placement.* (Hand placement?) And third, wouldn't it be more fun and relaxed with Tilda?

I'm getting some ideas, though. There's a great picture of a girl in a white negligee, arching her leg through a chair which is *just* like one of our kitchen chairs. I could do that. I'm peering at the screen, trying to work out her exact position, when I hear a heavy tread coming up the stairs.

Shit. It's him. The nephew. Robert. *Shit.*

I have literally about thirty windows open on my screen, each one containing a "boudoir photo" of a woman in a corset and fishnets or lying on a bed, wearing nothing but ten sets of false eyelashes and a wedding veil.

Heart thumping, I start closing the images down, but I'm all flustered and keep mis-clicking. The wretched women won't stop pouting at me, with their red lips and lacy bras and hands placed provocatively over their thongs. (Actually, I can see the point of *advice on hand placement.*)

As I'm frantically closing down the final photo, I'm aware that the tread on the staircase has stopped. He's here. But it's OK: I closed everything down in time. I'm sure I did. He didn't see anything.

Did he?

My back is prickling with embarrassment. I can't bring myself to turn round. Shall I pretend to be so engrossed in work that I haven't noticed he's here? Yes. Good plan.

I pick up the phone and dial a random number.

"Hello?" I say stagily. "It's Sylvie from Willoughby House, calling to talk about our event. Can you call me back? Thanks."

I put down the phone, turn round, and do an exaggerated double take at the sight of

Robert standing there in his monolithic dark suit, holding a briefcase.

"Oh, hi!" I exclaim gushingly. "Sorry. Didn't see you there."

His face remains impassive, but his eyes flicker to my computer screen, to the phone, and back to me. They're so dark and impenetrable I can't read them. In fact, his whole face has a kind of off-putting, closed-up air. As though what you see is the tip of the iceberg.

Not like Dan. Dan is open. His eyes are clear and true. If he frowns, I can usually guess why. If he smiles, I know what the joke is. This guy looks as if the joke might be that no one will ever guess it was *him* who severed all those heads and hid them in the coalpit.

Then instantly I chide myself. *Stop exaggerating. He's not that bad.*

"Most telephone numbers begin with a zero," he says matter-of-factly.

Damn.

And: bloody hell. He was watching my fingers deliberately, to catch me out. That shows how sneaky he is. I need to be on my guard.

"Some don't," I say vaguely, and call up a random document on my screen. It's a budget for a harpsichord concert we did last year, I belatedly realize, but if he queries it I'll say I'm doing an audit exercise. Yes.

I feel all fake and self-conscious, sitting here under his gaze — and it's his fault, I decide. He shouldn't have such a forbidding air. It's not conducive to . . . anything. At that moment, I hear Clarissa on the stairs — and as she enters she actually gives a little squeak of dismay at the sight of him.

"Good, you're here," he says to her. "I want a meeting with both of you. I want a few answers about a few things."

That's exactly what I mean. How aggressive does that sound?

"Fine," I say coolly. "Clarissa, why don't you make some coffee? I'll just finish up here."

I'm not going to jump when he says jump. We have busy lives. We have agendas. What does he think we do all day? I close down the harpsichord-concert budget and file a couple of stray documents which are littering the screen (Clarissa leaves everything on the desktop), then thoughtlessly click on some JPEG which has been minimized.

At once the screen is filled with the image of a woman with a massive trout pout and a see-through bra, her fingers splayed over her breasts (excellent hand placement). My stomach heaves in horror. *Shit. I'm an IDIOT.*

Close down, close down. . . . My face is puce as I dementedly click my mouse, trying to get rid of the picture for good. At last it disappears, and I swivel round in my chair with a shrill laugh.

"Ha ha! You're probably wondering why I had that picture up on the screen! It was actually . . ." My mind casts around desperately. "Research. For a possible exhibition of . . . erotica."

Now my face is flaming even harder. I should never have attempted to say *erotica* out loud. It's a bad word, *erotica,* almost as bad as *moist.*

"Erotica?" Robert sounds a bit stunned.

"Historical. Through the ages. Victorian, Edwardian, compared to modern . . . er . . . It's only at the early planning stages," I finish lamely.

There's a bit of a silence.

"Does Willoughby House contain any erotica?" says Robert at last, frowning. "I wouldn't have thought it was my aunt's thing."

Of course it isn't her bloody thing! But I have to say something, and from the depths of my memory I pluck an image.

"There's a picture of a girl on a swing in one of the archived print collections," I tell him.

"A girl on a swing?" He raises his eyebrows. "Doesn't sound very . . ."

"She's naked," I elaborate. "And fairly . . . you know. Fulsome. I guess for a Victorian man, she'd be quite alluring."

"What about for a modern man?" His dark eyes gleam at me.

Is that appropriate, for his eyes to gleam? I'm going to pretend I didn't notice. Or hear the question. Or start this conversation.

"Shall we begin the meeting?" I say instead. "What exactly do you want to know?"

"I want to know what the hell you do all day," he says pleasantly, and at once I bristle.

"We run Willoughby House's administration and fundraising," I say with a slight glare.

"Good. Then you'll be able to tell me what that is."

He's pointing to the Ladder. It's a wooden library ladder, set against the wall, with boxes of cards on the three steps. As I follow his gaze, I gulp inwardly. I have to admit, the Ladder is idiosyncratic, even by our standards.

"It's our Christmas-card system," I explain. "Christmas cards are a big deal for Mrs. Kendrick. The top step is for the cards we received last year. The middle step is for this year's cards, unsigned. The bottom step is for this year's cards, signed. We each sign five a day."

"This is what you spend your days doing?" He turns from me to Clarissa, who has brought over three cups of coffee and almost jumps in alarm. "Signing Christmas cards? In *May*?"

"It's not *all* we do!" I say, nettled, as I take my coffee.

"What about social media, marketing strategy, positioning?" he suddenly fires at me.

"Oh," I say, caught off guard. "Well. Our social-media presence is . . . subtle."

"*Subtle?*" he echoes incredulously. "*That's* what you call it?"

"Discreet," puts in Clarissa.

"I've looked at the website," he says flatly. "I couldn't believe my eyes."

"Ah." I try to think of a comeback to this. I was rather hoping he wouldn't look at the website.

"Do you have *any* explanation?" he asks, in tones that say, "I'm trying to be reasonable here."

"Mrs. Kendrick didn't really like the idea of a website," I say defensively. "She was the one who came up with the eventual . . . concept."

"Let's have a look at it again, shall we?" Robert says in ominous tones. He pulls a spare office chair toward him and sits down. Then he takes out a laptop from his briefcase, opens it, and types in the Web address — and after a few seconds our home page appears. It's a beautiful black-and-white line drawing of Willoughby House, and on the front door is a very small notice, which reads: *Inquiries: Please apply in writing to Willoughby House, Willoughby Street, London W1.*

"You see, what I'm wondering . . ." says Robert in the same studiedly calm tone, "is where the information pages are, the gallery of photos, the FAQ, the subscription form, and, in fact, the whole bloody website?" He erupts. "Where's the *website*? This —" He jabs at the page. "This looks like a classified ad from *The Times,* 1923! Apply in writing? *Apply in writing?*"

I can't help wincing. He's right. I mean, he's right. It's a ridiculous website.

"Mrs. Kendrick liked *Apply in writing,*" volunteers Clarissa, who has perched on the corner of the computer desk. "Sylvie tried to get her to have an email form, but . . ." She glances at me.

"We tried," I affirm.

"You didn't try hard enough," Robert

shoots back, unrelenting. "What about Twitter? You have a handle, I've seen that, but where are the tweets? Where are the followers?"

"I'm in charge of Twitter," says Clarissa, almost in a whisper. "I did tweet once, but I didn't know what to say, so I just said, *Hello.*"

Robert looks like he doesn't even know how to respond to this.

"I don't think our clientele are on Twitter," I say, coming to Clarissa's defense. "They prefer letters."

"Your clientele are dying out," says Robert, looking unimpressed. "Willoughby House is dying out. This entire concern is dying out and you can't even see it. You all live in a bubble, my aunt included."

"That's not fair!" I say hotly. "We don't live in a bubble. We interact with a lot of external organizations, benefactors. . . . And we're not dying out! We're a thriving, vibrant, exciting . . ."

"You are *not* thriving!" Robert suddenly roars. "You are *not* thriving." His voice is huge in the low-ceilinged office, and we both gape at him. He rubs the back of his neck, wincing, not looking either of us in the eye. "My aunt's been desperate to keep the truth from you," he continues in a calmer voice. "But you need to know. This place is in big financial trouble."

"*Trouble?*" echoes Clarissa with a little gasp.

"For the last few years my aunt's been subsidizing it out of her own money. It can't go on. And that's why I've stepped in."

I stare at him, so flabbergasted that I can't speak. My throat has actually closed up in shock. Mrs. Kendrick's been *subsidizing* us?

"But we raise funds!" says Clarissa, looking pink and distressed, her voice practically a squeak. "We've done really well this year!"

"Exactly." I find my voice. "We raise funds all the time!"

"Not enough," says Robert flatly. "This place costs a fortune to run. Heating, lighting, insurance, biscuits, salaries . . ." He gives me a pointed look.

"But Mrs. Pritchett-Williams!" says Clarissa. "She donated half a million!"

"Exactly!" I say. "Mrs. Pritchett-Williams!"

"Long gone," says Robert, folding his arms.

Long gone?

I feel shaken to my core. I had no idea. No idea.

I suppose Mrs. Kendrick *has* been rather

cagey about the financial situation of the charity. But, then, she's cagey about so many things. (Like, for example, she won't let us have the address of Lady Chapman, one of our supporters, for the database. She says Lady Chapman wouldn't like it. So we have to write *By hand* on the envelope every time we want to send Lady Chapman anything, and Mrs. Kendrick delivers it personally to her house.)

As I stare at Robert, I realize I've never once doubted the financial strength of Willoughby House. Mrs. Kendrick has always told us that we're doing well. We've seen the headline figure for the year and it's always been great. It never occurred to me that Mrs. Kendrick might have contributed to it.

And now suddenly everything makes sense. Robert's suspicious frown. Mrs. Kendrick's anxious, defensive manner. Everything.

"So you *are* going to shut us down and build condos." I blurt the thought out before I can stop myself, and Robert gives me a long look.

"Is that what you've been expecting?" he says at last.

"Well, are you?" I challenge him, and there's a long silence. My stomach is becoming heavy with foreboding. This is feeling like a real threat. I don't know what to worry about first: Mrs. Kendrick, the art collection, the volunteers, the patrons, or my job. OK, I'll admit it; it's my job. I may not have as big an income as Dan does — but we need it.

"Maybe," says Robert at last. "I won't pretend it's not an option. But it's not the only option. I would love this place to work. The whole family would. But . . ."

He gestures around the office, and I can suddenly see the situation from his point of view. An old-fashioned, idiosyncratic, yet successful charity is one thing. An old-fashioned, idiosyncratic, failing money pit is something else.

"We can save it," I say, trying to sound robust. "It has stacks of potential. We can turn it around."

"That's a good attitude," says Robert. "But we need more than that. We need practical, solid ideas to start the cash flow. Your erotica exhibition might be a start," he adds to me. "That's the first good idea I've heard in this place."

"Erotica exhibition?" Clarissa gapes at me.

"It was only a thought," I try to backtrack.

"I found Sylvie conducting some pretty thorough research on erotic images," puts in Robert. He sounds so deadpan that I glance up at him in suspicion — and instantly know: He saw the "boudoir photos" on my screen. All thirty of them.

Great.

"Well." I clear my throat. "I like to do things thoroughly."

"Evidently." His eyebrows raise, and I hastily look away. I fumble in my pocket for my lip-balm case and pretend to be engrossed in that. It was Dan who gave me my pink leather lip-balm case, because I am, truthfully, addicted to lip balm. (Which, if Toby is correct, is due to evil Big Pharma. I must google that one day. Maybe there'll be some class-action suit and we'll all win millions.)

"*PS.*" Robert reads aloud the gold-embossed letters on my lip-balm case. "Why *PS*?"

"It stands for 'Princess Sylvie,' " says Clarissa brightly. "That's Sylvie's nickname."

I feel an instant surge of embarrassment. Why did she have to blab that little detail?

" 'Princess Sylvie'?" echoes Robert in an amused tone that flicks me on the raw.

"It's just my husband's nickname for me," I say quickly. "It's silly. It's . . . nothing."

"Princess Sylvie," repeats Robert, as though I haven't spoken. He surveys me for a few moments. I can feel his eyes running over my sprigged silk top and my pearl necklace and waist-length blond hair. Then he nods his head. "Yup."

Yup? What does he mean, *yup?* I want to know. But I also want not to know. So I say, "How long have we got? I mean, when will you make a decision about Willoughby House?"

Even as I'm speaking, my thoughts are circling uneasily. What would I do if I lost my job? Where would I apply? I haven't even *looked* to see what's out there at the moment. I haven't wanted to. I've been safe in my haven.

"I don't know," says Robert. "Let's see what you come up with. Maybe you'll perform a miracle."

But he sounds unconvinced. He's probably mentally choosing kitchen fittings for his luxury condos already. I see him glancing at our hand-drawn home page again, his eyes expressionless, and feel a fresh wave of mortification.

"You know, we *have* tried to modernize," I say. "But Mrs. Kendrick just wouldn't do it."

"I'm afraid my aunt has the commercial nous of a teapot," says Robert flatly. "That's not your fault, but it hasn't helped matters."

"Where is Mrs. Kendrick?" asks Clarissa timidly, and Robert's face creases slightly. I can't tell if he's amused or exasperated.

"She's hired a full-time computer teacher."

"What!" I exclaim before I can stop myself — and I can see Clarissa's jaw has dropped. "What's she learning, exactly?" I add, and Robert's face creases again. I think he wants to laugh.

"I was there when he arrived," he says. "She said, 'Young man, I wish to be modern.' "

I feel simultaneously amused and chastened. Mrs. Kendrick has been more pro-active than any of us. If I'd *known* things were this bad, I wouldn't have sat here defending our nonexistent website and our quirky charming ways. I would have . . .

What, exactly?

I bite my lip, trying to think. I'm not sure yet. I need to get on top of this, quickly. I need to have ideas. If Mrs. Kendrick can modernize, we all can.

Toby, I think suddenly. I'll ask Toby; he'll know.

"So that's my aunt's contribution to the situation." Robert surveys first Clarissa, then me. "What about you? Any specific ideas other than erotica?"

"Well." I rack my brain feverishly. "Obviously the website is an issue."

"We all know that," says Robert heavily. "Anything else?"

"We need a decent sign outside." I pluck an old, buried thought out of my brain. "People walk past the house and have no idea what it is. We did try to suggest it to Mrs. Kendrick, but —"

"I can imagine." Robert rolls his eyes.

"And we could do something creative?" I'm feeling my way now. "Like . . . a podcast set in Willoughby House? A ghost story?"

"A ghost story." He looks quizzical. "Are you going to write a ghost story?"

"Well, OK . . . probably not," I allow. "We'd have to get someone to do it."

"How much income would it generate? Or publicity?"

"I don't know," I admit, losing faith in the idea even as I'm talking. "But it's just the first idea of many. Many, many ideas," I reiterate, as though to reassure myself.

"Good," says Robert, sounding unconvinced. "I look forward to your many ideas."

"Great." I try to sound bullish. "Well . . . you'll be impressed."

NINE

Everything's got so *stressful.* It's three days later, and I've just about had enough. Why is life like this? Just as you relax and start enjoying yourself, smiling, having fun . . . life looms up like a mean teacher in the playground shouting, "Playtime is *over!*" and everyone trails off to be miserable and bored again.

Dan is constantly strained but he won't tell me why. He got home at midnight the other night and smelled of whiskey. He sits gazing into the snake tank quite a lot, and his default expression has become a frown.

I joked yesterday morning, "Don't worry, only another sixty-seven years and fifty weeks to go," and he just looked up blankly as though he didn't get it. Then, when I said more gently, "Come on, Dan, what's the matter?" he sprang up and left the room, replying, "Nothing," over his shoulder.

How many divorces are caused by the

word *nothing*? I think this would be a very interesting statistic. When Dan says, "Nothing," I get this jab of total frusture, like a little twisty knife. *Frusture* is my word for the exquisite fury that only your husband can give you. Not only are you furious, you feel like he's doing it all on purpose, *in order to torment you.*

I raised this theory with Dan, once. I was — in hindsight — a bit stressed out. The babies had been up all night, in my defense. And I yelled, "Do you *deliberately* find the most annoying thing to say to me, Dan? Is this your plan?" Whereupon he looked all hunted and said, "No. I don't know. I wasn't quite following what you said. You look really nice in that dress."

Which kind of appeased me and didn't appease me, all at once. I mean, I had gone off topic. I will admit that. I sometimes do. But couldn't he see that our holiday plans and the problem with the recycling bins and his mother's birthday present were *all the same issue*?

(Also, it wasn't a dress; it was a nondescript breastfeeding tunic top that I'd worn fifty times before. So how on earth could he say I looked *nice* in it?)

Probably we should have agendas for our arguments. Probably we should decide to have an argument every Thursday evening and buy in snacks and hire a mediator. We should take ownership of the arguing process. But until we do, we're stuck with Dan saying, "Nothing," and me seething, and the air all crackly with static resentment.

Anyway, I'm hoping my boudoir pictures will change everything. Or change some things, at least.

Meanwhile, the office is pretty stressful too. Robert has been hanging around every day, going through figures and files and basically insulting everything we've ever done. He isn't scary, exactly, but he's businesslike. He asks short, brusque questions. He expects short, brusque answers. Poor Clarissa can't cope at all and communicates in whispers. I'm more resilient — but doesn't he realize? We don't make the big decisions. It wasn't *our* idea to commission a special Willoughby House Christmas Pudding last year as a gift to supporters (total loss: £379); it was Mrs. Kendrick's idea.

Shamed by Mrs. Kendrick's positive and adaptable attitude, I've done some research on websites and online shops and all the things I think we should be doing. I've spent every waking moment trying to think of creative ideas other than a ghost-story podcast. (The trouble is, once you *try* to have an idea, they all fly away.) I've also been round to see Toby, but he wasn't in, so I emailed him and haven't heard back yet.

Then Mummy keeps phoning me about the opening ceremony. She's nearly as bad as Esme, with her endless questions. Today she wanted to know: 1. What color shoes should she wear, and 2. How will she remember everyone's name? (Answers: 1. No one will be looking at her shoes, and 2. Name badges.) Esme, on the other hand, wanted to know: 3. Do I require a radio microphone, and 4. What kind of snacks would I like in the "green-room area"? (Answers: 3. I'm really not bothered, and 4. A bowl of M&M's with all the blue ones taken out. *Joke.*)

Just to add to the fraught atmosphere, Tilda and Toby had a massive shouting match last night. I could hear them through the wall and it made me wince. (I also decided it would be tactless for me to pop straight round and say, "Oh, Toby, you're in; did you get my email?" So I left it half an hour and by then he'd gone out again. Typical.)

I know it's tough for Toby and that his generation have it hard. I know all that. But I think Tilda's going to have to be firm. He needs to get a job. A place to live. A life, basically.

I'm actually quite apprehensive as I knock on her door on Thursday evening, in case I come across her and Toby mid-row again. But as she opens the door she looks quite calm — mellow, even, and there's music playing in the background.

"He's out," she says succinctly. "Staying over with friends. We're fine. All ready?"

"I guess!" I give a nervous laugh. "Ready as I ever will be."

"And Dan?" She peers round to next door, as though he might suddenly pop up.

"He thinks I'm at book group." I grin. "You might have to bullshit about our interesting discussion on Flaubert."

"Flaubert!" She gives a short laugh. "Well, come on in, Madame Bovary."

I've been googling *boudoir photos* pretty solidly over the last three days, and, as a result, I'm equipped. *More* than equipped. I have procured: a spray tan, a manicure, a pedicure, blow-dried hair, false eyelashes, a bag of pretty underwear, a bag of racy underwear, a bag of super-racy/trashy-whore underwear, and a massive long string of fake pearls from Topshop. I also have a few new accessories, which arrived in a plainly packaged box — I told Dan they were new ballet shoes for the girls — but I'm not sure about those. (In fact, I'm thinking the "vintage fur rabbit mask" was a definite mistake.)

Every chance I've got, I've been posing in the mirror, squinting at my bum to see how big it looks and practicing an alluring expression. Although I think I'll need a glass of prosecco beforehand to loosen up. (I've brought that too.)

"What do you think?" Tilda bustles me into her sitting room, and I gasp. She's moved half the furniture out and it looks like a photographer's studio. There are big lights on stands, and a white umbrella-type thing, and a single sofa in the center of the room, plus a folding screen and a full-length mirror.

"Amazing!"

"Isn't it?" Tilda looks pleased. "I thought if this goes well, I might go into the business properly. It's quite a racket, this boudoir photography."

"Have you ever used equipment like this before?" I ask, curiously touching the umbrella-type thing.

"No, but it's all fairly obvious." Tilda waves an airy hand. "I've been googling. Is the house warm enough for you?"

"It's sweltering!" I've never known Tilda's

house so hot. Usually she's of the "heating is for wimps" mentality.

"You want to be nice and warm and relaxed. Nice eyelashes, by the way," adds Tilda admiringly. "And what have you brought?" She reaches into one of my bags and pulls out the string of pearls. "Ah, very good. A classic. The 'draping shot,' as we boudoir photographers call it."

She sounds so expert, I want to laugh. I'm also quite touched she's taking it so seriously.

"You can change behind the screen," Tilda continues, opening up the prosecco and pouring it out. "And then we'll go into the first pose." She hands me a glass and consults a handwritten list headed *Sylvie — Poses.* "Sit on the sofa, then gradually slide off. Your head should be thrust upward, right leg bent, left leg relaxed, back arched, shoe dangling. . . ."

"Uh-huh," I say doubtfully. "Can you show me?"

"Show you?" Tilda looks aghast. "Well, I can try, but I'm not very supple."

She sits on the sofa, then slides off. Halfway toward the floor she freezes, one leg pinned to the floor, the other swinging akimbo, and her head thrust back in a painful-looking rictus. She looks like she's giving birth. That *can't* be right.

"Ow." She flops to the floor. "You see?"

"Er . . . kind of," I say, after a pause.

"It'll be fine!" she says breezily. "I'll direct you. Now, what are you going to wear?"

Choosing the first outfit is a lot of fun and takes us nearly half an hour. I went a bit overboard with the underwear shopping, so we have lots of choice and eventually get it down to a white lace set with white seamed stockings and suspenders. As I emerge from behind the screen, I feel genuinely sexy and excited. Dan won't believe his eyes!

"Amazing!" says Tilda, who is fiddling with her light counter. "Now, if you get into position . . ."

I sit on the sofa, slide down, and freeze in the same way that Tilda did. Almost at once, my thighs start burning. I should have done the boudoir workout.

"Ready?" I say, after what seems like ten minutes.

"Sorry," says Tilda, glancing up. "Oh, you look gorgeous. Lovely!" She takes a few pictures, peering at me between shots.

"Really? Are you sure?"

I want to say, *Do I look like I'm giving birth?* Only that might sound weird.

"Try putting your hands behind your head," suggests Tilda, snapping away. "Oh yes! Now sweep your hair back. Lovely! Do it again!"

Twenty hair-sweeps later, my legs can't take it anymore and I collapse onto the floor.

"Great!" says Tilda. "Shall we have a look?"

"Yes!" I scrabble to my feet and hurry over to the camera. Tilda scrolls back through the shots and we both gaze in silence.

The images are so far from what I imagined that I'm speechless. You can barely see my face. You can barely see the sexy underwear. The whole photo is dominated by my legs in their white stockings, which are lit up so brightly, they look like luminous surgical stockings. In half the photos, my hair is over my face, not in a sexy way but a disheveled, crap-looking way. And I *do* look like I'm giving birth.

"My legs look quite . . ." I say at last.

I don't want to say "huge, fat, and white." But that's the truth.

"I didn't *quite* get the lighting right," says Tilda after another long pause. Her ebullience has dimmed and there's a crinkle in her brow. "Not *exactly* right. Never mind. Let's go on to the second pose."

I put on a new outfit — red lace teddy — and get onto all fours, following Tilda's directions.

"Now, lean forward on your knees . . . legs apart . . . further apart . . ."

"They won't *go* any further apart," I gasp. "I'm not a bloody gymnast!"

"OK, now raise your chin," instructs Tilda, ignoring me. "Put your weight all on one arm if you can . . . boost your boobs with the other arm . . . give me a sexy look. . . ."

My knees are killing me. My arm is killing me. And now I have to produce a sexy look? I flutter my eyelashes and the camera flashes a few times. "Hmm," says Tilda, doubtfully squinting at her screen. "Could you lift your bum up for a better angle?"

With a huge effort, I try to arch my back and thrust my bum farther into the air.

"Hmm," says Tilda again. "No. Maybe I meant, lift up your head." She stares at her screen as though perplexed. "Can you get a bit more curve into your bum, somehow?"

Get more curve into my bum? What does that even mean? My bum is my bum.

"No." I sit back and rub my knees. "Ow. I need kneepads." I get to my feet and rub at my legs. "Can I have a look?"

"No," says Tilda hurriedly as I approach. "No, better not see these ones. I mean, they're *lovely,* absolutely *gorgeous,* but I might just delete them. . . ." She jabs quickly at her camera, then looks up with a bright smile. "That pose wasn't quite working. But I've got another idea. We'll use the doorway."

The doorway is the worst of all. This time I insist on seeing the shots, and I look like a gorilla. A pale, hairless gorilla in a blond wig, hanging from a doorframe in a black lace bra and knickers. This time, all the light pools harshly on my stomach. You can't see my face but you can see my stretch marks in glorious detail. If Dan saw this photo, we'd probably never have sex again.

"I can *absolutely* photoshop these," Tilda keeps saying as we scroll through, but I can tell she's slightly losing confidence. "It's harder than I thought," she says, heaving a sigh. "I mean, taking the photos is easy enough; it's making them *look* good." She gazes at a particularly ghoulish image of me, winces, and pours more prosecco into our glasses.

We both take a few gulps, and Tilda idly experiments with my black satin corset, wrapping it around herself this way and that.

"Maybe we need something simpler," she says at last. "We'll use the fail-safe pose."

"What's the fail-safe pose?"

"It's for all shapes and sizes," she says,

more confidently. "I read about it on a website. You lie on the sofa, legs crossed, and gaze up at the camera. I've got lighting instructions too."

Lying on the sofa sounds a lot better than kneeling on the floor, or hanging upside down off the back of a chair, which was her other idea.

"OK." I nod. "What shall I wear?"

But Tilda is still preoccupied with my corset.

"*How* does this thing work?" she says suddenly. "I can't work it out at all. Where's the top? Where's the boobs bit?"

"It doesn't have a boobs bit," I tell her. "It's an underbust corset. You can wear a bra with it. Or not."

"Oh, I *see*. Well, perfect!" Her imagination seems seized. "Wear this and a pair of knickers and nothing more. Lie on the sofa. Play with your pearls. It'll look great. Dan will go wild."

"Right." I hesitate. "So . . . a topless shot, you mean."

"Exactly! It'll be gorgeous!"

I'm not too sure. Posing in underwear is one thing. But topless? In front of Tilda?

"Won't that make you uncomfortable?" I venture.

"Of course not!" she says airily. "I've seen

your boobs before, haven't I?"

"Have you?"

"Well, haven't I?" She wrinkles her brow. "Out shopping or something? Glimpsed them in the changing room?"

I'm fairly sure Tilda hasn't glimpsed my boobs in the changing room. And I'm still not comfortable about this idea. I mean, I'm not *prudish.* I'm not. Really. It's just . . .

"Are you uncomfortable?" Tilda peers at me as though the thought is just dawning on her.

"Well . . ." I shrug awkwardly.

"Well, how about I show you mine? Fair's fair." I gape, stunned, as she whips up her top and unclasps her front-fastening bra, exposing two quite large, veiny breasts. "Ghastly, aren't they?" she adds dispassionately. "I breastfed Toby for two years, you know, like the idiot I was. No wonder he won't leave home."

I'm not sure what to reply. Or where to look. Do I say, "They're lovely"? What *do* you say about your friend's breasts? The truth is, they're not lovely in a conventional sense, but they're lovely because they look exactly like Tilda. Comforting and voluminous and Tilda-ish.

Luckily, she doesn't seem to require an answer. She fastens her bra up again, drops down her shirt, and grins. "OK, sexy Sylvie," she says. "Your turn."

And suddenly I feel stupid for even hesitating. This is Tilda. They're just boobs, for God's sake.

"OK!" I grab the corset. "Let's do it!"

"I'm going to get my extra pack of filters," says Tilda. "Be back in a moment."

I quickly strip off the bra I'm wearing, fit the satin corset around me, and cinch it so tight I can hardly breathe. I put on my highest stripper heels, drape the pearls around my neck, and survey myself in the mirror. I have to say, this corset is very flattering. I actually look quite hot. My boobs are . . . well, they're OK. Bearing in mind what they've done. Still perky-ish. As I hear Tilda returning, I sashay to the door.

"So what do you think of *this*?" I say, and fling it open, one hand on my hip.

Toby is standing in front of me. In the split second before I can react, I see his eyes fix on my nipples and his pupils dilate and his jaw slacken.

"Argh!" I hear myself scream before I realize I'm doing it. "Argh! Sorry!" I clutch my hands over my naked breasts, which probably looks *exactly* like a boudoir shot.

A hoarse sound is coming from Toby too. "Oh God!" He sounds even more aghast than I do and puts a hand up to shield his eyes. "Sylvie, I'm sorry! Argh! Mum . . ."

"Toby!" Tilda comes into the hall, scolding him. She tosses me a pashmina from the banister and I hastily wrap it round myself. "What are you doing back? I told you Sylvie was coming over!"

"I thought you were just going to drink wine, like you normally do!" Toby retorts defensively. "Not . . ." He peers past me. "Are you taking *photos*?"

"Don't tell Dan," I blurt out.

"Right." His eyes drift down to my stripper heels and back up again. "Right."

This is mortifying. I have never felt more like a tragic suburban wife, desperately trying to keep her husband interested because otherwise he'll shag his secretary; in fact, he probably has done already and, guess what, she wears nothing but his boxer shorts to bed, but, then, she's twenty-one and a natural 34D.

(OK, that was a *really* unhelpful train of thought.)

"Anyway!" I say in brittle tones. "So. Um. We're pretty much finished up, aren't we, Tilda? Nice to see you, Toby."

"Nice to see you, too, Sylvie," says Toby politely. "Oh, and I got your email about your website. What kind of CMS were you

271

thinking of?"

"CMS?" I echo blankly.

"Content management system? Because you'll need to think about scalability, plug-ins, e-commerce . . . Do you know what kind of functionality you're after?"

"You know, maybe we should discuss this another time?" I say in a shrill voice. *Like, when I've got clothes on?* "That would be great."

"No problem," says Toby easily. "Any-time."

He thuds upstairs and Tilda and I glance at each other. Suddenly Tilda makes an exploding noise, clutches at her mouth, and starts jiggling with suppressed laughter.

"You've got to admit," she says, when she's regained control of herself. "It's quite funny."

"No, it's not!" I say reproachfully. "I'm traumatized! Toby's traumatized! We'll all have to have therapy after this!"

"Oh, Sylvie." Tilda gives a final gurgle. "Don't be traumatized. And as for Toby, it's good for him to see that the older genera-tion still has a bit of oomph. Come on, let's take a picture of you in that corset. You look great," she adds.

"No." I wrap the pashmina more tightly around me, feeling deflated. "I'm not in the mood anymore. I feel old and stupid and . . . you know. Desperate."

Tilda's silent for a moment, surveying me with her shrewd, kind eyes.

"Go home," she says. "Sylvie, you don't need a book of boudoir photos. I'm a crap photographer, anyway."

"No, you're not," I begin politely, but Tilda makes a snorting sound.

"I could not have made you look more terrible if I'd tried! And why take pictures anyway? Just go home, wearing that." She nods at me. "Believe me, if that doesn't make Dan's day, there's something wrong with him."

I glance toward the party wall and imagine Dan on the other side of it, eating his single salmon fillet, watching sports on the kitchen telly, believing sincerely that Tilda and I are discussing Flaubert.

"You're right." I feel a surge of optimism and adrenaline. "You're right!"

Suddenly this whole endeavor seems artificial and weird and kind of *too much.*

"Leave all your stuff here," says Tilda. "Get it tomorrow." She hands me my handbag. "If I were you, I'd head home right now in that pashmina, peel it off, and ravish Dan. I'll turn up the TV loud," she adds with a wink. "We won't hear anything."

■ ■ ■ ■

Dan is sitting at the kitchen table as I enter, exactly as I pictured him. Discarded plate with salmon skin. Football on. Beer open. Feet up on a chair. If Vermeer had been around, he could have made a perfect study of him: *Man with Wife at Book Club.*

"Hi." He looks up with an absent smile. "You're home early."

"We wrapped it up." I smile back. "There's only so much you can say about Flaubert."

"Mmm." His attention shifts back toward the screen and he takes a slug of beer.

Isn't he going to say, "Why are you dressed only in a pashmina and high heels?"

Clearly not. Clearly he thinks it's a dress.

"Dan." I plant myself in his field of vision and start to unwrap the pashmina in my most tantalizing, boudoir-photo style. "Come *on*. . . ."

I don't believe it. He's peering around me at the screen, as if I'm some annoying obstacle, because something far more exciting is obviously happening on the football pitch. "Come on!" He clenches a fist. "Come on!"

"Dan!" I say sharply, and let the pashmina fall to the ground in one go.

OK, *now* I've got his attention.

There's silence, except for the roar of the football crowd. Dan is goggling up at me. He's actually speechless. He lifts a hand to caress one of my boobs, as though he's never seen it before.

"Well," he says at last, his voice a little thick. "This is interesting."

"Surprise." I shrug nonchalantly.

"So I see."

Slowly, he starts playing with the pearl necklace. He presses the pearls into my cleavage, rubs my nipples with them, runs them up and down my skin, his eyes fixed on mine. And I *know* the pearl necklace is a boudoir-photo cliché or whatever, but actually this is pretty sexy. It's all pretty sexy. The stripper heels, the corset — and Dan's expression in particular. He hasn't looked like this in a long time — as though something huge and powerful is overcoming him and no one can stop it.

"The children are asleep," I say huskily, reaching for the remote and snapping off the TV. "We can do anything. Try anything. Go anywhere. Be anyone."

Dan is already eyeing up a nearby barstool with intent. He's very keen on doing it on those barstools. Me, not so much. They always end up digging into my thighs.

"Maybe something different," I say quickly. "Something we've never done. Something adventurous. Surprise me."

There's another tense silence, broken only by the clicking of the pearls in Dan's fingers. His eyes are distant. I can tell he's hugely preoccupied. My own mind is ranging around various delicious possibilities and fixing on that chocolate body paint I bought once for Valentine's Day — hmm, I wonder where it is — when Dan's eyes seem to snap.

"Right," he says. "Get your coat on. I'm asking Tilda to babysit."

"What are we doing?"

"You'll find out." He flashes me a gaze that makes me shiver in anticipation.

"Do I need clothes on?"

"Just put a coat on." His eyes drop to my lacy black knickers. "You won't need those."

OK, this *totally* beats a book of boudoir photos. By the time I've removed my knickers, selected my sexiest coat, and made sure that passersby won't get an X-rated view of me as I walk along, Dan is back, with Tilda in tow.

"Going out to supper, I hear, Sylvie?" says Tilda in super-innocent tones. "Or is it more like dessert *alfresco*?" She eyes my stripper heels so comically, I bite my lip.

"Dan's in charge." I match her innocent

tone. "So. Who knows?"

"Good man." Her eyes sparkle wickedly at me. "Well, have a good time. Don't rush back."

Dan hires a taxi and gives an address to the driver that I can't hear. We travel along in silence, my pulse rising as Dan's hand roams idly up inside my coat. I'm feeling almost faint with lust. We haven't done anything like this for ages. Maybe ever. And I'm not even sure what "this" is yet.

After a short drive, we get out on a street corner in Vauxhall. Vauxhall? This is all very unlikely.

"What?" I begin, looking around. "Where are we —"

"Shhh." Dan cuts me off. "This way."

He leads me briskly through an unfamiliar garden square, just as though he's been here a million times. He ushers me past the church in the corner. We walk through the little graveyard and approach an old wooden gate, set in a brick wall, with a keypad next to it.

"OK," says Dan to himself, as we come to a halt. "The only question is, have they changed the code?"

I'm too bemused to answer. Where the hell are we?

Dan punches in a code, and I hear an

unlocking sound from the gate. Then he slowly pushes it open. And I don't believe it: It's a garden. A totally deserted little garden. I stare ahead, openmouthed, and Dan surveys me with a twinkle of satisfaction.

"Surprise," he says.

I follow him in, looking around in wonderment. What *is* this place? There are raised beds. Trellises. Pleached apple trees. Roses. It's a little haven in the heart of London. And in the center of it all is an arrangement of five abstract modern sculptures — all twisting, sinuous hardwood curves.

It's toward these that Dan is leading me, authoritatively, as though he owns the place. Without speaking, he pushes me up against a sculpture and starts to kiss me with determination, peeling off my coat, cupping my naked breasts, not saying a word. The smooth sweep of the sculpture melds to me perfectly. The air is fresh against my skin. I can smell roses in the air, hear the laughter of passersby on the other side of the wall. They've got no idea what we're up to. This is surreal.

I want to ask, "Where are we?" and "How did you know about this place?" and "Why haven't we been here before?" but already Dan is pulling me onto another of the sculptures. He fits my limbs expertly to its curves as though it's custom-made. For thirty seconds he just stares at me splayed on the wood, like his own private boudoir shot. A million miles from white suspenders and prosecco.

Then he's stripping off his own clothes, no pausing, no hesitating, no wondering, his face urgent. Businesslike. Serious. Was this sculpture *designed* for sex? I can't help wondering. And how does Dan know about it? And what — Why . . . ?

Moments later, I inhale in shock as Dan bodily lifts me onto a third, even more strangely curved sculpture. With firm hands, still not speaking, he maneuvers me into the weirdest ever . . . Wait, *what* does he want me to do? I'm getting a head rush. My limbs are twitching in this unfamiliar position. I've never *known* . . . How did he even *think* of . . . If the boudoir shots were "soft," this is full-on, X-rated. . . .

I had no idea Dan even . . .

Oh God. My thoughts putter out. I can hear my breath coming in short gasps. I'm clutching hard at the wood. I'm going to explode. This isn't "surprise." This is "seismic."

I don't think I've ever felt so sated in my

life. I'm shaky. What *was* that?

When we're finally, finally done, we nestle in the curve of one of the sculptures (they are *so* designed for sex) and stare up into the sky. There aren't any stars to speak of — too cloudy — but there's the floral, earthy scent of the garden and the trickle of a water feature that I didn't notice before.

"Wow," I say at last. "Best surprise ever. You win."

"Well, if you will dress up like a hooker . . ." I can sense Dan grinning into the darkness.

"So, what is this place?" I gesture around with a bare arm. "How did you know about it?"

"I just knew about it. It's great, isn't it?"

"Amazing."

I nod, feeling my heart rate subside. I'm still suffused with a rosy glow, with endorphins coursing round my body. (Do I mean pheromones? Sexy loving hormones, anyway.) In fact, I feel pretty euphoric. Finally it's all worked out! Project Surprise Me has led to this astounding, sublime, and transcendental evening, which we'll remember forever. I feel so *connected* to Dan right now. When's the last time we lay naked in the fresh night air? We should do this more. All the time.

How *did* he know about this place, anyway? I wonder idly. He didn't really answer
the question.

"How exactly did you know about it?" I
nudge Dan.

"Oh," says Dan, yawning. "Well, in actual
fact, I helped to create it."

"You *what*?" I raise myself on an elbow to
stare at him.

"During university, the summer after my
first year. I volunteered for a while." He
shrugs. "It's a community garden. They let
groups in to study horticulture, herbology,
that kind of thing."

"But . . . how come? Why a garden?"

"Well," Dan says, as though it's obvious,
"you know I'm into gardening."

I know *what*?

"No, I don't." I peer at him in astonishment. "What do you mean, 'I'm into
gardening'? You've never been into gardening. You never garden at home."

"That's true." Dan makes a regretful face.
"Too busy with work, I suppose. And the
twins. And now our garden's basically a
playground, what with the Wendy houses."

"Right." I pull my coat around my shoulders, digesting this. "My husband, the
gardener. I never knew."

"It's not a big thing." Dan shrugs. "Maybe

281

I'll take it up again when I retire."

"But wait." A fresh thought strikes me. "How did you know these sculptures were so . . . fit for purpose?"

"I didn't," says Dan. "But I always looked at them and wondered." He twinkles at me wickedly. "I wondered a *lot*."

"Ha." I smile back, running an affectionate hand over his shoulder. "I wish I'd been your girlfriend back then. But that year . . ." I wrinkle my brow, trying to remember. "Yes. I was attached."

"Well, so was I," says Dan. "And I don't wish we'd known each other back then. I think we found each other at exactly the right time." He kisses me tenderly and I smile absently back. But my brain is snagging on something. He was attached?

"Who were you attached to?" I ask, puzzled. My mind is already running through the roster of Dan's previous girlfriends. (I've quizzed him quite extensively on this subject.) "Charlotte? Amanda?"

Surely neither of those works, timing-wise?

"Actually, no." He stretches, with another huge yawn, then pulls me closer. "Does it matter who it was?"

My mind tussles with two answers. The not-ruining-the-moment answer: *no*. And the I-have-to-know-this answer: *yes.*

"It doesn't *matter,*" I say at last, in a light, breezy tone. "I'm not saying it *matters.* I'm just wondering. Who it was."

"Mary."

He smiles at me and kisses my forehead, but I don't react. All my internal radar have sprung into action. Mary? Mary?

"Mary?" I try a little laugh. "I don't remember you mentioning a Mary, ever."

"I'm sure I told you about her," he says easily.

"No, you didn't."

"I'm sure I did."

"You *didn't.*" A hint of steel is in my voice. I have all Dan's former girlfriends logged in my brain, in the same way that FBI agents have America's Most Wanted. There is not and has never been a Mary. Until now.

"Well, maybe I forgot about her," says Dan. "To be honest, I'd forgotten about this place. I'd forgotten about that whole part of my life. It was only when you said, 'Something adventurous'. . . ." He leans over me again, his eyes mischievous. "It woke something up in me."

"Clearly!" I say, matching his tone, deciding to leave the issue of Mary. "Come on, then, give me a tour."

As Dan leads me around the paths, gesturing at plants, I'm slightly gobsmacked at his knowledge. I thought I knew Dan inside out. And yet here's this rich seam of passion which he's never shared with me.

I mean, it's great, because we could definitely do more with our own garden. We can turn it into a family hobby. He can teach the girls to weed . . . hoe. . . . And presents! Yes! I have to resist a sudden urge to fist-pump. All his presents are solved for the next twenty years! I can buy him gardening tools and plants and all those witty items saying HEAD GARDENER.

But I must bone up on gardening myself. As we progress, I'm realizing quite how inexpert I am. I keep thinking he's talking about a shrub when he's referring to a climber, or vice versa. (The Latin names *really* don't help.)

"Amazing tree," I say as we reach the far corner. (I can get "tree" right.)

"That was Mary's idea." Dan's eyes soften. "She had a thing about hawthorn trees."

"Right," I say, forcing a polite smile. This is the third time he's mentioned Mary. "Gorgeous. And that arbor is lovely! I didn't even notice it at first, tucked away there."

"Mary and I put that up," says Dan reminiscently, patting the wooden structure.

"We used reclaimed wood. It took us a whole weekend."

"Well done, Mary!" I say sarcastically, before I can stop myself, and Dan turns his head in surprise. "I mean . . . amazing!"

I link my arm in Dan's and smile up at him, to cover the fact that all these little mentions of Mary are feeling like pinpricks of irritation. For a woman I'd never even heard about three minutes ago, she seems to be remarkably present in our conversation.

"So, was it serious, you and Mary?" I can't help asking.

"It was, for a bit." Dan nods. "But she was studying at Manchester, which is why we broke up eventually, I guess." He shrugs. "Long way from Exeter."

They didn't break up because they had a row or slept with other people, I register silently. It was logistics.

"We had all kinds of dreams," Dan continues. "We were going to set up a smallholding together. Organic veg, that kind of thing. Change the world. Like I say, it was a different me." Dan looks around the garden and shakes his head with a wry smile. "Coming in here is strange. It's taken me back to the person I was then."

"Were you *so* different?" I say, feeling

285

disconcerted again. He's got a light in his eye I've never seen before. Distant and kind of wistful. Wistful for what, exactly? This was supposed to be a sublime and transcendental evening about *us,* not some long-ago relationship.

"Oh, I was different, all right." He laughs. "Wait. There might be a picture. . . ."

He searches for a while on his phone, then holds it out. "Here." I take it and find myself looking at a website headed *The St. Philip's Garden: How We Started.*

"See?" Dan points to a dated-looking photo of young people in jeans, clutching muddy spades and forks. "That's Mary . . . and that's me."

I've seen pictures of Dan in his youth before. But never from this era. He looks so *skinny.* He's wearing a checked shirt and some weird bandanna round his head, and his arm is firmly squeezing Mary. I zoom in and survey her critically. Apart from the frizzy hair, she's pretty. Really pretty. In a wholesome, organic, dimpled way. Very long, lean legs, I notice. Her smile is radiant and her cheeks are flushed and her jeans are filthy. I can't imagine her doing a boudoir shoot. But, then, I can't imagine Dan the gardener either.

"I wonder what she's doing now?" Dan

muses. "It's crazy to think I just *forgot* about her. I mean, for a while we were —" He breaks off as though realizing where this is taking him. "Anyway."

"Crazy!" I say, with a shrill little laugh. "Well, here you are. Are you getting cold?"

I hold his phone out to him, but he doesn't take it. He's staring, transfixed, at the arbor. He seems lost in . . . what? Thought? Memories? Memories of him and Mary, aged nineteen, all lithe and idealistic, building their reclaimed-wood arbor?

Shagging in the arbor? When everyone else had gone home?

No. Do *not* have that thought.

"What are you thinking about?" I say, trying to sound light and carefree. *If he says "Mary," I will . . .*

"Oh." Dan comes to and darts an evasive look at me. "Nothing. Really. Nothing."

TEN

It woke something up in me.

I keep recalling Dan's words, and every time, it's with a sense of foreboding. I can't stop picturing his transported face. Transported away from me, to some other golden halcyon time of scented flowers and honest earthy work and nineteen-year-old girls with radiant smiles and dimples.

Whatever that secret garden "woke up in him," I would be quite keen on it going back to sleep now, thank you very much. I would be quite keen on him forgetting all about the garden, and Mary, and whatever "different person" he was back then. Because, newsflash, this isn't then; it's now. He's not nineteen anymore. He's married and a father. Has he forgotten all that?

I know I shouldn't leap to conclusions without evidence. But there *is* evidence. I know for a fact that in the five days since we visited the garden, Dan has been utterly preoccupied by Mary. *Secretly* preoccupied with her, I should clarify. On his own. Away from me.

I'm not a suspicious woman. I'm not. It's perfectly reasonable for me to glance at my husband's browsing history. It's part of the intimate ebb and flow of married life. He sees my used tissues, thrown in the bin . . . I see the workings of his mind, all there for me to find on his laptop with no attempt at concealment.

Honestly. You'd *think* he'd have been more discreet.

I can't decide if I'm pleased or not pleased that he didn't clear his history. On the one hand it could mean he doesn't have anything to hide. On the other hand it could mean he doesn't have any sense of women, or any sense of anything, or even a brain, maybe. What did he think? That I *wasn't* going to check his laptop after he revealed a secret long-lost girlfriend with dimples whom he'd failed to mention?

I *mean.*

He's searched for her in various different ways: *Mary Holland. Mary Holland job. Mary Holland husband.* One might ask: Why does he need to know about Mary Holland's (as it happens, nonexistent) husband? But I'm not going to be so undignified as to bring the subject up. I'm not that needy. I'm not that kind of wife.

Instead, I deliberately googled one of *my* old boyfriends — I typed in *Matt Quinton flash job big car really sexy* — and left my laptop out on the kitchen table. As far as I could tell, Dan didn't even notice. He is *so annoying.*

So then I decided on another tack. I bought a gardening magazine and tried to start a conversation about our garden and whether we should go for hardy annuals. I persevered for about ten minutes and even used a couple of Latin names, and at the end Dan said, "Hmm, maybe," in this absent way.

Hmm, maybe?

I thought he loved gardening. I thought that was his undeclared passion. He should have *leapt* at the chance to talk about hardy annuals.

And it left a question burning in my mind. A more concerning question. If it wasn't gardening that he was thinking about so wistfully the other night . . . what was it?

I haven't addressed this. Not directly. I just said, "I thought you wanted to garden more, Dan?" and Dan said, "Oh, I do, I do. We should make a plan," and went off to send some emails.

And now, of course, he's in a filthy mood because it's the opening ceremony at the hospital this afternoon and he has to take time off work and dress up super-smart and be nice to my mother and basically all the things he hates most in life.

The girls woke even earlier than usual and begged to play in the garden before school, so Dan and I are sitting in an unusual quietness at breakfast, while I tweak my speech about Daddy. I'm lurching between thinking it's too sentimental and not sentimental enough. Every time I read it through, I get misty about the eyes, but I'm determined that at the actual event I am not going to cry. I am going to be a dignified representative of the family.

It is taking me back, though. Life with Daddy was golden, somehow. Or do I mean gilded? I just remember endless summers and sunshine and being out on the boat and corner tables at restaurants and special ice-cream sundaes for "Miss Sylvie." Daddy's wink. Daddy's firm hand holding mine. Daddy putting the world to rights.

I mean, OK, he had a few forthright political views that I didn't *totally* agree with. And he wasn't wild about being argued with. I remember arriving at his office once as a child with Mummy and witnessing him tearing into some hapless employee. I was so shocked that tears actually sprang into my eyes.

But Mummy hurried me away and explained that all bosses had to shout at their staff sometimes. And then Daddy joined us and kissed and cuddled me and let me buy two chocolate bars out of the vending machine. Then he took me into a meeting room and told his assembled employees I was going to run the world one day, and they all clapped while Daddy lifted my hand up like a champion. It's one of the best memories of my childhood.

And as for the shouting — well, everyone loses their temper once in a while. It's simply a human flaw. And Daddy was such a positive force the rest of the time. Such a jolt of sunshine.

"Dan," I say suddenly, as I reread my anecdote about Daddy and the golf buggy. "Let's go on holiday to Spain next year."

"Spain?" He flinches. "Why?"

"Back to Los Bosques Antiguos," I explain. "Or nearby, anyway."

There's no way we could afford to stay at Los Bosques Antiguos. I've looked it up — the houses are way out of our league. But we could find a little hotel and go to Los Bosques Antiguos for the day, at least.

Wander among the white houses. Dip our feet in the communal lake. Crush the scented pine needles of the neighboring forest underfoot. Revisit my past.

"Why?" says Dan again.

"Lots of people go on holiday there," I assert.

"I just don't think it's a good idea." His face is closed up and tentery. Of course it is. "It's too hot, too expensive. . . ."

He's talking nonsense. It's only expensive if we stay somewhere expensive.

"Flights to Spain are cheap," I retort. "We could probably find a campsite. And I could go back to Los Bosques Antiguos. See what it's like now."

"I'm just not keen," Dan says at length, and I feel sudden fury boiling over.

"What is your *problem*?" I yell, and Anna comes hurtling in from the garden.

"Mummy!" She looks at me with wide eyes. "Don't shout! You'll scare Dora!"

I stare at her blankly. Dora? Oh, the bloody *snake*. Well, I hope I *do* scare it. I hope it has a heart attack out of fright.

"Don't worry, darling!" I say, as soothingly as I can. "I was just trying to make Daddy understand something. And I got a bit loud. Go and play with your Stomp Rocket."

Anna runs outside again and I pour out more tea. But my words are still hanging in the air, unanswered. *What is your problem?*

And of course, deep down, I know what his problem is. We'll walk among those huge white houses and Dan will see the wealth that I had when I was a child and it'll somehow spoil everything. Not for me, but for him.

"I just wanted to go and see where I went as a child," I say, staring down at my new tablecloth. "Nothing else. I don't want to spend any money, I don't want to go there every year, I just want to visit."

In my peripheral vision, I can see Dan gathering himself.

"Sylvie," he says, in what is clearly an effort to be reasonable, "you can't possibly remember Los Bosques Antiguos. You only went there until the age of four."

"Of course I remember it!" I protest impatiently. "It made a huge impression on me. I remember our house with the veranda and the lake, and sitting on the jetty and the smell of the forest and the sea views. . . ."

I want to add what I really feel, which is: "I wish Daddy had never sold that house," but it probably wouldn't go down well. Nor will I admit that my memories are a tad hazy. The point is, I want to go back.

Dan's silent. His face is motionless. It's as if he can't hear me. Or maybe he *can* hear me but something else in his head is louder and more insistent.

My energy levels are sinking. There's only so many times you can try. Sometimes I feel like his issue with my father is like a huge boulder, and I'm going to have to push it and drag it and heave it along beside us our whole marriage.

"Fine," I say at last. "Where *shall* we go next year?"

"I don't know," says Dan, and I can tell he feels defensive. "Somewhere in Britain, maybe."

"Like an organic garden?" I say pointedly, but I'm not sure Dan gets my little dig. I'm about to add, "I hope you've got your snake-sitter lined up," when Tessa comes running in, her mouth an *O* of horror.

"Mummy!" she cries. "Mummeeee! We've lost our Stomp Rocket!"

As Professor Russell answers the front door, his eyes seem to have a glint of humor in them, and I suddenly wonder: Did he hear me yelling at Dan just now? Oh God, of course he did. They're not deaf at all, are they? He and Owen probably sit and listen to Dan and me as though we're *The Archers.*

"Hello," I begin politely. "I'm so sorry to disturb you, but I think my daughter's rocket has landed on your greenhouse. I do apologize."

"My Stomp Rocket," clarifies Tessa, who was determined to accompany me on this little visit and is clutching my hand.

"Ah. Oh dear." Professor Russell's eyes dim, and I can tell he's got visions of Dan climbing up and cracking his glass.

"I've brought this," I say hastily, and I gesture at the telescopic broom in my hand. "I'll be really gentle, I promise. And if I can't reach it, then we'll get the window cleaner to do it."

"Very well." The professor's face relaxes into a smile. "Let's 'give it a go,' as they say."

As he leads us through the house, I look curiously about. Wow. Lots of books. *Lots* of books. We pass through a bare little kitchen and a tiny conservatory furnished with two Ercol chairs and a radio. And there, dominating the garden, is the greenhouse. It's a modernist structure of metal and glass, and if you put a kitchen in it, it could totally go in an interiors magazine.

I can already see our Stomp Rocket, looking incongruous and childlike on the glass roof, but I'm more interested in what's inside. It's not like other people's green-houses. There aren't any tomatoes or flowers or wrought-iron furniture. It's more lab-like. I can see functional tables and rows of pots — all containing what looks like the same kind of fern at different stages of growth — and a computer. No, two computers.

"This is amazing," I say as we approach. "Are these all the same kind of plant?"

"They are all varieties of fern," says Professor Russell with that glimmering smile he has, as though sharing a private joke with someone. (His plants, probably.) "Ferns are my particular interest."

"Look, Tessa." I point through the glass panes. "Professor Russell has written books about these ferns. He knows everything about them."

" 'Knows everything about them'?" Professor Russell echoes. "Oh my goodness, no. Oh no, no, no. I'm only just beginning to fathom their mysteries."

"You've been studying plants at school, haven't you, darling?" I say to Tessa. "You grew cress, didn't you?" I'm suddenly wondering if we could get Professor Russell to go into the girls' primary school and give a talk. I would get *major* brownie points.

"Plants need water," recites Tessa, on cue.

"Plants grow toward the light."

"Quite right." Professor Russell beams benevolently at her, and I feel a swell of pride. Look at my five-year-old, discussing botany with an Oxford professor!

"Do people grow toward the light?" Tessa, says, in that joking way she has.

I'm about to say, "Of course not, darling!" and share an amused glance with Professor Russell. But he says mildly, "Yes, my dear. I believe we do."

Oh, OK. That tells me.

"We have, of course, many different kinds of light," Professor Russell continues, almost dreamily. "Sometimes our light might be a faith, or an ideology, or even a person, and we grow toward that."

"We grow toward a *person*?" Tessa finds this hilarious. "Toward a *person*?"

"Of course." His eyes focus on something beyond my shoulder, and I turn to see Owen coming down the path.

I haven't seen Owen close up for a while, and there's something about him that makes me catch my breath. He looks translucent, somehow. Frailer than I remember. His white hair is sparse and his bony hands are painfully thin.

"Good morning," he says to me in a charming though hoarse voice. "I came to see if our visitors would like coffee."

"Oh, no, thanks," I say quickly. "We're just here to get our toy. Sorry for all the noise," I add. "I know we make a bit of a racket."

I can see Professor Russell's eyes meeting Owen's briefly, and I'm suddenly sure without a doubt that they've heard Dan and me fighting. *Great.* But almost at once, Owen smiles kindly at me.

"Not at all. Nothing to apologize for. We enjoy hearing the children play." He eyes the broom in my hand. "Ah. Now, that's ingenious."

"Well," I say doubtfully. "We'll see."

"Don't wait out here." Professor Russell pats Owen's hand. "You can watch our efforts from the conservatory."

As Owen retreats toward the house, I extend the broom handle and reach up, and after just a few jabs, the Stomp Rocket falls down into my arms.

"Well done!" applauds Professor Russell. Then he turns to Tessa. "And now, my dear, may I give you a little plant as a souvenir? You'll have to water it, mind, and look after it."

"Oh, that would be lovely!" I exclaim. "Thank you!"

I'm thinking: *I'll put Dan in charge of the plant.* That is, if he really *is* into gardening and not just into dimpled ex-girlfriends.

Professor Russell potters into the greenhouse and emerges with a small green frondy thing in a pot.

"Give it some light but not too much," he says, his eyes twinkling at her. "And watch how it grows."

Tessa takes the pot, then looks up at him expectantly. "But we need one for Anna," she says.

"Tessa!" I exclaim, appalled. "You don't say that! You say, 'Thank you for the lovely plant.' Anna's her twin," I explain apologetically to Professor Russell. "They look out for each other. You can *share* it with Anna," I add to Tessa.

"Not at all!" says Professor Russell at once. "Tessa's quite right. How could we forget Anna?"

He darts back into the greenhouse and produces a second little plant.

"I'm so sorry." I wince. "Tessa, you mustn't ask for things."

"Nonsense!" Professor Russell winks at Tessa. "If we don't stick up for the ones we love, then what are we good for?"

As Tessa sinks to her haunches and begins examining the plants more closely, Professor Russell's gaze drifts again over my shoulder. I turn and see that he's watching

Owen, who is settling himself in one of the Ercol chairs in the conservatory, a blanket over his knees. I can see Professor Russell mouthing, *Are you all right?* and Owen nodding.

"How long have you two been . . ." I ask softly, not quite sure how to put it. I'm *fairly* sure they're not just friends, but you can never be sure.

"We knew each other as schoolboys," says Professor Russell mildly.

"Oh, right," I say, taken aback. "Wow. That's a long time. So . . ."

"At that time, Owen didn't realize his . . . true nature, shall we say." Professor Russell blinks at me. "He married. . . . I devoted myself to research. . . . We found each other again eight years ago. In answer to what I believe you are asking, I have loved him for fifty-nine years. Much of it from afar, of course." He gives that glimmering smile again.

I'm speechless. *Fifty-nine years?* As I survey his wrinkled face, I feel like Professor Russell towers above me in every way. He has a towering intellect. A towering love. I have an urge to stay here and ask him lots of questions and soak up some of his wisdom.

Then, suddenly, I notice that Tessa is

shredding a frond from one of the plants. Shit. There's five-year-old intellectual curiosity for you.

"Anyway, we must go," I say hastily. "We've taken up too much of your time. Thank you so much, Professor Russell."

"Please." He beams at me. "Do call me John."

"John."

John leads us back through the house and we say goodbye with lots of warm hand-shaking and promises to have tea sometime. As I'm opening our own front door, I'm so busy trying to picture him and Owen as gangly teenage boys that Tilda's voice makes me jump.

"Sylvie!" She's striding down the path, dressed in a rather dated maroon work suit, and beckons me over vigorously. "How's things?"

"Oh, hi!" I greet her. "I've just been in Professor Russell's garden. He's really lovely. We should have drinks or something." I release Tessa's hand. "Go and show Anna her plant, darling. I'll be there in a minute."

"So?" Tilda's eyes flash at me as Tessa scampers inside the house. "How was dessert *alfresco*? I haven't had the full debrief yet."

This is true. Apart from a thirty-second

hello-thank-you-goodbye when we got back from the sculpture garden, I haven't seen Tilda. She's been working for one of her clients onsite in his Andover office, so we've missed our morning walks. Which means she has no idea what's been going on. I glance cautiously toward the house, but there's no sign of Dan. Still, just to be sure, I pull the front door to.

"Don't you have to get to Andover?" I say, eyeing up her suit.

"I'll go in a moment." Tilda waves an airy hand. "Spill."

"Well." I sit on her garden wall and wrap my arms around myself. "Slight backfire, if you must know."

"Really?" She sounds surprised. "Dan looked pretty revved up to me. Didn't he like the corset?"

"It's not that." I shake my head. "The *sex* was good. We went to this special secret garden and it was all pretty spectacular, in fact."

"So, what's the problem?"

I'm silent for a few moments. The truth is, although I'm trying to be breezy and matter-of-fact, I am feeling the odd flicker of genuine worry. And saying it out loud is going to make it twenty times worse.

"It 'woke something up' in Dan," I say at

303

last. "Apparently."

"Woke what up?" Tilda stares at me.

"The whole thing reminded him of this ex-girlfriend. An ex-girlfriend he'd never even *told* me about. And now he's been googling her. Loads of times." I'm speaking calmly, but I feel a tremor in my face, as if my worries can't be contained. "In secret."

"Oh." Tilda looks disconcerted for a moment, then rallies. "Oh, but googling means nothing. Everyone googles. I google Adam about three times a week. I like to torture myself," she adds with a wry shrug.

"But he's never googled her before. He's never even thought about her before. And it's all my own doing!" I add in self-castigation. "I brought this on myself!"

"No, you didn't!" Tilda gives an incredulous laugh. "What, by dressing up in sexy gear?"

"By poking our marriage with a stick! By pushing him to be adventurous! It made him *think*. And that's what he thought of! His ex!"

"Ah." Tilda pulls a wry, comical expression. "Well, yes. Maybe that wasn't such a wild idea. You don't want husbands to start *thinking*."

"You warned me," I say miserably. "You said, 'Surprises have a bad habit of going wrong.' Well, you were right."

"Sylvie, I didn't mean it!" says Tilda in dismay. "And you mustn't worry. Look at the facts. Dan loves you and you had great sex. A lot of couples would die to be having great sex," she adds pointedly.

"Yes, but even the sex . . ." I bite my lip and glance toward my front door again.

"What?" Tilda leans forward, looking fascinated, and I hesitate. I'm not really one for spilling intimate details. But since the boudoir shoot, there doesn't seem any point in being coy with Tilda.

"Well," I say, my voice almost a whisper, "it was super-hot, but it was . . . different. *He* was different. At the time, I thought: *Great, I'm turning him on.* But now I'm thinking: Was it the memory of her?" I give a little shudder. "Was it all about her?"

"I'm sure it wasn't —"

"I said I wanted a surprise," I cut her off in agitation. "Well, what if his 'surprise' is, he goes and shags someone else?"

"Enough!" says Tilda briskly, putting a hand on my arm. "Sylvie, you're overreacting. All Dan's *actually* done is google his ex. If you ask me, he'll never mention her again. In a month, he'll have forgotten her."

"You really think so?"

"I'm positive. What's her name?" Tilda

adds casually.

"Mary."

"Well, there you go." Tilda rolls her eyes. "He's never going to be unfaithful with someone called Mary."

I can't help laughing. Tilda has a knack of cheering me up, whatever the situation.

"How are you two getting on otherwise?" she queries.

"Oh, you know." I shrug. "Up and down . . ." But there's something quizzical in her expression, which makes me add, "Did *you* hear me yelling at him this morning?"

"Hard to miss it." Tilda's mouth is clamped together as though she's trying not to smile. Or laugh.

Great. So Dan and I really are the resident street soap opera.

"You'll be fine." Tilda pats me on the hand. "But promise me one thing. No more surprises."

She doesn't add *I told you so,* but it's sitting there, unspoken in the air. And she did.

"Don't worry," I say in heartfelt tones. "I'm totally over surprises. *Totally.*"

I've never met Esme in person and for some reason I'm expecting someone small and thin, in a slimline jacket and heels. But the girl waiting for me at the New London Hospital is large and fair and wearing endearingly childish clothes — a skirt covered in a sheep print and rubber-soled Mary Janes. She has one of those broad, well-structured faces which look naturally cheerful, but she has a giveaway furrowed brow.

"I *think* I've planned for everything," she says about five times as we walk through the lobby. "So, the green-room area has got coffee, tea, water, snacks . . ." She counts off on her fingers. "Biscuits . . . croissants . . . Oh, fizzy water, of course . . ."

I bite my lip, wanting to laugh. We're talking about a small seating area which we'll use for half an hour, if that. Not a polar expedition.

"That's very kind," I say.

"And your husband's on his way?" She blinks anxiously at me. "Because we *do* have a parking space reserved for him."

"Thank you. Yes, he's bringing our girls and his own parents."

Dan's parents suddenly decided they wanted to come to this event, about three days ago. Dan mentioned it to his mother on the phone, and apparently she got all prickly and wondered why she and Neville hadn't been asked? Were they not considered part of the extended family? Had it not occurred to Dan that they might like to pay their respects too? (Which is weird, because they never got on with Daddy when he was alive.) Dan looked all beleaguered and I could hear him saying, "Mum, it's not . . . No, it's not a *party.* . . . I mean, I never thought you'd want to come down from Leicester. . . . I mean, of course you can come. We'd love you to!"

Dan's parents can be a bit tricky. Although, to be fair, my mother can be tricky too. I expect the twins think Dan and I are tricky. In fact, I suppose all people are tricky, full stop. Sometimes I wonder how we all get anything done as a human race, there are so many misunderstandings and sore points and people taking umbrage all over the place.

I'm so busy thinking, it takes me a moment to realize that Esme is conveying information to me.

"I'll take you to the green room," she says, ushering me along, "then we'll have a quick rehearsal and sound check and you can comb your hair or whatever . . . not that you need it," she adds, giving my hair a sidelong look. "It's *amazing,* your hair."

It does look quite spectacular. I had it blow-dried earlier, and it's been tonged into ringlets, just how Daddy loved it.

"Thanks." I smile back.

"It must take *forever* to wash," she says next, just as I knew she would.

"Oh, it's not too bad," I reply, silently predicting her next remark: *How long did it take you to grow it?*

"How long did it take you to grow it?" she asks breathlessly as we turn a corner.

"I've always had really long hair. Just like Rapunzel!" I add swiftly, preempting any Rapunzel remarks. "So, is Sinead Brook here yet?"

"Not yet, but she does have a very busy schedule. She's lovely," Esme adds. "Really lovely. She does loads for the hospital. She had her three children here; that's the connection."

"She looks lovely on the TV," I say politely.

"Oh, she's even more lovely in real life," Esme says, so quickly that I instantly wonder if Sinead is in fact a total bitch. "Now, I *think* I've planned for everything. . . ." As she leads me down a hospital corridor filled with bright artworks, her brow is furrowed again. "So here's the green room. . . ." She ushers me into a tiny room with visitors printed on the door. "You can leave your things here."

I don't really have any "things." But to

make Esme feel that everything is going to plan, I take off my jacket and put it on a chair. I can see her mentally checking off *leave things in green room* and relaxing a little. Poor Esme. I've organized events myself. I know what it's like.

"Good!" she says, and bustles me along the corridor again. "So, come this way . . . and here it is!" We've stopped in a circular area, facing a new-looking set of double doors. There's a podium and a microphone in front of the doors — and above them is a sign reading THE MARCUS LOWE SUITE in the standard hospital-blue Helvetica. And as soon I see it, my throat clogs up.

I thought I was prepared for today. I thought I had my mental armor on. But I hadn't imagined actually seeing Daddy's name up there like that.

"That's what your dad achieved," says Esme gently, and I nod. I don't dare to speak.

I wasn't going to get emotional, but how do you not get emotional when your father paid for a facility which will help save lives, then lost his own life? The sharp, antiseptic hospital smell everywhere is reminding me of that last, terrible night, three days after the crash, when it became clear that *catastrophic* really did mean catastrophic.

No. I can't think about that. Not now.

"Darling, you're not going *sleeveless*?" Mummy's voice hails me, and instantly my throat unclogs. Trust Mummy to puncture the moment.

She's approaching down the corridor with a smooth, suited man whom I've met before. He's called Cedric and he's in charge of all development, so presumably he's Esme's boss. He must have been plying Mummy with coffee.

"No," I say defensively. "I just took my jacket off for a moment."

I want to add: "Why *shouldn't* I go sleeveless? Are you body-shaming me? What if the girls heard you and got a complex?" (But, time and place.)

"Your hair looks good," Mummy allows, and I instinctively run a hand through my ringlets.

"Thanks. You look very nice too," I say in return — and she does, all in mauve with matching shoes. I'm in powder blue, because Daddy loved that color. "Are you all right?" I add in an undertone, because this is a pretty momentous day, and if *I'm* feeling like I might crumble into bits, what about her?

"I'm fine, darling." She nods with a resolutely bright smile. "I'll be fine. Absolutely fine. Although I *am* rather looking forward to my glass of champagne."

"Is the podium all right?" Esme asks me anxiously.

"It's perfect." I beam at her, trying to boost her confidence. "Everything looks wonderful." I step up onto the podium, switch on the mike, and say, "One-two-one-two," into it, my voice booming through the speakers.

"Brilliant." Esme consults a document in her hand. "Then Sinead will come forward and unveil the plaque." She gestures at a small pair of red velvet curtains positioned on the wall to the side of the double doors. There are two tasseled cords hanging down, with a pink ribbon tied on one.

"What's the ribbon for?" I ask curiously.

"So that Sinead knows which tassel to pull," explains Esme. "It's a bit of a confusing system. Maybe you could be Sinead and we can check it all works?"

"Of course." I head over to the curtains, then glance at Cedric, to make sure he's listening. "But first, Esme, I want to thank you. You've organized every detail of this event so meticulously. You've been *beyond* thorough."

"Well." Esme flushes modestly. "You know. I *think* I've planned for everything. . . ."

"You certainly have." I reach for the tassel. "OK, pretend I'm Sinead. I now pronounce this scanner suite open!"

I tug on the tassel with the ribbon, the red velvet curtains swish open, and we all stare at . . . nothing.

It's bare wall. What?

I glance at Esme, and she's staring at the wall with horrified bulging eyes. I swish the curtains back and forth as though the plaque might somehow be hiding — but there's nothing there.

"It's going to be a *little* tricky for Sinead Brook to unveil a nonexistent plaque," says Mummy in that sweet, pointed way she has when she wants.

"Esme!" barks Cedric. "Where's the plaque?"

"I don't know!" whispers Esme, staring at the wall as though it's a mirage. "It should be there. Maintenance were supposed to . . ." She jabs feverishly at her phone. "Trev? It's Esme. Trev, where's the plaque? The plaque! For the new scanner suite! Well, it was supposed to be here this morning. They're going to unveil it. Yes! Yes, you *did* know that!" Her voice rises almost to a shriek. Then, with a weird, over-calm air, she puts her phone away and turns to the rest of us. "They're looking for it."

"*Looking* for it?" expostulates Cedric. "What time does the ceremony begin?"

"Twenty minutes." Esme gulps. Her face has turned a kind of pale green and I feel incredibly sorry for her, although at the same time . . . hello? Didn't it even *occur* to her to check the plaque?

"What happens if they can't find it?" snaps Cedric. "Esme, we have Sinead Brook coming to unveil this plaque, do you realize?"

"Um . . . um . . ." Esme swallows desperately. "We could . . . make a temporary one?"

"A temporary one?" he bellows. "With what, a Sharpie and some cardboard?"

"Sylvie!" Dan's voice greets me, and I see him approaching with Tessa, Anna, and his parents. There's a general greeting as we all kiss each other and exclaim over how long it's been. Dan's mother, Sue, has clearly been to the hairdresser for the occasion and her hair looks lovely — all auburn and shiny. Meanwhile, Dan's dad, Neville, is surveying everything with that measured look he has. When he was an accountant he audited big companies, and he's still in the habit of assessing. Everywhere he goes, he hangs back, looks around, and gauges things before he proceeds. I can see him doing it now. He's eyeing up the sign with Daddy's name on it. He's looking at the podium and the velvet curtains and now at Cedric, who is berating Esme in the corner.

"Something up?" he says at last.

"Bit of a drama," I say. "Let's get out of the way for a few moments." As we walk to the green room, it occurs to me again that Sue and Neville have been married for thirty-eight years. And I *know* Dan says they're "hardly a good example," and I *know* they went through that dicey patch . . . but they're together, aren't they? They must be doing something right. Maybe we can learn from them.

But, oh God.

I'd forgotten. I always forget. The atmosphere of Dan's parents. It's like a crackly, invisible veil of just . . . *tension.* It's not that they don't smile and laugh and make jokes. But everything is so barbed. There are so many little flashes of resentment and simmering fury. It's exhausting. They're talking about their recent trip to Switzerland, which you'd think would be innocuous enough. But, no.

"Then we got out at Lausanne," Neville is saying to Tessa (as though Tessa has the first idea what Lausanne is). "And we started climbing the mountain, but then Granny Sue suddenly changed her mind. So that was a shame, wasn't it? Grandpa had to go up all alone."

"Granny Sue didn't 'suddenly change her mind.' " Sue prickles all over. "Grandpa's remembering everything wrong, as usual. Granny Sue was never supposed to be climbing the mountain. Granny Sue had a bad foot, which Grandpa kept forgetting about!" She flashes an unnerving smile at Anna. "Poor Granny!"

The girls are both silenced by their grandparents' double act. They can pick up on the hostile undertones, even if they don't know what Lausanne is. Even Dan's spirits are descending, and you'd think he'd be used to it. His shoulders look cowed and he glances at me as though for rescue.

"Well!" I say brightly. "Maybe we should head along to the reception. It must have started by now. Girls, finish your biscuits."

Mummy's already left the green room — she had one nibble of a grape and then said she was going to visit the ladies'. The truth is, she can't really connect with Neville and Sue. She doesn't understand their concerns and they don't understand hers. Sue, in particular, got in a real huff after she came to one of Mummy's jewelry parties, all the way from Leicester, and there was a misunderstanding over the pricing of a necklace.

Unfortunately, it was the one party I couldn't make, so I couldn't smooth things over. I'm sure it was Mummy's fault. Sue isn't married to an accountant for nothing — she would have clocked the price exactly. But Mummy would just think, *Well, what's twenty pounds?* and not even *notice* there was a problem, because she's infuriating that way.

"Lovely outfit, Sylvie," says Sue, as I slip on my powder-blue jacket. "Really super. And your *hair* . . ." She shakes her head admiringly. "Your dad would be proud, love. I know he always loved your hair. Your 'glory.' "

The thing about Sue is, when she's talking to anyone but her spouse, she's charming. Neville too.

"Thanks, Sue," I say gratefully. "You look gorgeous too." I stroke her creamy silk shirtsleeve. "This is pretty."

"You do look good, Mum," Dan joins in, and I see Sue's face pinken with pleasure.

"Very nice," says Neville, his gaze sweeping over her without really looking. "All right. Into the fray."

He never properly looks at her, I think idly. Then this thought hits me again, with more vigor. Or maybe it's a theory. A hypothesis. *Neville never properly looks at Sue.* His gaze always seems to skate past her, like a magnet being repelled. I can't picture them making proper eye contact. I don't think it ever happens. Neville, the man who surveys everything so carefully, doesn't look at his wife. Isn't that a bit weird? A bit sad?

And now I'm stricken by a new thought: Will Dan and I be like that one day? Raging silently against each other as we trudge up Swiss mountains?

No.

No. Definitely not. We won't let that happen.

But isn't that what every young couple thinks, and then suddenly, boom, they're old and bitter and not looking at each other properly? According to Dan, Neville and Sue used to have a great relationship. They made jokes and did ballroom dancing and all sorts.

Oh God. *How* can we prevent it happening? What do we *do*? Clearly, surprising each other isn't the answer. So what is?

As we walk to the reception area, hospital staff are gathering and waitresses are handing out drinks. A lady in a purple jacket and heavy gold chain is chatting to Mummy; she must be the mayoress. There's also a loud sound of drilling as a guy in overalls, on a stepladder, fixes screws into the wall. The plaque is at his feet, propped against the wall, but everyone is politely ignoring it and trying to make conversation above the din. Esme is standing at the foot of the ladder, saying, "Hurry! Hurry!" and I shoot her a sympathetic smile.

I take a glass of water, have a sip, and unfold my speech. I must concentrate. I must do this occasion justice and stop obsessing about my marriage, because today isn't about that — it's about Daddy. The workman has finally finished screwing the plaque to the wall, and there's an excited hubbub in the corridor, which must be Sinead Brook arriving. I'll be on, any moment.

I skim over the words I wrote, wondering if they're OK, knowing they're not, and realizing I could never do justice to Daddy in a six-minute speech, anyway. It's all so arbitrary. Three sides of A4. Such a tiny sliver of a man and his life and all he did.

Should I have mentioned his childhood? Or the story about the horses?

Too late now. A familiar, celebrity-type woman in a red clingy dress is suddenly in front of me, shaking my hand, and Esme is saying, "Sylvie, I'm delighted to introduce

Sinead Brook," in awestruck tones, and we barely have time to exchange a word before Cedric mounts the podium and taps the microphone.

"My Lady Mayoress, ladies and gentlemen," he begins, "welcome to what is a very special occasion."

Hmph. He's pinched *my* opening.

"A lot of you here today knew Marcus Lowe," he continues more somberly. "Some, sadly, did not. Marcus was known to all of us here at the New London Hospital as a man of commitment, charm, great intelligence, and an inability to take no for an answer." His eyes glint, and a lot of the guests laugh knowingly. "He masterminded the fundraising for this scanner suite with tremendous tenacity, and quite simply it would not exist today without him. I'm now going to hand you over to his daughter, Sylvie Winter, who will say a few words."

I mount the podium and look at the faces — some familiar but most not — and take a breath.

"Hello, everyone," I say simply. "Thank you for coming today to celebrate both this wonderful scanner suite and my father, who was so determined to make it happen. Those of you who met my father know that he was a remarkable man. He had the looks of Robert Redford . . . the dash of Errol Flynn . . . and the persistence of Columbus. Or maybe I mean Columbo. Or both."

Even as I'm finishing my speech, I know it was crap.

No, I'm being too hard on myself. It wasn't crap, but it wasn't what it could have been. People nodded and smiled and even laughed, but they didn't look fired up. They didn't get *who Daddy was.* I have a sudden urge to take a week off and rewrite my thoughts until I get to the real, *real* essence of him . . . and then invite everyone back and tell them properly.

But everyone's clapping and smiling approvingly, and Mummy looks all misty-eyed, and the honest truth is, no one cares about the real essence of Daddy, do they? They just want to swig champagne and start using the scanners and saving lives. The world moves on. As I've been told, about 56,000 times.

I think I need a drink. As soon as the curtains have been opened, I'm having a drink.

We all watch as the mayoress takes the podium and introduces Sinead Brook, mispronouncing her name twice. (It's obvious she doesn't really know who Sinead

Brook is.) Sinead Brook gives what is clearly a standard-issue speech about the hospital, then pulls the cord, and the plaque is there this time. There's another round of applause and a few photos. Then, at last, the glasses of champagne start coming around again, and everyone disperses into groups.

The children are being entertained by some younger members of hospital staff blowing up disposable gloves. Cedric is telling me about the new children's wing campaign, which does sound an amazing project, and I find myself drinking three glasses in quick succession. Dan's promised to drive home. It's fine.

Where is Dan, come to that?

I glance around the gathering and notice him with Mummy, huddled right over in the corner. At once I stiffen. Why are they huddled together? What are they talking about?

I can't escape Cedric's constant stream of facts on children's hospital beds in London, and I *am* genuinely interested in what he's saying. But, by reaching for a canapé, I'm also able to move subtly toward Dan and Mummy. I'm also able to tilt my head and just about pick up snippets of their conversation.

". . . certain that's the right course . . . ?"

she's saying, in a sharpish, anxious sort of tone.

". . . this is the reality of the . . ." I can't hear the end of the sentence, but Dan sounds fairly tense too.

". . . really don't understand why . . ."

". . . discussed this . . ."

". . . so what exactly . . ."

The conversation seems to die out, and I turn in time to see Dan mouthing, *A million pounds, maybe two?* at my mother.

My lungs seem to freeze. The next moment I'm choking on my champagne. A million pounds, maybe two? What does that mean? What "million pounds, maybe two"?

"Sylvie!" Cedric halts his flood of statistics. "Are you all right?"

"Fine!" I swivel back. "Sorry! Just went down the wrong way. Please do carry on." I smile at Cedric, but my head is whirring in a nasty, ominous way.

Is Dan borrowing money? Is Dan borrowing money without telling me, *from my own mother?* A *million pounds, maybe two?*

I don't want to be a suspicious wife. I don't. I'm not. There's an explanation; I know there is. Maybe he's won the lottery.

No. He and Mummy did not look like lottery winners. Quite the opposite, in fact.

At last Cedric presses his business card

on me and disappears. I glance over at the girls, who are playing safely with Esme, then head toward Dan. He's on his own now, all hunched and miserable-looking, gazing at his phone.

"Hi!" I say in a breezy, non-suspicious way. "I saw you chatting to Mummy just now."

Dan's eyes lift to mine and for an instant — only an instant — I see undiluted fear in them. But then it's gone. His eyes have closed up. Did I imagine it?

"Right," he says with a discouraging frown.

"Nice to see you two getting along." I try again.

"Right. Actually, Sylvie, I've got to make a call. Great speech, by the way," he shoots back over his shoulder as he strides away.

For a few seconds I watch him go, trying to keep my breath steady, while my brain begins on an angry-fishwife rant. He didn't look me in the eye. He rushed off. He barely had anything to say about my speech, which, after all, was quite a big deal for me, even if it was crap. He was all frowning and tentery while I was making it. (I noticed.) *Nor* did he even clap very hard when I finished. (I noticed that too.)

At last I wheel round, head to the drinks

table, and grab a spare bottle of champagne. I head to where three lurid-red foam chairs have been pushed together to form a kind of sofa. Sue is sitting down (her shoes have uncomfortable-looking stiletto heels, I now notice) and her cheeks are rosy. I guess she's been necking the champagne too.

"Hi," I say, flopping down beside her. "How are you doing, Sue?"

"Oh, Sylvie." She regards me with slightly bloodshot eyes. "What a speech; I was quite choked up."

"Thanks," I say, touched.

"It must be hard for you." She pats my knee. "So hard. Dan says you do marvelously, coping with everything."

Dan does? I blink at her, trying not to give away my surprise. My fury is sliding away. The truth is, I'd always assumed Dan thought I was a complete shambles. Now I want to know more. I want to ask, "What else does Dan say about me?" And, "Do *you* know about this million quid, maybe two?" But that might cause more problems. So, instead, I fill her glass up and lean back with a massive sigh.

"It is hard," I say, nodding. "It is. It's hard."

As I take yet another gulp of champagne, I feel my brain cells gently tipping over the edge from pleasantly-relaxed to actually-quite-drunk. Glancing at Sue, I'd guess hers are in the same state too. Is this a good moment for a full-and-frank?

"The thing is . . ." I begin thoughtfully — then stop. There are so many things. I'll pick one. Thing One. "The thing is, how *do* you stay married forever?" I say, more plaintively than I meant to.

"Forever?" Sue laughs.

"For a long time. Sixty-eight years," I clarify. Sue gives me a puzzled glance, but I press on. "Dan and I look at the future, and we think . . . we *worry,* you know?" I gesture with my glass for emphasis, and a little champagne spills out. "We think, how do we sustain it? And we look at you, still married after all this time, and we think . . ." I trail off awkwardly. (Obviously I can't say what we *really* think, which is, *Oh my God, how do you stand it?*)

But I don't need to say anything more. Sue has sat up, her face more alert than I've ever seen it. As though finally, after all this time, I'm tapping into her special area of expertise.

"It's all about retirement," she says, and swigs her champagne with fresh determination. "All about retirement."

"Right," I say uncertainly. I wasn't expecting that, somehow. "What exactly do you . . ."

"When he retires . . ." She eyes me firmly. "Don't let him in the house."

"Huh?" I gape at her.

"Hobbies. Interests. They need interests. Travel. You can manage if you travel. Travel separately!" she adds. "Find some girl-friends. Weekends to Dublin, that kind of thing."

"But —"

"Golf," she cuts me off. "Neville never would take up golf. Why not? That's what I want to know. What's wrong with golf?" Her mouth twists and her eyes go distant, as though she's mentally having an argument about golf — and winning. Then she comes to. "Just don't let him loaf about the house asking you what's for lunch every half hour. That's where it goes wrong. All my girl-friends agree. Fatal. Fatal!"

I'm dumbstruck. I hadn't even thought about retirement. And, anyway, why wouldn't I want Dan in the house?

"I'm looking *forward* to having Dan around more when he retires," I venture. "I mean, it's still a long way away, obvi-ously. . . ." Sue surveys me for a moment, then bursts into laughter.

"Oh, Sylvie, I do forget, you're very

young." She pats my knee again. "But bear my advice in mind, when the time comes. That's how to make it work."

She relaxes back and sips her champagne. And here's the thing. (Thing Two.) This is my mother-in-law talking. I should just nod. I should say, "I'm sure you're right, Sue," and move the conversation on. It would be polite. It would be easy.

But I can't. I can't buy into this version of marriage, or retirement, or whatever we're talking about. I mean, don't get me wrong, I'm totally up for some girlie trips to Dublin with Tilda and my mates from the school gate (excellent idea). But banning Dan from the house in case he asks for lunch? I mean, *really*? First of all, I'm more likely to ask *him* what's for lunch. He's the better cook. And second of all, we'd probably just make our own sandwiches. And third, why would you want your husband to take up a sport he didn't enjoy?

"But don't you lose intimacy if you create barriers like that?" I say, thinking aloud. "Don't you create wedges?"

"Wedges? What does that mean, *wedges*?" says Sue suspiciously, as though I might mean potato wedges.

"You know." My brain gropes for an explanation. "Things in the way. Things that stop you being what you should be as a partnership. As a relationship."

"Well." Sue sounds almost truculent. "What is a partnership? What is a relationship? What is a marriage? There are a thousand different answers to *that*." She takes another deep slug of champagne, and for a while we're both silent. My mind is chewing on what she's just said. I close my eyes and squint into the back of my brain, trying to work out what I think.

I could tell you what I think about the Kardashians in a heartbeat. But "What is a relationship?" not so much. I've neglected the subject. Or maybe I didn't ever realize I should be thinking about it.

"I think a relationship is like two stories," I say at last, feeling my way cautiously through my thoughts. "Like . . . two open books, pressing together, and all the words mingle into one big, epic story. But if they *stop* mingling . . ." I lift my glass for emphasis. "Then they turn into two stories again. And that's when it's over." I clap my hands together, spilling champagne. "The books shut. The End."

There's quite a long silence, and I wonder if I'm so drunk that I'm not making sense. But when at last I turn, I see to my horror that Sue has tears running down her cheeks.

Shit. Where did *they* come from?

"Oh my God!" I exclaim. "Sue! I'm sorry! What did I say?"

Sue just shakes her head. She produces a tissue from her snappy leather handbag and wipes her nose roughly with it.

We sit in silence for a while — then on impulse I put an arm around Sue's shoulders and squeeze.

"Let's have lunch," I say. "One of these days."

"Yes," says Sue. "Let's."

The reception goes on and on. Staff keep popping up from different hospital departments and wanting to say hello to Mummy and me and tell me about that time they met Daddy at some fundraiser or other and he was so charming/brilliant/amazing at darts. (Darts? I never knew he could play darts.)

During a lull, I find myself alone with Mummy, just the two of us. Mummy's color is high, too, although whether that's the champagne or the emotion, I can't tell.

"That was a lovely speech, Sylvie," she says. "Lovely."

"Thanks." I bite my lip. "I hope Daddy would have been proud."

"Oh, darling, he's looking down at you

now." Mummy nods emphatically, as though convincing herself. "He really is. He's looking down at his beautiful daughter and he's so, *so* proud. . . ." She reaches up and takes one of my blond ringlets. "He loved your hair," she says, almost absently.

"I know." I nod. "I know he did."

For a while, neither of us speaks, and a voice is telling me to leave the moment be. But another voice is urging me on to find out more. This is my chance.

"So . . . I saw you talking to Dan." I try to sound casual, as though I'm just making chitchat.

"Oh yes." Her eyes slide away from mine. "Poor Dan. Such a rock for us all."

"What were you talking about?"

"Talking about?" Mummy blinks at me. "Darling, I have no idea. This and that."

I feel a surge of frustration. "This and that"? *Really?* I saw Dan mouthing, *A million pounds, maybe two,* at her. In what universe could this be described as "this and that"?

"Nothing important, then?" I say more bluntly. "Nothing I should know about?"

Mummy gives me one of her most infuriating wide-eyed looks. I know she's hiding something. I know it. But what? Oh God, *she's* not in debt, is she? The idea hits me with sudden force. Has she bought so many stupid gadgets to sell that she owes QVC a million pounds, maybe two?

Stop it, Sylvie. Don't be ridiculous. But something else?

Gambling?

The thought comes to me in a flash. I remember Mummy blinking furiously in the kitchen when I'd just mentioned the play *Dealer's Choice.* Oh God. Please don't say that's been her way of assuaging her grief.

But . . . no. Surely not. I can't picture Mummy gambling. Even when we went to Monte Carlo that time, she wasn't interested in the casino. She preferred drinking cocktails and eyeing up people on their boats.

I take a gulp of champagne, my thoughts all over the place. Am I going to push it? Am I going to confront my mother at a reception honoring her dead husband?

No. Clearly I am not.

"Well, it was a lovely ceremony," I say, retreating into platitude. "Lovely."

Mummy nods. "Sinead Brook looked *older* than I'd imagined, don't you agree? Or was it all that makeup she was wearing?"

We bitch happily about Sinead Brook's makeup for a few minutes, then Mummy's car arrives for her and she leaves, and I look around for my family, who are all — including Dan — scoffing the mini-éclairs. I gather them up and find the children's inflated disposable-glove toys, which they've named "Glovey" and "Glover" and which have obviously become their most precious, treasured friends. (God knows what's going to happen when they burst this evening. Oh well, cross that bridge.) Then it's time for goodbyes and thank-yous and I start to feel I've really had enough of this event.

At last we emerge into the fresh air. I'm quite dazed and my head is pounding. There were too many bright lights and voices and faces and memories. Not to mention emotional encounters. Not to mention mystery conversations involving a million pounds, maybe two.

We stand in the hospital forecourt for the longest time, wondering whether to go for a cup of tea or not and looking cafés up on our phones, before Sue and Neville decide that, no, in fact they'll catch the earlier train to Leicester. So then we're into a round of hugs and future arrangements, and that takes forever too.

When, finally, we pile into the car, I feel exhausted. But I'm wired too. I've been waiting to be alone with Dan. I need to get to the bottom of this.

"So, you had a nice long chat with my

mother!" I say lightly as we pull up at some traffic lights. "And I thought I heard you talking about . . . money?"

"Money?" Dan gives me a quick, impenetrable glance. "No."

"You didn't talk about money at all?"

"Not at all."

"Right," I say after a long pause. "Must have made a mistake."

I stare out of the windscreen, feeling a heaviness in my stomach. He's lying. Dan's actually lying to me. What do I do? Do I call him out? Do I say, "Well, guess what, I saw you saying, 'A million pounds, maybe two,' " and see what he says?

No. Because . . . just, no.

If he wants to lie, he'll lie, even if I do throw "a million pounds, maybe two" at him. He'll say I misread his lips. Or he'll say, "Oh, *that*. We were talking about the local council." He'll have some explanation. And then he'll be on his guard. And I'll feel even more desperate than before. I'm just quelling an urge to wail, "Oh, Dan, please tell me, *please* tell me what's going on," when he wriggles in his seat and clears his throat and says, "By the way, I'm having some old friends round. But I've arranged it for your Pilates night so you won't be bored by us."

He gives a short little laugh, which doesn't ring quite true, and I stare at him with fresh concern. The million pounds (maybe two) feel instantly less urgent. I'm now more perturbed by these old friends. What old friends?

"Don't worry!" I say, attempting an easy tone. "I'll cancel Pilates. I'd love to meet your old friends! Which old friends are these?"

"Oh, just . . . friends," says Dan vaguely. "From back in the day. You don't know them."

"I don't know *any* of them?"

"I don't think so, no."

"What are their names?"

"Like I say, you don't know them." Dan frowns into his mirror as he changes lanes. "Adrian, Jeremy . . . There was a whole bunch of us. We volunteered at the St. Philip's Garden."

"Oh, right!" I shoot him a savage smile. "The St. Philip's Garden. Brilliant. What a *super* idea, to invite them round after all this time." And I leave it a full five seconds before I add in my lightest tones, "And what about Mary — did you ask her too?"

"Oh yes," Dan says, still apparently preoccupied by the road. "Of course."

"Of course!" My savage smile gets even

brighter. "Of course you invited Mary! Why wouldn't you?"

Of course he bloody did.

ELEVEN

This is officially a Marital Situation. And actually I'm quite freaked out, in a way I really didn't expect to be.

I feel as though our whole marriage, I've been playing around with worries. They were amateur worries. Mini-worries. I used to sigh and roll my eyes and exclaim, "I'm so *stressed*!" without knowing what "stressed" really was.

But now a real, genuine, scary worry is looming at me, like Everest. Ten days have passed since the hospital event. Things haven't got any better. And I can't sigh or roll my eyes or exclaim, "I'm so *stressed*!" because they, I now realize, are things you do when you're not really worried. When you're really worried, you go silent and pick at your fingernails and forget to put your lipstick on. You stare at your husband and try to read his mind. You google *Mary Holland* a hundred times a day. Then you google *husband lying what does it mean?* Then you google *husband affair how common?* And you flinch at the answers you receive.

God, I hate the Internet.

I especially hate the photo of Mary Holland that pops up every time I google her. She looks like an angel. She's beautiful, successful, and basically perfect all round. She runs an environmental consultancy and she's done a TED Talk on emissions and is on some House of Commons committee *and* she's run the London Marathon three times. In all the photos I can find of her, she's wearing what look like eco clothes — lots of natural linens and ethnic-looking cotton tops. She has clear pale skin and blunt yet gorgeous features and wavy dark hair (she's got rid of the frizz), which sits around her face in a pre-Raphaelite cloud. Dimples when she smiles, obviously. Plus a single silver ring, which she does *not* wear on her left hand.

Previously, I might have thought: *Well, she's not Dan's type.* All his other exes are more like me — fine-featured, fairly conventional, and mostly blond. But clearly she *is* his type. Clearly I know my husband far less well than I thought I did. He's into gardening. He has a bunch of old friends I've never heard of. He fancies dark-haired girls in eco clothes. What else?

Dan, meanwhile, seems to have no idea what I'm going through. He seems locked in his own little bubble, preoccupied and even snarly. So, last night I decided I had to take action. I had to break through this weird vibe between us. At supper I produced notepads and paper and said, as brightly as I could, "Let's each choose a new hobby for next year. Then we'll compare and contrast."

I thought it would be a fun thing to do. I thought it might trigger some lighthearted discussions or at least loosen the atmosphere.

But it didn't work. Dan just scowled and said, "Jeez, Sylvie, *really*? I'm knackered." Then he took his supper off to eat in front of the computer, which is something we really try not to do, because we've always said couples who don't eat together . . .

Anyway.

I don't often cry. But I did blink away a couple of tears, because he sounded so hostile. So impatient. So un-Dan-like.

And now it's Friday and we're having breakfast and Dan's just told me he has to work all weekend.

"*All* weekend?" I say, before I can stop

myself. I'm aware I sound plaintive and even a bit whiny, which is something I always swore I'd never be.

"Huge project," Dan says, draining his coffee. "I need all my wits to focus on it."

"Is that the Limehouse one?" I say, trying to show an interest. "I'd love to see the drawings."

"No." Dan shrugs on his jacket.

No. Just *no.* Really charming, Dan.

"Oh, and I've done an extra supermarket order," he adds. "For this supper party I'm having on Tuesday."

"Really?" I peer at him in surprise. "That's very forward-thinking of you."

"It's all arriving on Monday," he continues as though I haven't spoken. "I'll do the Ottolenghi lamb recipe — you know, the slow-roast one with all the spices."

The slow-roast Ottolenghi lamb. The recipe he rolls out for special occasions or when he wants to impress. And I know Tilda would say I'm overreacting, but I can't help it. My chest is burning with hurt. He hasn't got time to spend at home with his family, but he has got time to plan a menu and do an Ocado order and make slow-roast Ottolenghi lamb?

"That'll be nice." I try to sound pleasant. "Quite a lot of effort, though, just for some old friends you haven't seen for ages."

"It's no effort." His eyes are light and unreadable. "See you later."

He kisses me in a perfunctory way and heads to the door, just as Tessa comes charging in.

"What's your wish?" she says, holding a piece of paper up at him. "What's your wish? Your *wish*, Daddy?"

Oh God. I'd forgotten about that. The girls' homework task was all about wishes. Anna's began *My Mummy's wish is,* and I carefully spelled out *world peace* for her, rather than *to know what the fuck is up with my husband.*

"What's your wish, Dan?" I echo her. "We're all waiting with bated breath."

And if there's a challenging, almost searing note in my voice, then so be it. Let him pick up on it any way he likes. (Except, let's be truthful, he won't pick up on it at all. He never picks up on searing notes in voices, nor sidelong glances, nor pointed pauses. It's all for my own benefit.)

Dan takes the piece of paper and scans it briefly.

"Oh, I see. Well. I wish . . ." He stops as his phone buzzes, glances at it, then winces and shoves it away again. Usually I'd ask, "What's wrong?" but today there's no point.

I know the reply I'd get: "Nothing."

"What *is* your wish, Daddy?" demands Tessa. "What *is* your wish?" She's sitting at the kitchen table, pencil poised over her sheet.

"I wish that . . . I could . . ." Dan speaks slowly, distractedly, as though his mind is grappling with some other, far-off problem.

"How do you spell *could*?" asks Tessa promptly, and I spell it out, because it's obvious Dan isn't paying attention. The morning sun is catching the fine lines etched around his eyes. His gaze is distant and he looks almost bleak.

"Could what?" Tessa is banging her pencil on her sheet. "Could what?"

"Escape," Dan says, so absently that I wonder if he's even aware he said it. My stomach clenches in dismay. *Escape?*

"Escape?" Tessa surveys him, as though suspecting a grown-up joke. "You're not in a cage, Daddy! People who escape are in a cage!"

"Escape." Dan comes to and sees me staring at him. "Escape!" he repeats, in a more upbeat tone. "Escape to the jungle and see the lions. I have to go."

"That's a stupid wish!" Tessa calls after him as he disappears toward the front door.

"Just write, *See some lions,*" I tell Tessa,

trying to stay calm. But my voice is shaky. My whole being is shaky. Dan wants to escape? Well, thanks for the heads-up.

It's my turn to do the school run this morning, and I'm so preoccupied, I drive the wrong way, twice.

"Why are we going this way, Mummy?" says Tess beadily from the back seat.

"It's nice to try different things," I say defensively. "Otherwise, life gets boring."

The minute the words are out of my mouth, I realize their ghastly significance. Is Dan "trying different things"? Is Mary a "different thing"?

I don't quite know what's happened to me. I feel like a pinball machine. Suspicions and worries and theories are careering around my brain in a way they never have before. I trusted Dan. I *knew* Dan. We were *us.* Solid. So what's changed?

Or am I inventing problems for myself? The idea hits me as I head into a snarl of traffic, all heading to school. It's entirely possible. Maybe I'm Othello, obsessing over a handkerchief. Dan is totally innocent, yet my irrational jealousy is an unstoppable force and I'll only realize it, in anguish, once I've killed him. (Divorced him and got the children and the house. It's the Wandsworth equivalent.)

My head is spinning more than ever. What would Tilda say? She'd say, "Focus on what you actually *know.*" So. OK. Here goes. I know that I encouraged Dan to be adventur-ous. (Huge mistake — what was I think-ing?) I know that this "woke something up" inside him. I know that he's cooking Mary his flashest lamb recipe and suggested that I be out of the house for the evening. I know he googled *Mary Holland husband.* And, of course, now I know he wants to escape.

It's more than a handkerchief.

Isn't it?

Is it?

I pause at a set of traffic lights, my heart thumping and my brows knotted. My hands are clenched around the wheel; my entire body is engaged in this mental process.

OK, here's the thing: I'm not saying I think he's having an affair. Yet. What I'm saying is, he's *in that zone.* He's primed. He's vulnerable. He may not even realize it himself, but he is.

"Mummy! Mummeee! The cars are hoot-ing!" Suddenly I'm aware I'm being beeped. Shit. (And trust Tessa to notice, not me.)

I hastily move on, then start looking for a parking space, all thoughts of marriage temporarily swept from my head. Bloody London. It's impossible to park. It's impossible to do anything. Why are there so many people on the roads? What are they all *doing*?

At last I find a spot, three streets away from the school, and hustle the girls along, trailing book bags, recorders, and gym kit. As I head through the playground, I wave and smile to various mums I know, all clustered in gossiping groups. They basically fall into three categories, the mums at school. There are the working mums. There are the at-home mums. And there are the exercise-*is*-their-work mums, who never wear anything except leggings and trainers.

What are *their* marriages like? I find myself wondering as I survey all the jolly, chatting faces. How many of them are hiding worries under their smiles?

"Oh, Sylvie!" calls Jane Moffat, our class rep, as I pass by. "Can I put you down for a quiche for the year group picnic?"

"Sure," I say absently, before cursing myself. Quiches are vile. Why does anyone want quiche at a picnic anyway? It's impossible to eat. I'll email her later and suggest sushi instead, which has the advantage that no one expects you to make sushi.

Tessa and Anna are already at the door of their classroom, which is on the ground floor and opens straight onto the playground. I head over and help them put gym-kit bags onto pegs, book bags into the basket, and recorders onto the special recorder shelf.

"Oh, Mrs. Winter," says Mrs. Pickford, their teacher. She's a gentle, kindly woman with graying hair cut in layers and a lot of waterfall cardigans in different colors. "The girls have been telling us that you have a new snake in the family! How exciting!"

Here's the thing about five-year-old children: They tell their teachers *everything*.

"That's right!" I try to look positive. "We do indeed have a snake in the family."

"We were wondering if you might bring it in for show-and-tell? I'm sure the children would love to see . . . her, is it?"

"Maybe," I say, after a pause. "She's really more my husband's thing. He feeds her and everything."

"I see." Mrs. Pickford nods. "Well, perhaps you could ask him?" She hesitates. "I mean, it would be *safe*? It is a *safe* snake?"

I resist the temptation to answer, "No, it's a ten-foot lethal boa constrictor; that's why we have it in our family home."

"Quite safe." I nod reassuringly.

"Apparently it was a complete surprise?" Mrs. Pickford adds chattily. "Tessa told us all that you were quite shocked! I don't know how I'd react if my husband brought home a snake out of the blue!"

She gives a little laugh, and I know she's only making conversation, but I feel flicked on the raw.

"Well, we have a very strong marriage," I say before I can stop myself. "Very strong and happy. Very stable. We're in a really good place, actually. We don't get rocked by stuff like snakes or other . . ." I clear my throat. "So."

As I stop talking, I can see a slightly odd look on Mrs. Pickford's face.

Oh God. I am actually losing it.

"Right," she says, her voice a little too bright. "Well, let me know about the show-and-tell. Girls, say goodbye to Mummy."

I hug each of the girls in turn, then walk away, my mind churning. I smile and wave goodbye to the other mums, and I probably look relaxed and jolly, just like them, but inside, the tension is ratcheting up. What I really need right now is a distraction.

OK, Toby is definitely a distraction. When I arrive at work, he's already there, wandering round the hall, peering up the staircase, looking totally incongruous in his shabby black T-shirt.

Thank God he's here. He's already canceled on me twice. Always with a good excuse, but still.

"Hi, Toby!" I say, greeting him with a handshake — and just for a moment there's a weird little frisson between us. The last time I saw Toby, I was half naked, and I can tell he's remembering that, too, from the way his eyeballs are darting up and down. Then I see him gather himself, and the next instant he's making a valiant effort at saying, "Hello, Sylvie."

"Thank you so much for coming by. I usually take the stairs; is that OK?"

"No problem," he says, following me up the staircase two steps at a time. "This place is mad! All those suits of armor!"

"They're great, aren't they?" I nod. "You should see the basement."

"You know, I never knew about this place," Toby continues blithely. "Never even heard of it. I've probably walked past a million times, but I've never noticed it, my friends have never noticed it . . . like, literally, I didn't know it existed. If you said 'Willoughby House' to me, I'd be like, 'What's that?' "

Does he have to sound *quite* so emphatic? Thank God neither Robert nor Mrs. Kendrick is in earshot. And also thank God we've already commissioned a BIG WIL-

LOUGHBY HOUSE MUSEUM sign for the exterior of the house. It's going to be gray-painted wood and very tasteful, and it only took us a week of solid discussion to nail Mrs. Kendrick on the style and font.

How are we ever going to agree on a whole website redesign?

No. Don't think like that. Be positive.

"I'm sure your mum must have mentioned this place to you a few times?" I suggest. Tilda's been to loads of events here; she's very loyal.

"Yeah, maybe she has," he says agreeably. "But it never stuck in my mind. It's not *famous,* is it? It's not like the V&A."

"Right." I try to find a smile. "Well, that's the trouble. That's the problem we're trying to solve."

Clarissa's out this morning and Robert hasn't shown up either, so we have the office to ourselves. I show Toby our home page saying *Apply in writing,* and he bursts into laughter.

"I love that," he says, about fifty times. "I love that. That is so cool." He takes a photo of the home page and shares it with all his techie friends and reads me out all the comments which instantly stream in. And I'm torn between feeling pride that we have something so distinctive and embarrassment that a whole group of tech whizzes are laughing at us.

"Anyway," I say at last, "as you see, we're behind the times. We can't carry on like this. So . . . what can we do? What are the possibilities?"

"Well," says Toby vaguely, still laughing at some comment on his phone, "there are loads. Depends what you want to achieve. Like, manage a database, an interactive experience, an e-shop, what?"

"I don't know!" I say, my appetite whetted. "Show me!"

"I looked at a few museum websites," he says, getting out his laptop. "Like, globally. It was pretty interesting."

He starts loading up websites, one after another. I thought I'd done my research pretty well, but some of these I missed. And they're *amazing.* There are photos that spring to life, 360-degree videos, interactive apps, spectacular graphics, celebrity audio tours. . . .

"Like I say," Toby concludes, "the sky's the limit. You can have anything you want. Depends on what you want. What your priorities are. Oh, and budget," he adds as an afterthought.

Budget. I should have *started* with budget.

"Right." I wrench my gaze away from the

website of an American museum which has extraordinary 3-D photos of exhibits spinning slowly round on the screen. They're so vivid that you really feel you're there in the room with them. Imagine if we could do that! "So, like . . . how much would that one have cost?"

"Actually, I read about that one in a tech magazine," Toby says, nodding. "It was half a million. Oh, don't worry," he adds at my expression. "Not pounds, dollars."

"Half a *million*?" I feel like he's punched me in the chest.

"But that was, like, with a whole big rebrand and everything," he adds hastily. "Like I say, it depends what you want."

I feel betrayed. All I've seen online are adverts saying how cheap and easy it is to make websites.

"I thought these days you could make websites in your bedroom for half nothing," I say, almost accusingly. "I thought that was the whole *point.*"

"You can!" Toby nods earnestly. "Totally. But they won't work like that one does. You don't need to spend half a million, though." He's obviously trying to sound reassuring. "You could spend a hundred grand, fifty grand, ten grand, one grand. . . ." His eyes drift back to our home page again. "I mean, *this* is cool," he says. "Just a drawing. It's subversive."

Mrs. Kendrick, subversive? I'd laugh if I weren't still pole-axed by half a million.

"Maybe it is." I sigh. "But it doesn't bring in any customers. It doesn't make any *money.*"

"So how do you get customers?"

"Lots of ways. Little adverts here and there. Or word of mouth."

"Oh, word of mouth." Toby perks up. "That's the Holy Grail. That's what you want."

"Yes, but there aren't enough words. Or mouths." I look at the American website longingly for a few more moments. "So, basically, we need money in order to afford the website which we need to make money."

"Golden goose." Toby nods sagely. "No, I mean chicken and egg. So, did you think about a platform yet?"

I rub my face, feeling my energy ebbing away. Why is it that everything in life is just a bit harder than you think it'll be? Icing cakes, having children, keeping marriages together, saving museums, building websites. All hard. The only thing that's ever turned out easier than I expected was my Italian final exam. (Oh, and lasering my legs — that was a doddle.)

"I think I'd better put a budget together,"
I say at last. "Then we can talk about
platforms or whatever."

Put a budget together. It's such a euphe-
mism. It sounds as if I just need to collect
the bits together from where they've been
scattered and assemble them. But I don't
have any bits. I have nothing.

It crosses my mind that we could sell off
some pieces of art. But would Mrs. Kendrick ever agree to that?

"Sure thing, Sylvie, whenever you're
ready," says Toby, and a wave of sympathy
passes over his face. "It's tough, isn't it?" he
adds, suddenly sounding more serious, as if
he gets it.

Well, of course he gets it. He's trying to
launch a start-up. He's got enough struggles
and obstacles of his own.

I give him a wry smile in return and shut
his laptop.

"Yes. Yes, it is. It's all pretty tough."

TWELVE

It's all pretty tough. And it hasn't got any easier.

It's the following Tuesday and the most positive development in my life right now is the WILLOUGHBY HOUSE MUSEUM sign, which arrived yesterday and is gorgeous. Far better than we expected. We all keep going outside to gaze adoringly at it, and the volunteers are convinced it's bringing in more visitors already, and even Robert gave a kind-of-impressed grunt when he saw it.

But at home, forget it. I'm not sure who's most stressed out right now, me or Dan. He's permanently taut, stroppy, tentery, and generally hard to live with. When his phone rings, he grabs for it so fast it makes me wince. I've got home twice to find him striding around the kitchen having intense phone conversations, which he immediately breaks off from. And when I ask, "What was that?" he replies, "Nothing," in discouraging tones, as though I'm somehow trespassing on his privacy. Whereupon I feel such a surge of frusture that I want to *hit* something.

I feel as if I don't know anything anymore. I don't know what Dan's thinking; I don't know what he wants; I still don't know what this "million pounds, maybe two" is. I don't know why he's been huddling with my mother. If it was to arrange a surprise, then where is that surprise?

I used to think our marriage was a solid entity. Firm and dense, with maybe just the odd little fault line. But are those fault lines bigger than I thought? Are they chasms? And if so, *why can't I see them?*

Sometimes, honestly and truly, I feel like a color-blind person. It's as if everyone else can see something I can't. Even Mummy. Sometimes she takes a breath to speak, then stops herself and says, "Oh, I've lost my train of thought," in an unconvincing way, and her eyes slide away from mine and I think, What? *What?*

On the other hand, I may be going paranoid. It's possible.

I could really do with a sensible friend to talk to, but the only person who knows all the ins and outs is Tilda, and she's still commuting to Andover. Yesterday I felt so desperate, I found myself googling *How to keep your husband,* and the answer that came back was essentially: *You can't. If he wants to leave you, he will.* (I hate the Internet.)

The infamous dinner party is tonight, and Dan is totally obsessed — about the food, the wine, even the coffee cups. (When has he ever taken any notice of coffee cups?)

Meanwhile, I'm ratty and snappy and dying for the whole thing to be over. I keep telling myself: *It can't be that bad.* Then: *Yes, it can.* And then: *Actually, it can be worse.* (I'm not sure what "worse" might consist of, but it won't be good, surely?)

Dan's picked up on my tension; how could he not? Although — silver lining — I've blamed it on my problems at work, which are still massive, despite the sign. My nonexistent website budget is still nonexistent. I've made approaches to every single supporter, patron, and philanthropist I can think of. But so far we've received nothing except a hundred pounds in cash, pushed anonymously through the letterbox in an envelope (I totally suspect Mrs. Kendrick), and a big crate of Fortnum's biscuits. One of our volunteers apparently "pulled some strings." (Robert's face when he saw them was quite funny; in fact, it's the only thing I've laughed at for ages.)

And now I've got to get ready to confront my nemesis over Ottolenghi slow-cooked lamb.

No. I don't have any *proof* she's my nemesis. I have to remember this.

As I enter the kitchen, I'm wearing my most casually elegant outfit — slim white trousers and a print top with a flash of cleavage — and wafting perfume. I'm hoping Dan will turn from the stove and his eyes will light up and maybe we'll sink into each other's arms in a bonding, imprinting way, which will inoculate him against Mary.

But he's not by the stove. I can see him through the window, out in the garden, picking some mint from our straggly bush which grows by one of the Wendy houses. (I do know mint. Mint and rosemary. Any other herbs, forget it: I'd need to see them in a Tesco packet to identify them.)

I head through the back door and make my way over our crappy grass, picking my brain for something to say. As I reach him, I blurt out, "Mint is lovely, isn't it?"

Which is such a bland comment I instantly regret it — but, then, I'm not sure Dan even heard. He's rubbing a mint leaf in his fingers, and his eyes have got that faraway look again. Where is he now? Back in his youth? With her?

And yet again I feel a stab of anxiety. OK, I have no proof of anything, but that's not the point. The point is, Dan is vulnerable. I believe it more than ever. Something happened in that garden. Something was stirred up in him. And now this woman is going to arrive (and, if she's *anything* like she looks in her photo, still be totally gorgeous) and remind him of how it all used to be before marriage and kids and stretch marks. (I mean, she might have stretch marks. But I doubt it.)

I help Dan gather some more mint and we head back inside, and somehow I keep making innocuous conversation — but my mind is whirring.

"So, tell me about your friends," I say as he washes the mint. "Tell me about . . ." I make a heroic effort to sound casual. "Mary."

"Well, I haven't seen Jeremy or Adrian for *years,*" Dan says, and my brain gives a squeal of frustration.

I don't want to know about bloody Jeremy or Adrian; didn't you hear me say Mary? Mary?

"Jeremy's in tax law, as far as I know," Dan continues, "and Adrian's in teaching, I *think,* but it wasn't clear on LinkedIn. . . ."

My brain tunes out as he tells me all about Jeremy and Adrian and how much fun they used to be and the walk they once did in the Brecon Beacons.

"And Mary?" I say, as soon as I get a chance. "What's she like? Do I need to be worried? Old girlfriend and all that? Ha ha!" I try, unsuccessfully, to give an airy, natural laugh.

"Don't be ridiculous," snaps Dan, and there's a defensive flare to his voice that makes me stare at him in sudden genuine fear. He clearly realizes that he's over-reacted, because the next moment he's looking up from his mint and smiling like any loving husband would and saying, "I don't worry about you seeing Nick Reese every day, do I?"

I keep on smiling, but inside I'm seething. Nick Reese is a *totally different case.* Yes, he is my ex-boyfriend and, yes, I run into him a fair amount, but that's because he has a daughter in the girls' class at school. I run into him at school events, because I have to. Not because I've invited him to my house for a special Ottolenghi dinner and taken special care over my outfit. (Yes, I *have* noticed that Dan's wearing his nicest, most flattering shirt. I *have* noticed.)

"I just wondered what she was like." I shrug casually.

"Oh, she's . . ." Dan pauses and his eyes

become distant. "She's a life-enhancer. She's wise. Calm. Some people just have that quality, you know? A kind of goodness. A kind of down-to-earth . . . soothing . . . She's like a tranquil lake."

I stare at him, stricken. Mary's a tranquil lake. Whereas I'm what? Some burbling, frantic river with white-water rapids round every corner?

Is he simply tired of me? Does he want a lake, not a river? Is *that* the massive great chasm in our marriage that I can't see? Tears suddenly prick my eyes again and I look away. I *have* to get a grip. What would Tilda say? She'd say, "Stop overthinking, you silly idiot, and have a glass of wine."

"I'm having a glass of wine," I say, opening the fridge. "You want one?"

"I'll just finish this mint," says Dan, glancing at his watch. "They'll be here soon."

I pour myself a glass of sauvignon blanc and check the table, trying to calm myself down. And as I walk round, straightening napkins that didn't need to be straightened, something new occurs to me. I've been focusing entirely on him. What about *her*? From her photo, she looks like a good person. She looks like a person who wouldn't steal her friend's husband. So maybe my best bet is to become her friend.

Bond with her. Show her that I'm a really nice person. Show her that even if Dan says, "My wife doesn't understand me" — which, to be fair, sometimes I don't — I'm still doing my best.

(I mean, he is quite hard to understand, in my defense. That mania he has about turning radiators down — I will never get that.)

I'm just telling myself that this is a good strategy and there's no need to be anxious, when the doorbell rings and I start so hard, my sauvignon blanc nearly spills out of my glass.

"She's here!" I say shrilly. "I mean . . . they're here. Someone's here."

Dan goes to get the front door and I soon hear the boom of cheery male voices from the hall.

"Adrian! Jeremy! Long time! Come on in!" Dan is saying, and my heart unclenches a little. It's not her. Not yet.

I look up with a smile as Adrian and Jeremy appear — both standard-issue nice guys with stubbly beards. Adrian has glasses, Jeremy has red suede shoes, and apart from that I can't really tell the difference. Dan pours drinks and hands round crisps while I half-listen to their conversation, which is all about people I've never even heard of . . .

and then they're on to Mary.

"She works for an environmental consultancy?" Adrian is saying. "That makes sense."

"I can't think how we all lost touch." Dan shakes his head. "Have you been back to the garden?"

"A few times." Jeremy nods. "You know —" He breaks off as the doorbell rings, and I swear a frisson runs through every one of us. It's her. It's Mary.

"Right!" says Dan, and I can tell he's keyed up, from his voice. "Well, that must be her. I'll just go and . . ."

Is he deliberately avoiding my eye as he heads out to the hall? I can't tell. I top up everyone's glass with wine — especially my own. I think we're going to need it.

And then suddenly there she is, coming into the kitchen with Dan, and my heart plummets. She's a vision, an absolute vision, taller than I expected, all cloudy dark hair and kind eyes and those amazing dimples.

"Hello," she says with a radiant smile, and extends a hand. "Sylvie? I'm Mary."

I blink at her, feeling overwhelmed. She's gorgeous. She really does look like an angel. An angel in a white shirt with an oversize collar and soft linen trousers.

"Hi." I clasp her hand and shake it. "Yes. I'm Dan's wife."

"You're so sweet to have us all over," says Mary, then adds to Dan, "Oh, white wine, please. What a treat. Jeremy, Adrian, you both look wonderful."

She has that gift of putting people at their ease, I instantly realize. I glance downward and see that she's wearing amazing gray leather pumps, which manage to look fashionable and ethical and expensive but non-showy, all at the same time.

I'm in the sling-back kitten heels I always wear for supper parties. I liked them ten minutes ago — but they suddenly seem really obvious and inferior.

"I love your kitchen," says Mary, in her soft voice. "It has a wonderful family atmosphere. And that blue is stunning. Did you choose that?"

She has the most soothing voice. She really is a tranquil lake. Oh God, I think *I* have a crush on this woman, never mind Dan.

"We tried loads of different blues before we got it right," I say, and her face breaks into another dimpled smile.

"I can imagine. And look at your garden. Those adorable Wendy houses!"

She heads toward the back door to peer

out, and I'm struck by her supple walk. She's not skinny, but she possesses her body perfectly. I can just imagine her aged nineteen, her pre-Raphaelite hair around her shoulders, her skin pale and perfect. . . .

No. *Stop* it. I need to bond with her. I'll talk about gardening.

"Come out and see!" I say, opening the back door and ushering her out onto the tiny patio. "I mean, we don't do much with it. . . . Do you have a boyfriend?"

Oh God. That just popped out before I could stop it. Did that sound unnatural?

No. It's fine. It's a normal question. It's what you do when you meet people. You ask them about themselves.

"No." Mary's face twists into a rueful expression, and she wanders over to look at our sole tree, a silver birch. "Not for a while."

"Ah." I try to sound understanding, like a member of the sisterhood, not like the suspicious wife who's mentally logging, *No boyfriend.*

"Men can let you down so badly," Mary continues in her melodious voice. "Or maybe it's just the men I've come across. They seem to have an extra capacity for deceit. This is lovely," she adds, stroking the tree.

She has picked the *one* thing in our garden you could describe as lovely.

"And yarrow!" she exclaims, reaching for some nondescript plant I've never even noticed. "Gorgeous. So healing. Do you ever use it in your bath?"

"Er . . . no," I admit. Use that scraggy plant in my bath?

"Never let anyone tell you that it's a weed. You can make a wonderful tincture with the flowers. It helps with sleep . . . fevers . . . everything." She looks up, her eyes shining, and I stare back, slightly mesmerized. "It's one of my passions, natural healing. And energy healing."

"Energy healing?"

"Using the body's own energy to rebalance." Mary gives me her beatific smile again. "I'm only a beginner, but I believe passionately in the mind–body connection. In the flow." She gestures down her body in one beautiful movement.

"Here you are!" Dan's voice interrupts us, and we both turn to see him stepping out of the back door. "What are you two gossiping about?"

He sounds self-conscious, I instantly register. Too hearty.

"Sylvie was asking me about my love life," says Mary with that same rueful expression, and I see Dan's gaze dart to me sharply.

Great. So now it looks like I've led Mary outside, away from the group, to demand if she's single.

Which is totally not what I did.

I mean, it's not what I *meant* to do. It just came up.

"I wasn't!" I say a little shrilly. "I mean . . . who cares about that?" I attempt a laugh, which doesn't quite come off. "Anyway, tell Dan about your natural healing, Mary! It sounds amazing!"

OK. So I'm being a bit Machiavellian here. If I had to vote for Person Least Into Alternative Medicine, it would be Dan, by a million miles. His view on medicine is basically: Take paracetamol and see your GP if you really must. He doesn't take vitamins, he doesn't meditate, and he thinks homeopathy is a massive con trick.

So what I'm hoping as we sit down to dinner is that as Mary talks about "mind–body flow" and "clearing energy blockages," Dan will adopt his usual cynical stance and the two will end up arguing. Or at least disagreeing. (Dream scenario: Mary stomping out of the house, shouting, "How dare you say Reiki is all a load of bollocks!")

But it doesn't happen like that. As Dan

doles out the lamb, Mary tells us about her healing in such an intelligent, compelling way that we all listen, riveted. She sounds like a Shakespearean actress. She even looks like one. I start to think maybe there *is* something in healing after all, and even Dan seems quite open-minded. Then she moves onto yoga and teaches us all a shoulder stretch at the table. And then she tells funny stories about going on a herbalism course and making some kind of beech-leaf liqueur and everyone getting totally drunk.

She's not just angelic; she's sassy. She exudes positive energy. Everyone is charmed. *I'm* charmed. I want her to be my friend.

As the evening progresses, I find myself relaxing. My fears seem to float away. There's no special vibe between her and Dan that I can make out. Dan has relaxed, too, and he seems just as interested in catching up with Jeremy and Adrian as he does in Mary. By the time we're onto the Green & Black's chocolates, I'm thinking, *We must do this again,* and *What nice new friends,* and *I'll ask Mary where she got those gray pumps.*

I'm just pouring out fresh mint tea when I realize that a shrill voice is calling for me: "Mummy! Mummy!" I excuse myself and find Anna standing on the stairs, clutching the banisters, her face wet with tears, telling me, "It was coming after me, it was coming, it was coming."

Poor Anna. She always takes ages to calm after a nightmare, and so I settle down to a good twenty minutes of sitting on her bed, soothing, patting, singing, and talking in a low voice. She seems to drift off, then opens her eyes again in panic and searches for me . . . then drifts off again . . . then opens her eyes again . . . and I just sit there, patiently waiting. And at last she's truly asleep, her breaths coming deeply, her fingers still clutching the edge of her duvet.

I feel tempted to climb in with her. I'm suddenly quite shattered. But, after all, we still have guests, and those Green & Black's chocolates won't hand themselves round. So at last I get to my feet and head out of her room . . . and freeze dead. From where I'm standing on the landing, I have a view into the mirror in the hall, and in that mirror I can see the sitting room reflected.

And in the sitting room are Dan and Mary. Just them.

They must have no idea I can see them, that anyone can see them. They're alone and standing close together. Mary's listening to Dan, her head tilted with an intent, understanding expression. He's talking softly to her — so softly, I can't hear his actual words. I can pick up on the vibe between them, though. It's a vibe of closeness. Of familiarity. Of everything I was afraid of.

For a few moments I'm motionless, my thoughts lurching this way and that. I want to confront them. No, I can't face confronting them. I might be wrong. Wrong about what, anyway? What do I imagine is happening? Might they not just be two old friends sharing a moment?

But why hide away from everyone?

A burst of male laughter from the kitchen brings me to, and automatically I start walking forward. I can't stay upstairs forever. As I head downstairs, the stairs creak, and at once Dan appears at the sitting room door.

"Sylvie!" he exclaims, too loudly. "I was just showing Mary . . ." He trails off as though unable to think of a convincing story. Then Mary appears in the doorway — and the look she gives me makes me feel chilled. It's unmistakable. It's a look of pity.

For a moment our eyes are locked, and I swallow, my throat tight, unable to speak.

"Actually, I must be going," says Mary, in that soft voice.

"Already?" says Dan, but he doesn't sound too sorry, and as we head back into the kitchen, the other two are also standing up, talking about tubes and Ubers and thanking us for a wonderful time.

This evening has got away from me. I want it to slow down. Press PAUSE. I need to gather my thoughts. But before I have a chance to, we're in the hall, finding everyone's coats and exchanging kisses. Mary won't look me in the eye. I'm desperate to pull her aside and ask, "What were you talking to Dan about just now?" And "Why did you two go off like that?" But I'm not brave enough.

Am I?

"Mummy! I woked up!"

Tessa's shrill voice interrupts my thoughts, and my heart sinks.

"Tessa! Not you too!"

I hurry upstairs instinctively, scooping her back before she decides to join in the party. Children being out of bed is like the five-second rule — you have to be swift. I bundle her back into bed and sit there until she's closed her eyes, listening to all the final goodbyes below in the hall and the front door closing. When Tessa is gently snoring, I creep back out onto the landing. And I'm about to head downstairs, when something stops me. Something hard and splintery and suspicious. Instead, I move silently into the bathroom, which overlooks the front of the house, and peep out. Dan and Mary are on the pavement, talking, just the two of them.

How did I know they would be there?

I just knew.

There's a horrible squeezing feeling in my chest as I crouch down by the window and silently open it a crack. Mary has wrapped herself up in a pashmina, and her face under the streetlight is wreathed with concern.

I lean my head against the windowsill, trying desperately to pick up scraps of conversation.

"*Now* you understand," Dan is saying in a low voice. "I just feel . . . pinned in a corner."

My throat tightens in shock. Pinned in a corner? He feels *pinned in a corner*?

"Yes. I get it," Mary is saying. "I do. I just . . ."

Their voices descend lower, and I can only pick out the odd word. ". . . talk . . ."

". . . find out . . ."

". . . she won't . . ."

". . . be careful . . ."

My heart is thudding as I peep out of the window again, to see that Mary is clasping Dan in a hug. A tight hug. A passionate hug.

I sink back on my heels. I feel faint. Dark shapes are scudding across my brain. Am I the ultimate trusting fool? Were the pair of them playing me all evening? I'm rerunning Mary's friendly, charming air. Her soft voice. The hand she kept putting on my arm. Was it all an act? Men have "an extra capacity for deceit," she said — and now I remember the look she gave me. Was that a hint? A warning?

I hear the front door closing and hastily come out of the bathroom to see Dan in the hall, staring up at me. There are shadows on his face and I can't read his expression and all I can think is, *He feels pinned in a corner.*

"You go to bed," he says. "I'll just stack a few plates; we can do the rest tomorrow."

Normally I'd say, "Don't be silly, I'll help!" and we'd clear away companionably and pick over the evening and start laughing over something or other.

Not tonight.

I get ready for bed, feeling a bit numb, and I'm still lying there, totally rigid, wondering what on earth I do next, how on earth I proceed . . . when Dan finally gets in beside me.

"Well, that went well," he says.

"Yes." Somehow I manage to speak. "The lamb was delicious."

"They're a fun crowd."

"Yes."

There's another long, weird silence, then Dan suddenly says, "Oh. I need to send an email. Sorry."

He gets out of bed and pads out of the room in his bare feet. And for ten seconds I lie still, my mind trying to self-soothe. Dan is always sending emails. He's always getting out of bed with some late-night thought. He's a busy man. It doesn't mean anything. It *really* doesn't mean anything. . . .

But I can't help it. My suspicion is like a desperate hunger; I have to obey it. Without making a sound, I swing my legs round, stand up, and move silently to the door of our bedroom. The door of Dan's study is open and the light is on. I lean forward noiselessly until I glimpse him — and feel another profound shock.

He's standing in his study, tapping away on a phone I've never seen before. A Samsung. What's that phone? Why does he need two phones? As I watch, he drops it into a drawer and locks it with a little key. It's on the same key ring as his house keys. I never even knew he had that little key. I didn't know he kept a drawer of his desk locked.

Why does he need to lock a drawer? What's he hiding from me? What?

For a few moments, we're both motionless. Dan seems transfixed by his thoughts. I'm transfixed by Dan. Then he suddenly turns and in fright I leap backward, skittering silently away. I'm back in bed within ten seconds, the duvet pulled right over me, my heart banging furiously.

"Everything OK?" I ask as he gets back into bed.

"Oh, fine."

And I don't know if it's my desperate optimism surfacing or my belief in giving everyone a fair chance, but I can't rest until I've given him an opportunity to make this all OK again.

"Dan, listen." I prod his shoulder until he turns, his face all tired and ready-for-sleep-ish. "Seriously. Is everything all right? Please. You look so stressed. If there's anything, *anything,* wrong . . . or worrying you . . . I mean, you would tell me, wouldn't you? You're not ill, are you?" I say with a gasp of horror. "Because if you were . . ." Tears have started to my eyes. For God's sake. I'm a nervous wreck.

"Of course I'm not *ill.*" He stares at me. "Why would I be ill?"

"Because you seem so . . ." I trail away desperately.

Because you were hugging Mary. Because you're hiding something. Because you feel pinned in a corner. Because I don't know what to think.

I gaze at him silently, willing him to see the words in my eyes. To react. To feel my pain. I thought we were psychic. I thought he would pick up on my every fear and reassure me. But he seems impervious.

"I'm fine," he says shortly. "It's all good. Let's get some sleep."

He turns over and within moments he's breathing the heavy, regular breaths of someone who was so tired, they couldn't hang about being awake any longer.

But I don't. I lie awake, staring at the ceiling, my resolve hardening. Because I know what I'm going to do now. I know exactly what I'm going to do.

Tomorrow I'm going to steal his keys.

THIRTEEN

I've never stolen anything before. I feel so guilty I don't know what to do with myself. I swiped Dan's keys while he was in the shower and put them at the back of my underwear drawer. Now I'm hovering round the kitchen, wiping things that don't need wiping, talking to the girls in a false high-pitched voice, and dropping spoons every five minutes.

"Where are my keys?" Dan comes scowling into the kitchen. "They aren't anywhere. Tessa? Anna? Have you taken Daddy's keys?"

"Of course they haven't!" I exclaim defensively. "You probably just . . . misplaced them. Have you checked your jacket pockets?"

I turn hastily away before he can see the telltale blush in my cheeks. I would *so* not make an arch-criminal.

"I had them." Dan is rummaging through

the fruit bowl. "I *had* them."

"Yes, but we were all distracted by the guests, weren't we?" I say, deftly inserting a plausible reason for him to have lost them. "Just use your spares for now. I'm sure your proper set will turn up."

"I'm not using my spares," says Dan in horror. "I need to find my *keys.*"

"It's only for now," I say soothingly. "Look, here are your spares, in the cupboard."

I double-checked the spares before I pinched his proper keys. So in some ways I *would* make a good arch-criminal.

I can see Dan is torn between two huge yet opposing principles: Never admit defeat when something's lost, and don't be late for work. At last, making an impatient noise, he grabs the spares. Between us we chivy the girls into their school sweatshirts and check their book bags, and at last all three of them are out of the house. As Dan is closing the car door, I call out, "I'll have another look for your keys before I leave," which is a genius stroke, because 1. If Dan unexpectedly returns, it explains why I'm in his study, 2. It deflects suspicion away from me, and 3. I can now "find them" and leave them on the kitchen table, job done.

Let's face it, I would make an *excellent*

arch-criminal.

I watch as the car pulls away. I wait another five minutes, just in case. Then, feeling totally surreal, I tiptoe upstairs, not even sure why I'm tiptoeing. I hesitate for a moment on the landing, trying to stay calm, then slowly venture into Dan's study.

I know exactly where I'm heading — but I pretend to myself that I'm just having a general look round. I shuffle through some papers about a planning decision. I examine a brochure from a rival office-construction company. I discover an old school report of Anna's in Dan's in-tray and find myself reading comments on her handwriting.

Then, at last, my pulse beating quickly, I find the little key on his key ring. I stare at it for a moment, thinking, *Do I really want to do this? What if I find . . . ?*

The truth is, I don't know what I'll find. My mind won't even go there.

But I'm here. I'm on a mission. I'm going to see it through. At last, swiftly, I bend down and unlock his secret desk drawer, my hand trembling so much that I have to try three times. But then I've got it open and I'm staring at what's inside.

I'm not sure what I was expecting to find — but it's the phone. The Samsung phone I saw last night. Just that; nothing else. I take it out, thinking wildly, *Wait, what about fin-gerprints?* and then *Don't be ridiculous; this isn't* CSI. I press in Dan's usual passcode and get straight in. Clearly he never expected me to find it. Which kind of comforts me. And kind of doesn't.

It's a pretty new phone. There are only twenty-four texts on it, back and forth. As I scroll down, I see they're all to the same person — *Mary.* And I just stare, unable to process the enormity of what I'm seeing. It's the nightmare, worst-case scenario.

My shoulders are rising and falling. My brain is shouting panicky messages at me, like, *What?* And: *Does that mean . . . ?* And: *Please. No. This is wrong. This has to be wrong.*

And, almost worst of all: *Was Tilda right all along? Did I bring this on myself?*

I can feel rising tears, mixed with rising incredulity. And rising dread. I'm not sure yet which is winning. Actually, yes, I am. Incredulity is winning, and it's joining forces with anger. "Really?" I feel like shouting. "*Really,* Dan?"

Everything else, I could rationalize. The moods . . . the familiar vibe between Dan and Mary . . . even the hug. But not this. Not these messages in black and white.

Gd to talk in 5.

10 am Starbucks?

It's ok have distracted S.

Today was a bit tricky.

At home can't talk

Remember PS factor

Going insane today she is NUTS

11 am Villandry

Running late, sorry

Thank God for you

And so it goes on. I read all twenty-four messages twice. I take photos of everything with my phone, because . . . just because. Might come in useful. Then I put the Samsung back with my fingertips, feeling as though it's contaminated. I shut the desk drawer, lock it carefully, check it again, and back away, as though from the crime scene.

On the landing I look around, feeling dazed, as though seeing our house for the first time. Our home. Our little nest, with its wedding presents and prints we bought on holiday and photos of the girls everywhere. All this time I've spent trying to make it cozy, trying to make it *hygge,* trying to create a place for us as a couple to retreat from the world. Now I look at my stupid candles and throws and carefully placed cushions . . . and I want to shred them all. I want to destroy them and throw them onto the street and yell, "OK, well, *fuck you, then, Dan, FUCK YOU.*"

Dan doesn't want to escape with me. He wants to escape *from* me. Maybe it was our session in the secret garden that triggered a sudden latent passion for Mary. Maybe this is all really new and exciting for him. Or maybe she's the latest in a long line of extracurricular affairs that I've been too blind to see. Either way: Sixty-eight more years of marriage? Sixty-eight more years of Dan and me together? It's a joke, a terrible, horrible joke, and I'm not laughing, I'm crying.

For a while I stand motionless, watching dust motes float by. Then I blink and half an hour has gone by, and I really should be getting to work. Not that this is the biggest priority in my life, quite frankly.

Like an automaton, I get my things together, double-check the hob is turned off (OCD), and even leave a jaunty Post-it for Dan with his keys, saying, *Found them!*

Because what else am I going to write? *Found them, and found your secret texts to Mary, too, you cheating bastard?*

As I shut the front door, I see Toby emerging from Tilda's house in black jeans and a trilby. He's holding a massive great laundry bag, spilling over with things, and has a magazine in his mouth, like a dog.

"Toby, can I help you?" I say.

Toby shakes his head cheerfully and heads down the street, unaware that he's leaving a trail behind him of T-shirts, underwear, and vinyl records.

"Toby!" Despite everything, I can't help smiling. "Your stuff! It's all falling out!"

I gather his things up and follow him along the street to where a white van is parked. He dumps the laundry bag in the back, where I see several more laundry bags, plus a desk, chair, and computer.

"Wow," I say in astonishment. "What's going on?"

"I'm moving out," he says, his eyes gleaming. "Moooooving out. Oh yeah."

"Oh my God!" I stare at him. "That's incredible! Where to?"

"Hackney. My new job's in Shoreditch, so. Makes sense."

"You've got a *job*?" I gape at him.

"Job, flat, cat," he says in satisfaction. "Shared cat," he amends. "It's called Treacle. It belongs to Michi."

"Michi?"

"Michiko. My girlfriend."

Toby has a girlfriend? Since when?

"Well . . . congratulations!" I say, stuffing his pants into the laundry bag and zipping it up. "But what about the start-up?"

"It never did start up," says Toby frankly. "That was the trouble with it."

We walk back from the van just as Tilda emerges from her front door, and I wave to get her attention. She texted me last night, I suddenly remember, and told me her commute to Andover had finished for now, but I never texted back.

As I get near, I can see that she's bright pink in the face and has a kind of suppressed energy about her. She's actually quivering. Which makes sense. She must be so jubilant. At *last.* At last he's going! And he has a job! And a girlfriend! No more noise, no more rows, no more midnight pizza deliveries . . . . I mean, I feel quite relieved, so I can only imagine how Tilda must feel.

"This is amazing news!" I greet her. "Toby seems so *together* all of a sudden."

"Oh, I know." Tilda nods vigorously. "He just announced it over supper two nights ago: 'I'm moving out.' No warning, no buildup, just 'Boom, I'm off.' "

"I'm so pleased for you! God, it's been a long time coming!" I lean forward to hug Tilda — then look more closely. Is she quivering with jubilation? Or . . .

Her eyes are bloodshot, I suddenly notice. Oh my God.

"Tilda?"

"I'm fine. Fine. Stupid." She bats away my concerned look.

"Oh, Tilda." I peer into her kind, crumpled face, and of course now I can see it beneath her bustling, energetic, Tilda-ish manner. Grief. Because she's losing him. Finally.

"It just hit me," she says in a low voice, perching on the garden wall. "Ridiculous! I've been begging him to move out, but . . ."

"He's your baby," I say quietly, sitting down next to her, and we both watch as Toby makes another journey to the white van, carrying a kettle, a sandwich toaster, and a NutriBullet, all trailing wires along the street.

"That's *my* NutriBullet," says Tilda, and I

384

can't help laughing at her expression. "I know he has to move out," she adds, her eyes not moving from him. "I know he has to grow up. I know I pushed him to do all this. But . . ." Tears start spilling from her eyes, and she pulls a tissue out of her pocket. "Stupid," she says, shaking her head. "Stupid."

I watch Toby returning to the house, oblivious of his mother's grief, bouncing up and down in his hipster trainers, humming a happy tune, ready to start his *proper* life.

"The girls will move out," I say, stricken. "They'll move out one day, without looking back."

I can suddenly see a grown-up Tessa and Anna. Beautiful, leggy women in their twenties. Brisk. Checking their phones constantly. Discounting everything I say, because I'm their mother — what do I know?

I'm half-hoping Tilda will say something comforting, like, "Don't worry, your girls will be different," but she just shakes her head.

"It's not even that simple. They'll try you. Hate you. Scream at you. Need you. Tangle your heart up in theirs. *Then* they'll move out without looking back."

There's silence for a while. She's right. And I don't know how I can dodge it.

"Some people make it look so *easy,*" I say at last, exhaling hard. But Tilda shakes her head wryly.

"If love is easy, then you're not doing it right."

We both watch as Toby carts a double duvet out of the front door.

"Hey, did you want to talk any more about your website, Sylvie?" he says as he nears us, and I shake my head.

"We're not ready just yet. Thanks, though."

"Sure," says Toby, and carries on down the street, the corners dragging on the dusty pavement.

"Mind the *corners!*" Tilda yells after him — then she shakes her head. "Whatever. He's got a washing machine."

"I think Dan's having an affair," I say, staring straight ahead, my voice oddly calm. "I found texts. Secret texts. A locked drawer. The whole bit."

"Oh fuck." Tilda grabs my arm. "*Fuck.* Sylvie, you should have said —"

"No. It's fine. It's fine. I'm going to . . ." As I say the words, I realize I don't have the first idea what I'm going to do. "It's fine," I say again. "It'll be fine."

"Oh, love." Tilda's arm clamps around my shoulders and squeezes hard. "It's shitty.

You two seemed so . . . Of all the couples, I would have said . . ."

"I know!" I give a tremulous laugh. "We were *that couple.* In fact, you know the really funny thing about Dan and me? I thought I knew him *too* well." I give a mirthless laugh. "I thought we were *too* close. I wanted him to surprise me. Well, guess what, he did. He did."

"Look . . ." Tilda sighs. "Are you sure about this? Could there be any other . . . Have you talked about it with Dan?"

"No. Not yet." The very thought of "talking about it with Dan" makes my stomach turn over. "I guess you just don't ever know the truth about people."

"But Dan." Tilda is shaking her head incredulously. "*Dan.* The most loving, thoughtful . . . I remember him coming over to ours after your father died. He was so worried about you. Obsessed by keeping the noise down so you could sleep. Asked us to walk around in our socks. Which we did," she adds with a grin.

"Sorry about that." I wince. A depressing new thought hits me and I sag. "Maybe that's Dan's problem. My breakdown was all too much for him."

There's a long, heavy silence between us. I can see Tilda's brow knitting.

"Hmm," she says at last. "Your 'breakdown.' "

"Episode," I amend awkwardly. "However you describe it."

"Yes, I've heard you talk about your 'episode.' But . . ." Tilda's brow is still deeply knitted. "I mean . . . weren't you just going through grief?"

"Well, yes, of course I was," I say, puzzled. "But I didn't cope well."

"That's what you've always said. And I've never wanted to contradict you, but . . ." Tilda sighs and turns to face me. "Sylvie, I don't know if this will help right now, but here goes anyway. I don't think you had a breakdown. I think you went through grief like any normal person."

I stare back at her, discomfited, not knowing how to respond.

"But I wrote that letter," I say at last. "I went to Gary Butler's house."

"So what? A couple of erratic moments."

"But . . . Dan. My mother. They both said . . . they called a doctor —"

"I wouldn't say your mother is any great judge of anything," Tilda cuts me off crisply. "And Dan . . . Dan was always very protective of you. Maybe too much so. Has he ever lost anyone? Been bereaved?"

"Well . . . no," I say, thinking aloud. "No,

he hasn't. No one close."

"So he doesn't know. He wasn't prepared. He couldn't bear to see you suffering and he wanted to cure you. Sylvie, grief is long and messy and horrible — but it's not an illness. And you cope how you cope. There's no 'well' about it."

She links her arm in mine and we sit there silently for a while. And despite everything, I feel strengthened by what she's just said. It feels true.

"I don't know if that helps," she says at last. "Probably not."

"No, it does," I say. "It does. You always help." I squeeze her tight and give her an impulsive kiss, then get to my feet. "I have to go. I'm late."

"Shall I walk with you?" offers Tilda at once, and I feel another wave of affection for her.

"No, no." I pat her shoulder. "Stay. Say a proper goodbye to Toby. He'll be back," I add over my shoulder as I set off. "He'll be back to see you. You wait."

Fourteen

As I travel to work, the maelstrom in my mind gradually, gradually calms down. Walking along the London pavements, I feel as though with every step I'm pushing my problems down. Away. I mean, I have to get on with life, don't I? I can't sit crying and shaking at work.

To my surprise, as I enter Willoughby House, Mrs. Kendrick is in the hall, along with Robert and an unfamiliar guy in a blue suit with a shaven head. The guy is looking around the spacious tiled hall with a practiced eye, and I instantly know he's in property.

"Hello, Mrs. Kendrick!" I say. "How lovely to see you here. It's been a while!"

"Sylvie, I'm so sorry." She puts a hand on my arm. "I know I've left you in the lurch recently. I've been rather busy."

"Robert said you've been learning to use a computer?"

"Indeed I have! I have an Apple Mac." She says the words carefully, as though enunciating a foreign language. *Ap-ple Mac.*

"Wow!" I say. "Amazing."

"Oh, you can do all sorts of things on it. I bought this 'online,' you know." She plucks at the white frilly shirt she's wearing. "Do you see? They delivered it straight to my house from the shop. I just had to type in my credit-card number. So convenient." She nods, as though satisfied with herself. "And then I reviewed it on Review Your Stuff. Four stars out of five. Nice fabric, but the buttons are a little cheap. You can read my review, if you like."

I feel a bit speechless. Mrs. Kendrick has gone from barely knowing what a computer is to reviewing products online?

"Right," I say at last. "Well, I don't know that particular website —"

"Oh, but you must, you *must.*" She fixes me with a glittering eye. "Reviewing is the most marvelous hobby. You can review anything. I reviewed the policeman standing outside my block of flats yesterday."

Robert turns and stares at her incredulously. "Aunt Margaret, you can't review *policemen.*"

"Of course you can," says Mrs. Kendrick crisply. "In the General category you can

391

review anything you like. Tea bags . . . holidays . . . policemen . . . I'm afraid I only gave him three stars. He was slightly dull about the eyes and wore his uniform badly."

As she speaks, she eyes the shaven-headed guy meaningfully, and I bite my lip. Mrs. Kendrick is back on form. Thank God for that. And I'm definitely going to look up some of her reviews. I just love the idea of Mrs. Kendrick's views on life being disseminated across the Internet.

The shaven-headed guy moves toward the rear of the hall and I say quietly, "Who's that?"

"That is Robert's guest. I believe his name is 'Mike.' " She enunciates *Mike* with slight disdain.

"You know his name is Mike," says Robert patiently.

"Really, Robert, this has nothing to do with me," says Mrs. Kendrick frostily. "You may proceed however you wish. When I'm dead, it will all be yours anyway."

"Are you selling up?" I stare at Robert. "Weren't you going to give us a chance first?"

"I'm finding out our options," he says, a little testily. "Gathering information."

"Some people give up." Mrs. Kendrick gives Robert a scathing look. "Others think outside the space."

" 'Outside the space'?" As Robert confronts Mrs. Kendrick, he seems beleaguered, and I wonder if this disagreement has been going on all morning. " 'Outside the space' isn't even a saying! As I've told you, all I'm doing is getting a valuation —"

"And as I have told *you,* Robert," Mrs. Kendrick retorts crisply, "I have come up with an ingenious plan, in which you do not seem interested. You may think I'm a dinosaur, but I can move with the times."

Robert sighs. "Look, I am interested, but I need to deal with this first. . . ."

"It is a forward-looking idea." Mrs. Kendrick turns to me. "It involves a smart phone."

I clamp my lips together, trying not to smile. Mrs. Kendrick enunciates *smart phone* with the same care as *Apple Mac,* accentuating *phone* instead of *smart.*

"Mavis, where is your smart *phone?*" She raises her voice. "We need the smart *phone.*"

Mavis is one of our most stalwart volunteers, a plump lady with dark bobbed hair, shapeless dresses, and sturdy shoes which she wears all year round. She's clutching an iPhone and brandishes it at Mrs. Kendrick.

"Here you are, Margaret. Are you ready?"

"Well, not quite." Mrs. Kendrick looks

around the hall, as though seeing the occasional tables and porcelain urns and eighteenth-century paintings for the first time.

What on earth is she planning to do? Take a selfie? Post a picture of Willoughby House online? Write a review?

"Where shall I stand?" Mavis looks around. "A few steps back, I think?"

"Yes." Mrs. Kendrick nods. "Perfect."

I'm watching, intrigued, as they maneuver themselves round the hall. Mavis keeps holding her iPhone up as though to frame Mrs. Kendrick, and the pair of them seem to have something quite specific in mind.

"Robert, to the left," says Mrs. Kendrick suddenly. "Just a little. And 'Mike'?" Even as she addresses him, she manages to make his name sound ridiculous. "Could you possibly stand on the stairs? Now, quiet, everyone, I'm going to film."

Before anyone can protest, she draws breath, beams at the iPhone, and begins speaking, while simultaneously walking backward over the black-and-white-tiled floor, like a TV presenter.

"Welcome to Willoughby House," she says in clear, distinct tones. "A hidden gem in London. A treasure trove of art and antiquities. And a snapshot of what life was really like . . . Argh!"

"Shit!"

"Oh my God!"

Everyone cries out in horror as Mrs. Kendrick stumbles on the tiled floor and crashes heavily into a little circular table, knocking a blue-and-white urn flying. It seems almost to stop, poised in midair, before Robert, in a flying rugby tackle, hurls himself at it. He grasps the urn, rolls on the hard floor, and there's an audible crack as his head hits the stair banister.

"Robert!" Mrs. Kendrick shrieks. "That's twenty thousand pounds you've just saved!"

"Twenty grand?" Robert stares at the urn with such an expression of horror I want to laugh. "What's wrong with the bloody world? Who would pay twenty grand for *this*?"

"Are you all right, mate?" Mike descends the stairs.

"Fine. Fine." Slowly, grasping the urn tightly, Robert gets to his feet.

"Are *you* all right, Mrs. Kendrick?" I ask, because, after all, she got a bit of a bump too.

"Of course I'm all right," says Mrs. Kendrick impatiently. "Play it back, Mavis. Let's see it."

We all crane over Mavis's shoulder and

watch Mrs. Kendrick backing over the tiles, talking in distinct, serene tones, stumbling . . . and then the total chaos that followed. Oh God, you can't help but laugh.

"Next time, try walking forward," says Robert pointedly to his aunt as it finishes.

"Well, at least the urn didn't break," I remind him.

"Twenty grand." Robert is still staring incredulously at the urn. "For a pot. Is that insured separately? I mean, shouldn't it be in a locked case?"

But Mrs. Kendrick isn't listening to any of us. She's saying, "Put it on Twitter, Mavis! And YouTube. Load it up! Now." She looks at Robert and me. "Everyone must start twittering," she says firmly. "Sharing. Whatever you call it."

"What?" I say stupidly.

"Twittering! If we want to go viral, we have to twitter. Now, what shall we call it?"

Viral?

A sudden suspicion is forming in my mind — and as I glance at Robert I see he's thinking the same way.

"Aunt Margaret," he says in even tones. "Was that *faked*?"

"Of course it was faked," says Mrs. Kendrick with asperity. "Robert, as I said, I'm not a dinosaur. The more people see this video, the more people will know the name of Willoughby House."

"I've just asked my grandson's advice," announces Mavis breathlessly, looking up from her phone. "He suggests, 'That awkward moment when your priceless urn nearly breaks.'"

"Marvelous." Mrs. Kendrick nods at Mavis. "Type it in, dear."

"But you let me dive to the floor! I bumped my head!" Robert sounds really quite aggrieved.

"I was afraid you wouldn't be able to act." Mrs. Kendrick gives him a frosty smile.

"And what if the urn had broken?" he demands. "That would have been twenty grand. You risked twenty grand for a viral video!"

"Oh, Robert." Mrs. Kendrick gives him a supremely pitying look. "Have a little sense. It's not really worth twenty thousand pounds. I bought it from John Lewis."

Robert looks so apoplectic, I want to laugh, although I'm not sure if it's because his aunt has got one over on him, or because his head is still sore, or because Mike gives a sudden snort of laughter.

"I'll leave you to it," I say diplomatically, and head upstairs to the office — and the whole thing has almost, kind of, sort of, cheered me up.

Sure enough, the video is soon up on YouTube, and every time I check, it's been viewed by another fifty or so people. It's not exactly a sneezing panda, but I do think Mrs. Kendrick has the right idea.

But even a viral video can't keep my spirits up. I get through the day on a kind of autopilot, and by 4:00 P.M. I'm really in the pits. Clarissa has gone out to see a prospect, and it's started to rain, and I'm sitting at the computer desk, head slumped in my arms, when I hear the tread of Robert on the stairs. Hastily, I sit up and resume the email I started about three hours ago.

"Oh, hello," I say as he appears, in an absent sort of voice, as though I'm in the middle of concentrating. "Has 'Mike' gone, then?" I can't help calling him "Mike" with a sardonic tone, just like Mrs. Kendrick did.

"Yes, 'Mike' has gone." Robert sounds amused.

"And have you sold the place for twenty million?" I add, without looking up.

"Oh, at least."

"Good. Because I wouldn't want you to starve." I briskly sign off my email.

"It's OK," he says, deadpan. "The orphans that I trample over on my way to cash my ill-gotten money can cook me some roast suckling pig while they're sweeping my capitalist chimneys."

I can't help a tiny smile curving my lips. He's funnier than he lets on, Robert. I finally raise my head and wince at the sight of the bruise which has sprouted on his forehead.

"You hurt yourself!" I say.

"Yes! Thank you," he says in mock-aggrieved tones. "That's what I was trying to say."

"Has Mrs. Kendrick gone too?"

"Yes, she's in a meeting with Elon Musk," he says, and I nearly exclaim, "Really?" before I realize he's joking.

"Ha," I say.

"On the plus side," Robert says, "while I was showing Mike around, we found this." He lifts up a bottle of wine in his right hand.

"Oh yes," I say, without much interest, "that's the Christmas wine. We give it to the volunteers every year."

"Château Lafite," repeats Robert, and I realize he's making a point. "Château La-fucking-*fite.*"

"Well, you know." I shrug. "Mrs. Kendrick likes the best."

Robert looks at me, then stares at the wine bottle, then shakes his head incredulously. "Every time I think this place can't get any madder, it does. Well, let's see if it is the best, shall we? Got any glasses?"

I fetch a couple of cut-crystal glasses from the Trolley, which is where we keep our sherry, nuts, and crisps.

"You're well kitted out," says Robert, watching me. "Don't tell me — Mrs. Kendrick . . ."

"She likes to have a glass of sherry if we stay late," I explain.

"Of course she does." Robert pours out two glasses of the Château Lafite, and even though I'm not a wine buff, I can tell from the smell alone that it's special.

"Cheers." Robert holds up his glass and I clink it with mine, and I suddenly need a drink so badly, I gulp down about half.

"Have some snacks," I say, decanting some little cheesy biscuits into a cut-glass bowl. Robert sits down on an office chair and we drink silently, hoovering the cheesy biscuits. After a while, I open another packet and Robert replenishes our glasses. He still looks incongruous up here, with his big shoes and deep voice and way of pushing things aside without even noticing.

"Careful!" I say, as he leans back, his elbow casually on the computer desk, and knocks over Clarissa's pile of leather-bound exercise books. "Those are the Books."

"The Books?"

"We write summaries of all our meetings," I explain. "Time, person, subject. They're actually incredibly useful. They go back years and years."

Robert picks up the exercise books. He flicks through one of them, reading Clarissa's careful entries in fountain pen, then puts it back with a sigh.

"You're all getting under my skin, you know that? The Dish, the Ladder, the Books, the Wine . . . It's like bloody *Alice in Wonderland* up here." He looks around the office with what seems like genuine ruefulness. "I don't *want* to force this place into the real world. But I have to. We can't stave off reality forever."

"I'm looking into websites," I say quickly. "I've done another appeal to supporters. Or we could sell off some pieces, raise some cash that way —" I break off as Robert shakes his head.

"That would take us so far," he says. "But what then? Sell three paintings every year till they're all gone? This place needs to be sustainable."

"It needs an injection of cash," I counter. "Just one lump sum would really help us —"

"It's *had* injections of cash!" Robert

sounds frustrated. "Year after year! There's a limit! Do you realize how much my aunt —" He stops himself, and I feel an uneasy twinge. I have no idea how much Mrs. Kendrick has spent propping us up.

"So you're really going to sell?" I can't help a catch in my voice. "You said you'd give us a chance."

"I haven't said I won't," Robert says after a pause. "Nothing's definite. It's just . . ." He exhales. "It's a big job. Bigger than I first imagined. It's not just turning round an ocean liner. It's turning round an ocean liner while also saving the ocean liner from sinking. YouTube videos won't save us. A new website . . . well, maybe. But maybe not."

The rain is drumming on the windows as he refreshes my glass. I can feel sadness settling about me like a cloud. So that's it. The end of an era. At home, maybe it's the end of another era. And suddenly I can't stop tears rolling down my cheeks. I was so *happy.* My life made sense. Now I feel like the whole lot is unraveling. Job, income, husband . . .

"Oh God. Sylvie — I'm sorry." Robert looks perturbed. "Look, as I say, it's not for definite . . . it won't be for a while . . . we'll help you find new positions. . . ."

"It's not that." I take out my hanky and wipe my face. "Sorry. It's . . . personal stuff."

"Ah," he says — and there's an immediate shift in the air. I can actually feel the molecules changing. It's as if my professional life was a beaker of clear water and now I've introduced a drop of home-life color and it's slowly seeping through everything.

I glance up, as though to reassure myself that Robert isn't remotely interested in my ridiculous private affairs — but he's leaning forward, a crease in his forehead as though he *is* interested. Very interested.

His hair is about twice the thickness of Dan's, I find myself noticing randomly. Thick and dark and shiny. And I can smell his aftershave from here. It's expensive. Nice.

"I won't pry," says Robert, after a long pause.

"It's not . . ." I shrug. "I just . . ." I wipe my nose, trying to get control of myself. "Are you married?" I find myself asking; I don't even know why.

"No." He pauses. "I was with someone."

"Right."

"But even that wasn't easy. Marriage . . ." He shrugs too.

"Yup."

"But I *will* say one thing." Robert gulps his wine. "I probably shouldn't, but I will. If your husband has, in any way . . . If he for one moment . . . If he doesn't realize what he has —" He breaks off and looks at me full on, his eyes dark and unreadable. "Then he's mad. He's mad."

I can feel my skin shimmer under Robert's gaze. I'm transfixed by his eyes. His shiny hair. His forthright manner. He's so different from Dan. He's a different variety of man. A different flavor altogether.

If life is like a box of chocolates, then getting married is like choosing a chocolate and saying, "That's it, done," and slamming the lid closed. When you make your vows, what you're basically saying is: "That's all I want, ever. That one flavor. Even if it goes off. Yum. I can't even *see* any other flavors anymore, la-la-la."

And it might be your favorite flavor. And you might truly love it. But can you help it if you sometimes look over at the honeycomb crunch and think . . . *mmm*?

"He's mad," Robert repeats, his eyes still locked on mine. "Do you want to get something to eat?" he adds more tentatively.

In a flash, a door in my mind seems to open. Through it, I can see a glittering, beckoning chain of events, starting right now. Dinner. More drinks. Laughter and a blurred head and a screw-you-Dan kind of exhilaration. A hand on my arm, murmurings in my ear . . . dancing? A taxi? The dimly lit corridor of a hotel . . . unfamiliar lips on mine . . . hands peeling off my clothes . . . a new body against mine . . .

It would be good.

And it would be terrible.

It would screw me up. I'm just not in that place. I don't know what place I *am* in . . . but it's not that one.

"No, thanks," I say at last, my breath a little jagged. "I'd better go and . . . But thanks. Thanks. Really. Thanks."

I get home before Dan, say goodbye to Karen with a cheery smile, put the children to bed, and then just wait in the kitchen, feeling like a Bond villain.

I've been expecting you, Mr. Winter. That's my line. Except it's not true. Until last night I didn't expect any of this. Extramarital affairs? Secret drawers? Little messages? Are you kidding? I've looked at the photos on my phone about a thousand times today. I've read Dan's texts over and over. They're so familiar-sounding. So Dan-like. Just like the kind of texts he'd send to me . . . but not to me.

The one that really makes my stomach clench is *Remember PS factor.* The "Princess Sylvie" factor. I'm not his beloved wife; I'm a *factor.* Not to mention the fact that Princess Sylvie is a very private little nickname that makes me flinch for all sorts of reasons, and now he's using it with her.

I just don't get it. The Dan I know is caring and solicitous. Protective of us: Of what we've made together. Our home. Our family. Our world. Can you really not know someone you've been so close to? Can you really be so blind?

I don't know exactly what I'm going to say. What I do know is, I'm *not* going to greet him by waving the evidence in his face. Because what do I gain by doing that? Nothing, except a momentary flash of vindictive glee. (Which, actually, is fairly appealing right now.)

But then what happens? I've caught him out. I win. Except it doesn't feel like winning.

Winning would be: He decides to confess everything, totally spontaneously, and is really sorry and has some explanation which makes everything right. (What explanation? Don't know. Not my job.)

Or, even better, we go back in time and

none of this ever happened.

The sound of his key in the lock makes me jump. Fuck. I'm not ready. I hastily smooth down my hair and take a few deep breaths. My heart is pounding so hard, I feel like it must be audible — but as Dan comes in, he doesn't seem to hear it. Or notice anything. He looks knackered, and his brow is screwed up as though he can't escape his thoughts. As he drops his briefcase, he exhales with a weary sigh. Any other night I'd say, "Are you OK?" and get him a cup of tea or a drink.

But not tonight. If he's knackered, *maybe he shouldn't make so many complicated arrangements in his private life.* I spit the words out in the privacy of my own brain and almost wish he could hear them.

"All right?" I say shortly.

"I've had better days." Dan rubs his brow and I feel a flare of fury, which I quell.

"I think we need to talk," I say.

"Sylvie . . ." Dan looks up as though this is the last straw. "I'm shattered, it's been a fuck of a day, I have calls I need to make —"

"Oh, *calls,*" I retort sarcastically before I can stop myself.

"Yes, calls." He stares at me.

"What kind of calls?"

"Just calls."

I'm breathing hard. My thoughts are skittering around. I need to gather myself.

"I just think . . . we should be . . . honest with each other," I say, feeling my way. "Really, really honest. Let's have a new project where we confess everything. Project Clean Slate."

"For fuck's sake," Dan mutters. "I need a drink." He looks as if Project Clean Slate is the last thing he wants in his life, but I press on determinedly as he gets a beer from the fridge.

"We need to connect. And to connect you need to be totally straightforward and not hide anything. Like . . ." I scrabble hastily around. "Like, I found a Post-it that I'd written for myself the other day. Your mum had called and I *totally* forgot to tell you. Sorry."

There's silence, and I look at Dan expectantly.

"What?" he says.

"Your turn! Project Clean Slate! There must be something you . . . something you haven't told me . . . it could be anything. . . ."

I trail off, my heart beating even faster. Already I know this isn't going to work. It was a stupid idea. I confess a missed phone message and he confesses an entire affair?

"Sylvie, I *really* don't have time for this," Dan says, and something about his terse, dismissive tone makes me see red.

"You don't have time for your marriage?" I explode. "You don't have time to talk about the hiccups in our relationship?"

"What hiccups?" Dan sounds irritable. "Why are you always inventing problems?"

"Inventing?" I want to scream. "Did I invent your texts?"

There's silence in the kitchen, apart from the ticking of our wall clock. We bought it together in Ikea, before we were married. We didn't even need to discuss it. We were both instantly drawn to the same one, with a big black rim and no numerals. I remember thinking, *God, we're so in sync.*

What a joke.

Dan pulls up a chair and sits down and he looks exactly like the husband I've known and loved all these years, except he's not, is he? He's stuffed full of secrets.

I'm bubbling over again. I need to confront him. If I can't bring myself to brandish his texts to Mary, I can brandish something else.

"I know you're cooking up something at work," I fling out at him. "I heard you at the hospital, talking to my mother. 'A million pounds, maybe two,' huh, Dan? Is that what you're borrowing? Without telling me? Is this for that Copenhagen business?"

"For *fuck's* sake." Dan's eyes widen.

"I heard you!" I know my voice is shrill, but I can't help it. " 'One million, maybe two!' Jesus, Dan! This is our future you're gambling on! And I know exactly what it's about really —"

"Oh yes?" Dan says in ominous tones. "What's it about really?"

Seriously? He's asking this?

"My father!" I almost yell. "What do you *think*? It's always about my father! You can't stand that Daddy was rich and successful, you can't stand that he was admired, you look miserable anytime anyone says anything nice about him —"

"I do not," snaps Dan.

"Oh my God, Dan, are you for real?" I almost want to laugh, except it's not funny. "Have you seen yourself? It's completely obvious. And that's why you want to expand your company, not because it's good for us, as a family, but because you've got to compete with my father, who by the way, is dead. *Dead.* You're so bloody *chippy,* and I'm sick of it."

I break off, panting, tears rising, half terrified. I can't believe I called Dan chippy. It's a word I vowed never, ever to use. But now I have. I've crossed a line.

A vein is twitching in Dan's forehead. He stares at me for a few silent moments and I can see a million thoughts passing through his eyes, but I can't read any of them.

"I can't do this," he says abruptly, pushing back his chair.

"Can't do *what*?" I throw after him, but he doesn't answer, just strides into the hall and up the stairs.

"Dan!" I hurry after him furiously. "Come back! We need to talk!"

"Jesus, Sylvie!" Dan pauses halfway up the stairs and wheels round. "Are *you* for real? We do *not* need to talk. I'm fucking talked out. I need to have some space. Some space. To think. To . . . I need space. Space." He clutches his head. "Space."

"Oh, *space*," I say as scathingly as I can, because my heart is beating a tattoo of panic.

This has all gone far worse than I expected, far more quickly. I want to pull it back. I want to say, "Please. Please, Dan. Tell me you don't love her." But I'm petrified of what he might say. So much for knowing him inside out; for being psychic; for finishing off his sentences. I have no idea what he's about to say anymore.

I feel almost faint with fear, standing here in my familiar hall, staring up at my unfamiliar husband. He's gazing at me with a wry expression that makes my hair stand on end, because it's not one of our looks. It's the kind of look he might give to a stranger.

"I meant to tell you," he says at last, in a voice that doesn't ring true. "I've got a trip tomorrow. I need to fly up to . . . Glasgow. I might as well go and stay at an airport hotel tonight."

"Glasgow?" I stare at him. "Why Glasgow?"

"Possible new supplier," he says, looking away, and my heart plunges. He's lying. I can tell.

He's going to her.

"Fine." I manage the single syllable, even though my lungs feel like they're packing up.

"Tell the girls I'll be back soon. Give them a kiss."

"Fine."

He turns and trudges up the stairs and I stand, motionless, replaying our conversation in my head on a loop, feeling as if any move I make might be wrong. After a few minutes he's back, holding the leather weekend bag I gave him our first Christmas together.

"Dan, listen." I swallow, trying not to sound desperate. "Why don't you stay here tonight? Couldn't you drive to the airport in the morning?"

"I have stuff I need to do," he says, staring resolutely past me. "It'll be simpler if . . . I'll text Karen. I'm sure she'll do some extra hours, take care of the school run. . . ."

The school run? Is that what he thinks I'm worried about? The *school run*?

"OK." I can barely get the word out.

"I'll be a day or two. I'll keep you posted." He kisses me on the forehead, then heads to the front door with his swift, determined stride. Within ten seconds he's gone, and I'm still standing motionless, almost light-headed with shock. What just happened?

A sudden thought comes to me and I dart upstairs to his study. I wrench open his top drawer — and his passport is inside, where it's always kept. Dan's not the type to forget his passport. He's not flying anywhere.

I pick up the passport, open it, and stare at Dan's impassive photo face, feeling sick. The man I thought couldn't keep secrets from me turns out to be a pretty good liar.

And now humiliation is descending upon me like a suffocating blanket. It's so sordid. So predictable. My husband has walked out on me for his mistress, leaving me to look after the kids. This is my reality. I thought we were different. Special. But we're just like every other tedious messed-up marriage in southwest London. With a sudden half sob, half scream, I grab my phone and start texting him with stabby fingers:

Go off and enjoy yourself, then. Talk about surprising each other. You're such a predictable, boring fucking cliché.

I send the text, then collapse down onto the floor. I'm beyond crying. I'm beyond thought.

We were that couple. We were always *that couple.*

Now we're *that couple.*

FIFTEEN

I remember this from when Daddy died: At first you're numb. You function perfectly. You smile and crack jokes. You think, *Wow, it's actually all fine, I must be a really strong person, who knew?* And it's only later that the pain swallows you up and you start dry-heaving into your sink.

I'm still at the numb stage. I've got the girls ready for school. I've chatted merrily with Karen and mentioned Dan being really busy with work. I've waved at Professor Russell — John — through the window.

I could easily have done the school run, but Dan clearly texted Karen last night claiming a state of emergency, because she pitched up at 7:00 A.M., all ready to swing into action. They've just left, and the house has that super-silent feeling it gets whenever the children leave it. It's just me and the snake. Which, thank God, does not need feeding for another five days. If Dan isn't

415

back by then, I'm giving it to the RSPCA.

I put on more makeup than usual, savagely jabbing at my eyes with the mascara wand. I step into a pair of high heels, because I feel height will help me today. I'm in my jacket, ready to leave for work, when the post rattles through the letterbox and I pick it up, thinking dazedly, *What do I do if there's post for Dan? Forward it on? Where?*

But it's just a couple of catalogs and a handwritten envelope. Creamy and expensive. Nice handwriting, slanted and elegant. I stare at it in mounting suspicion. That can't be from . . . She wouldn't have . . .

I rip it open and something seems to stab my stomach. It is. It's from her. She's written us a bloody thank-you letter. I scan the anodyne words, but I can't digest them. I can't focus. All I can think is: *How dare you, how dare you?*

Both of them.

Him.

Her.

With their texts and secret hugs. Treating me like a fool.

A new energy is suffusing me. A new, incandescent fury. Last night I played it all wrong. I was wrong-footed. I didn't react quickly enough. I didn't say the stuff I should have said. I keep going over the scene, wishing I *had* confronted Dan with those texts, that I *had* shoved everything out in the open. What was I thinking of, waiting for him to confess? Why was he ever going to do that?

So today I'm taking charge. My husband's lover may get to do a lot of things. But she does *not* get to write me a two-faced thank-you letter, laughing at me behind my back. She does *not* get to do that.

I send a text to Clarissa: *Just popping to London Library for research,* then google Mary's company, Green Pear Consulting. It's in Bloomsbury. Easy. As I emerge from the tube at Goodge Street, I'm walking snappily, my legs like scissors. My fists are clenched at my sides. My jaw is tight. I feel ready for body blows.

I arrive at the address to find one of those tall London houses with about ten companies on five different floors and a rickety lift and a receptionist whose aim seems to be to misunderstand you at every turn. But at last, after an excruciating conversation between the receptionist and someone on the phone at Green Pear Consulting ("No, she don't have no appointment. No. No appointment. She called Sylvie. Syl-vee Winter. For Mary. Ma-ree"), I'm on my way up the stairs to the fourth floor. I'm pretty fit, but my heart is already pounding and my skin keeps breaking out in goose-bumps. I feel unreal. Finally, *finally,* I'm going to get some answers. Or some payback. Or *something . . .*

I get to the top and push my way through a heavy fire door. And there's Mary, waiting for me on a tiny landing, as beautiful as ever, in a gray linen shift dress. She looks shocked to see me, I notice with satisfaction. Not so tranquil *now.*

"Sylvie!" she says. "They phoned up and told me someone called Sylvie was here, but I didn't . . . I mean . . ."

"You didn't know why I was here?" I say scathingly. "Really? You have no idea?"

There's silence and I can see Mary's dark eyes flickering with thought. Then she says, "Maybe we should go to my office."

She leads me to a tiny room and gestures to a chair opposite her desk. It's quite a bare space — all pale wood and posters for environmental causes and a striking abstract painting, which I would ask her about in different circumstances.

Mary sits down, but I don't. I want the advantage of height.

"So," I say, in my most cutting tones. "Thanks for your *letter.*" I take it out of my bag and throw it onto her desk and she

418

flinches, startled.

"Right." She picks the envelope up warily, then replaces it on her desk. "Is there a . . . Are you . . ." She tries a third time. "Sylvie . . ."

"Yes?" I say, as unforgivingly as I can. I'm certainly not making this easy for her.

"Is something . . . wrong?"

Is something *wrong*?

"Oh, come on, Mary," I snap. "So you're having a secret thing with him. An affair. He's moved in with you. Whatever. But *don't* send me a letter saying thank you for the lovely dinner, OK?" I break off, breathing hard, and Mary stares at me, her jaw dropped.

"Moved *in* with me? What on earth . . . ?"

"Nice try."

"Oh God." Mary clutches her head. "I need to unpick all this. Sylvie, I'm *not* having an affair with Dan, and he *hasn't* moved in with me. OK?"

"Oh, right," I say icily. "I suppose he hasn't sent you secret texts either. I suppose he didn't tell you he feels 'pinned in a corner.' I saw you talking, Mary. I saw you hugging. So you can stop the playacting, OK? I *know*."

There's silence, and I can see I've got to Mary. I've punctured her serene veneer. She looks quite rattled, for an angel.

"We did talk that night," she says at last. "And, yes, we did hug. But as old friends, nothing more. Dan wanted to open up to me . . . and I found myself listening. Talking." She suddenly rises from her chair, so she's at eye level with me. "But Dan and I are not having an affair. We're really, really not. Please believe me."

"Old friends." I echo the words sarcastically.

"Yes!" Her face suddenly flushes. "Just that. I don't have affairs with married men. I wouldn't do that."

"What about the texts?" I fling back at her.

"I've only sent him a couple of texts. We've chatted. Nothing more. I promise."

"But you've met up. At Starbucks. At Villandry."

"No." She shakes her head. "At your house we talked about meeting up, possibly . . . that's all. He just wanted to talk to me. Download. That's all."

"Download about what?" There's an edge to my voice. "About how I'm 'nuts'?"

"What?" She blinks at me in shock. "No!"

"Stop denying it!" I erupt. "I've seen the texts! *Running late, sorry. It's ok have distracted S.*" I make jabbing, quotey gestures at her. "*Remember PS factor. I've read them! There's no point lying!*"

"I have no idea what you're talking about!" She appears baffled. "What's the PS factor? And he's never been 'running late,' because we've never met up."

I'm breathing hard. *Seriously?*

"Look." I summon up the photos I took of Dan's secret phone and thrust them in front of her. "Remember these?"

Mary looks down, her forehead delicately wrinkled, then shakes her head. "I've never seen these texts in my life."

"What?" I'm almost shouting. "But they're to *Mary!* Look! *Mary!*"

"I don't care. They're not to me."

For a moment we just stare at each other. My mind is scrabbling around and around, trying to find an explanation. Then Mary grabs the phone. She flicks through the photos until she comes to a text from *Mary* reading, *New mobile no. from tomorrow,* followed by a string of digits.

"That's not my number," she says calmly. "Those aren't my texts. I'll show you my phone, if you like. You can read the texts Dan sent me, all three of them, and you'll *see* how innocent they are." She grabs an iPhone from where it's charging and swipes it open.

A moment later I'm looking at three texts from Dan, all beginning *Hi Mary* and all along the lines of *So great to make contact.* Mary's right. They're all innocent and even quite formal. Nothing like the intimate, casual ease of the other texts.

"I don't know who *this* is" — she jerks a thumb at the photos on my phone — "but you have the wrong woman."

"But . . ."

I sink into a chair, my legs trembling. I feel shoffed. I feel so shoffed, I'm breathless. Who's this other Mary? How many Marys does Dan *have* in his life? At last I glance up at Mary, who seems equally perplexed. She's swiping slowly through my photos, and I can see her grimacing.

"I can see why you're . . . alarmed," she says. "What are you going to do?"

"Don't know." I lift a helpless hand and drop it. "Dan went off somewhere last night. He said it was a work trip, but I don't believe him. Is he with *her*?"

"No," says Mary at once. "I can't believe it. He wouldn't do that. I think more likely —" She stops as though a thought has occurred to her, and I sit up, alert.

"What?" I demand. "What did he say to you? Did he confide in you?"

"Not exactly. He started to . . . but then

he stopped himself." Mary sighs. "I felt bad for him. He's really stressed out at the moment."

"I *know* he's stressed out!" I exclaim in frustration. "But he won't tell me why. I don't even know where to start. It's like there's some massive great secret. But how can I help him if I don't know what's going on?"

Mary is swiping through the photos again, reading the texts carefully. Her brow is furrowed and she seems troubled. She looks as though she's wrestling with a dilemma. She looks as though —

"Oh my God." I stare at her. "He *did* tell you something. Didn't he? What?"

Mary looks up and I can tell I've hit the mark. Her mouth is clamped shut. Her eyes are pained. Clearly he revealed something to her and she's protecting him because she's a good person and she thinks it's the right thing to do. But it's the *wrong* thing to do.

"Please, Mary." I lean forward, trying to convey the urgency of the situation. "I know you're his friend and you want to respect Dan's confidence. But maybe the best way to help him is to *break* his confidence. I'll never ever say it was you who told me," I add hurriedly. "And I'll do the same for you,

I promise."

I can't see how an equivalent situation will ever arise, but I mean it. If it does, I will *totally* reveal everything to Mary.

"He didn't tell me any details," says Mary reluctantly. "Not properly. But, yes, there is . . . something. He said it was clogging up his life. He called it his 'ongoing nightmare.' "

"His 'ongoing nightmare'?" I echo in dismay. Dan has an ongoing nightmare that I don't know about? But how can he? What is it? What hasn't he told me?

"That's the phrase he used. He didn't give any other details. Except . . ." She bites her soft pink lip, looking uncomfortable.

"What?" I'm nearly popping with frustration.

"OK." She exhales. "Whatever it is . . . it has to do with your mother."

"My mother?" I gape at her.

"I'd talk to her. Ask her. I got the feeling —" Again Mary stops herself. "Talk to her."

I can't face work. I text Clarissa, *Still researching, back later,* and head straight home. By the time I reach Wandsworth I've left Mummy three voicemails, texted, and sent her an email — entitled *We need to talk!!!* — but I haven't had a response. I'll go round there in person if I have to. Right now, though, I need some quiet time to digest what I've just heard. An "ongoing nightmare." How long has Dan been dealing with an ongoing nightmare?

It's something to do with my mother, Mary said. Is this the "million pounds, maybe two"? Oh God, what's going on, *what*?

And — worse — what if Mary's wrong? What if *I'm* the ongoing nightmare? The thought makes me feel cold and rather small inside. I'm remembering Dan's face last night. The way he said, "I can't do this," as though he was at the end of his tether.

Every time I remember last night, I cringe inside. I called him a *boring fucking cliché*. I assumed he was just following the same old tedious trope: Husband Hooks Up with Old Flame, Lies to Wife. But there's more. There's something else. As I'm walking, I pull out my phone, wanting to text him again, wanting to make it right. I even get as far as *Dear Dan . . .* but then I stop. What do I say? Phrases shoot into my mind but I instantly discard them, one by one.

Tell me who the other Mary is. Please don't shut me out anymore. I know you have an ongoing nightmare — what is it?

If he wanted to tell me, he would have

told me. Which brings me back to the question that fills me with foreboding: Am I his ongoing nightmare?

As I walk along our street, tears are running down my face, but when I see Toby, I hastily scrub them away. He's standing outside Tilda's house, clutching a pair of Rollerblades and a helmet.

"Hi, Toby!" I say. "I knew you'd be back."

"Getting my blades." He nods. "I forgot to take them." He dumps them in the boot of an open Corsa, which I don't recognize.

"Is that your car?" I say curiously, as he locks it.

"Michi's. Actually, I'd better tell her I took it." He perches on the garden wall, sending a text. The sun has come out, and when he's finished texting he leans back, savoring the warmth, seeming utterly unhurried.

"Don't you have a job?"

"I'll go in later. It's fine." He shrugs. "We normally work, like, noon to midnight?"

Midnight? I suddenly feel very ancient.

"Right. Well, make sure you see your mum while you're here. Is she around?"

"Yeah, she's making me spaghetti Bolognese." His face lights up and I can't help smiling. He must have made Tilda's day, coming home so soon. Either that, or they're yelling at each other again.

"D'you want to come for lunch?" he adds politely. "I'm sure we've got some spare."

"No, thanks." I try to smile. "I've got some stuff to . . . I'm . . . It's all a bit . . ." Without intending to, I sigh heavily and sit down next to him on the wall. "Do you ever feel like there's a conspiracy?"

I'm not really expecting an answer, but Toby nods gravely. "There is a conspiracy. I've told you, Sylvie, it's *all* a conspiracy."

The sun's getting hotter on our faces. He must be sweltering, with his beard. I get out my sunglasses and reach for my lip balm, and as I unbutton the pink case, Toby nods at it, as though that proves everything. "Big Pharma, Sylvie. You see?"

I don't respond. I'm gazing at the gold-embossed *PS*. I can't believe Dan used my private nickname in texts to another woman. I can't believe he referred to me as the "PS factor." The "Princess Sylvie factor." Just the idea of some other woman calling me that makes me cringe. It's almost the worst betrayal.

Who is she? Who *is* she?

"What would you do if you'd found a whole load of texts on a phone and you didn't know who they were to?" I say, staring up at the blue sky.

"Get the number off contacts," says Toby

427

with a shrug.

"A number doesn't tell you anything," I object.

"Google it, then. See if anything comes up."

I turn to stare at him. Google it? I never even thought of googling it.

"Mobile phone numbers aren't on Google," I say warily.

"Sometimes they are. Worth a try. Whose phone?" he asks with interest, and my defenses instantly rise.

"Oh, just a girl at work," I say. "Her cousin," I add for good measure. "Half cousin. It's not a big deal."

I could google the number. Suddenly I'm all jittery. I need to get to a computer *now.*

"Well, see you, Tobes," I say, getting to my feet. "Bring Michi over! We'd like to meet her."

"Sure. Bye, Sylvie."

I hurry into the house, fumbling with my key in my haste. It seems to take forever for my computer to fire up, and I actually start saying, "Come on, come *on,*" under my breath.

I type in the phone number from the text and wait breathlessly for the results, although if I was hoping for an instant answer, I was an idiot. There's a lot of garbage to wade through. Entries about car serial numbers and phone-directory pages without any actual information. But on page five, I see something that makes me lean forward.

St. Savior's School Rugby Club. Parent rep: Mary Smith-Sullivan.

It's her. The same mobile number. The same first name. Oh God, she exists. Can I find out anything else about her? Does she have a job, maybe?

My heart beating wildly, I look up Mary Smith-Sullivan on LinkedIn. And there she is. *Mary Smith-Sullivan, Partner, Avory Milton. Specialism: defamation, privacy, and other media-related litigation.* She looks to be in her early fifties, with close-cropped dark hair and a boxy jacket. Minimal makeup. She's smiling but not in a warm way, more in a businesslike "I have to smile for this photo" way.

This is who Dan is sending endless texts to?

He can't be having an affair with her. He can't. I mean . . .

He *can't.*

I stare at the page, trying and failing to make sense of it. Then at last, with a trembling hand, I reach for my phone and dial.

"Avory Milton, how can I help you?" a singsong voice greets me.

"I'd like to make an appointment with Ms. Smith-Sullivan," I say in a rush. "Today. As soon as possible, please."

Avory Milton is a medium-sized law firm, off Chancery Lane, with a reception area on the fourteenth floor. It has a big floor-to-ceiling window, showing off an impressive view over London, which made my legs nearly give way when I stepped out of the lift. People should *not* just put terrifying windows there like that.

But somehow I made it to the front desk and got my visitor's pass. And now I'm in the seating area, firmly turned away from the view.

As I sit there, pretending to read a magazine, I look around carefully. I study the slate-gray sofas and the people in suits striding through and even the water dispenser . . . but there aren't any clues. I have no idea what this place has to do with Dan. I am also unimpressed by their timekeeping. I've been sitting here for at least half an hour.

"Mrs. Tilda?"

My chest seizes up in apprehension as I see a woman approaching me. It's her. She has the same close-cropped hair that she did on LinkedIn. She's wearing a navy jacket and a blue striped shirt I recognize from Zara. Expensive shoes. A wedding ring.

"I'm Mary Smith-Sullivan." She smiles professionally and holds out a manicured hand. "Apologies for keeping you. How d'you do."

"Oh, hi." My voice catches, and I can only produce a squawk. "Hi," I try again, scrambling to my feet. "Yes. Thank you. How do you do."

My pseudonym is Mrs. Tilda. Which is not ideal, but I was so flustered as I made the appointment that I wasn't thinking straight. When the receptionist asked, "And the name?" I panicked and blurted out, "Tilda." Then I quickly amended, "Mrs. Tilda. Er . . . Mrs. Penelope Tilda."

Penelope Tilda? What was I thinking? No one's called Penelope Tilda. But I haven't been challenged yet. Although, as we walk along a neutral, pale-carpeted corridor, Mary Smith-Sullivan shoots me the odd appraising look. I didn't say why I wanted the appointment on the phone. I just kept saying it was "highly confidential" and "highly urgent," until the receptionist said, "Of course, Mrs. Tilda. I've booked you in for two-thirty P.M."

Mary Smith-Sullivan ushers me into a fairly large office — with, thankfully, quite a small window — and I sit down on a blue upholstered chair. There's a still, unbearable pause as she pours us each a glass of water.

"So." At last she faces me properly and gives one of those professional smiles again. "Mrs. Tilda. How can I help you?"

This is exactly what I predicted she'd say, and I have my line all ready to fling at her, just like a soap-opera heroine: *I want to know why my husband's been texting you, BITCH.*

(OK, not *bitch.* Not in real life.)

"Mrs. Tilda?" she prompts pleasantly.

"I want to know . . ." I break off and swallow. *Shit.* I promised myself I was going to be calm and steely, but my voice is already wobbling.

OK. Take a moment. No rush.

Actually, there is a rush. This woman probably costs a thousand pounds an hour and she'll bill me even if she is Dan's mistress. *Especially* then. And I haven't even thought about how I'll afford it. Shit. Why didn't I find out the fee? Quick, Sylvie, *talk.*

I take a deep breath, gathering my thoughts, and glance out of the window of her door. And what I see makes me nearly pass out.

It's Mummy.

She's wearing a pink suit and walking

quickly toward this room with a hugely fat guy in pinstripes, talking animatedly while he cocks his head to listen.

What the fuck is my mother doing here?

Already my legs are propelling me to the door of Mary Smith-Sullivan's office. I'm grabbing the handle like a demented person.

"Mummy?" I demand, my voice strident. *"Mummy?"*

Both Mummy and the fat pinstriped guy stop dead, and Mummy's face freezes in a rictus of dismay.

"So it *is* you," she says.

"It *is* me?" I look from her to the fat pinstriped guy. "What does that mean, 'It *is* me'? Of course it's me. Mummy, why are you here?"

"I'm the one who called your mother, Sylvie," says Mary Smith-Sullivan, behind me, and I swivel round to face her.

"You *know* me?"

"I thought it was you as soon as I saw you in reception. I've seen photos, and your hair's quite distinctive. Although, of course, the false name . . ." She shrugs. "But, still, I was sure it was you."

"Darling, why are you here?" demands Mummy, almost accusingly. "What brought you here?"

"Because . . ." I stare at her, bewildered,

433

then turn back to Mary Smith-Sullivan. "I want to know why my husband's been texting you."

Finally I've managed to get my line out. But it's lost its sting. Everything has lost its meaning. I feel as though I've walked into a stage play and I don't know my part.

"Yes, I expect you do," says Mary, and she regards me with a kind of pity. The same kind of pity Dan had. "I always *said* you should know, but —"

"Mrs. Winter." The fat pinstriped guy speaks in a booming voice as he approaches me. "I do apologize; let me introduce myself. I'm Roderick Rice, and I've been dealing with this issue, along with Mary, of course —"

"What issue?" I feel as though I might scream. Or kill someone. *"What bloody issue?"* I look from Mary Smith-Sullivan to Roderick to Mummy, who is hovering outside the office door, with one of her evasive Mummy looks. "What is it? *What?*"

I can see eyes meeting, silent consultations flying around.

"Is anyone in touch with Dan?" Mary says to Roderick at length.

"He's gone to Devon. To see what he can do down there. I tried him earlier, but . . ." Roderick shrugs. "No signal, probably."

Devon? Why's Dan gone to Devon? But Mary nods as though this makes total sense.

"Just thinking of the PS factor," she says quietly.

The PS factor. Again. I can't bear it.

"Please don't call me that!" My voice explodes out of me like a rocket. "I'm *not* a princess; I'm *not* Princess Sylvie; I wish Dan had never *given* me that stupid nickname."

Both lawyers turn to survey me in what seems like genuine surprise.

"PS doesn't stand for 'Princess Sylvie,' " says Mary Smith-Sullivan at last. "Not in this office."

"But . . ." I stare at her, taken aback. "Then what . . ."

There's silence. And once again she gives me that odd, pitying look, as though she knows far more about me than I do.

"Protect Sylvie," she says. "It stands for 'Protect Sylvie.' "

For an instant, I can't speak. My mouth won't work. *Protect* me?

"From what?" I manage at last and turn to Mummy, who's still standing at the doorway. "Mummy?"

"Oh, darling." She starts blinking furiously. "It's been so difficult to know what to do. . . ."

"Your husband loves you very much," says

Mary Smith-Sullivan. "And I think he's been acting for all the right reasons. But —" She breaks off and looks at Roderick, then at Mummy. "This is ridiculous. She's got to know."

We sit in Mary's little seating area with cups of tea in proper cups and saucers, brought in by an assistant. I cradle mine in my hands, not drinking it, just gripping it tightly. It's something tangible. It's something real. When nothing else in my life seems to be.

"Let me give you the bare facts," says Mary, in her measured way, when at last the assistant leaves. "It has been alleged that your father had an affair, many years ago, with a sixteen-year-old girl."

I look back at her silently. I don't know what I was expecting. Not this.

Daddy? A sixteen-year-old girl?

I glance at Mummy, who is staring at a distant corner of the room.

"Is it . . . true?" I manage.

"Of course it's not true," snaps Mummy. "The whole thing is falsehood. Wretched, evil falsehood." She starts to blink furiously again. "When I *think* of your father . . ."

"The girl in question, who is now an adult," continues Mary impassively, "threatened to expose this affair in a book. This was . . . prevented."

"What book?" I say, confused. "A book about my father?"

"Not exactly, no. Have you heard of a writer called Joss Burton?"

Through the High Maze. I stare at her. "I've read it. She had a really hard time before her success. She had an eating disorder; she had to drop out of university. . . ." I swallow, feeling ill. "Did Daddy . . . *No.*"

"It's all lies," says Mummy tearfully. "It was all in her head. She became fixated by your father because he was so handsome."

"An early draft contained an account of her alleged affair with your father and its effect upon her," Mary resumes. "Obviously, at sixteen she wasn't underage; nevertheless, it's . . ." She hesitates. "Not particularly easy reading."

Not particularly easy reading. My mind registers this phrase and then veers away from it. There's only so much I can deal with at one time.

"Your father became aware of the book and engaged our firm. We applied for an injunction on his behalf, although in the event, the author was persuaded to excise the relevant passages."

"Persuaded?"

"Dan was very helpful," says Mummy, wiping her nose.

"Dan?" I look from face to face.

"Your father wished to keep the matter within the family, so he enlisted Dan's help." There's something about Mary's tone that makes me look sharply at her. "I would say that Dan worked above and beyond for your father," she says. "He became our contact. He read every document. He attended every meeting with Joss Burton and her lawyers and managed to turn what were . . . fairly difficult discussions . . . into something more constructive. As your mother says, it was his personal intervention which, in the end, persuaded Joss Burton to retract the relevant passages."

"Dan was pleased to help," says Mummy defensively. "Only too pleased to help."

My head is spinning like a kaleidoscope. Daddy. Dan. Joss Burton. That book, lying in Mummy's kitchen. Dan's tension. All the whispers, all the huddling . . . I knew there was something, I knew it. . . .

"Why didn't you tell me? Why didn't anyone *tell* me?" My voice bursts forth in a roar. "Why am I the only person sitting here who doesn't know any of this?"

"Darling," says Mummy hastily. "Daddy

was appalled by this . . . this vicious slander. He didn't want you hearing salacious invented stories. We decided to keep the whole matter under wraps."

"And then, just as things were settled, your father died," puts in Roderick, in a ponderous, heavy way. "And everything changed again."

"You were so fragile, Sylvie." Mummy reaches out a hand and squeezes mine. "You were so devastated. We *couldn't* tell you. Any of us. Besides which, we thought the whole thing was over." She starts blinking again.

"And isn't it? No," I answer myself, thinking aloud. "Of course it's not — otherwise, why are you here?" I stare around at the faces again, thoughts springing up in my brain so fast, I can barely get them out. "Why's Dan in Devon? What's the 'one million, maybe two'?" I round on Mummy. "Is that to do with this? What's been happening?"

"Oh, sweetheart," says Mummy vaguely, her eyes swiveling away, and I quell a sharp response. She's *so frustrating.*

"Joss Burton has written another memoir," says Mary. "A 'prequel,' describing her earlier life. She is adamant that this time she will describe her alleged relationship with your father. Apparently it is 'key' to her story. It's due to be published in a year's time, when the film of *Through the High Maze* comes out."

"A film," says Mummy in distaste. "Who wants to watch a film about her?"

I bite back the retort, "Who wants to watch a story about a woman who overcame her demons to become a massive global businesswoman? Oh, no one, I should think."

"The new book will be very high profile," continues Mary. "Serialized in a national newspaper, no doubt. And your father's name with it."

"Her advance is a million," puts in Roderick. "Although of course she says it's not about the money, it's about the truth."

"The truth!" says Mummy, a vicious edge to her voice. "If this book is published, if your father is remembered for *that* . . . after all his charity work . . ." Her voice rises shrilly. "It's wicked! And, anyway, how could she remember after all these years?"

"So, why is Dan in Devon?" I'm looking from face to face. "I still don't understand —"

"He's talking to Joss Burton again," says Mummy, dabbing at her nose with a tiny lace handkerchief. "She lives in Devon."

"He went down on the sleeper train last

night." Mary gives me a kind look. "I think one of the biggest strains for Dan in all of this has been keeping the truth from you."

The sleeper train. I thought he was with his lover. When all the time . . .

My throat is suddenly clogged as I picture Dan getting on a train, all alone. Shouldering this, all alone. I stare into my tea, my eyes getting hot, trying to stay composed.

"He never breathed a word," I say at last. "Not a word."

"His biggest concern, all along, has been that you might find out and 'not cope,' as he put it," says Mary.

"Have another . . . episode," puts in Roderick tactfully.

"It wasn't an episode!" My voice rockets out, and I see Roderick exchanging startled looks with Mummy. "It wasn't an episode or a breakdown or whatever everyone said," I say more calmly. "It was grief. Just that. Yes, I was devastated. But just because I found Daddy's death hard to process . . . it doesn't mean I was *unstable.* Dan worried about me too much. He was overprotective. Far too overprotective."

"We were all worried, darling!" says Mummy defensively.

"You were worried I might embarrass you," I snap, and turn to Mary, who I sense

441

is the most receptive to what I'm saying. "Dan had the best possible motives, and I don't blame him — but he got it wrong. I could have coped and he should have told me. You all should have told me." I put my cup down on the coffee table with a bang. "So now I want to know. Everything."

I meet Mary's eyes, and I can see her taking the measure of me. At last she nods.

"Very well. I'll give you access to all the files. You'll have to look at them here, in the office, but I can give you a room to sit in."

"Thank you," I match her businesslike tone.

"Sylvie, darling." Mummy makes an anguished face. "I really wouldn't. You really don't need to know —"

"I do!" I cut her off furiously. "I've been living in a bubble. Well, now I'm stepping out of it. I don't need protecting. I don't need shielding. 'Protect Sylvie' is over." I shoot a savage look around the room. *"Over."*

I sit alone, reading and reading. My eyes blur over. My head starts to hurt. An assistant brings me three more cups of tea, but they all sit going cold, undrunk, because I'm too wrapped up in what I'm seeing, what I'm understanding. My head is a whirl. How can all this have been happening and I had no idea? What kind of blind, oblivious moron have I been?

Joss Burton used to go on holiday to Los Bosques Antiguos. That's where she apparently met Daddy. None of this is in doubt. Her family genuinely did have a house there, very close to ours. Her parents did socialize with Mummy and Daddy. I don't remember them, but, then again, I was only three or four at the time.

Then there's all the stuff she alleges: stuff about Daddy giving her presents, plying her with cocktails, leading her into the woods . . . and I couldn't bring myself to read that properly. Just the *idea* of it made me feel ill. I skimmed only a few pages, taking in phrases here and there, and felt even more sickened. My father? With a naïve, inexperienced teenage girl, who'd never even . . .

Mary Smith-Sullivan was right. It's not particularly easy reading.

So I hastened on to the emails, the present-day correspondence, the actual case. There are hundreds of emails in the files. Thousands, even. Daddy to Dan, Dan back to Daddy, Roderick to both of them, Dan to Mary, Mary back to Dan . . . And the more I read, the more shocked I am. Daddy's emails are so abrupt. Demanding.

Entitled. Dan is resolutely polite, resolutely charming, but Daddy . . . Daddy pushes him around. He expects Dan to drop everything. He swears at him when things go wrong. He's a bully.

I can't believe I'm having these thoughts about my father. My charming, twinkly father — a *bully*? I mean, yes, he sometimes lost it with his staff . . . but never with his family.

Surely?

I keep reading, hoping desperately to discover the email where he's appreciative. Where he thanks Dan for all his efforts. Where he gushes. He was a charming person. Where's the charm here?

After 258 emails, I haven't yet found it, and my stomach is heavy. Everything makes horrible sense. This is why Dan's relationship with Daddy deteriorated. Because Daddy dragged him into his problems and made them his and treated him like mud.

No wonder Dan talked about an "ongoing nightmare." Daddy was the nightmare.

At last I raise my head, my cheeks flaming. I'm churned up. I want to wade in. I want to confront Daddy. I want to have it out. Phrases are flying around my head: *How could you? Apologize! You can't speak to Dan like that! That's my husband!*

444

But Daddy's dead. He's dead. It's too late. I can't confront him; I can't talk to him; I can't demand to know why he behaved like that, or have it out, or make it right. It's all too late, far too late.

And guilt is rising in me, making my face still warmer. Because I didn't help Dan, did I? All along I blanked out Daddy's flaws, I glorified him, I made it impossible for Dan ever to speak the truth. And *that* was the chasm.

"Are you OK?"

I jump, shocked, at Mary's voice, and abruptly realize I'm rocking back and forth in my chair, my jaw jutting out as though for a fight.

"Fine!" I hastily sit upright. "Fine. It's . . . quite heavy stuff."

"Yes." She gives me a sympathetic look. "Probably a bit much to try to digest it all."

"I need to go, anyway." I glance at my watch. "School-pickup time."

"Ah." She nods. "Well, come back anytime you'd like. Ask me anything you'd like to know."

"Have you heard from Dan?" The question spills out before I can stop it.

"No." She gives me a neutral look. "I'm sure he's doing everything he can."

I have about ten thousand questions I

445

want to bombard her with, but as we walk to the lifts, two are circling high above the rest.

"My father," I say, as I press the lift button.

"Yes?"

"Did he . . . Is it . . . You don't think . . ." I can't say it out loud. But Mary understands exactly.

"Your father always maintained that Jocelyn Burton has a fertile imagination and the affair was entirely fictitious," she says. "Her full account is all there in the files for you to read. Thousands of words. Very descriptive. However, you may feel that it's not helpful for you."

"Right," I say. "Well . . . maybe." I watch the lift indicator changing — 26, 25, 24 — then draw breath. "My father," I say again.

"Yes?"

I bite my lip. I don't know what I want to ask, exactly.

"I've been reading the emails between Dan and my father." I try again. "And . . ."

"Yes." Mary meets my eye and I have a feeling that, again, she knows exactly what I'm driving at. "Dan is very patient. Very smart. I hope your father knew how much he did for him."

"But he didn't, though, did he?" I say

bluntly. "I've seen it in those emails. Daddy was awful to him. I can't believe Dan stuck it out." Tears suddenly spring to my eyes as I think of Dan, uncomplainingly dealing with Daddy's charmless missives. Never telling me a word. "I mean, why would he? Why *would* he?"

"Oh, Sylvie." Mary shakes her head with an odd little laugh. "If you don't know —" She breaks off, surveying me with such a wry gaze I almost feel uncomfortable. "You know, I've been intrigued to meet you all this time. To meet Dan's Sylvie."

"Dan's Sylvie?" A painful laugh rises through me. "I don't feel like Dan's Sylvie right now. If I were him I would have left me ages ago."

The doors open, and as I get in, Mary holds out her hand.

"Very nice to meet you at last, Sylvie," she says. "Please don't worry about this second book. I'm sure it will all be resolved. And if there's any more information I can give you about Joss, or Lynn . . ."

"What?" I stare at her, puzzled. "What do you mean, Lynn?"

"Oh, sorry. I know it's confusing." Mary raises her eyes ruefully. "Jocelyn is her full name, but she was known as Lynn as a

teenager. For legal purposes, obviously, we
—"

"Wait." My hand jams the HOLD button
before I'm even aware I'm reacting. "Lynn?
Are you telling me . . . she was called *Lynn*?"

"Well, we generally refer to her as Joss,
obviously." Mary seems puzzled by my reaction. "But she was Lynn then. I thought
you might remember her, in fact. In her account, she certainly mentions you. She used
to play with you. Sing songs with you.
'Kumbaya,' that kind of thing." Mary's face
changes. "Sylvie? Are you all right?"

I've been living inside a bubble inside a
bubble. I feel surreal. As I stride along
Lower Sloane Street, the same phrase keeps
running through my head: *What's real?
What's real?*

When I finally left the Avory Milton offices, I tried Dan's phone about five times.
But he wasn't picking up, or didn't have
signal, or something. So at last I left a
desperate, frantic voicemail: "Dan, I've just
found out, I can't believe it, I had no idea,
I'm so sorry, I got it all wrong. Dan, we
need to talk, Dan, please ring me, I'm so,
so sorry . . ." and kept on in that vein until
the beep went.

Now I'm heading to Mummy's flat. I'm in

a bit of a state and should probably pause for a calming drink of something — but I'm not going to. I have to see her. I have to have this out. I've already phoned up the school and put the girls into after-school club. (They're pretty good about last-minute phone calls from frazzled London working parents.)

I let myself into Mummy's flat with my latchkey, stalk into the drawing room with no greeting, and say in unforgiving tones, "You lied."

Mummy jumps and looks round from where she was sitting, staring into space, a cushion clutched to her chest. She seems suddenly small and vulnerable against the vast expanse of the sofa, but I thrust that thought from my mind.

"Lynn," I say, my eyes searing into hers. "Lynn, Mummy. *Lynn.*"

To her credit, she doesn't say, "What do you mean, Lynn?" She gazes past me as though she's looking at a ghost, her face slowly creasing up in anxiety.

"Lynn!" I practically yell. "You told me she was imaginary! You screwed me up! She was real! She was *real!*"

"Oh, darling." Mummy's hand nervously crushes the fabric of her jacket.

"Why would you *do* that?" My voice is

perilously close to a wail, a childlike wail. "Why would you make me feel so terrible? You wouldn't let me talk about her, you made me feel so guilty . . . and all the time you knew she was real! It's sick! It's messed up!"

As I'm talking, an image flashes into my head of Tessa and Anna. My gorgeous girls with their precious thoughts and dreams and ideas. The idea of messing with them, altering them, making them feel bad about *anything* . . . is just anathema.

Mummy isn't answering. I stalk round to the front of the sofa so that I'm facing her, breathing hard.

"Why? *Why?*"

"You were so small," says Mummy at last.

"Small? What's that got to do with it?"

"We thought it would make things simpler."

"Why simpler?" I stare at her. "What do you mean, simpler?"

"Because we had to leave so hurriedly. Because . . ."

"Why did we have to leave so hurriedly?"

"Because that girl was making . . . *accusations*!" Mummy's voice is suddenly raw and harsh and her face takes on the ugliest expression I've ever seen, a kind of contorted disgust, which chills me to my heart.

The next moment it's disappeared. But I saw it. I can't unsee it. I can't unhear that voice.

Our life was so glittery. I could never see anything but the gloss, the fun, the luxury. My handsome father and beautiful mother. My charmed, enviable family. But now I'm seeing hectoring emails. Lying parents. An ugliness lurking underneath everything.

"Is there any . . ." I swallow hard. "Is there any . . . truth in what she says?"

"Of course not." Mummy's voice is harsh again, making me flinch. "Of course not. Of *course* not."

"So why . . ."

"We had to leave Los Bosques Antiguos." Mummy turns her head away, staring at the corner of the room. "It was all so unpleasant. Unbearable. The girl told her parents her story, and obviously they believed her lurid tale. Well, you can imagine how they reacted. And they spread such vicious rumors among our friends. We couldn't have that kind of . . . We had to leave."

"So you sold the house."

"I expect we would have sold anyway."

"And you told me Lynn was imaginary. You messed around with the mind of a four-year-old." My voice is pitiless.

"You kept *asking* about her, Sylvie."

451

Mummy has developed a twitch in her left eye, and she smooths it away repeatedly. "Always asking, 'Where's Lynn?' Singing that wretched song."

" 'Kumbaya,' " I say quietly.

"It drove your father mad. It drove both of us mad. How could we put everything behind us? It was your father's idea to tell you she was imaginary. And I thought, what would it matter? Real . . . imaginary . . . you were never going to see her again. It was a harmless white lie."

"A *harmless white lie*?"

I feel incandescent with rage. I'm replaying a million moments from my childhood. I'm remembering Daddy's bristling, silent fury whenever Lynn came up. Mummy hastily glossing over the moment and changing the subject. But, then, that's been her life, hasn't it? Glossing over the moment.

There's silence in the room. I can't stay, but I can't bring myself to move either. For some reason I'm fixating on Mummy's sofa. It's large and cream, with fringing and lots of bespoke cushions in pink velvet and damask and linen prints. It's beautiful. And she looks so blond and pretty, sitting there in her pink suit. The whole picture is adorable. On the surface.

And that's what Mummy has always been

to me, I realize. Surface, all surface. Shine and reflection. Bright smiles, designed to deflect. The pair of us have echoed the same lines to each other over the years, never pausing or examining them. *Lovely skirt. Delicious wine. Daddy was a hero.* When did we last have a deep, empathetic conversation that actually *went* somewhere?

Never.

"What about Dan?" I say flatly.

"Dan?" Mummy crinkles her brow as though perhaps she's forgotten who Dan is, and I feel another flare of anger at her.

"Dan who's been working his socks off for you. Dan who's in Devon right now, trying to protect Daddy's name. Again. Dan who is the hero in all this, but you treat him like . . . like . . ." I flounder. "Like . . . a joke."

As I say the word, I realize it's exactly right. Mummy has never taken Dan seriously. Never respected him. She's been polite and charming and everything else, but there's always been that slight curve to her mouth. That slight pitying air. *Poor Dan.*

"Darling, don't be ridiculous," says Mummy crisply. "We all feel for poor Dan."

I don't believe it. She's doing it again.

"Don't call him 'poor Dan'!" I snap. "You're so patronizing!"

"Sylvie, darling, calm down."

"I'll calm down when you treat my husband with respect! You're as bad as Daddy. I saw his emails to Dan, and they were rude. *Rude.* All this time, we've been behaving as though Daddy's the saint. Daddy's the star. Well, Dan's the star! He's the star, and he hasn't had any recognition, any thanks. . . ."

Anger is spilling out, but it's anger at myself too. I feel hot all over with self-reproach, mortification. I'm remembering the number of times I defended Daddy to Dan. The assumptions I made. The unforgivable things I said.

You can't stand that Daddy was rich and successful. . . . You're so bloody chippy, and I'm sick of it. . . .

I called Dan, who patiently put up with all that shit, *chippy.*

I can't bear it. I can't bear myself. No wonder he got all tentery. No wonder he felt pinned in a corner. No wonder he couldn't stand us watching the wedding DVD, wallowing in the Daddy Show.

Shame keeps crawling over me. I thought I was so clever. I thought I was psychic Sylvie. I knew *nothing.*

And even now Mummy won't see it. She won't acknowledge any of it. I can tell it from her distant gaze. She's reordering events in her mind to suit herself, like some algorithm, placing Daddy and herself in the center and everyone else just floats to the sides.

"You sat here in this very room," I continue, "and you said Dan's 'hardly the life and soul, is he?' Well, he *is* the life and soul." My voice gives a sudden wobble. "He's the genuine life and soul. Not flashing around, not showing off . . . but being there for his family. You've underestimated him. I've underestimated him." Tears prick my eyes. "And I can't believe how Daddy just took him for granted. Swore at him. Treated him like —"

"Sylvie, enough of this!" snaps Mummy, cutting me off. "You're overreacting. Dan is very lucky to have married into this family, very lucky indeed."

"What?" I stare at her, not sure I heard that right. *"What?"*

"Your father was a wonderful, generous, remarkable man. Think what he achieved. He would be distraught to hear you talking of him this way!"

"Well, too bad!" I explode. "And what do you mean, Dan's lucky? He hasn't touched a penny of my family money, he's provided for me and the girls, he's put up with watching that bloody wedding DVD every time we come here, watching Daddy steal the show. . . . *Lucky?* You and Daddy were lucky to gain such a fantastic son-in-law! Did you ever think of that?"

I break off, panting. I'm starting to lose control of myself. I don't know what I'm going to say next. But I don't care.

"Don't speak about your father like that!" Mummy's voice rockets shrilly through the room. "Do you know how much he loved you? Do you know how proud he was of you?"

"If he'd loved me, he would have respected the man I love! He would have treated Dan like a proper family member, not like some . . . underling! He wouldn't have lied about my imaginary friend because it was convenient for him!" I stare at Mummy, my breath suddenly caught, my thoughts assembling themselves into a pattern which makes horrible sense. "I'm not even sure he loved me as a person in my own right. He loved me as a reflection of him. As part of the Marcus Lowe Show. The princess to his king. But I'm me. I'm *Sylvie.*"

As I speak, I glance into one of Mummy's gilt-framed mirrors and see my reflection. My waist-long blond hair, as girlish and wavy and princess-like as ever. It was Daddy who loved my hair. Daddy who stopped me cutting it.

Do I even like long hair?

Does long hair even *suit* me?

For a few moments I just stare at myself, barely breathing. Then, feeling heady and unreal, I walk to Mummy's writing desk and reach for the handmade scissors I bought her for Christmas one year. I grab my hair with one hand and start to cut.

I've never felt so empowered in my life. In my *life*.

"Sylvie." Mummy inhales in horror. "Sylvie. *Sylvie!*" Her voice rises to a hysterical shriek. "What are you *doing*?"

I pause, my hand mid-snip, a length of blond hair already on the floor. I look at it dispassionately, then raise my head to meet her eyes. "I'm growing up."

Sixteen

I get through the rest of the day on autopilot. I pick the girls up from after-school
club and try to laugh off their dismayed
exclamations:

"Mummy, what's happened to your *hair*?"

"Where's your *hair* gone?"

"When will you put it back?" (Anna,
blinking anxiously at me.) "Will you put it
back now, Mummy? Now?"

And my first instinct is somehow to protect them. Soften the blow. I even find
myself thinking, *Should I buy a long blond
wig?* Until reality hits me. I can't protect
the girls forever, and I shouldn't. Stuff will
happen in their lives that they don't like.
Shit happens. And they will have to cope.
We all have to cope.

We eat supper and I put them to bed and
then just sit on my bed — our bed — staring at the wall, until the events of the last
few days overcome me like a wave over my

head and I succumb to crying. Deep, heaving sobbing, my head buried in a pillow, as though I'm grieving all over again.

And I suppose I am grieving, in a way. But for what? For my lost real/imaginary friend, Lynn? For the heroic father I thought I knew? For Dan? For our battered marriage? For the Sylvie I used to be, so blithe and innocent, tripping about the world with no bloody idea about anything?

My thoughts keep veering toward Daddy and Lynn and that whole issue . . . fabrication . . . whatever it was . . . but then I mentally jump away. I can't deal with thinking about it. The whole thing is just surreal. Surreal.

And what I really care about — what I'm really fixating on, like a crazy obsessed person — is Dan. As evening turns into night and I finally get into bed, I can't sleep. I'm staring up at the ceiling, words and phrases churning round my brain. *I'm so sorry . . . I didn't understand . . . You should have told me . . . If I'd known . . . If I'd only known . . .*

He hasn't replied to my voicemail. He hasn't been in touch at all. I don't blame him.

By morning I've dozed for a couple of hours and my face is deathly pale, but I get up as soon as the alarm goes, feeling wired. As I'm getting dressed for work, I automatically reach for one of my Mrs. Kendrick–friendly sprigged dresses. Then I pause, my mind working hard. I push all my dresses aside and reach for a black suit with slim trousers and a well-cut jacket. I haven't worn it for years. It's very much not a Mrs. Kendrick sort of outfit. Which is exactly what I want.

My head has clarified overnight. I can see everything differently in the pale morning light. Not just Dan and me . . . and our marriage . . . and Daddy . . . but work. Who I am. What I've been doing.

And it needs changing. No more ladylike steps. No more convention. No more caution. I need to stride. I need to *grab* life. I need to make up for lost time.

I drop the girls at school and nod, smiling tightly, as everyone gasps over my new chopped hair. Parents, teachers — even Miss Blake, the headmistress, as she passes by — all of them blench in shock, then rearrange their faces hastily as they greet me. The truth is, it does look quite brutal. Even I was shocked anew when I saw myself in the mirror this morning — I've never had cropped hair before in my *life.* I say pleasantly, "Yes, I fancied a change," and "It needs a bit of tidying up," about six hundred times — and then escape.

I must book a proper haircut. I will do. But I have other things to do first.

As I arrive at Willoughby House, Clarissa's jaw drops in horror.

"Your hair, Sylvie!" she exclaims. "Your *hair*!"

"Yes." I nod. "My hair. I cut it off."

"Right. Gosh." She swallows. "It looks . . . lovely!"

"You don't have to lie." I smile, touched by her efforts. "It doesn't look lovely. But it looks right. For me."

Clarissa clearly has no idea what I mean — but, then, why should she?

"Robert was wondering what you were up to yesterday," she says, eyeing me warily. "In fact, we were all wondering."

"I was cutting my hair off," I say, and head to the computer desk. The Books are stacked neatly in a pile and I grab them. They go back twelve years. That should be enough. Surely?

"What are you doing?" Clarissa is watching me curiously.

"It's time for somebody to take action," I say. "It's time for one of us to *do* something." I swivel to face her. "Not just safe little actions — but big actions. Risky ac-

461

tions. Things we should have done a long time ago."

"Right," says Clarissa, looking taken aback. "Yes. Absolutely."

"I'll be back later." I put the Books carefully into a tote bag. "Wish me luck."

"Good luck," echoes Clarissa obediently. "You look very *businesslike,*" she adds suddenly, peering at me as though this is a new and alien idea. "That trouser suit. And the hair."

"Yes, well." I give her a wry smile. "It's about time."

I arrive at the Wilson-Cross Foundation with twenty minutes to spare. It's an office in a white stucco house in Mayfair and has a staff of about twenty people. I have no idea what they all do — apart from having coffee with idiots like me at Claridge's — but I don't care. It's not their staff I'm interested in. It's their money.

The trustees' meeting begins at eleven o'clock, as I know from consulting the diary of events that Susie Jackson sent me at the beginning of the year. I've heard her describe trustees' meetings many times, over coffee, and she's quite funny about them. The way the trustees won't get down to business but keep chatting about schools and holidays. The way they misread figures but then pretend they haven't. The way they'll make a decision about a million pounds in a heartbeat — but then argue for half an hour about some tiny grant of five hundred pounds and whether it "fulfills the brief of the foundation." The way they gang up on one another. The trustees of the Wilson-Cross Foundation are very grand and important people — I've seen the list, and it's all Sir This and Dame That — but apparently they can behave like little children.

So, I know all this. I also know that today the trustees are making grants of up to five million pounds. And that they'll be listening to recommendations, including from Susie Jackson herself.

And what I know, above all, is that she owes us.

I've told the girl at the front desk that I have an appointment, and as Susie comes into the reception area, holding a thick white folder, she looks confused.

"Sylvie! Hi! Your *hair.*" Her eyes widen in revulsion, and I mentally allot her a 2 out of 10 in the Tactful Response category. (A 10 out of 10 goes to the girls' headmistress, Miss Blake, who caught sight of me and was clearly shocked but almost instantly said,

"Mrs. Winter, what dramatic hair you have today, most inspiring.")

"Yes. My hair. Whatever."

"Did we have an appointment?" Susie's brow furrows as she consults her phone. "I don't *think* we did. Oh, I'm sorry I haven't replied to your email yet —"

"Don't worry about the email." I cut her off. "And, no, we didn't have an appointment. I just want to borrow you quickly and ask how much of a grant you're planning to give Willoughby House today."

"I'm sorry?" Susie looks perplexed.

"It was so great to see you at Claridge's for our meeting, and I do hope you enjoyed your *cake*," I say meaningfully, and a pink tinge comes over her face.

"Oh. Yes." She addresses the floor. "Thank you."

"I do believe in quid pro quo, don't you?" I add sweetly. "Cashing in favors. Payback."

"Look, Sylvie, this isn't a good time," begins Susie, but I press on.

"And what I've realized is, we've been waiting *quite a long time* for our payback." I reach into my bag and pull out the Books. I marked them up with sticky notes before I came here, and I now flick to an old entry written in faded fountain pen. "We first had a meeting with one of your predecessors eleven years ago. *Eleven years ago.* She was called Marian, and she said that Willoughby House was exactly the sort of cause you should be supporting but unfortunately the time wasn't quite right. She said that for three years." I flick to another of the Books. "Then Fiona took over from Marian. Look, on May twelfth, 2011, Mrs. Kendrick treated her to lunch at the Savoy." I run a finger down the relevant handwritten entry. "They had three courses and wine, and Fiona promised that the foundation would support us. But, of course, it never happened. And then you took over from Fiona and I've had, what, eight meetings with you? You've been treated to coffee, cakes, parties, and receptions. We apply every year for a grant. And not a penny."

"Right," says Susie, her manner becoming more formal. "Well. As you know, we have many demands upon us, and we treat each application with great care —"

"Don't give me the bloody spiel!" I say impatiently. "Why have you donated constantly to the V&A, the Wallace Collection, Handel House, the Museum Van Loon in Amsterdam . . . and never Willoughby House?"

I've done my homework, and I can see I've hit home. But instantly Susie rallies.

"Sylvie," she says, a little pompously. "If you think there's some kind of vendetta against Willoughby House —"

"No. I don't think that," I cut her off. "But I think we've been too polite and unassuming. We're as deserving as any other museum, and we're about to go bust."

I can feel my inner Mrs. Kendrick wincing at that word, *bust.* But the time has come to be blunt. Blunt hair, blunt talk.

"Bust?" Susie stares at me, looking genuinely shocked. "How can you be going bust? I thought you were rolling in it! Didn't you have some huge private donation?"

"Long gone. We're about to be sold off to be condos."

"Oh my God." She seems aghast. *"Condos?* I didn't — I thought — We all thought —"

"Well. So did we." I shrug.

There's a long silence. Susie seems truly chastened. She looks at the folder in her hand, then up at me, her face troubled.

"There's nothing I can do today. All the budgets are worked out. The recommendations have been made. Everything's been planned out to the last penny."

"But it hasn't been agreed upon." I gesture at her white folder. "These are just recommendations. You could unplan. Un-

466

recommend."

"No, I couldn't!"

"You could make an amendment. An extra proposal."

"It's too late." She's shaking her head. "It's too late."

"The meeting hasn't begun yet!" I suddenly flip out. "How can it be too late? All you need to do is walk in there and say, 'Hey, trustees, guess what, I've just heard some terrible news about Willoughby House going bust and I think we've somewhat overlooked them, so let's make a donation, hands up, who agrees?' "

I can see this idea lodging in Susie's brain, although she still looks resistant.

"That would be the right thing to do," I say for emphasis. "And you know it. Here's a document with some useful information." I hand her a sheet with a few bullet points about Willoughby House written neatly on it. "I'm going to leave this with you, Susie, and wait to hear from you, because I trust you. Have a good meeting."

Somehow I force myself to turn and leave, even though there are hundreds more arguments I could make. Less is more, and if I stay, I'll only launch into some rant, which will piss Susie off.

Besides, I'm on a mission today. That was

only part one. Now on to parts two, three, and four.

By five o'clock I'm exhausted. But I'm on a roll too. In all the time I've worked for Willoughby House, I've never put myself out like I have today. I've never pitched so much, or cajoled so much, or talked so passionately to so many people. And now I'm wondering: What have I been *doing* all this time?

I feel like I've been sleepwalking for years. Doing everything according to Mrs. Kendrick's Way. Even in these last few weeks, even knowing we were under threat, I didn't strike out boldly enough. I didn't *challenge* anything; I didn't *change* anything.

Well, today I have. Today it's been Sylvie's Way. And Sylvie's Way is quite different, it turns out.

I've never called the shots here before. But today I've summoned Mrs. Kendrick and Robert for a meeting and I've stipulated the time and place and I've drawn up the agenda and basically I'm in charge. I'm on it. I've been steely and focused all day.

OK, not "all day." It would be more truthful to say I've been steely and focused "in patches." Sometimes I've been concentrating on Willoughby House. And sometimes

I've been checking my phone five hundred times to see if Dan has texted, and trying his number another five hundred times, and imagining what he must think of me, and imagining worst-case scenarios while my eyes fill with tears.

But I can't afford tears now. So I've somehow put Dan from my mind. As I walk into the library, my chin is firm and my gaze is stern, and I can tell from the expressions of Mrs. Kendrick and Robert that they're both shocked at my appearance.

"Sylvie!" Mrs. Kendrick gasps in horror. "Your —"

"I know," I preempt her. "My hair."

"Looks good," says Robert, and I shoot him a suspicious glance, but his face is impassive. Without any further niceties, I get out my scribbled notes and take up a position by the fireplace.

"I've brought you both here," I say, "to discuss the future. Willoughby House is a valuable, uniquely educational museum, full of potential. Full of assets. Full of capability." I put my notes down and look each of them in the eye. "We need to realize that capability, tap into that potential, and monetize those assets." *Monetize* is so *not* a Mrs. Kendrick word that I repeat it for emphasis: "We need to monetize our assets if we're to survive."

"Hear, hear," says Robert firmly, and I shoot him a brief, grateful smile.

"I have a number of ideas, which I would like to run past you," I continue. "First: The basement has been criminally overlooked. I suggest an *Upstairs Downstairs* exhibition, tapping into the fascination that people have with how the different classes used to live and work. Second: In the kitchen is an old housemaid's diary, itemizing her day. I rang up two publishers today, and both expressed interest in publishing the diary. This could link in with the exhibition. Perhaps we find the diary of her employer of the time and publish the two together?"

"That's inspired!" exclaims Robert, but I carry on without pausing.

"Third: We need to get more schools in and develop the educational side. Fourth: We need to get this whole place online. Fifth: We rent it out as a party venue."

"A party venue?" Mrs. Kendrick's face drops.

"Sixth: We hire it out as a movie set."

"Yes." Robert nods. *"Yes."*

"Seventh: We put on the erotica exhibit and make a media splash. And eighth: We focus our fundraising more tightly, because at the moment it's all over the place. That's it." I look up from my list.

"Well." Robert raises his eyebrows. "You've been busy."

"I know the condo merchants are circling." I appeal to him directly. "But can't we at least give this place a *chance* to become a modern functioning museum?"

"I like it," says Robert slowly. "I like all your ideas. Although, again, money. Do *not* commit any money, Aunt Margaret," he adds quickly to Mrs. Kendrick as she opens her mouth. "You have done *enough.*"

"I agree," I reply. "She has. And we don't need it." I can't help smiling at them both. "Because today we were awarded a grant of thirty thousand pounds from the Wilson-Cross Foundation."

Susie texted me with the good news an hour ago. And I'll be honest: My initial reaction was, *Great. But . . . is that all?* I'd been secretly hoping for a magical, problem-solving, fairy-godmother amount, like another half million.

But you have to be thankful for what you can get.

"Well done, Sylvie!" Mrs. Kendrick claps her hands together.

"Good work," agrees Robert.

"It'll tide us over," I say, "until some of these projects start generating income."

Robert holds out his hand for the list and I pass it to him. He runs his eyes down it and nods a few times. "You'll spearhead all of this?"

"Can't wait." I nod vigorously.

And I mean it: I can't wait to get cracking. I want to kick-start these projects and see them into fruition. More than that, I want to see them save Willoughby House.

But at the same time, there's a weird feeling inside me that's been growing all day. A sense that my time here might be nearing its final stage. That I might, sometime in the not-too-distant future, move on to a new environment. Challenge myself even more. See what I'm capable of.

I catch Robert's eye and have the strangest conviction that he can tell what I'm thinking. So I hastily look away. Instead, I focus on the Adam fireplace, with the two huge shells brought back from Polynesia by Sir Walter Kendrick. It's where we gather every year for Mrs. Kendrick's Staff Christmas Stockings. She wraps up little gifts and makes special marzipan cakes. . . .

I feel a sudden wrench. *God,* this place gets under your skin, with all its quirks and traditions. But you can't stay somewhere just for the sake of tradition, can you? You can't stay put just for a few sentimental reasons.

Is that how Dan feels about me?

Am I a sentimental reason?

My eyes start to feel hot again. It's been such a day, I'm not sure I can hold it together.

"If you don't mind, I'll be going," I say, my voice husky. "I'll send you an email summarizing everything we've discussed. It's just . . . I think I need to get home."

"Of course, Sylvie!" says Mrs. Kendrick. "You go and have a lovely evening. And well done!" She claps her hands together again.

I head out of the library, and Robert comes along with me.

"Are you OK?" he says in a low voice, and I curse him for being so perceptive.

"Yes," I say. "Kind of. I mean, not really."

I pause by the stairs, and Robert stares at me as though he wants to say something else.

"What did he do?" he says at last.

And this is all so upside down, I want to laugh. Except it's not funny. What did Dan do? He worked tirelessly for my family with no credit, while I called him "chippy" and a "fucking cliché" and drove him away.

"Nothing. He did nothing wrong. Nothing. Sorry." I start to walk again. "I have to go."

■ ■ ■ ■

As I walk along our street, I feel numb. Flat. All the adrenaline of the day has dissipated. For a while I was distracted by the stimulation of doing stuff and achieving change and making decisions. But now that's all faded away. It doesn't seem important. Only one thing seems important. One person. And I don't know where he is or what he's thinking or what the future holds.

I don't even have my girls waiting for me at home. If I did, I could hug them tightly to me and hear their little stories and jokes and troubles, read their books, cook their suppers, and distract myself that way. But they're at a birthday party with Karen.

I'm walking along in a mist of preoccupation, unaware of my surroundings — but as I near home, I focus in dismay. There's an ambulance outside John and Owen's house, and two paramedics are lifting Owen out of it in a wheelchair. He looks frailer than ever and there's a small plastic tube running into his nose.

"Oh my God." I hurry over to John, who keeps trying to put a hand on Owen's arm and is being firmly but gently batted away by the paramedics. "What happened?"

"Owen is not well," says John simply. There's almost a warning note to his voice, and I sense he doesn't want to be quizzed on "What? How? When?"

"I'm sorry," I say. "If there's anything I can do . . ." Even as I say the words, they sound hollow. We all say them, but what do they mean?

"You're very kind." John nods, his face almost, but not quite, breaking into a smile. "Very kind indeed."

He follows Owen and the paramedics into the house and I watch them, stricken, not wanting to be the nosy neighbor who stares but not wanting to be the callous neighbor who turns away either.

And as I'm standing there, it occurs to me: There *is* something I could do. I hurry home, dash into the empty, silent kitchen, and start rooting around in the fridge. We had a supermarket order recently and it's pretty full, and to be honest, I've never felt less like eating.

I load up a tray with a packet of ham, a pot of guacamole, a bag of "perfectly ripe pears," two frozen baguettes that just need eight minutes in the oven, a jar of nuts left over from Christmas, a packet of dates also left over from Christmas, and a bar of chocolate. Then, balancing it on one hand,

I head outside and along to John and Owen's house. The ambulance has gone. Everything seems very silent.

Should I leave the tray on the doorstep and not disturb them? No. They might not realize it's there until it's tomorrow and the foxes have ripped it to bits.

Cautiously, I ring the bell and form my face into an apologetic expression as John answers. His eyes are red-rimmed, I instantly notice. They weren't before. I feel a jab through my heart and want to back away instantly, leaving him in his private space. But I'm here now. And so I clear my throat a couple of times and say awkwardly, "I just thought you might like . . . You might not have thought about food. . . ."

"My dear." His face crinkles. "My dear, you are too kind."

"Shall I bring it in?"

Slowly I proceed through the house, afraid of disturbing Owen, but John nods toward the closed sitting room door and says, "He's resting."

I put the tray on the kitchen counter and the cold items in the fridge, noticing how bare it is. I'm going to get Tilda in on this too. We'll make sure they're permanently stocked up.

As I finish, I turn to see that John seems

lost in a reverie. I wait in wary silence, not wanting to break his thoughts.

"Your daughter." He suddenly comes to. "I believe she left . . . a small rabbit. Small . . . white . . . large ears . . ." He describes vaguely with his hands. "Not a breed I recognize . . ."

"Oh! You mean her Sylvanian Families. I'm sorry. She leaves them everywhere."

"I'll fetch it for you."

"Let me!"

I follow him out to his greenhouse, where sure enough one of Tessa's Sylvanian rabbits is standing incongruously by the rows of frondy plants. As I pick it up, John seems lost again, this time transfixed by one of the plants, and I remember something Tilda told me the other day. She said she'd googled John and apparently his research on plants has led to a breakthrough in gene therapy, which could help millions of people. (I have no idea how that works, but there you go.)

"It's an amazing life's work you've achieved," I venture, wanting to say something positive.

"Oh, my work will never be done," he says, almost as though amused. His face softens and he rubs a leaf between his fingers lovingly. "These wonders will never reveal all their secrets. I've been learning about them ever since I was a boy. Every time I look at them I learn a little more. And as a result I love them a little more." He moves a pot tenderly, patting its fronds. "Tiny miracles. Much like people."

I'm not quite sure if he's talking to me or to himself, but every word he says feels like a drop of Wise Potion. I want to hear more. I want him to tell me all the answers to life.

"I don't know how you —" I break off, rubbing my nose, inhaling the earthy, greeny smell of the plants. "You're very inspiring. Dan and I have . . ." I swallow hard. "Anyway, it doesn't matter about us. I just want you to know, you're inspiring. Fifty-nine years." I look straight at him. "Fifty-nine years, loving one person. It's something. It's an achievement."

John is silent for a few moments, his hands moving absently around his plants, his eyes far off with thought.

"I am an early riser," he says at last. "So I watch Owen wake up every morning. And each morning reveals something new. The light catches his face in a particular way; he has a fresh thought; he shares a memory. Love is finding one person infinitely fascinating." John seems lost in thought again — then comes to. "And so . . . not an achievement, my dear." He gives me a mild, kind smile. "Rather, a privilege."

I stare back at him, feeling choked up. John's hands are trembling as he rearranges his pots. He knocks one over, then rights it, and I can tell he doesn't quite know what he's doing. I recall Owen just now, pale and shrunken, the tube in his nose, and have a sudden horrible fear that it's bad, really bad.

On impulse I grab John's shaky hands and hold them in mine till they're still.

"If you ever want company," I say. "Help. Lifts in the car. Anything. We're here."

He nods and squeezes my hands. And we go back into the house, and I make two cups of tea, because that's something else I can do. And as I leave, promising to return tomorrow, all I can think is: Dan. I need to talk to Dan. I need to communicate. Even if he's still in Devon. Even if he has no signal. Even if it's a one-sided conversation.

As I get inside our house I'm already reaching for the phone. I dial his number, sinking down onto the bottom step of the stairs, desperate to let him know, desperate to make him understand . . . what?

"Dan," I say as the phone beeps. "It's me. And I'm so sorry." I swallow, my throat all lumpy. "I just . . . I wish . . . I just . . ."

Oh God. Terrible. Why am I so bloody

inarticulate? John, with all his worries, manages to sound like some elegiac poet, whereas I flounder around like an idiot. I click off, dial again, and start another voice-mail.

"Dan." I swallow the lumps down. "It's me. And I just called to say . . ." No. I sound like Stevie Wonder. *Bad.* I click off and try again.

"Dan, it's me. I mean, you knew that, right? Because you saw *Sylvie* pop up on your screen. Which means you're listening to a message from me. Which I suppose is a good sign . . ."

What am I going on about? I click off before I can sound any more like a rambling moron and dial a fourth time.

"Dan. Please ignore all those other messages. Sorry. I don't know what I was trying to say. What I *am* trying to say is . . ." I pause, trying to untangle my thoughts. "Well, I suppose it's that all I can think about is you. Where you are. What you're doing. What you're thinking. Because I have no idea anymore. None." My voice wobbles and I take a few seconds to calm myself. "It's ironic, I guess, because I used to think I knew you *too* well. But now . . ." A tear suddenly runs down my cheek. "Anyway. Above all, Dan . . . and I don't know if you're even still listening . . . but above all, I wanted to say . . ."

The door opens and I'm so startled, I drop my phone in shock, thinking, Dan? *Dan?*

But it's Karen, wearing sneakers and earbuds and her cycling backpack.

"Oh, hi," she says, looking surprised to see me sitting on the stairs. "I forgot my iPad. Shit, Sylvie, your *hair.*"

"Yes. My hair." I peer at her in confusion. "But, wait, aren't you supposed to be with the girls?"

"Dan's with them," she says casually — then at my reaction, her expression changes. "Oh. Wasn't I supposed to say? He just turned up and said he'd do the party."

"Dan's here?" My heart is thudding so hard, I can hardly breathe. "He's here? Where? *Where?*"

"Battersea Park," says Karen, eyeing me weirdly. "Climb On? You know, the climbing place?"

My legs are already moving. I'm scrambling to my feet. I need to get there.

SEVENTEEN

Battersea Park is one of the reasons we like southwest London. It's an amazing resource — huge and green and full of activities. It's a fine evening as I reach the gates, and people are out in force enjoying themselves. They're strolling, cycling, rollerblading, riding recumbent bikes, and hitting tennis balls. Everyone's relaxed and smiling at one another. But not me. I'm desperate. I'm not smiling. I'm a woman on a mission.

I don't know what's propelling me — maybe some marriage-in-crisis superpower that causes all your muscles to explode in strength? But somehow I'm speeding along, past all the joggers, tottering in my black high heels, panting and red-faced. My lungs are on fire and there's a blister on my heel, but the more it hurts, the harder I run. I don't know what I'm going to say when I see him. I'm not even sure I can string a sentence together — all I have is the odd random word landing in my brain as I run. *Love. Forever. Please.*

"Argh!" Suddenly, without warning, I feel a massive jolt and crash to the ground, scraping my face painfully against the tarmac. "Ow! *Ow!*" I manage to get to my feet and see a little boy on a recumbent bike, who has clearly just bashed into me and doesn't look remotely sorry.

"Sorry!" A woman is running over. "Josh, I've told you to be careful on that bike —" She surveys me in dismay. "Oh dear. You've cut your forehead. You should see a medic. Do they have a first-aid place?"

"It's fine," I say hoarsely, and start running again. Now she mentions it, I can feel blood running down my face. But whatever. I'll find a Band-Aid later.

Climb On is a massive adventure playground for children, full of ropes, dangling ladders, and dangerous, hideous swaying bridges. As it comes into view, the very sight of it makes my stomach turn. Why on earth would you have a party here? What's wrong with safe activities on the ground?

As I get near, I can see Dan. He's standing on a bridge, at the top of a tower, with a couple of other dads, all wearing safety helmets. But while the dads are joking about something, Dan seems oblivious to the party. He's staring ahead, his face shadowed, his brow taut.

"Dan!" I yell, but the place is full of clamoring children and he doesn't turn. "Dan! *Dan!*" I scream so loud that my throat catches, and still he doesn't hear me. I have no choice. Dodging past the entrance barrier and ignoring the cry of the attendant, I run at the structure, kick off my heels, and start climbing up a monstrous set of rope steps that will lead me to the platform that Dan is on. I'm not even thinking about what I'm doing. I'm just getting to Dan in the only way possible.

And it's only when I'm about ten feet off the ground that I realize what I'm doing. Oh God. No. I can't . . . no.

My fingers freeze around the ropes. I start to breathe more quickly. I look down at the ground and think I might vomit. Dan is another twenty feet up. I need to keep climbing. But I can't. But I have to.

"Hey!" An irate voice is calling me from the ground. "Who are you? Are you with the party? You need a helmet!"

Somehow I force myself up another step. And up. Tears have started to my eyes. *Don't look down. Don't look. Another step.* The rope steps keep wobbling perilously, and a whimper escapes from me.

"Sylvie? *Sylvie?*" Dan's voice hits my ears. "What the *fuck* . . ." I raise my head to see him peering down at me incredulously.

"We need a manager," someone is saying on the ground. "Gavin, you're deputy manager. You climb up after her."

"I'm not climbing after her!" an indignant voice replies. "We're supposed to use the emergency ladder, anyway. Jamie, get out the emergency ladder."

Every sinew of my body is begging me to stop. My head is spinning. But somehow I push on, step after step, higher and higher, ignoring the fact that I'm twenty feet off the ground. Twenty-five feet. That I don't have any harness. Or any helmet. That if I fall . . . *No. Stop. Don't think about falling. Keep going.*

I'm aware of the atmosphere becoming quieter. Everyone must be watching. Are the girls watching? My hands have started sweating. My breath is coming in fast, harsh little gasps.

Now the platform is only a few feet away. Only a few more steps will do it. But a new tremor comes over me. My legs are shaking so hard that I feel the hugest wash of fear I have yet. I can't control my limbs. I can't do this. *I'm going to fall, I'm going to fall, how can I not fall?*

485

"You're nearly there." Dan's voice is in my ears. Solid. Familiar. Something to cling to mentally. "You're nearly there," he repeats. "You're not going to fall. One more step. Hand on the platform. Nearly there, Sylvie, nearly there."

And suddenly I'm there, and his strong hand is grasping mine and I'm collapsing on the wooden platform, and for a few moments I can't move. At last I raise my head to see Dan staring at me, with such a scrubcious face that I want to laugh, except I can't, because tears are streaming down my face.

"What the fuck?" he demands, and grabs me so tightly, I gasp. "What the fuck? Sylvie, you could have . . . What were you *doing*?" He stares at me, looking quite aghast. I suppose I am quite an apparition, what with the shorn hair and the blood dripping down my face. "Were you trying to surprise me? Or shock me? Or give me a heart attack? Is this *real*?" He touches my cheek, and as blood comes away on his fingers, he looks even more shocked. "Jesus Christ."

"I wasn't trying to surprise you," I manage, my breaths still short and fast. "That's not what this is. I just . . . I just had to see you. Didn't you get my messages?"

"Messages?" His hand goes automatically

to his pocket. "No. My phone's fucked. Sylvie . . . what *is* this? You can't do heights." He looks at the ground, thirty feet below, then at me. "You can't even do a stepladder."

"Well." I rub my bloody face. "Looks like I did them."

"But . . . your face. Your hair. What's *happened*? Sylvie, what the hell —" He turns ashen. "Have you been attacked?"

"No." I shake my head. "No. I cut my hair off myself. Dan, listen. I know. About . . ." I have to get this through to him, urgently. "I *know.*"

"You 'know'?" A familiar guarded expression comes across his face, as though he's ready to bat away my questions. And in that moment I realize just how much he's been keeping from me. What a constant pressure it must have been. No wonder he's fed up.

"I *know,* OK? Believe me. I know."

The other dads who were on the platform with Dan have tactfully headed off to the zip-wire platform, where all the children, including our two, are clustering with play leaders in branded T-shirts. We're alone.

"What do you know, exactly, Sylvie?" says Dan cautiously. And his willingness to protect me, even now, makes my eyes hot. I stare back at him, thoughts swirling around my mind. What exactly do I know? Nothing, it feels like, most of the time.

"I know that you're not the man I thought you were." I gaze into his guarded blue eyes, trying to get beneath the surface. "You're so, so much more than I ever realized." My throat is tight, but I press on. "I know what you've been doing, Dan. I know what all the secrets are. I know about my father. Joss Burton. The whole thing. I read the emails." I take a deep breath. "I know my father was a liar and a shit."

Dan visibly flinches and stares at me incredulously. "*What* did you say?"

"My father was a liar. And a shit."

There's silence as my words sit in the air. I've never seen Dan look so shoffed. I don't think he can speak. But that's OK, because I have more to say.

"I've been living in a bubble." I swallow hard. "A climate-controlled, safe bubble. But now it's burst. And the weather has blown in. And it's . . . exhilarating."

"I can see." Dan nods slowly. "Your face. It's different."

"Bad different?"

"No. *Real* different. You look more *real*." He surveys me, as though trying to work it out. "Your eyes. Your expression. Your *hair*."

I put up a hand and feel my bare neck. It

488

still feels unfamiliar. Exposed. It feels like a new me.

"Princess Sylvie is dead," I say abruptly, and there must be something about my tone, because Dan nods gravely and says, "Agreed."

I suddenly become aware of an extendable ladder being placed against the platform we're on. A few moments later, a guy in his twenties appears, holding a helmet. As he sees my bloody face, he recoils, aghast.

"Did that injury happen on our premises?" He has a reedy voice and sounds freaked out. "Because you are not an authorized client, you have not undergone the health-and-safety briefing, you are not wearing approved headwear —"

"It's OK." I cut him off. "I didn't injure myself on your premises."

"Well." He gives me a resentful look and holds out the helmet to me. "All clients must wear protective helmets at all times. All clients must register before using any apparatus and be fitted for a harness."

"Sorry," I say humbly. I take the helmet from him and put it on.

"Please descend from the apparatus," the guy adds, in such a disapproving voice that I feel an involuntary giggle. "Forthwith."

Forthwith? I glance at Dan and see that he's hiding a smile too.

"OK," I say. "I'm going." I eye the extendable ladder and feel a wave of nausea. "In a minute."

"I can show you a gentler way down," Dan says to me. "Unless you felt like hurling yourself down the rope ladder headfirst?"

"Not today," I match his deadpan tone. "Another time."

I follow Dan across a rickety ropy bridge to a lower platform. My legs are trembling violently in a kind of aftershock state. Every time I glance down, I want to heave. But I smile brightly at Dan whenever he looks round, and somehow I keep going and we make it. *Vincit qui se vincit,* keeps running through my head. *She conquers who conquers herself.*

And then we descend an easier ladder and pretty soon we're on the ground. And I am really, *really* glad. In fact, I slightly want to hug the ground in gratitude.

Not that I would ever admit this to anyone.

"OK." Dan rounds on me. "Now we're on the ground and you're not going to fall off in fright, I'm going to say it again: What the *fuck*?" His eyes are wide and I realize he's genuinely freaked out. "What happened

490

to your face, your hair . . ." He's counting off on his fingers. "How do you know about your dad? I leave you for two nights and all hell breaks loose."

Two nights? It feels like an eternity.

"I knew you were lying about going to Glasgow," I say, a familiar pain washing over me. "I thought you'd gone to . . . I thought you were leaving me. You said you needed space; you said you needed to escape. . . ."

"Oh God. Yes." Dan closes his eyes. "Yes, I didn't mean that. I just . . ." He pauses and I wait fearfully. "It was all becoming . . ." He breaks off again, looking toward the sky.

I can't finish his sentence in perfect, overlapping sync. Psychic Sylvie, who knew everything, has vanished. And now that the exhilaration of climbing up thirty feet has worn off, I can see us for what we are. A married couple from southwest London who have hit the buffers. Trying to sort it out. Finding our way. Not there yet.

"I know it's been an 'ongoing nightmare,' " I say at last. "Mary Holland told me."

"Oh, 'nightmare' is probably too strong." Dan rubs his face, looking suddenly weary. "But it's endless. I have your mother on at me every day. Emails from the lawyers, Joss

Burton's agent . . . This book is going to happen. And it's going to be huge. She's a big deal, Sylvie, and I'm not sure I can stop it this time."

He looks so troubled, I should say something sympathetic, but my residual anger's too great and I can't help rounding on him in turn:

"So why didn't you *tell* me?" Because it's Dan who kept secrets, who drove wedges between us, who kept flicking to another page when I tried to read his whole story. "You should have told me right from the start. As soon as my father came to you, you should have said, 'We need to tell Sylvie.' Then everything would have been different."

I can't help sounding accusing. I've developed a whole alternate universe in my head, where this is what happened, and somehow the situation made Dan and me stronger as a couple instead of nearly splitting us up.

"I should have *told* you?" Dan stares at me incredulously, almost angrily. "Sylvie, do you have *any* idea . . . Your father would have killed me, for a start. The whole thing was a total secret from everybody. Even your mother didn't want to know. All we were trying to do, round the clock, was contain it. Shut it down. Your father was after a *knighthood,* for God's sake. He was adamant that no one could know about this scandal, least of all his daughter. And he really meant it. Can you imagine what kind of rage he was in?"

There's a pause — then silently I nod. I can still remember the white-hot fury that would come into Daddy's eyes. Not with me, never with his princess, but with others. And the idea of Daddy caged in by possible scandal . . . Yes, I can imagine.

"And then, just when we were in the middle of it all . . . he had the crash. He was gone." Dan stops abruptly and I can see the remembered shock pass through him. "And there was no way I could have told you then."

"Yes, you could," I say robustly. "That was the perfect time."

"Sylvie, you couldn't cope as it was!" Dan erupts furiously. "Do you *remember* what that time was like? Do you realize how worried I was? You were a bloody mess! If I'd come along and said, 'Hey, guess what, you know your adored dad? The one you've gone into extreme grief over? Well, apparently he preyed on a sixteen-year-old girl, or maybe he didn't.' " Dan rubs his face, hard. "I mean, Jesus. You were in meltdown; your mum was on another planet — what was I supposed to do? What was I *supposed* to do?"

He appeals to me directly, his face twisted up, as tentery as I've ever known it, and I can see years of strain in him. I can see all the decisions he's been wrestling with. All alone.

"I'm sorry," I say, chastened. "I know. You did what you thought was best. And I realize it was out of love for me. But, Dan . . . you were too protective."

I can see Dan smarting at my words. All this time, he's thought he was doing the right thing, the gallant thing, the best possible thing. It's hard to hear that it wasn't.

"Perhaps," he allows after a pause.

"You were," I insist. "And we need to stop talking about my 'episode.' We need to accept that grief happens. Shit happens; life happens. And glossing over it or trying to say it's an illness isn't the way to go. Better to acknowledge it. Cope with it. Clear it up together."

I have a sudden image of Dan and me working together with brooms, side by side, hot and sweaty and determined. It's not the most romantic, Hallmark image of marriage . . . but it's what I want us to be.

I can see Dan digesting what I'm saying

494

— or at least trying to. It'll probably take a while.

"Fair enough," he says at last. "Maybe you're right." Then his face changes, becomes a little more tense. "Have you seen what she wrote?"

"Skimmed it," I say, looking at the ground.

The big question is sitting there in the air between us. I know he's never going to broach it, so I have to. I take a breath, gearing myself up, preparing myself for his answer, whatever it is. "Do you think it's true?"

At once his face closes up again, like a clam. "Don't know," he says distantly. "It's his word against hers. It's a long time ago. Probably not worth speculating."

"But you've read everything she wrote." I peer at his face, trying to read it. "What do you *think*?"

Dan looks even more tortured. "I don't like talking about this with you. It's . . ."

"Sordid," I say flatly. "It's not what my family was supposed to be about. We were supposed to be the gilded, perfect ones, right?"

Dan winces but doesn't contradict me. God, he's had a fucked-up view of my family. Ridiculous brunches with Mummy. Endless viewings of Daddy on that DVD, all golden and handsome. And all the while, scrabbling around with lawyers to keep our dirty washing out of sight.

"I'm going to read all the files," I say. "Everything she's written, everything she's said. Every word."

Dan looks appalled. "That's not a good idea —"

"I'm going to." I cut him off. "I have to know. Don't worry, I won't flip out. You know she was Lynn?" I add, hunching my arms round my body. "My parents lied to me."

"I know." Dan grimaces. "That was the worst bit of all. Hearing you talk about your imaginary friend, and knowing . . ." He shakes his head. "That was messed up."

"I felt guilty about Lynn my whole childhood. I felt ashamed and confused and stupid." My jaw grows tight at the memory. "And I will never forgive him for that, *never.*" I speak the words viciously and look up to see Dan regarding me anxiously.

"Sylvie, don't go overboard. Don't go too far the other way. I know this is all shocking. But he was still your dad, remember? You loved him, remember?"

I prod my feelings. My feelings about Daddy. I wait for the familiar torrent of grief and love and fury that he's been taken from us. But there's nothing. It's as though the flow has been cut off at the mains.

"Maybe I did." I watch a guy on Rollerblades in the park trying to go backward. "Maybe I will one day again. That's all I can say for now." I shoot him a sidelong look. "I never understood what went wrong with you and Daddy. Now I get it."

"I thought I concealed my feelings perfectly." Dan gives me a wry smile.

"Not so much." I return his smile, but inside I'm rewinding over the years, back to when Dan discovered all this and got dragged into a side street of our family map that he was never expecting. "It must have been awful for you."

"It wasn't great," says Dan, his eyes distant. "I idolized your dad, too, you know, in my own way. He was such a hero. So when these allegations came along, at first I was shocked. I wanted to defend him. I was *glad* to defend him. I actually thought it would be a way for us to become closer. Until . . ." He gives a humorless laugh. "Well. Let's just say . . . we didn't."

"I've read his emails to you." I nod bleakly. "I know."

"He didn't like that I'd seen beneath the glossy veneer," says Dan slowly. "He couldn't really stand it."

The sound of shrieking heralds the children, who are being ushered off the apparatus and into a room decorated with balloons. As they pass by, both Tessa and Anna gasp at the sight of us, as though it's been several days since we saw each other.

"Mummy, you got a hurt!" says Tessa.

"Just a tiny one!" I call back. "I'll get a Band-Aid and it will all get better."

"Look, that's my daddy! He's there!" Anna points at Dan, and all the children turn to gawp at us as though we're celebrities, despite the fact that they see us pretty much every day at school and that all the other parents are here too.

"Should we go in with them?" I say to Dan, my parental radar tweaking. "Are we supposed to be at the tea?"

"No. They'll be fine."

We wave as they file into the party room — I can just about hear Tessa boasting, "My mummy *always* climbs up ladders" — and then look at each other, as though we're starting again.

I feel like another layer has been stripped off. The guarded look has gone from Dan's eyes. As he meets my gaze, there's a new honesty in them. With every revelation, I understand Dan better; I learn more about him; I *want* to learn more about him. John's voice runs through my head: *Love is finding one person infinitely fascinating.*

He's my man. My Dan. The sun in my solar system. And I know he used to be eclipsed at times by a bigger, showier sun, and maybe that was always our problem. But now I can't think how I *ever* compared Daddy to Dan, even in the privacy of my own brain, and found Dan lesser. Dan is my sun. Dan wins on every, every, *every* count. . . .

"Sylvie?" Dan interrupts my thoughts and I realize that tears are streaming down my face.

"Sorry," I gulp, brushing at my cheeks. "Just thinking about . . . You know. Us."

"Oh, *us.*" His eyes lock on to mine and, again, there's that new truth to his gaze: an acknowledgment. It's a different connection. We're different. Both of us.

"So what now?" I venture at last.

"Sixty-eight years minus, what, a few weeks?" says Dan in unreadable tones. "It's still a long time."

"I know." I nod.

"Bloody long time. I mean, jeez."

"Yup."

Dan's silent for a moment, and I almost can't breathe. Then he looks up and there's something in his eyes which makes my heart twitch and tangle up in knots.

"I'm up for it if you are."

"I am." I nod, barely able to speak. "I am. I'm up for it."

"OK, then."

"OK."

Dan hesitates, then lifts his hand and gently touches my fingertips, and my skin starts fizzing in a way I really wasn't expecting. What's happened to my nerve endings? To *me*? Everything feels brand new. Unpredictable. Dan starts nibbling my fingers, his eyes never leaving mine, and I stare back, transfixed, wanting more. Wanting to get a room. Wanting to rediscover this man that I love.

"Sylvie? Dan? Are you coming in for tea?" A cheery voice hails us, and we both jerk round in shock to see the birthday girl's mother, a woman called Gill, waving at us from the door of the party room. "We've got nibbles for parents, prosecco. . . ."

"Maybe in a minute!" calls back Dan politely. "By which I mean, 'Can't you see we're busy?' " he adds in a voice that only I can hear.

"Don't be like that," I say reprovingly. "She's offering prosecco."

"I don't want prosecco, I want you. Now." His eyes are running over me with a greed I

500

haven't seen in years, an urgency that makes me shiver. He grips me by the hips and he's breathing hard and I think he would have me right here, right now. But we're in Battersea Park, at a children's party. Sometimes I think Dan forgets these things.

"We've got another sixty-seven years and some," I remind him. "We'll find another moment."

"I don't want another moment." He buries his face in my neck.

"Dan!" I bat at him. "We'll get arrested."

"Fine." He rolls his eyes comically. *"Fine.* Let's go and drink our prosecco. You could wash your face too," he adds, as we start slowly walking up the balloon-decorated path. "Not that 'bloodstained zombie' isn't a good look."

"Or else I could scare the children," I suggest. "I could be the slasher zombie clown."

"I like it." He nods and reaches a hand to ruffle the hair at the nape of my neck. "I like this too. I like it a lot."

"Good."

"A *lot.*" He can't seem to remove his hand from my shorn neck and his voice has descended to a kind of dark growl, and I suddenly think: *Oh my God, was Dan a short-hair guy all the time and I never even knew?*

"The girls hate it, of course," I tell him.

"Of course they do." Dan looks amused. "And Mrs. Kendrick?"

"Hates it too. Oh, that's the other thing," I add. "I'm thinking of leaving my job."

Dan stops dead and stares at me incredulously.

"OK," he says at last. "Where is my wife and what have you done with her?"

"Why?" I meet his gaze head-on, challenging. "Do you want her back?" I have another image of the princess-haired bubble Sylvie that I was. She already feels a lifetime ago.

"No," says Dan without missing a beat. "You can keep her. This is the version I like."

"Me too." I nod. He still can't keep his hands off my bare nape, and I don't want him to stop. My whole neck is tingling. My whole *me* is tingling. I should have cut my hair off *years* ago.

We've reached the party building by now. I can hear the shrieks of children and the chatter of parents and all the conversations that will swallow us up as soon as we enter. Dan pauses on the doorstep, his fingers resting on the back of my neck, and I can see a deeply concentrating, scrubcious look pass over his face.

"It's not easy, is it?" he says heavily, as though coming to some almighty conclusion. "Marriage. Love. It's not *easy.*"

As he says it, Tilda's words come back to me, and they've never seemed so true.

"If love is easy . . ." I hesitate. "You're not doing it right."

Dan looks down at me silently, and even though I'm not psychic Sylvie anymore, I can see emotions jumbling through his eyes. Old anger. Tenderness. Love.

"Well, then, we must be fucking masters." He pulls me to him and kisses me hard, almost fiercely, like a statement of intent. A vow, almost. Then, at last, he releases me. "Come on. Let's get that prosecco."

EIGHTEEN

The house is all alone on a cliff, with huge glass windows framing the sea view and a vast linen wraparound sofa and beautifully scented air. I'm sitting on one end of the sofa and Lynn is sitting facing me.

Jocelyn, I mean. I know she's Joss. That's what I call her to her face. But as I stare at her, all I can think is: *Lynn.*

It's like looking at a Magic Eye picture. There's Joss. Famous Joss Burton, founder of Maze, who I've seen on book covers and in magazine articles, with her trademark white streak of hair and dark, intelligent eyes. And then, glimmering underneath, there's Lynn. Traces of my Lynn. In her smile, especially. Her laugh. The way she crinkles up her nose in thought. The way she uses her hands when she talks.

She's Lynn. My made-up Lynn, come to life, never imaginary at all. It's like seeing Father Christmas and my fairy godmother, all wrapped up in one elegant, real-life woman.

It's not the first time I've seen her as an adult. We met up for the first time a month ago. But I'm still finding it surreal, being here, being with her.

"I used to talk to you every day," I say, my hands wrapped around a cup of Maze chamomile tisane. "I used to tell you my problems. I used to lie in bed and conjure you up and just . . . talk to you."

"Was I helpful?" Joss smiles in that way I remember: warm and just a little bit teasing.

"Yes." I smile back. "You always made me feel better."

"Good. More tea?"

"Thanks."

As Joss pours fresh tisane into my cup, I glance toward the stunning view of a cliff top giving way to endless pale-gray December sky with churning sea beneath. I'm deliberately testing myself, and to my own satisfaction, my heart remains quite steady. I've had a full course of therapy and lots of practice — and while I'll never be the type to dance merrily across a tightrope, I'm a lot better with heights now. A *lot* better.

And I still see the counselor who helped me. Once a week I knock on her door, looking forward to the session, knowing I should have done this years ago. Because it turns out she's pretty good at talking about issues other than heights. Like fathers. Imaginary friends. Old alleged affairs. That kind of thing.

Of course, I've read everything now. First I read *Through the High Maze* cover to cover, twice over, searching for clues, reading between the lines. Then I went into Avory Milton and read Joss's whole account of the episode with Daddy. It took a morning, because I kept breaking off. I couldn't believe it. I wouldn't believe it. I *did* believe it. I hated myself for believing it.

It was weeks before everything properly shook down in my head. And now I think . . .

What do I think?

I exhale, as my thoughts describe the same circle they have done constantly, ever since that day I went to see Mary Smith-Sullivan.

I think Joss is a truthful person. That's what I think. Whether every single detail is accurate, I can't know. But she's truthful. Mary Smith-Sullivan isn't as convinced. She keeps saying to me: "It's her word against his." Which is right, and it's her job as a lawyer to protect her client, and I understand that.

But the thing is, it's Joss's words which feel true. As I read her story, little details of what he'd said and how he'd behaved kept jumping out at me. I kept thinking: *That's Daddy*. And, *Yes, that's just how it was*. And then I found myself thinking: *How would our sixteen-year-old holiday neighbor know Daddy so well?* And it led me logically to one place.

I came to that conclusion four months ago and went to bed feeling numb. I couldn't even talk to Dan about it. But the next day I woke up with total clarity, and before I'd even left for work, I'd written a letter to Joss. She phoned me up as soon as she got it, and we spoke for an hour. I cried. I'm not sure if she did, because she's one of those very tranquil people who have found their way through the maelstrom. (That's a quote from *Through the High Maze*.) But her voice shook. Her voice definitely shook. She said she'd thought of me a lot over the years.

Then we met in London and had a cup of tea together. We were both nervous, I think, although Joss hid it better than I did. Dan said he was happy to come as moral support, but I said, "No." And actually, if he'd been there, I would never have had that amazing chat I did with Joss. She told me that Dan, all along, had been the one posi-

507

tive force in the whole matter. She said he'd persuaded her that the affair with my father wasn't necessary to the powerful story she was telling in *Through the High Maze,* and it might even detract.

"Do you know," she said then, her eyes shining, "he was right. I know he was trying to defend your father, but he made a good point too. I'm glad I didn't make that book about my teenage self."

There was a pause, and I wondered if she was about to say she wouldn't ever tell that part of her story and I needn't worry anymore. But then she pulled out a huge bound sheaf of papers, and I could see the wary look in her eye, and I instantly knew. "This is the proof of the new book," she said. "I want you to read it."

And so I read it.

I don't know how I did it so calmly. If I'd read it a few months ago, with no warning, it would have freaked me out. I probably would have thrown it across the room. But I've changed. Everything's changed.

"Sylvie, your last email troubled me," Joss says as she puts down the teapot. She has a way of talking which is very calming. She says something and then pauses and lets the words breathe, so you actually *think* about them.

"Why? What exactly?"

Joss cradles her own cup and gazes out to sea for a moment. She's calling her new book *Into the Wide Open Air,* and right now I can't think of a better title.

"You seemed to be assuming culpability. Feeling guilt." She turns and fixes me with a clear look. "Sylvie, I am not saying and I never will say that your father caused my eating disorder."

"Well, maybe you're not." My stomach twists up in a familiar gnarl of bad feelings. "But surely —"

"It's far more complex than that. He was part of my story, but he wasn't the *cause* of anything. You must understand that." She sounds quite firm, and just for a moment she's sixteen and I'm four, and she's Lynn, magical Lynn, who knows everything.

"But he didn't exactly help."

"Well, no. But you could say that of so many things, including my own personality quirks." Joss's eyes crease in that kind way she has. "It's hard for you. I know. It's all new. But I've been processing all these events for years."

My eyes travel around the room, looking at the huge flickering candles everywhere. Those candles cost a *fortune* — they're big-ticket presents in southwest London — yet she has eight of them on the go. I've been sitting here for fifteen minutes and already I feel almost hypnotized by the scent. I feel soothed. I feel finally able to address the subject looming between us.

"So, as I said in my email . . . I've read the whole thing now," I say slowly. "The new book."

"Yes," says Joss. And it's only one syllable, but I can hear the increased alertness in her voice and see how her head has tilted, like a bird's.

"I think it's . . . powerful. Empowering. No . . ." I can't find the right word. "I think I can see why you wanted to write it. I think women will read it and see how you can fall into a trap and maybe it'll stop them falling into that trap."

"Exactly." Joss leans forward, her eyes glowing intensely. "Sylvie, I'm so glad you realize . . . this isn't supposed to be a sensationalist book. And I'm not trying to expose your father. If I'm exposing anyone, it's me, my sixteen-year-old self, my hang-ups and my misconceptions, and the wrong thought patterns I had. And I hope a new generation of girls can learn from them."

"I think you should publish it."

There. The words are out. We've been dancing around this for weeks. I've been dealing with Mummy and the lawyers and Dan and my own terrible confusion. I've been trying, first, to have my voice heard — then trying to work out what I really think.

It was only when I actually *read* the proof that I realized what Joss was doing, what she was saying, how she was trying to set out her story as a tale to help others. Mummy couldn't see beyond the mention of Daddy. Dan couldn't see beyond wanting to protect me. The lawyers couldn't see beyond doing their jobs. But I could see Lynn. Wise, kind, humorous, talented Lynn, taking a negative situation and turning it into something inspiring. How can I silence Lynn?

I know Mummy thinks I'm a traitor. She'll always believe that Joss is a liar, that the whole story is malicious fiction designed to upset our family and nothing more. When I asked her if she'd actually read Joss's words, she just started ranting at me: "*How* can it be true? *How* can it be true?"

I wanted to retort, "Well, how can my imaginary friend be real?" But I didn't.

Joss bows her head. "Thank you," she says quietly, and for a while we're both silent.

"Do you remember going out on the Mastersons' boat?" I say at last.

"Of course." She looks up, her eyes shining. "Oh, Sylvie, you were so sweet in your little life jacket."

"I *so* wanted to see a dolphin," I say with a laugh. "I never did, though."

I've always kept snatches of that day in my memory. Blue sky, glittering water, sitting on Lynn's lap, hearing her sing "Kumbaya." Then it turned into an "imaginary" memory, and I clung to it all the harder. I invented conversations and games. I built up our secret friendship. I created a whole fantasy world of Lynn and me, a place where I could escape.

The irony is, if my parents had never told me Lynn was imaginary, I probably would have forgotten all about her.

"I'd love to meet your children," says Joss, breaking the silence. "Please bring them to visit."

"I will, definitely."

"We sometimes get dolphins here," she adds, twinkling. "I'll do my best."

"I ought to go." I get to my feet reluctantly. Devon's a long way from London and I need to be back tonight.

"Come again, soon. Bring the family. And good luck on Saturday," she adds.

"Thanks." I smile. "I'm sorry I couldn't invite you."

Seeing Joss on my own is one thing. Having her in the same room as Mummy would be a step too far. Mummy does know that I've been in touch with Joss, but it's firmly in the category of things she won't acknowledge.

"It's fine." Joss nods. "I'll be thinking of you, though," she says, and draws me in for a tight hug, and I feel like, out of all of this, something good came. A new friendship. Or a new old one.

A real one.

And then, in a blink, it's Saturday and I'm getting ready. Makeup: done. Dress: on. Hair: sprayed. There's nothing else I can do with it. Even flowers or a jeweled comb would look ridiculous.

My hair is even shorter than it was when I first hacked it off. I went to the hairdresser and, after gaping in shock, my regular stylist, Neil, pointed out how jagged it was and how he'd need to "really go in there" to even it up. He calls it my "Twiggy" look, which is sweet of him because I don't look anything like Twiggy. On the other hand, it does suit my face. That's the general view. Everyone who blenched when they first saw it is now saying, "You know, I actually *prefer* it this way." Apart from Mummy, of course.

I've tried to talk to Mummy a lot over the

last six months. Many times, I've sat on that sofa of hers and tried to bring up different subjects. I've tried to explain why I cut my hair off. And why I flipped out. And why I can't be treated like a child anymore — shut out while the grown-ups confer. I've tried to explain how wrong the whole "Lynn" thing was. I've tried to explain how mixed up my feelings are about Daddy. I've tried over and over to have a proper, empathetic conversation, the kind I feel we *should* be having.

But everything bounces off. Nothing lands. She won't meet my eyes or acknowledge the past or shift position an inch. For her, Daddy is still the golden untouchable hero of our family, Joss is the villain, and I'm the turncoat. She's locked in a kind of ossified reality, surrounded by her photos of Daddy and the wedding DVD, which she still plays when the girls visit. (I won't watch it anymore. I'm done with it. Maybe I'll revisit it in ten years' time or so.)

So, the last time I went round for brunch — just me — we didn't even talk about any of it. We talked about where Mummy might go on holiday with Lorna, and she made Bellinis, and I bought a set of stacking rings — so versatile — at the special one-off price of £39.99 (normal price for all five items:

£120.95). And at the end, she said, "Darling, this has been *so* lovely," and I think she really meant it. She likes the bubble. She's happy there. She's not interested in bursting it.

"Mummy!" Tessa comes running into my room, dressed in her chosen outfit — Chelsea top, tutu skirt, and glittery trainers. There was just a nanosecond when I considered laying down the law and forcing her into the adorable dusty-pink Wild & Gorgeous dress I'd seen online. But then I stopped myself. I'm not going to force my girls into dresses, or hairstyles, or thoughts that aren't theirs. Let everyone be who they want to be. Let Tessa wear her Chelsea top and Anna her Gruffalo costume. They'll make perfect bridesmaids. Or whatever they are.

"Daddy says, 'See you there,' " she announces.

"OK." I beam at her. "Thanks."

We haven't done the whole spend-the-night-apart thing — I mean, this is a renewal of vows, not a wedding — but we decided to arrive at the venue separately. Keep some magic, at least.

And Dan hasn't seen my dress either, so he doesn't know that I've splashed out on the most elegant, strapless pale-gray Vera

Wang concoction. Well, it wasn't me who splashed out. Mummy offered to buy me a big-ticket dress for the occasion, and I agreed without hesitation. It's Daddy's money that's paid for it. I reckoned he owed us.

Dan and I had a bit of a money conversation a few weeks after I cut my hair off. I admitted I'd thought for a long time that he was prickly about my father's wealth, and he shrugged, looking uncomfortable.

"Maybe," he said. "It's fair to say I was prickly about a lot of things regarding your father." Then he confessed that he does have a bit of a hang-up about providing for the family, and I said, "Like your dad," and he didn't contradict me.

So then I tried to prove that we could in fact live on my income (if we made a *lot* of changes), so the old stereotypes were dead. And if he was a real feminist he wouldn't feel the need to be the breadwinner but could support the family unit in other ways. And Dan listened politely and agreed with everything and then said, "Actually, we've got a big new order coming in, so is it OK if I carry on contributing financially, just for the moment?"

Thank *God*.

I spray myself with Maze lily of the valley

perfume — a gift from Joss — then step into my shoes and head downstairs to find the girls peering at Dora.

"I want her to talk," says Tessa, who has just seen *Harry Potter* for the first time. "Dora, talk." She addresses the snake bossily. *"Talk."*

"Talking snakes are not in real life," says Anna, glancing at me for confirmation. "Made-up things are not in real life, are they, Mummy?"

"No," I say. "They're not."

I'm never going to tell them that my made-up friend came to life. They don't need that kind of complicated, weird stuff in their heads. When they meet Joss, she'll be Joss.

"See you, Dora," I say, shepherding the girls out of the kitchen. I won't say I've got fond of Dora, exactly, but I can look at her. I can kind of appreciate that she's an amazing creature. Especially as I know she's moving out of the kitchen. (*Yes! Result!*)

Basically, our whole garden is being revamped. The Wendy houses have already gone, and the girls barely noticed. Instead, we're having a new outdoor room for Dan, all glass and wood, in which he'll have his office and a special space for Dora. And we're starting a vegetable patch.

"If you're such a bloody gardening expert," I said to Dan one night, "why aren't we eating home-grown rocket every day?" And he laughed and phoned up his mate Pete, who does landscaping, and together they drew up a whole garden design. They even planned to put in some hardy annuals. Whereupon Dan suddenly remembered me trying to interest him in the garden before and apologized for having been so distracted. He didn't need to. I get it — he had a few other things on his mind.

Then we invited Mary Holland round to have lunch and help plan the herb garden. (Partly to show her — and each other — that there are no hard feelings or misunderstandings left.) It was great, because John looked over the fence from next door and started joining in the discussion. So then he came over too. And we ended up with this rather high-powered gardening forum, all to discuss a tiny herb bed.

Since then, Mary's been back to visit us a few times — she gets on well with Tilda too. ("I can *see* why you were worried," Tilda breathed in my ear, about five seconds after meeting her.) Meanwhile, Dan has taken to popping over to see John and talking about his work (while quietly making sure the fridge is full), and I do feel as though our existence has opened up a bit. We're doing a bit less watching our past life on DVDs. A bit more building our own present life.

The girls can even have their own bedrooms now that Dan won't need the study. (Except, of course, they don't want their own bedrooms and wept when we mentioned it, and Tessa wailed, "But I will *miss* Anna!" clinging to her as though we'd suggested Anna go and sleep in the gulag.)

The car is waiting in the road, and as I shut the front door, I have a flashback to our wedding. Daddy leading me out of the house. Me looking like a Disney princess. Like so many things, it seems a lifetime ago. A different me. Today, there's no one to lead the girls and me out of the house. There's no one to "give me away." I'm not a thing to be handed over; I'm a person. And I want to commit to another person. And that's the end of it.

Quite nice to be in a posh car, though. As we glide along, the girls wave at passersby, and I redo my lip gloss several times and run over what I'm going to say. Then, before I feel quite ready, we're pulling up in front of Willoughby House. And even though I know this isn't my actual wedding and I'm not a bride, and it's really not a big deal . . .

I still feel a *whoosh* of sudden nerves.

The driver opens the door and I emerge as elegantly as I can, and passersby stop to point and take pictures, especially when Anna gets out in her Gruffalo costume, holding her bouquet. We've all got winter bouquets of eucalyptus wound with ivy, which Mary dropped round this morning, together with a buttonhole for Dan. All from the St. Philip's Garden. She gave me a massive hug and said, "I'm so, *so* pleased for you," and I could tell she genuinely meant it.

"Come on, girls," I say, when we're all in place. "Let's do it." And I push open the door to Willoughby House.

It looks phenomenal. There are flowers and greenery everywhere, cascading down the banisters and arranged in sprays. Guests are seated on gold chairs in rows, in the hall and through into the drawing room. Music begins and I process slowly between the chairs, up what is almost an aisle.

I can see lots of volunteers, watching with misty smiles, all wearing pastel hats. Dan's parents are dressed up smartly and I beam at Sue. I had lunch with her a couple of weeks ago, and apparently she and Neville have taken ballroom dancing up again. She seemed quite excited about it. Certainly they look a lot more relaxed today than they have for ages.

There's Mary, looking gorgeous in a pale aquamarine dress . . . Tilda, in a jeweled shawl . . . Toby and Michi . . . Mummy in a new pink suit, talking animatedly to Michi (probably selling her stacking rings). My heart catches as I see John, with his distinctive white, tufty hair, sitting on his own at the end of a row. He came. Even though Owen's really not well these days, he still came.

Clarissa is standing to one side, capturing everything on video, and Robert is at the other side, recording from that angle. He meets my eye and nods as I pass. He's a good guy, Robert.

And there ahead of me, standing on a small carpeted platform, is Dan. He's dressed in an elegant blue suit, which brings out his eyes. His hair is glowing in the sunshine, filtered through the famous golden stained-glass window. And as he stands there proudly, watching the girls and me approach, he suddenly reminds me of a lion. A victorious lion. Happy and noble. Head of his pride.

(At least, joint head with me, obviously. I think that's understood.)

The inspiration to use Willoughby House

as a wedding venue came originally from me. Dan and I had decided to renew our vows and I was googling places, and they all promised elegant rooms and reception space "steeped in history," and I thought, *Hang on, hang on, hang on. . . .*

Talk about monetizing Willoughby House. It's made for weddings!

It took a bit of time for the license to come through, but since then we've already had three weddings (all daughters of supporters), and there are more inquiries every day. It's changed the whole nature of the house. We have constant influxes of flowers and visiting brides and all the hope and excitement that weddings bring. It's fun. It makes it feel like a proper, living space again.

Not just that, the website is up and running! A proper, functioning website, where you can book tickets and read about events and everything. (The online shop will come.) And it makes me feel joyful every time I log on, because it's not like every other website — it's *us.* We couldn't afford 3-D spinning pictures or celebrity audio tours . . . but what we've got is beautiful line drawings on every page. There are drawings of the house and artifacts and even a sketch of Mrs. Kendrick on the *History of the Family* page. Every page is more charming than the last, and it feels like the perfect alchemy of old and new. Just like Willoughby House. (Indeed, just like Mrs. Kendrick, who has recently discovered texting and now sends Clarissa and me emojis pretty much on the hour.)

"Welcome, everybody." Mrs. Kendrick steps forward and I stifle a giggle, because she's gone and bought a robe. A kind of high school graduation robe, in deep purple, with trailing arms and a square neck.

I mean, really, it quite suits her.

When it came to the question of who would be the officiant at our renewal, it occurred to us that this isn't a legal ceremony, so anyone could do it. And actually I couldn't think of anyone I would rather have than Mrs. Kendrick. She was very touched. Then she asked me about a hundred questions a day about it, until I wished I'd asked *anyone* else.

But now she's standing, beaming around as though she owns the place — which of course she does — saying, "Today we are delighted to welcome Dan and Sylvie to this historic house to renew their marriage vows. Which is an honorable estate, not to be undertaken lightly," she adds, making dramatic gestures with her capacious robe sleeves. "Those whom God hath joined together, let no man put asunder."

OK . . . what? This all sounds very random. But she seems to be having a good time, swirling her robe sleeves, so what does it matter?

"Now!" she continues. "Sylvie and Dan have written their own vows, so I will pass you over to them." She steps to one side, and I turn to face Dan.

My Dan. He's haloed in the golden light. His eyes are all crinkly and loving. And I thought I was on top of this, no problem . . . but suddenly I can't speak.

As though sensing this, Dan draws breath, and I can tell he's choked up too. Why the *hell* did we decide to make emotional vows to each other in front of other people? Why did we think this was a good idea?

"Sylvie," he says, his voice a little crackly. "Before I make my vows, I want to tell you one thing." He leans forward and whispers in my ear, "We're going to St. Lucia tomorrow; it's all fixed up. All four of us. Family-moon. Surprise."

What? *What?* I thought we were *done* with surprises. He was *not* supposed to do that. Although, oh my God, St. Lucia! I blink a couple of times, then lean forward and whisper in his ear.

"I'm not wearing any knickers. Surprise."

Ha! His expression!

Dan seems temporarily to have forgotten about making his vows, so I'm about to launch in with my own set, when there's a slight kerfuffle from the entrance hall. The next moment, Dr. Bamford is making his way into the room. He waves at us cheerily and takes his place on a chair.

"Surprise," I say to Dan. "I thought he ought to be here. He started this all off, after all."

"Good call." Dan nods, his eyes softening. "Good call."

And then somehow we've said all our vows and not cried or tripped up, and everyone has applauded, and we're all on the champagne. Clarissa is playing jazz records on the old gramophone, and some of the volunteers are dancing in a makeshift dancing space. I can see Robert talking intently to Mary — hmm, *there's* an idea — and Dan's parents doing a rather flashy quickstep. Neville's eyes are fixed on Sue's, and the sight of them moving in perfect time with each other makes me blink. Then, as if she can sense me watching, Sue meets my eye and smiles over Neville's shoulder and I wave back.

I catch Clarissa's eye as she changes a

record on the gramophone and give her a fond smile. Clarissa has been another revelation. Three months ago she stunned us by revealing she'd written a ghost story set in Willoughby House and recorded it as a podcast! Without telling anyone! She said she'd heard me suggesting it and it had stuck in her mind and she thought she'd "have a bash." It's up on the website now and keeps being downloaded, and we all know that Clarissa will end up going into writing full time one day. She just doesn't seem to know it herself yet.

As I'm standing there with Dan, watching everyone, he leans over and murmurs, "Have you told Mrs. Kendrick yet? Or Clarissa?"

I know what he means and shake my head. "Not the time," I say quietly. "After we get back."

I'm so proud of everything we've achieved at Willoughby House. And I love the place more than ever now it has a new lease of life. But nothing changes if nothing changes. I saw that slogan on a T-shirt the other day, and it really resonated. I've changed. My horizons have shifted. And if I want to keep on growing and changing, I need to challenge myself.

It's taken a while to work out what to do

next — but I've finally found the perfect thing. I'm masterminding the campaign for the new children's wing at the New London Hospital. I saw the advert for the post and instantly thought, *yes.* It's a big job, and I had to persuade Cedric and his board that my skills would transfer from the world of art history — but every time I think about it I feel a surge of adrenaline. I'll be helping children. I'll be achieving a whole new level of fundraising. And someone else can take on my work here — someone with fresh eyes and energy.

Sometimes you need to poke things with a stick. If I hadn't poked our marriage with a stick, what would have happened, long term? I don't like thinking this much, because it's irrelevant now that everything did come out and we're OK. But let's just say . . . I don't think it would have been great.

When I look back at ourselves, I feel that the Dan and Sylvie who were married for all those years, who were so pleased with each other, who thought life was such a breeze . . . they're different people. They had no idea.

"Congratulations!" A booming voice greets us and I see Dr. Bamford approaching, glass in hand. "How nice to see you again, and thank you for the invitation! I've always meant to visit this place but never have. Wonderful collection of books. And the basement kitchen! Fascinating!"

"You probably think it's strange that we invited you today." I smile up at him. "But as I think I said in my letter, you really started something when we saw you all those months ago."

"Oh dear!" exclaims Dr. Bamford, and I can tell he doesn't remember at all.

"No, it was good," Dan reassures him. "In the end."

"In the end." I nod. "You told us we would have another sixty-eight years of marriage, and it kind of kick-started . . . Well, we didn't react brilliantly."

"We freaked out," says Dan honestly. "I mean, sixty-eight years. That's a *lot* of box sets." He laughs at his own joke, but Dr. Bamford doesn't seem to hear. He's peering thoughtfully at Dan. He transfers his gaze to me, then back to Dan.

"Sixty-eight years?" he says at last. "Dear me. Hmm. I may possibly have overestimated a tad. I tend to do that. My colleague Alan McKenzie is forever chiding me on the matter."

Overestimated?

"What do you mean, 'overestimated'?" I

say, staring at him.

"What do you mean, 'overestimated'?" Dan echoes, only half a second behind me.

"Dr. McKenzie recently advised me to shave a good half percent off my calculations. Which would mean you have closer to, let's say . . . sixty-four years." He beams cheerfully, then notices a tray of canapés passing by. "Ah, smoked salmon! Excuse me a moment. . . ."

As Dr. Bamford pursues the canapés, Dan and I stare at each other, stricken. I feel cheated. I had sixty-eight years and now I only have sixty-four.

"Sixty-four years?" I gulp at last. "*Sixty-four?* That's no time!"

Dan looks equally traumatized. He seizes me to him as though we're counting every second, crushing me against him.

"OK, so we only have sixty-four years," he says. "Let's make them count."

"No more wasting time," I agree fervently.

"No more petty arguments."

"Live every moment."

"Set the alarm earlier," says Dan urgently. "Ten minutes a day. We can claw back some time that way." And he looks so worked up that something inside me says, *Wait a minute. We're overreacting again.*

"Dan . . ." I say more gently. "No one

actually *knows*. We could have seventy-two more years together. Or two. Or two days."

My gaze travels around the room, suddenly seeing everyone here in a different light. There's Mummy, with her brittle smile, who thought she would be with Daddy for a lot longer. John, facing a future without Owen, his eyes sad even as he talks to Tilda — who herself had to cope with a life that didn't pan out the way she'd hoped. Dan's parents, still dancing, faces determined, making it work. Mary and Robert, chatting closely with shy smiles, maybe at the start of something. And my girls, dancing joyously in their Chelsea top and Gruffalo costume. Out of all of us, they've got the right idea.

"Come on." I put a hand on his arm and squeeze it fondly. "Come on, Dan. Let's just get on with life."

And I lead him onto the dance floor, where everyone breaks off to applaud us. Dan throws some shapes and Tilda whoops and the girls spin round and round with me, laughing.

And we get on with life.

ACKNOWLEDGMENTS

While writing this book, I reflected a lot on longevity, loyalty, and partnership.

I am lucky enough to have been writing books for many years, for which I'm endlessly grateful to my wonderful and loyal readers. Writers don't really have the facility to "renew their vows" with their readers — but I'm lifting a glass to you all, anyway. Thank you so much for reading.

I would also like to take this opportunity to acknowledge and thank my publishers around the world. I am, again, lucky enough to be published in many countries, from the UK, the United States, and Canada, throughout Europe, to South America, Asia, and Australasia. I have worked closely with many of my publishers and have built up fantastic long-term relationships with them. Other countries I'm yet to visit — but I'm still very aware of how much energy and enthusiasm goes into publishing my books.

I will be forever grateful.

I would like to thank in particular my agenting team — a group of very talented and supportive people, who could only ever surprise me in a good way. (This is not a challenge!) Araminta Whitley, Marina de Pass, Kim Witherspoon, Jessica Mileo, Maria Whelan, Nicki Kennedy, Sam Edenborough, Katherine West, Jenny Robson, Simone Smith, and Florence Dodd: thank you.

Thanks also to The Board, which has been in my life nearly as long as I have been writing. Can't imagine doing it without you.

Jenny Colgan, thank you for being my *Doctor Who* expert.

And, finally, as this is a book about marriage, I would like to credit my constantly amazing husband, Henry, and our children, Freddy, Hugo, Oscar, Rex, and Sissy, for supporting me, cheering me on, making me laugh, and teaching me what long-term love looks like.

ABOUT THE AUTHOR

Sophie Kinsella is the author of the best-selling Shopaholic series, as well as the novels *Can You Keep a Secret?*, *The Undomestic Goddess*, *Remember Me?*, *Twenties Girl*, *I've Got Your Number*, *Wedding Night*, *Finding Audrey*, and *My Not So Perfect Life*. She lives in the UK.

sophiekinsella.com
Facebook.com/SophieKinsellaOfficial
Twitter: @KinsellaSophie
Instagram: @sophiekinsellawriter

The employees of Thorndike Press hope you have enjoyed this Large Print book. All our Thorndike, Wheeler, and Kennebec Large Print titles are designed for easy reading, and all our books are made to last. Other Thorndike Press Large Print books are available at your library, through selected bookstores, or directly from us.

For information about titles, please call:
  (800) 223-1244

or visit our website at:
  gale.com/thorndike

To share your comments, please write:
  Publisher
  Thorndike Press
  10 Water St., Suite 310
  Waterville, ME 04901

FEB 2018